THE ORIENTAL BOUQUET

KITTY LIU

Author: Kitty Liu

Title: The Oriental Boutique

Website: kittyliu.com.au

Copyright © 2023

First Published February 2023

The moral rights of the author have been asserted.

All rights reserved.

This novel is a work of fiction. Space and time have been rearranged to suit the convenience of the book. While the author has drawn upon the experiences of both herself and others, names, characteristics, events, and dialogue have been changed and recreated throughout. The opinions expressed are those of the characters, and should not be confused with the author or publisher's personal or professional views.

The publisher accepts no responsibility, and is not liable for recollections drawn upon for inspiration from the author or stories within the book.

ISBN 978-0-6456843-5-3

A LETTER FROM THE AUTHOR, KITTY LIU

As a single mother, for many years, I focused on being the best mother I could possibly be to provide, protect and guide my children. Since my children gained independence, I seized what I'd refer to as a "God-given" second chance.

Throughout the journey of writing The Oriental Bouquet, little did I know that I was also writing the next chapter of my new life.

Given that English is my second language, I've faced and had to overcome many obstacles and challenges in completing this book. Countless times, I stopped writing because of my fear of language barriers and my English not being good enough. But I soon realised that my mission and purpose far outweighed my lingering fears. I truly hope you enjoy The Oriental Bouquet—a story about female empowerment, cultural acclimation and survival. It's a book that covers themes of immigration, cultural mishaps, survival, forgiveness, and self-love. It's also a series of fables— each chapter a story in itself. One of the poignant lessons The Oriental Bouquet highlights, is that everyone is deserving of a second chance.

I sincerely hope my book will inspire and encourage you to understand that it's not where we come from but where we are headed that matters. It's not about years in life, but life in years. It's not what we have but rather, what we choose to give. It's not the situation but the extent of our determination that can power us through. It's not about the setback, but rather, possessing the courage of resilience, and persistence. And last but not least, it's not how we start but how we choose to finish that matters.

Love,
Kitty Liu
xx

CONTENTS

CHAPTER 1

Three young Chinese girls filed in, found their seats, and settled for the lengthy flight on the Qantas Boeing 747 from Hong Kong to Sydney. They were seated in different parts of the aircraft and did not know one another. However, they were all travelling to Australia with the same purpose—to create a better future. A range of thoughts and emotions crept into their minds and bodies as their plane drew closer to Sydney in the early morning—fear, uncertainty, worry. They were concerned about potential issues that may arise and had anxiety about facing the unknown. On the other hand, every one of them was brimming with enthusiasm and hope for a better life.

Lili, a tall, gorgeous, slender woman with flawless light skin and silky black hair that almost reached to her waist, was fast asleep. As the aircraft started to descend, she woke up. Lili didn't care about anything other than leaving China and her past behind her. In order to start her life over, she needed to go to a new location where no one knew who she was.

Jasmine pulled down her scarlet T-shirt with sparkling embroidery while rubbing her hands over her worn-out high-waisted jeans from the 1980s. Despite her lack of sleep and anxiety, she continued to hold hope for a better future. She was adamant that she would flourish in Australia and show her father that she wasn't the waste of space he'd told her she was.

Peony's sparkling big black eyes widened further as she gazed out of the window at the pearly glow of the early morning sky. The first rays of sunlight slowly decanted through the rosy clouds. 'What a magical morning to start my new journey in this new country,' Peony thought.

"Ladies and Gentlemen. Boys and girls. Welcome to Sydney, Australia...." The captain announced.

Everyone got their carry-on luggage and started to make their way through to the customs checkpoints and into the expansive halls and Duty-Free. Lili was instructed to move forward by a customs official. "Lili," he murmured as he opened her passport. "Do you have any dairy products—fresh or dried seeds, herbs, or nuts in your luggage?"

"Ha?" Lili looked at him, puzzled.

"Can you speak English?" The officer spoke with a slow and clear tone.

Lili turned around and looked behind her. She desperately hoped someone who could speak Chinese would come to her aid.

"Putonghua? (Mandarin?)" Peony asked who was standing in the queue.

"She de (Yes)," Lili replied.

"He asked if you have any fresh or dry fruits, seeds, plants, nuts, or dairy products. Those things are forbidden to bring into Australia." Peony explained in Mandarin.

"Mei you! (No!)" Lili answered in a loud and offended voice.

"She said no, sir," Peony translated.

"Ok, thanks. You can go," he said.

Jasmine, who was standing behind Peony, panicked. "Can I go before you in case I need your help?"

"Yes, sure." Peony let her move in front.

"Next, please." Jasmine stepped to the counter and passed her passport and the declaration to him. He looked at the passport.

"Moli (Jasmine in Chinese) Yang, can… you… speak… English? Any fresh or dry fruits, seeds or plants, nuts, or dairy products?"

"Shenmue? (What?)," She turned around and looked at Peony.

"You mieyou Zhiwu, Shuiguo, Ganguo. Ru zhipin," Peony translated.

"Meiyou (No)," she replied and shook her head.

"She said none of them, Sir."

He stamped the passport and gave it back to her. "Next, please." He waved his hand and signalled Peony to come to the counter.

"Mudan (Peony in Chinese) Chen, you can speak English. Right?" he asked.

"A little bit, Sir," Peony answered with a nervous smile.

"Any fresh or dry fruit, seeds or plants, nuts or dairy products?"

"No, Sir," she replied calmly.

"Well, you can understand what I asked. That means you speak good English. Welcome to Sydney."

"Thank you, Sir."

"No worries." Now he sounded cheery.

"Pardon, Sir?" She looked confused.

"Oh, it means you are welcome." He gave Peony a friendly smile.

When Peony walked past Customs towards the luggage carousels, she noticed that Lili and Jasmine were following her.

"Lucky you could speak some English." Lili conversed in Mandarin, ensuring she hung on to Peony in case she needed more help.

"At the moment, very limited. Still a long way to go," Peony continued in Mandarin.

"How long have you been learning English?" Jasmine asked.

"About a year," Peony grabbed her suitcase from the luggage carousel and continued, "When I decided to move to Australia to pursue my education, I asked my mother to send some English study materials from Hong Kong. I tried to pick up the language as quickly as I could. I think we must learn the language and culture of a new place when we move there".

Jasmine smiled gratefully and remarked, "At least you could speak some English. I looked like a stupid idiot at Customs. Thank you for being so helpful." She then noticed that her luggage had arrived. Seizing it, she asked, "Have we all got our bags?"

"Yes." Then Lili introduced herself. "By the way, I am Lili from Shanghai."

"Ni hao (hello in Chinese), I am Jasmine from Beijing."

"Ni hao, I am Peony, What a coincidence! My parents chose my name after a flower as well. My mum told me that Peony represents purity, humanity, and honour. Oh, I am from Guangzhou." she said with a warm smile. "Hey, do you realise that Lily, Jasmine, and Peony, together we can make the most beautiful Chinese bouquet? I am so glad to meet some new friends in this new country," she concluded.

"Are you here to study?" Lili asked.

"Yes, and you?" Peony responded.

"Yes. Me, too," Lili said.

"Which college?" Peony asked.

"Broadway English College," Lili said.

"Same one! That is so good. How about you, Jasmine?"

"Oh! I am so happy, yes! The same college! Did they ask you to stand in front of the bank with, umm... a big red W and wait there for someone to come to pick you up?"

"Yes. The Westpac Bank," Peony replied.

"Now I feel much better knowing that I am not alone."

Jasmine breathed a sigh of relief.

"Let's find the bank first," Peony suggested.

They waited almost an hour. Finally, a Chinese-looking man with their Chinese names on a piece of cardboard walked toward them.

"Oh, he is coming to pick us up!" Jasmine cheered.

The man waved at them to come with him and directed them to an old van he unlocked and instructed them to enter before driving away. After about 30 minutes, he parked the van on a side street off Broadway. Motioning them to follow him, the three girls followed the driver and proceeded to a block of apartments. Walking along a bustling street, the driver came to a halt in front of an apartment building and unlocked one of the doors on the ground floor entrance. As they entered, the girls exchanged startled looks with one another. Inside was a unit, but it was bare. Nothing was inside, including furnishings!

"Where are our beds? Are you going to organise some beds for us to sleep in tonight?" Lili asked.

The driver shrugged and answered, "There are no beds, and it was like that for all of us who first came here. You will sleep on the floor until you find your place, my 'princesses'. I will come to pick you up at eight o'clock tomorrow morning and take you to the college."

"But wait!" Peony snapped. "I was told that accommodation would be provided when I arrived in Sydney. Four weeks' rent was included in the College fees. Accommodation means there are at least some simple basic things such as beds to sleep in, chairs to sit down on, plates, bowls, cutlery, jugs and cups."

The driver frowned. "Well, they don't want to make it too comfortable for students, so you don't waste time finding a place as soon as possible to move into and start your life here. You have four weeks. Unfortunately, the owner of the college is not a nice person. All the students who have come here to study in this college get the same treatment. They all sleep on the floor till they find their place. See you tomorrow." He waved his hand as he left.

For a long time, the three girls stood still in the unit. Jasmine leaned against the wall before sliding to the ground. She sobbed uncontrollably. "I thought I would have a new life in Australia. My mum borrowed a lot of money from our relatives to fund for me to get away from my abusive father. He frequently referred to my mother, my younger sister, and me as a group of useless women. He was devastated when I was born and accused my mother of not giving birth to a boy so he could continue the family name. I came here to show him that I am not useless."

Lili pushed her suitcase next to her. Then laid it on its side—flat, and sat on it. "Jasmine, at least you came here with clean money. You can pay them back later when you can. I sold my virginity, body, and soul to my scumbag boss to pay my college fees to study here." She blinked back tears. "I can never repurchase my virginity. Every time I think about it, I feel disgusted with myself. So just put up with it. We will start to look for our place tomorrow."

Peony opened her suitcase and took out a long coat. She laid it on the floor and asked Jasmine and Lili to join her. "This will be more comfortable. Have a little rest first. We will sort something out later."

Lili put her back against the wall. She closed her eyes and tried to sleep, doing her best to ignore the disturbing memories that plagued her from her past.

CHAPTER 2

Lili made a concerted effort to forget, but she couldn't help but recall the first night she worked as a waitress at Hung's Shanghai Night Restaurant. In one of his "exclusive" rooms that evening, Hung welcomed a group of business people for dinner. Lili was ignorant of the new Open Doors policy China had implemented in the 1980s to encourage people to create their own businesses, which led to a rise in wealth. Escorts and prostitutes were illegal in China, but individuals like Hung came up with the concept of posing as restaurants and hiring "waitresses" to act as escort girls. There were unique rooms in the restaurant. While the girls served the food in these special rooms, the guests would try to put their hands all over the girls' bodies. After eating and drinking, they'd select one or more girls and take them to hotels to have sex with them.

Hung often arranged a "fashion parade" where he would force young girls to wear bikinis and march around the restaurant holding a number. Customers would select one or more numbers and write their selections, along with the price they were willing to pay on a piece of provided paper which would be delivered to the manager after the parade. If more than one person had the same number, the girl would go to the highest bidder. The manager then directed the waitress to have sex with the client in a nearby hotel. That is how Hung became wealthy by exploiting young girls.

Hung was the first to notice Lili's beauty when she arrived for what she believed to be a waitressing job interview. She declined his invitation to join them at their table the first evening she was at work, feeling a bit nervous about joining him and the sizeable all-male group he had in his entourage. When she served him the second time, one of the older men gawked at Lili and reached under her short, black miniskirt to touch her bottom. She was so startled by it, the plate she was holding almost fell from her grasp. She crossed to the other side of the table in a flash to continue serving, well away from the groping customer. Lili remembered how Hung had laughed at this, and how he had winked at the old man and said, "don't even think about it; she is mine." She cringed as she remembered them all laughing out loud at his remark. Later that evening, Hung called her into his office to speak with her. As she entered the room, she saw him light a cigarette and slowly release the smoke to the ceiling in little rings. "What is your monthly wage as a waitress?"

"Three hundred yen," Lili replied.

"I remember during the job interview you told me that you want to save up for further study in Australia. Even if you worked for the next five years, you still couldn't accumulate enough money for even one year of college fees with the amount you are earning now. Not to mention the food and accommodation that needs to be added to it." He stood up and walked close to her. He put his hand around her slim waist and continued, "However, for a beautiful girl like you, there are fast ways to earn money. All you need to do is eat the best food, drink the finest wine, and make your clients happy. I guarantee you that by the end of this year, you will have enough money to pay for your college fees and the living expenditure as well."

Lili pushed his hand away from her waist; feeling very

uncomfortable, she said, "You want me to be that type of girl? A prostitute? No, I am still a virgin!"

"Fantastic! I like that! Virgins are my favourite. If you're a virgin here, Lili, you can attract the biggest money and become very rich faster than all the other girls. Why don't you be my courtesan? All you have to do is work for me, and you would have your very own apartment and not want or need for anything. I will take care of it." He said persuasively. Hung told her he would prepare an apartment for her where she could stay as long as she remained in his employment. "You will have all the freedom in the world, and every now and then, I will visit you, and sometimes, you will also get a visit from one or two of my special guests. It's a deal of a century that you can't pass up! Just think of the future you will have with the money you earn!"

Lili stood still, deliberating. While she didn't want to sell her body, she knew this could be the faster way to accumulate money to study overseas. She was fighting between her moral conscience and temptation. An apartment to stay in and money to spend. She could continue her studies at university during the weekdays. Moreover, she could achieve her dream of further studying in Australia the following year.

Hung's eyes sparkled. He knew she would agree, just like the dozens before her had. He waited and watched her struggle and battle with the decision, but was confident it would go in his favour, he just had to be patient.

Lili closed her eyes for a few seconds, feeling frozen in time. What to do? She looked at Hung, who was silent, waiting for her response. Finally, she gave in and agreed. Her future was where she wanted to be, and all that mattered. She would work for Hung for a year, save her money, and fly to Australia to begin her new life. "Ok," she said quietly. Hung jumped up and said, "Good! You've made the right decision!" Then he grabbed her by the hand and led her into a room she didn't even know existed, hidden behind his office, where he laid her on a bed and unemotionally took her virginity.

In the year that followed, Hung exploited her every opportunity he had. When she wasn't working in the restaurant, he'd barely give her time to dress before taking her to business meetings, where he'd use her and her beauty as bait to seal deals and sweeten them as well. If Hung's special guests showed a hint of interest in her, he would offer her for the night. He was a ruthless and callous man who had no regard for anyone. He used everyone around him to get what he wanted, including Lili.

Lili had been tricked, and she knew it, but it was too late. Thoughts of how to escape Hung consumed her from the moment she opened her eyes in the morning until the time she wearily closed them.

CHAPTER 3

"Let's get out for a meal. I could eat a full chicken right now; it's almost five o'clock!" Lili was jolted out of her memories by Jasmine's voice.

"Since we only speak a little English, I suggest Chinatown should be the first place we visit." Peony grinned at them both as if everything was fine. "Let's get out of here and explore this new city. The driver told us Chinatown is not far from here. I remember he said we would be there if we walked along Broadway for about twenty minutes. "Maybe we will meet some people who have a place for rent. Or we can buy a Chinese newspaper and see if there are other places to stay," she suggested.

"Are you serious?" Lili was so desperate that she nearly screamed. "Doesn't it disturb you that we are in this predicament? Tonight, everyone is going to sleep on the floor."

"Hey, there are three of us here. We are not alone; we're together and will be fine," Peony said, maintaining her optimistic attitude. "Where there is a will, there is a way! All things were brought together by HIM for the greater good." She said cryptically, but encouragingly as she turned her head to the sky."

"Who is HE? Your imaginary friend?" Lili rolled her eyes.

"As our bodies need food, so do our souls and spirit. I will tell you about Him later. Let's get some food first." Peony picked up her handbag. "Let's go!"

When they arrived in Chinatown, they looked around with astonishment. They passed through the two lions at the entrance. As they went a little further, they recognised Chinese writings, the decorations of the shops, and the familiar aroma of food from the restaurant. "Wow, I can't believe this. The atmosphere here is exactly like it is in China. I can hear so many people speaking Chinese." Lili shouted!

"Yes, I feel like I am back in China!" Jasmine agreed excitedly.

"Let's go up the stairs. Looks like there is a food court up there," Peony suggested.

They found a table at the food court and sat down. Jasmine looked at the menu. "Thank God, they are written in both English and Chinese. But ten dollars for a bowl of noodles?! It is too expensive! That's approximately forty-eight yens!" she carried on. "As you both know, we only pay five yen in China. I am not going to eat anything. I will find a Chinese food store around here and get some instant noodles later."

"I would like to buy both of you dinner if you don't mind me using the dirty money I earned from Hung," Lili said in an uneasy tone.

Following an early dinner, they spent some time exploring Chinatown before visiting a Chinese store to pick up some instant noodles, a packet of biscuits, and a few apples for the next morning's breakfast. "It's just seven o'clock," Peony said as they passed Victoria Park on the way back. "Should we remain in the park to see the stunning sunset?" she asked.

"Peony, are you joking! Why would you still be in the mood to watch the sunset when we are in such a bad situation? You are completely crazy!" Lili shook her head.

"Why not?! It is the first sunset we will experience in this new country, let's make it unforgettable."

"Yes! It is unforgettable!" Jasmine said. "We slept on the floor on our first night in Australia."

"Come on! Stay here for at least a little while with me," she pleaded. "How we live our lives is about choices. We can choose to go back to the unit and cry and feel sorry for ourselves and complain that life is not fair, or we can make the most out of today. This is the beautiful moment we choose to set in our minds that becomes a memory. If you start a new chapter of your book, how would you like to tell your story about the first day you were in Australia? Mine will start like this... It was a warm, beautiful summer day."

"Ok. You don't need to sell us on it. We will stay in the park with you." Lili gave Peony an impatient look.

"That's the way! You will not regret it!" Peony assured them.

They discovered a bench by a lovely pond when they got to the park. Two wild ducks were swimming around the water with their six ducklings. Peony could sense the warm embrace of the golden sunlight and the soft kiss of the summer breeze on her face. Lili and Jasmine held Peony's hands tightly as she gazed at the magnificent sunset. She said in a hushed voice, "Everything will be OK."

Back in the apartment, Lili started reading the accommodation section in the Chinese newspaper she had bought. She noticed one of the ads that stood out in the newspaper and read out loud:

"Free accommodation for the right Chinese female students. Plus, the opportunity to earn up to one thousand dollars or more per week. Weekend work only. Please call Madam B on 723 242 for an interview."

After much deliberation on what to do, Lili wrote the number down in her diary.

"Just be careful. It seems too good to be true," Peony, who was watching, warned Lili.

"I don't think I can sleep tonight," Lili said jokingly. "How about you tell us about HIM? Your invisible friend, and where you met Him."

"Well. When my mum was a professor at Guangzhou University in the seventies, one of the professors, Jade, was sent to England by the Chinese government to study. Not long after arriving there, one of her classmates invited her to the local church Sunday BBQ. This is where she met Jesus. She told my mum that He is the saviour of the world. Once you are friends with Him, you are friends forever. Because he promised that he would neither forsake you nor leave you till the end of time. Jade smuggled a Bible back with her, and Mum studied the Bible secretly with her. My mum used to come home and tell us stories from the Bible on quiet nights."

"Your mum was a professor and studied religion during the Cultural Revolution? She asked for double trouble!" Jasmine looked like she was watching a horror movie.

"Yes, you are right," Peony said. "The university found out later and reported her and her friend Jade to the local government. They took the Bible and burned it. They sent Mum and our family to Shun De province for 're-education' and 'confession'. Mum always said they can burn the Bible, but they cannot burn Jesus because He is living in the heart of whoever invited him to come into their lives."

"During the day, Mum and Dad were sent to the farm for 're-education'. At night, Mum was forced to carry a piece of cardboard with a picture of a Bible drawn on it. They forced Dad to walk behind her and shout, 'She is a religious witch!' It was a form of punishment for studying the Bible and being educated. Then both Mum and Dad had to kneel on the sharp stones till midnight for 'confession'. I was only four years old. I was left at home alone in the dark."

"Wow, that must have been hard for you and your family,"

Jasmine said.

"Yes, it was", Peony agreed. She smiled and drew a cross on her heart and continued. "The first few nights, I cried myself to sleep. Mum told me I only needed to remember what Jesus said if I was scared. 'Do not be afraid, for I am with you'. Eventually, I found myself no longer afraid at night. Even when I was by myself, somehow, I did not feel alone. After about a month, the village chief told the Red Guards that my Mum and Dad were dangerous and not to let them out at night. He ordered that they both be locked up at home during the night instead. He sent two Red Guards to the front of our house to ensure they were not trying to escape. Many years later, we found out that the village Chief used this to protect my mum and Dad from being tortured by other extremists Red Guards. Furthermore, I would no longer be left alone by myself at night anymore."

Peony looked up with a grateful smile and added. "So don't be afraid; His spirit will be here to guide and protect us." Peony took her thick woollen shawl, which her mum made for her, out of the suitcase, used it as a blanket, and spread it on top of Lili and Jasmine. Then she got under it beside them. "It will keep us warm. We have a big day tomorrow. Now let's try to get some sleep."

CHAPTER 4

The following day, the girls woke up stiff and sore from sleeping on the hard ground. At eight o'clock, the same driver came to collect them and drove them to the Broadway English College. While they were waiting to be allocated to their classroom, Peony went up to the receptionist and communicated with her in her limited English. "Good morning. My name is Peony. The unit we stayed in last night was no good, with no beds. Only walls and floor. Not happy!" she said to the receptionist.

The lady at the reception was in her 30s, blue eyes and with curly golden hair. She gave Peony a friendly smile. "Hi, I'm Linda. After your last class, please come back to see me. Hopefully, we can arrange something better for you."

"Thank you," Peony said as she followed a staff member to class with Lili and Jasmine.

Jasmine went to the park during the lunch break, where they watched the sunset opposite the College. She was tired and still upset that the student agent had lied about the accommodation, and her body ached from sleeping on the hard floor. They didn't even have a kettle to boil water for the instant noodles they'd bought, so she had to eat them dry or go hungry. She sat on the same bench she had sat on the night before and watched the wild ducks swimming in the pond. "Such a beautiful place. I thought I would have a better life here, but it seems I was wrong! I am so lost and uncertain of my future." She said quietly to herself and started to sob.

"Are… you… Chinese? Can… you… speak… English?" a male voice with a strong Australian accent spoke very slowly and loudly.

She saw a man in his 40s with a black and white striped polo shirt, boxer shorts, and a pair of thongs.

"No English… arrived… yesterday," Jasmine answered with a nervous voice.

"I… am… Bob. What… is… your… name? Where… are… you… from?" He still used a very loud voice, as if Jasmine would then understand his English better. He sat beside Jasmine and pointed to himself. "Bob," then he pointed to her, "Your name?"

"Jasmine," she said, moving further away from Bob to the very end of the bench.

"Why are you crying? What is upsetting you?" he asked.

"Place-stayed… no good. No bed, no chair, no kettle." She was still sobbing as she took a handkerchief out of her pocket to dry her tears.

"I live on my own. Come and stay at my place." He pointed to himself. Then he lifted six fingers. "Meet me here at six o'clock," then he pointed to the ground. "Here… this evening, and I will take you to my place. My… house… safe."

Jasmine shook her head while trying to dry her tears again.

As Bob was leaving, he put six fingers up again and repeated, "Six o'clock." Then pointed down again at the spot they were sitting and said, "Here."

At lunchtime, Lili went to the public phone booth to make the call to enquire about the free accommodation advertised in the Chinese newspaper.

"Hi, are you Madam B? I am Lili. I'm calling about your ad in the Chinese newspaper." She spoke nervously in Mandarin.

"Glad that you called. Do you have time to meet me?" a

female voice replied in Mandarin with a Vietnamese accent.

"Where do you want to meet?" Lili asked.

"Can you meet me in Chinatown?"

"Yes, I have just started my lunch break. I can meet you now, or after four o'clock when I finish my last class." Chinatown was the only place she knew so far. Plus, someone in the college had told her it was the Chinese students' gathering place which made her feel more at ease.

"I can meet... let me see... yes, I can meet you now. I'll see you at the Chinese arch? Do you know it? It's where the two big lions are at the entrance of Dixon Street."

"Yes, I have seen it. Thank you, I will see you there." Lili put the phone down and headed to Chinatown.

When she arrived, she found a woman in her late 50s standing under the arch beside one of the lions waiting. The woman was short and wore very thick makeup. She was dressed in a traditional Chinese cheongsam.

"Are you Madam B?" Lili walked up to her and asked.

"Yes. You must be Lili." Madam B looked Lili up and down, admiring her slim and curvy figure. "Nice to meet you. Let's talk over a Yum Cha."

She led Lili to what Madam B said was a well-known Chinese restaurant nearby. "This is the Golden Gate Chinese Restaurant, the best in Chinatown," she said proudly.

Lili took her word for it. She thought it certainly looked like a nice restaurant and followed Madam B through the doors. Tai, the manager, walked up to them, "Welcome, Madam B. Is this your new girl? She is so beeeeaaaautiful." He said, fixing his eyes on Lili's full breasts under her tight high-necked T-shirt.

Madam B gave him a flirty look but evaded his question; instead, she said, "Mr Tai, look after us please, and give us the best, quietest table so we can talk in private. We have some business to discuss." Then she turned to Lili. "You must be hungry. Order whatever you like. This lunch is on me. I will look after you."

The manager pointed to a side room and said, "This is perfect for you to discuss business."

Tai led them into the room "Please take a seat. I will bring your favourite Oolong tea to you." As he walked out, he closed the door behind him.

"In here is quiet. Now we can talk business," she said, pulling the chair out and sitting down.

"I live in a modern four-bedroom house in a suburb called Burwood. It is about fifteen minutes drive from here. If you work for me, you will have your very own room at my house. As I said in the ad, the rent is free for girls who work for me. If you decide to work for me, I can pick up your luggage after lunch," she said confidently.

"I need to go back to college for the next class soon," Lili said, trying to give herself some breathing space to collect her thoughts. "Please tell me about the weekend job you mentioned in your ad so I can decide."

"We will order some food first, Lili. We have plenty of time to discuss your job. Forget your class in the afternoon. I will teach you how to earn easy money. Ok?" While they were viewing the menu, Madam B continued. "As I mentioned, it is easy money. All you need to do is go out with men and do what they tell you to make them happy. Your body is your best asset, Lili. Trust me, you will have an easy life."

Lili instantly felt a chill run down her spine. Madame B's words took her back to the time Hung had said much the same to her.

"In other words, you want me to be a prostitute?" She said with disappointment. She thought being in Australia would mean a new start for her, and she could leave the ghosts of the past behind her.

Madam B frowned. "Don't be silly; we call it a high-class

escort."

"I came to Australia to start a new life. I plan to study one year of English and then study for an Honours degree in business management. I have already obtained a bachelor's degree in China." Lili explained.

"Girl like you with a beautiful body doesn't need to use her brain. Just use your body." Madame B scoffed.

Lili stared at her. This was all going wrong; Madam B wasn't listening. "I need to go back to college now. I can hardly speak any English. And I need to learn the language and culture as soon as possible."

"You don't need to speak good English," Madam B said. "You only need to learn how to please them. I can teach you all the best tricks." She winked at Lili.

Lili gazed out the window, deep in thought. She felt caught between a rock and a hard place. She didn't want to go back to that horrible unit and sleep on the floor again that night, and she didn't want to become a prostitute again. She sighed deeply, feeling depressed about the situation she had found herself in.

Madam B pointed to a waitress outside the window in the main dining area and said sharply, "look at that, the dim sum waitress out there. She pushes the dim sum trolley all day, earning about eighty dollars per hour. If she works six days, after tax, she will earn about three hundred and fifty dollars per week. That's only if you are lucky enough to get the job. At the moment, a lot of Chinese students are looking for jobs. As a student, you can only work no more than twenty-two hours. That means you will only earn about two hundred dollars per week. But if you work for me, I will get you the clients, you only need to work weekends or at night. You will earn at least one thousand dollars per week. Easy money!"

At that moment, the waitress pushed the dim sum trolley into the room, parked next to Lili, and opened the lids to show her the food. "Would you like spring rolls, Cha Siu Bao (steam BBQ pork buns), Cheong Fun (Rice noodle Rolls), or Har Gao (prawn dumplings)?" Madame B asked.

Lili stared at the trolley, then looked up at the waitress's tired face and thought for a long while. Finally, she put her head down dejectedly and said quietly, "All right, after yum cha, I will pick up my luggage, and I will go to your place."

Madam B patted Lili's shoulder with excitement. "That's my girl! From now on, your name is Lily. Tiger Lily, sexy and wild!"

Madam B happily signalled to the manager to come. "Mr Tai, could you cook us a lobster? Make half of it sashimi, and the other half with ginger and shallots. By the way, meet my new girl, Lili. My Tiger Lily."

Tai winked at her and said, "Congratulations! I hope Lili is available this weekend. I will be her first client." He lusted all over her body with his sinful eyes and laughed. Lili held back the tears. She felt worse than she ever had in her life as her hopes and dreams for a new life slipped away from her.

CHAPTER 5

Peony and Jasmine were worried they had not seen Lili; they searched around the college premises and couldn't find her. They returned to the unit after their last English class, hoping to see Lili. As they entered the unit, Peony saw a white paper on the floor. She walked towards it and picked it up. Reading it aloud, she said.

"Peony and Jasmine, I will not stay here tonight, as I have found new accommodation. Good luck with finding your place to stay. Lili."

"Peony," Jasmine said hesitantly. "I don't think I will stay here tonight either."

"Where are you going?" Peony asked with concern.

"I met a man at lunchtime at the same park where we watched the sunset yesterday evening. He saw me crying and said I could stay at his place tonight. I am going to meet him at the park at six o'clock this evening. I thought Lili would be here with you tonight. Now you'll be all alone. Will you be all right?" Jasmine asked, concerned.

"I will be ok. Don't worry. Are you sure you want to leave with a stranger? You barely know the person." Peony was worried.

"Well, he is the only one who has offered to help me at the moment. If I miss this opportunity, I don't know what I may end up doing. I haven't got much money, and I don't want to return to China."

"We can find a job once we settle in."

"Peony, you can speak some English. It's probably not hard for you to find a job. Look at me! Who wants to employ a woman like me? I can hardly speak English. Plus, I'm not as attractive as you and Lili; I won't have the opportunities you two can get."

"Looks like you have already made up your mind to go there. Please take care, and I will see you in college on Monday." Peony hugged her tightly as if she wouldn't see her again.

"See you." Tears streamed down Jasmine's face as she turned and left the bare unit.

Peony, now alone in the unit, retrieved an apple from the benchtop and started eating it. Digging out her notes of what she learned from the lessons at school that day, she went through them until she was too tired to read. Then she lay on the floor with a jumper rolled up under her head as a pillow, and her shawl covering herself like a blanket. She felt entirely enveloped by the darkness, with the violent storm and howling wind outside. Feeling very alone. It didn't matter how hard she tried; she could not fall asleep. She put one hand on top of her heart, and one hand on top of her belly button and started deep breathing with the Qigong technique. Then she slowly closed her eyes and prayed.

"Dear God, thank you in advance for giving me strength and clearing the path I need to take. I pray you will send angels to protect Lili and Jasmine and keep them safe. In your holy name. Amen."

As she was about to fall asleep, she heard a voice, "Do not be afraid my child, for I am with you. I want you to know that not all the storms come to distract you. Some of the storms come to clear your path. And some of the storms come to test your strength. At some point in your life, flying alone in the storm is necessary. This is the perfect opportunity to show your strength and courage. I will always be there to watch over you. For I promised you I will neither forsake you nor leave you till the end of time."

Peony opened her eyes and whispered, "Oh my Lord! Is that you? Or was I just dreaming?" Somehow, she felt a calm peace inside of her. She rolled on her side and fell fast asleep.

The next morning, Peony walked into the college feeling bright and cheerful. "Good morning, Linda."

"Good morning, Peony. I thought you were coming to see me yesterday after class. Have you found a place yet?"

"Not yet, I thought my two other friends… um… would stay in the flat, but it seems I was wrong… um… anyway, they found a new place to stay." Peony struggled to reply in English.

"Normally, I don't do this, but somehow I was guided to. We have a spare bedroom. Would you like to stay with us till you find a place?" Linda suggested.

"I don't want to bother you," Peony hesitated.

"We live at Newport, one of the nicest suburbs on the Northern Beaches. Located across the other side of the Harbour Bridge. The beautiful beaches there are destinations for many tourists from around the world." Linda smiled at her. "Come for a few days, and I will show you around. Come on! You will not be disappointed. I promise." Linda insisted with a smile.

"You sure?" Peony asked.

"Yes, when you finish your class, wait for me here. I will go with you to pick up your luggage."

"OK, thank you," Peony replied.

In the afternoon, Linda arrived at the unit with Peony, and she couldn't believe her eyes. "I am so glad that you agreed to come with me. This unit is not a suitable place for you to stay," she said angrily. "No furniture and utilities at all? Unbelievable!"

Linda helped Peony carry her luggage to her car as they both set off for Newport and soon approached the Harbour Bridge.

Peony looked out of the vehicle and shouted with excitement. "Wow! We are crossing the famous Sydney Harbour Bridge! Over there is the Opera House!" Then she looked back to the heart of the city. "The Sydney Tower. Linda, I still can't believe it's real. I am in Sydney, Australia! I feel I am in a dream!"

Linda laughed, "No, you are not in a dream. You are here in Sydney! Do you want me to pinch you?" She glanced at Peony's happy face and laughed. Continuing, she said, "Peony, you might want to know a bit more about my family and me. I live with my husband, Jason, and my two children. Hannah is five, and Raymond is three. Oh, on our way to Newport, we will pick up a BBQ chicken and some chips and salad from Mona Vale. They sell the best charcoal BBQ chicken. Normally we buy chicken there once a week. Jason works full-time as an engineer. I only work three days a week. With two young children, my life is full-on. But I like it because that three days' work keeps me in touch with the outside world. I enjoy my job because getting to know other cultures is fascinating. Jason is a wonderful husband and father; you'll like him and my children." Linda spoke as if Peony fully understood her English. Peony couldn't keep up with Linda's fast-talking. Still, she understood a few words here and there.

Linda parked the car next to the Mona Vale BBQ Chicken shop.

"Won't be long. Would you please wait for me in the car?" she said as she got out of the car.

"Ok," Peony replied with a smile, still trying to process what Linda said.

After a while, Linda came back and handed the bags of dinner to Peony. "You look a bit nervous. Don't worry. I have called Jason, and my family knows you are coming home with me. They can't wait to meet you. I am sure you will feel very welcome."

By the time Linda turned her car into the driveway of her house, it was about six thirty in the evening. There was still a lot of sunlight, so Peony could easily see Linda's charming beach-style home with the ocean view behind it. When Peony stepped into the front garden, she could smell the aroma of the gardenias that reminded her of the ones her mum planted in the front of their house in China. Immediately, she felt a kind of familiarity and warmness, safe and calmness, come over her.

As Linda opened the front door, Hannah and Raymond ran to greet their mummy. Linda gave both of her children a long hug. Then she turned to Peony. "This is my new friend, Peony, from China. I want you both to make her feel at home. Can you do that?"

Both children shouted, "Yeah!"

Jason came forward after the kids. He put his hand out to shake Peony's hand. "Hi, I am Jason. Nice to meet you."

Extending her hand to his, she said, "Hi, I am Peony. Nice to meet you, too." Peony tried hard not to show her nervousness.

At that moment, Hannah grabbed Peony's other hand. "Would you like to play with us in the backyard?"

"I want to show you how good I can swim!" Raymond ran to the entrance gate of the pool. "Could you please open the gate for us?"

Peony looked at the pool gate and tried to figure out how to open it.

"Just lift this button on the top." Hannah pointed.

"Only fifteen minutes, children!" Linda called. "Dinner will be served soon!" Then Linda returned to the kitchen to start setting up the table with Jason.

As Peony sat beside the pool and watched the kids swim and splash water at each other, she felt her nervousness evaporate. "I am so lucky to be here," she thought, smiling at the antics of Linda's children.

"Hey, guys! Dinner is ready!" Jason shouted.

"I want you to sit next to me," Hanna directed Peony to the table.

"I want to sit next to you, too," Raymond demanded.

"Peony can sit between you both. There is no need to fight over her," Linda said firmly.

Peony picked up the knife and fork and hesitated. She didn't want to show that she didn't know how to use them properly yet.

"Peony, you can eat with your fingers and lick the gravy off your fingers too, if you like. Just like this." Jason picked up the drumstick from his plate, dipped it in the gravy, then took a bite and licked his fingers.

"Daddy, where are your table manners?" Hannah asked giggling.

"Jason just exaggerated it a bit," Linda carried on. "Sometimes, we do use our fingers with a casual meal. Like tonight's dinner. But we do use the fork for the salad." Linda served some salad on Peony's plate, then picked up a chip with her fingers and put it in her mouth.

Peony picked up a chip and put it in her mouth as well. She felt more relaxed with the rest of her meal.

She was so grateful that Linda let her stay with them. A couple of days' stay turned into a couple of weeks. Peony made sure that she helped Linda as much as she could. Especially with cleaning the house and cooking dinners. She remembered what her father used to teach her.

"Peony, I want you to remember that wherever you go and whatever you do, in a family, a company, a community, or a country, make sure you are the asset, not a liability." Peony made sure that she was an asset to Linda's family. She was doing her best to contribute to the family and offered to look after the kids so Linda and Jason could spend time out as a couple. Both

Linda and Jason were very impressed by her Chinese dishes. Of course, the kids said she made the best vegetarian spring rolls and chicken dumplings.

Linda was very impressed with Peony and how she finely chopped different vegetables to make the spring roll mix.

"This is an excellent way to encourage the children to eat more vegetables. And those spring rolls taste delicious."

"Well, when I was little," Peony explained, "Most people could not afford to have meat daily. We only have meat dishes on special occasions such as the Moon Festival and the Chinese New Year." Listening intently to Peony's stories, Linda began to gain a great insight into her background.

After two weeks with the family, Peony still could not find a suitable place. On Saturday, Jason suggested he look after the kids so Linda could take Peony to the French Forest Farmers' Market to buy fresh produce from the farms.

As Linda drove out of the driveway, she blew a kiss to Jason, "You are the best! We appreciate you, Darling."

"Enjoy your time, lovely ladies. No need to rush back home." Jason blew a kiss back and waved.

On their way to the market, Linda said, "Peony, you are such a beautiful person, inside and out. We are so happy that you're staying with us. May I make a suggestion?"

"Yes. Please," Peony said enthusiastically. She was open to any advice she could get.

"Jason and I would like you to keep living with us. But only if you are happy to. We won't ask for any rent from you. In return, you can help us with some housework, and once a week, you can look after our kids so Jason and I can spend some quality time together. As you know, my kids love you. Think about it; you don't need to give me the answer right now."

Peony thought it was a perfect environment for her to learn the culture and the language. And she adored the kids. But she also felt that she was disrupting their family life.

"Ok, thank you, I will think about your offer. I don't want to burden you and your family."

They drove near the market area, and Linda started looking for a parking spot. Peony gazed at the rows of market stalls. "Wow, look over there. All these fresh fruits and vegetables. Linda, I wish one day I could have my herbs and vegetable garden, just like when I was a child in China. We used to grow all of our vegetables."

"I am glad you enjoy coming to the market with me and some of the things that remind you of your hometown."

Linda found a place to park her car. As they walked through the market, Linda pointed to the BBQ stand. "They make the most delicious burger. I am so hungry. Would you like a chicken burger for brunch?"

"What is brunch?" Peony asked curiously.

"That's Aussie slang. A meal between breakfast and lunch. We took the first two letters from breakfast and joined the lunch without the L that became brunch."

"Interesting! Yes, I would like one, but please let me pay," Peony insisted.

"Ah, ah! It's my shout. I am going to order two chicken burgers with the lot."

"Your shout?" Peony scratched her head and looked at Linda.

"Sorry, more slang; that means I will pay for the burgers."

Linda took a picnic rug out of her car and laid it on the ground in the nearby park, and then they sat down to eat their burgers. They tasted different from the ones she had eaten in the past, but they were delicious, and she eagerly devoured them. Peony felt the friendship between her and Linda grow day by day. She really wanted to stay at her home; she had become her closest friend.

"Linda, I am more than happy to stay at your home. I adore

you, Jason and the children, and you're teaching me so much about Australian culture and language. It's great for me. I need to improve my English for next year when I plan to study fashion design. Being at your home has helped me so much. It would be my honour to be part of your family if that's ok?" she asked.

Linda raised her arms and looked up at the sky, "Yay! Thank you, God!" She dropped the burger on the ground. "Oops! Holy God!" She picked it up and said, "I am not going to chuck it away. It tastes too good. In Australia, we have the five-seconds rule. This means when you drop your food, if you pick it up within five seconds, bacteria will not get in the food, so you still can eat it." She laughed and patted Peony's shoulder gently. "Thank you, Peony! I think we are going to have a BBQ this evening to celebrate you staying on with us."

"I like BBQ pork," Peony replied. "If you like it, too, I can make the Chinese style with the Chinese five spices."

"Peony, you will have your chance to shine with your Chinese BBQ. But I think we should have a true-blue Aussie BBQ. Let's walk back to the markets. There is a stall that sells organic meat, and we can get some pork chops and sausages there."

"Sounds great, and I would love to learn to cook Aussie BBQ," Peony said.

"When we arrive home, I want you to go to our next-door neighbour, Barry—he recently lost his wife to breast cancer, and say, "Hey, Mate come over this arvo for a barbie.""

"What do you mean by arvo and barbie?" Peony asked, confused.

"Come over this afternoon for a barbeque," clarified Linda.

"You must make sure I speak with the Aussie accent accurately!" Said Peony, loving the chance to be in on an Australian cultural joke.

"That would be so funny!" Linda laughed along with her

new friend. "An Asian lady speaking like an Aussie! I can't wait to see his facial expression when you say it."

Linda paused, looking at Peony enjoying the plan they had hatched. "I feel extremely comfortable with you Peony. The first time I met you at the college, I felt as if I had known you for a long time and had an instant connection with you. In Australia, they say when a girl is close to another girl, they are a sister from another Mister. It means we are close like sisters but have different parents." She giggled. Peony loved this. Smiling, she totally agreed with Linda and said she felt the same.

When they arrived home, Linda could not wait to share with Jason the good news. Linda rushed into the house and shouted, "Jason, Jason, Darling! Guess what?! Peony said she would stay with us! We are going to have a true-blue Aussie BBQ to show Peony the Aussie way of celebration!"

Jason hugged his wife, swung her around, then gently put her down and walked over to Peony. He gave Peony a very firm handshake as he thought that Peony might not feel comfortable yet if he hugged her. "Yes, definitely, an Aussie BBQ is in order. We will help you with your English and teach you the Australian culture while we have the privilege of learning and understanding yours," he said. "The best way to learn another culture starts with food. Linda and I have enjoyed your Chinese cooking in the last couple of weeks and look forward to sharing many more meals with you—both Aussie and Chinese," he said warmly.

"Today is such a hot day, Peony. Go and put your swimmers on and cool off in the pool while Jason and I prepare the BBQ," Linda suggested.

"I don't have a swimsuit," Peony replied.

"No problem, I will lend you one of mine." Linda went back to her bedroom to retrieve a black with white stripe bikini from her chest of drawers to give to Peony. "You'll also need some sunglasses Peony," she said, handing her a pair of old sunnies she had. "In Australia, the sun is harsh, and you need to protect your eyes as much as your body from the UV Rays; otherwise, you can get sunburnt and sick," she explained. "Relax and make yourself comfortable—this is your home now too. You can swim or lie on the pool chair, read your magazines, and chill out. Imagine that you're on holiday at a five-star resort. Let us take care of the BBQ." She insisted.

Peony looked at the bikini with an embarrassed smile and said, "I'm sorry, I don't think I can wear them. I don't feel comfortable in them. They look like … um, underwear," she said worriedly.

"Don't stress. I will get you another one." Linda took the bikini and swapped it for a black one-piece she had. "Try this one," she said.

It was about 3 pm, and the sunshine was growing hotter. Peony remembered Linda's comment about the sun being quite harsh in Australia, and she went into the bathroom to apply some sunscreen after changing into the one-piece. She felt a bit bare walking around in Linda's swimmers; she wasn't used to wearing or even swimming in a swimming costume. She put her white linen shirt on over the top and Linda's sunglasses on and headed for the pool. She lay by the pool, picked up one of the fashion magazines that Linda had bought, and started to read. It was so quiet without the kids in the pool, she noticed. They had gone into their rooms to finish off some homework they had.

"G'day, you must be Peony," a man's deep voice said, penetrating her thoughts.

Peony jumped, scared by the stranger's voice. She turned around and saw a tall man, over six feet, with wavy golden hair. He wore a white T-shirt and a pair of swimming boxer shorts. Casual but very smart. Peony sat up and tried to wrap the white shirt around her thighs. "Damn! I wish the shirt was longer," she thought.

"I'm Matt; very nice to meet you. My sister Linda has talked about you a lot in the last two weeks!" He extended his hand to Peony.

Peony stood up and shook hands with him. "Nice to meet you."

He pulled Peony close and gave her a friendly, warm hug that surprised her. "Linda invited Mum and me for BBQ, hope you don't mind. Welcome to Australia and our family Peony," he said with a smile.

"Thank you," Peony said as she stared at the magazine in her hand to avoid eye contact with him.

Matt took his T-shirt off, threw it casually onto the poolside chair next to Peony, and dived into the pool. The spray from the water splashed all over Peony. A bit embarrassed that her white top had become see-through, she quickly grabbed her towel and draped it around herself.

"The water is so cool. Hop in!" He said as he splashed more water on Peony.

Now both she and her towel were soaking wet. Her silhouette was showing under her wet shirt, and she felt more embarrassed and uncomfortable than ever. She tried to find an excuse not to get in the pool. It was far from an interaction she'd ever had with a boy before, and she was confused about what to do. She felt so awkward that she wanted to hide. "I... um... I better go and help Linda prepare the BBQ," Peony said, making a quick exit towards the back door.

"Hey! You'd better get used to me!" yelled out Matt with a huge grin. "I come here all the time," he added, laughing as he porpoised in and out of the water.

Peony turned around. His laughter made her smile. She popped her tongue out and made a funny face at him to show she'd understood his joke before walking to the kitchen.

Matt laughed again and whispered, "I like this girl."

CHAPTER 6

After staying with Linda's family, Peony found her first job selling roses in a Greek restaurant in a Sydney suburb called Narrabeen. It was Valentine's Day. She needed to earn some income to support herself while she studied the following year. She only had enough in her account to last this year and knew she had to begin planning ahead. In addition to earning enough to cover her college fees, her aim was to become as fluent in English as possible, so her chances of securing her dream job were achievable.

With her big basket containing 30 beautiful red roses, she walked into her first establishment—a restaurant hoping to sell them. Her employer had already got permission for her to enter a few businesses, so she wasn't walking in unannounced, but she was still very nervous as she awkwardly approached the first couple dining at the nearest table to the entry.

She walked towards them, gently asking, "Red roses for the lady?"

The man asked with a strong Australian accent, "How much love?"

"Ten dollars each, Sir."

"Forget it! Do you think money grows on trees? Just because today is Valentine's Day doesn't mean you can rip people off!" the man retorted as he picked up a piece of pita bread, dipped it in the tzatziki, and filled his mouth.

Peony was shocked. She didn't move and didn't know how to respond. She stood there like a statue wishing there was a hole she could dive into and hide in. She wanted to quit right then, but somehow her mind kept repeating, 'quitters don't win; winners don't quit'. Besides, she had promised herself that she would sell all 30 roses in her basket by the night's end. Taking a big breath, she tried to force her feet to move to the next table, but they seemed stuck to the floor.

"Excuse me. I would like to buy some roses," a voice said gently behind her.

Peony turned around to locate the voice. Sitting on the table behind her was a man in his early 30s, with olive skin, dark brown short hair, and a solid medium build. Beside him was an older man; they were both dressed in suits and ties. They looked like business men to Peony. They both stared at her waiting for her to respond.

Peony did her best to put on a fake smile to hide her nervousness and asked. "Thank you, certainly Sir; how many would you like?

"How many in the basket?" he asked.

"There are thirty," Peony replied.

"I would like to buy all of them," he said without hesitation.

Peony could hardly believe what she had just heard.

"Sir, they're ten dollars each. That would cost you three hundred dollars. Are you sure you want to buy all of them?"

He took his wallet out, counted out six $50 notes, and handed them to Peony politely. "Here is three hundred dollars."

Peony was astounded but took the man's money and set the basket on a table next to him. She carefully rolled all the roses into a large piece of paper so they wouldn't drip water everywhere and handed them to him, thanking him profusely.

Shocking her even more, the man declined the roses Peony held out to him. Instead, he said, "Keep them, please. I bought these roses for you. I know you girls must sell all of them before you go home for the night. Now, you can pack up and head home earlier." He said.

Peony didn't know what to say; he had completely surprised her. "Thank you so much for buying them," she gratefully said as she noticed his wedding ring glisten from the restaurant lights illuminating it. "Please, take them home to your wife," she said as she met eyes that seemed to penetrate right through her own. She could feel kindness mixed with sadness in his eyes. And there was something else, but she couldn't put her finger on it... "What was that?" she asked herself. "And why is my heart beating so fast?" she wondered silently.

"They are for you. I hope I will see you again," he said, his gaze never leaving hers.

"Thank you again," Peony shyly responded without losing contact with his eyes. She noticed his light brown eyes, flecked, but focused and mesmerising in a way. She thought they showed tenderness and passion. Peony was the first to break the connection. She could feel heat flowing through her body. It was the first time she had felt such an intense sensation and fluttery butterflies in her stomach. She walked to the doorway as fast as she could so the man wouldn't see her begin to blush. As she reached the door, she couldn't help herself; she turned around and stole a quick last look towards the man. Her heart skipped a beat when she saw he was still watching her. Their gaze connected before she nervously turned and raced through the open door onto the street.

When she arrived home, Linda was still awake. She had been marking some papers waiting for the time to go and pick Peony up from work.

"What happened? Why have you come home early and still with all those flowers? Are you ok?" Linda asked with concern.

Peony took the wad of money out of her bag and showed Linda. "I sold all the flowers."

"But you still have the roses. I don't quite understand."

"A gentleman bought all the roses and insisted I take them. He said he bought them for me." Peony told Linda.

"Aaahhhh! He must like you," Linda said with a cheeky wink.

"Well, I don't want to confuse myself with his kindness, but when our eyes met, I could feel something there. I don't know what, but it was something special. I don't think it will amount to anything because I saw a ring on his wedding finger. I think I will find another job elsewhere because I don't want to be involved with a married man, no matter how good-looking he is." Peony sighed dreamily.

The following week, Peony found another job as a dressmaker at Dee Why. She enjoyed the job because she could showcase her skills and creativity, plus the owner was very kind to her. One day Peony came home from work to announce to Linda. "Hey, guess what? My boss invited me to his place for a BBQ this evening. He asked me to bring a plate. Could I please borrow a plate from you? He must have so many guests and doesn't have enough plates."

Linda giggled, and then explained, "Australians sometimes shorten the sentences when they speak Peony. This is a classic example. Your boss said to bring a plate. He means a plate of food, not an empty plate."

"Oh! Gosh! Luckily you explained it to me. I would have been so embarrassed turning up with an empty plate! What should I bring?"

"Why not take the pack of chicken kebabs in the freezer? Normally you bring some drinks as well. People bring wine, beer, or any sort of alcohol. Since you don't drink alcohol, you can take juice with you," Linda said, moving toward the fridge to get a bottle of juice out for her.

"By the way," she said, "I have asked Matt to take you out to speed up your English, and you can learn more about Australian culture as well."

"I am not sure. Your brother is a bit of a...." Peony began to say.

"A bit of what?" Linda asked.

"Well, he is a cheeky monkey!" Peony giggled.

"Yes, indeed, I agree with you. However, you have met him a few times, and by now, you know he is a good man."

The first time Matt invited Peony out. He took her to a football match. Before they went into the football stadium, Matt said to Peony, "Stay here and wait for me. I am going over there to get us some hot dogs."

Horrified, Peony exclaimed, "No, thank you very much!" she said, offended. "I don't eat dog meat. Don't assume everybody from China eats dog meat!"

Matt couldn't stop laughing. Finally, he managed to stop and explained, "A hot dog is a sausage normally made with beef mince in a bread roll and topped up with cooked onion, mustard sauce, barbeque sauce, or tomato sauce. Or sometimes people called it a sausage roll or sausage in a blanket if they put it on bread."

"Ha, ha, ha," Peony laughed. "Remember Matt, I have just arrived in this country. There are so many things I don't know."

Matt shook his head and rolled his eyes. "Oh God, I have to teach you something important relating to sausages. If any man asks you to play hide the sausage in a blanket, you have to tell them to get lost. Will you promise me to do that?"

Peony was confused. "I don't understand! What do you mean?"

"It basically means they want to have sex with you. I don't want anyone taking advantage of you not knowing that one."

"Oh no! It is so complicated. I have to improve my English faster then, so I don't get into trouble from the sounds of it." She said as her face turned bright pink with embarrassment.

"Looks like I need to teach you not only English, but also more Aussie slang. The same words in different tones could have completely different meanings. Some are good, some bad. Also, you don't need to use some rude words unless you have to. But you must learn and understand them just in case. For example, fuck is a slang word for having sex. If you add a preposition behind this word, it means something different. When someone says fuck off, it means to get lost; fuckwit means idiot; fuck up means stuff things up and fuck me doesn't necessarily mean that someone wants you to fuck them; it could mean that they are astounded about something. Ok, this is enough for today's lesson. So, do you still want a hot dog?"

"I don't know if I'll like it, but I will try," she said before murmuring under her breath, "Sounds better than hiding a sausage in a blanket."

"I heard that. Don't worry! I don't want it with you either," Matt laughed as he walked off to get the hot dogs.

When they were sitting in the stadium eating their hot dogs, Matt explained to Peony, "Aussie football rules are different. I will explain to you as the game starts. One thing you must do tonight is to cheer our Aussie team. You follow me and say: 'Aussie, Aussie, Aussie, Oi, Oi, Oi!'"

"I can't fully understand those words. But it sounds like a lot of fun! Aussie. Aussie, Aussie, Oi, Oi, Oi! Do I sound right?" She took another bite of the hot dog. "Well, I like this hot dog."

Matt used his serviette to wipe the mustard sauce off her lips. "You sounded not only like a true Aussie, but it sounded very cute as well."

Peony did not fully understand the game, but she shouted as loud as possible and enjoyed the atmosphere.

On their way home, Peony stated, "I enjoy going out with you. Where will you take me next time?" She playfully hit Matt's arm gently.

"If you like, I will take you to the pub next Saturday. It's a good place to experience more Aussie culture."

"Yes, I would like to go; it should be fun."

On the following Saturday, Matt took Peony to a pub in Manly.

"This pub has a mix of all sorts of people," Matt explained.

As they entered the pub, Peony looked around. A live band played on the stage at the left-hand side of the corner. Some people were dancing in the middle of the room to the rhythm of the music. Some of them were drunk and doing out-of-rhythm crazy dancing. Each individual was expressing their emotion and releasing their energy. A group of men was sitting by the side of the bar bench. They seemed very drunk and were talking and laughing loudly.

"A bit lousy here!" Peony mentioned.

"If you don't like it, we can go somewhere else."

"No, no, that's ok. We stay."

While Matt went to the bar to get some drinks, a man from the group sitting by the bar walked up to Peony. "How much does he pay you, China Doll? Come with me. I'll pay you double." He grabbed her arm.

Peony stood up and pushed his hand away. She shouted at him, "Fuck off! You Fuckwit!"

At that moment, Matt returning with the drinks, momentarily froze with a look of shock, hearing Peony tell the drunk guy off. Seeing she was ok, he put the drinks on the table and turned to the drunk. "Did you hear what she just said? You just fucked up big time mate. You're lucky she didn't give you a Kung Fu kick! You'd never walk again, then you'd be royally fucked!"

With that, the man threw a big hay-maker punch at Matt's head. Ducking, Matt easily avoided the drunken punch and grabbed him by the collar and pushed him away. The man gave up and went back to his mates, who were all having a laugh at his expense.

"Let's get out of here. We'll go somewhere a little quieter and with less action, I think," he told Peony.

Once they got out of the pub, Matt put his hand up, "Give me five."

Peony reached for her handbag and took out her wallet. She took out a five-dollar note and handed it to Matt.

Matt laughed so hard that he began to cough. Finally, he was able to catch his breath. "I don't mean give me five dollars. In English, it means we're slapping palms above each other's heads as a celebration gesture. Firstly, I am so proud that you stood up for yourself. Secondly, you are a fast learner. You used the F word in a perfect situation." Matt put up his hand again. "Give me five."

Peony lifted her hand and slapped Matt's palm with a giggle.

"Hey, Peony, I like you a lot and enjoy being with you. I reckon I'll organise to take you to some places once a week—how does that sound?"

"I'd like that!" Peony replied.

They left the pub happy and headed for home.

CHAPTER 7

Lili arrived at Madam B's house. When the door was opened, she saw two women sitting on the sofa in the lounge room smoking cigarettes. Welcoming her was the smell of stale cigarettes and strong perfume. It was dingy and dark. The atmosphere made her feel extremely uncomfortable. She held on to the handle of her suitcase tightly and stood still in the middle of the room anxiously.

"This is my new girl, Lili." Madam B introduced.

"Hi, I am Tara." One of the women waved to Lili. The other women looked at her condescendingly and said nothing.

"Susan, what's your problem? You think she is so beautiful that she will steal all your clients?" Tara said and laughed.

"Don't worry. Lili can hardly speak English. She can only take clients that I hook her up with." Madam B explained to Susan.

"What are you talking about? I have no worries at all!" Susan protested.

"Then why do you ignore her? You did the same thing to me when I first came. It's rude." Tara asked.

"You are the one who should worry about her. I just don't like her look. That's all." Susan rolled her eyes.

"Well, you girls have a chat. Be nice! I am going to prepare a room for Lili." Madam B said, and went upstairs.

"I don't worry. I am only doing it part-time. I do this job because my husband works as a gardener, and he can't provide me with expensive lunches, French champagne and designer handbags and clothes that I love. It's convenient for me because I drop the kids at school and then come here, change into one of my sexy outfits, and then the driver picks me up and takes me to the hotel. I have lunch with one of the bastards who pay me, then he takes me to a hotel room, and he fucks me. I get a couple of hundred bucks, and I'm happy. Much easier than making bloody sandwiches in a café. Then I shower and change and pick my kids up from school. Easy!"

"Does your husband know about that?" Susan asked.

"I don't think so. And I don't care." Tara replied.

"What if he finds out?" Susan questioned further.

"He can't do much about it unless he can provide me the lifestyle that I want." Scoffed Tara, picking at her false fingernails.

"Tara, you are a bad girl!" Susan laughed.

"How's your client today? I bet he was not as ugly as mine." Tara joked.

"Let's be honest, any decent, good-looking man will not get women like us. In my experience, they are not only ugly outwardly but ugly inside as well. Most of them think money can buy everything! And...." Susan said.

"In our case, money does buy us," Tara interrupted her.

"I had one of the worst fucked up clients today. He was my regular client. But I don't think he will be my client after today." Susan stated.

"What happened? Tell me about it. I want to know about it before I pick up my kids." Tara said, collecting her things.

"Can you remember that bastard on television yesterday?" She whispered his name in Tara's ear.

Tara was shocked, with her eyes wide open, "You mean that politician with his adorable wife and children standing beside him?

"Yes, that's him!" Susan confirmed.

"I remembered that he made an impressive speech. His pitch was to end the sexual abuse of women and children. Help to build a better Australia where women and children are safe, secure, supported, and protected," Tara recounted.

"Well, I am telling you, he is the biggest hypocrite of all. You know what? He has been my client for quite some time. He usually drives to the hotel car park on his own and parks the car there. Then he gets the lift straight up to the room floor, and slides into the room when no one is looking to have sex with me. Normally at lunchtime. When I found out that he booked me for today, I called the Sydney News and spoke with a reporter. So, today after having sex with him, I deliberately did not put my clothes back on. I opened the door to let him out, and the reporter was outside waiting. He took photos of him with me naked in the background. I cannot wait and will be so satisfied to see him with me in the background on the front page of tomorrow's newspaper. Or even better on this evening's breaking news on TV," Susan laughed.

"Why did you do that? In our industry, we have an unwritten rule that we kiss but don't tell. Especially with the rich and famous." Tara said worriedly.

"Nice girls don't tell. A fucked-up woman like me from a worse fucked up family tells. The last time he was with me he said something that pissed me right off. I want to teach that stupid jerk a lesson. Last night when I saw him on television, I decided that I had to do something to ruin his family and career."

"I never heard you talk about your family before," Tara mentioned.

"That's because I am so ashamed to talk about them. Do you want to know why I chose to be a hooker? It's so complicated, I don't even know where to start, but I'll tell you this, after my grandpa passed away, my grandma got into a de facto relationship with a scumbag. Soon after, she moved into his house with my mother, who then was just fifteen years old. He groomed her to have sex with him behind my grandma's back.

"What? Your father, grandma, and your mum? I can't get it!" Tara was so shocked.

"When my grandma found out that that scumbag made my mum—her daughter-pregnant-Grandma was devastated and moved out. She never wanted to see either of them again. Soon after, Mum gave birth to me. Do you think that bastard would stay with my mum? Of course not. A dog is a dog; a dog never gives up eating shit. He is a typical playboy. Since I can remember, somehow, when I was a few years old, he started to share custody with my mum. Every time I had to go to his house for him to look after me, he sexually assaulted me. Anyway, that bastard does not deserve to be called my father. He tried to tell me it was a game between Daddy and his girl, and that it was our secret. He told me not to tell anyone. I didn't like it, but there was nothing I could do. When I was about thirteen years old, I realised what he did to me was not a game. I confronted him about it and never saw him again. Growing up with my mum, who changed men like changing her undies, did not help either. I was already broken and a mess. I started to have sex with different men, including my mum's boyfriends. One day I thought, why don't I get money from those scumbags in exchange for the sex I have with them?"

"So that's why today that bastard triggered you, and you wanted to expose him for his dirty secrets?" Tara asked.

"Yes, I asked him why he needed to use women like us. He said, 'To me, you are just like a piece of meat. Put it this way, I use hookers just like people go to different restaurants. I have different hookers to fulfil my physical need and feed my ego. I have the power to choose different women. I like to taste women from different cultural backgrounds; Chinese, Japanese, Thai, French, Italian, Indian—any nationality, you name it! Then I go back home to my wife just like that. Even if my wife knew what I did, she has to turn a blind eye to it and pretend to know nothing. She wouldn't do anything to stop me. I stripped her of her confidence years ago by keeping her as a stay-at-home mum and made sure she was a hundred percent reliant on me.' He had bragged and I told him that if he chose to be a playboy, he should not hold his wife hostage. I suggested he should divorce her and let her have the chance to pursue her happiness and find someone who respects and love her. That's when he became very angry with me and shouted, 'Are you kidding me? You are just a hooker. How dare you tell me what to do! Do you think I am that stupid? If I divorced her, I would lose half of my fortune. I created the perfect Stepford Wife; she knows her place, knows what to say, and does everything I expect of her at family and friends' gatherings, business, and public functions. I have to show in the public that I have a successful marriage, am a good husband and a wonderful father to continue my political career.' " Susan paused and took a breath.

"You are brilliant. You killed two birds with one stone. You not only ruined his reputation but, at the same time, you will get free publicity which will make more men desire you—you could increase your charge!" Tara said.

"I don't just have blonde hair and a pretty face; I got a brain as well!' Susan laughed sarcastically.

Then Tara realised Lili was still standing there quietly, trying to understand as much of the conversation as she could. "Lili, don't worry; we will teach you English and all the tricks to get as much money as you can from these bastards," she said.

"It will take ages! The first thing she needs to learn is to lie to those bastards and tell them what they want to hear to boost their egos. Because deep down, they are just a bunch of ugly bastards with severe insecurity and low self-esteem. If your client is short, tell him he has a strong and sexy body, if he is a big fat pig, tell him he's your type of man. If he is too bloody old, tell him you love a Sugar Daddy. If he is the wham bam, thank you ma'am type, tell him you had the best fuck you have ever had. But Tara, you are the one going to teach her, not me," Susan said. With a shake of her head, she got up and walked upstairs.

"What if they got a little chilli dick?" Tara yelled out after her, laughing.

"You work that one out!" Susan laughed and disappeared up the staircase that led to her bedroom.

"Come up. I will show you your room," Madam B called out from the top of the staircase. After Lili got to the room, Madam B opened the wardrobe. It was full of sexy outfits. "Take a shower and pick one of them to wear. I just lined up your first client for tonight," she said.

"That soon?" Lili questioned, unsure.

"Well, you have not come here to enjoy life. You have come here to make money; what is the difference whether you do it tonight or tomorrow night!" she said impatiently.

That night, before Madam B sent the first client to her room, Lili showered, chose one of the transparent lingerie pieces out of the wardrobe and put it on. She felt extremely uncomfortable, so she put on a bathrobe. She sat at the end of the bed shaking and thinking to herself, "Why did I agree to this?! Should I just leave and go back to the unit and sleep on the floor again?" Clasping and unclasping her hands, she tried to calm herself down. Just then, she heard the sound of the door opening. She was scared. She wanted to run out of the room but felt as if she was frozen.

"What's your name?" he asked as he moved closer to her, trying to undress her.

"Lili," she replied like a robot, wondering why she let him come at her like that.

"Where do you come from?"

"Ha?" Lili could not understand.

"Is it your first time?"

"Um...." By then, he had taken all her clothes off. Lili put her left arm across to touch her right armpit, so her arm covered her breasts and put her right hand down to cover her crutch.

"Don't be shy and do the job well. You are paid to please me, so do as I tell you." He pushed her onto the bed and then forced himself on top of her. Lili closed her eyes and focused on the tick-tock sound of the clock on the wall. Even though it was only a few minutes until the whole thing was over, Lili felt like it was forever. When he was done, he rolled off her body and lay beside her for a short while before trying to have another go at her. Despite how hard he tried, he couldn't do it the second time, so he got up. While he was putting his clothes back on, he complained. "Fucking hell, of all Madam B's newbies, you are the worst! You can't even speak bloody English. Without men like us, you don't even have a job. With one fuck the money you take will feed your whole family for a month in your poor fucking country. You should be grateful and at least make an effort!" he spat at her furiously and left the room.

She had no idea what the man said. She only knew that he was not satisfied by the tone of his voice.

"Welcome to hell again." She murmured while she covered her naked and used body with the bed sheet.

CHAPTER 8

Towards the end of the year, Peony was excited to book her air ticket to Hong Kong to see her mum and dad, who were invited to lecture at Hong Kong University. The travel agent, Sasha Bui, told Peony the ticket would be ready the following week, and she had to collect it from her mother's place in Burwood.

At the house in Burwood, the doorbell rang. Lili stumbled to the front door, nearly falling over on the way; she opened the door, holding onto it to regain her balance. Complete shock came across her as she saw Peony standing before her. "Peony?" she asked, not quite believing whom she was seeing.

"Lili!" Peony said, surprised, leaping forward to hug her long-lost friend. "So good to see you. Are you coming to pick up an air ticket as well?"

Lili's eyes were half-open, and she stared at Peony, trying to focus. She slurred, "No. I...live here."

Peony tried hard to understand the Lili she was looking at. "You look... um..." She swallowed back the words she was going to say. Instead, she asked, "How are you?"

"I am totally fine," Lili said with a sad smile.

Peony smiled back. "I have been thinking of you since the day you left the unit at Broadway. I thought I would see you at the English college the next day. Your disappearance worried me a lot. I am very happy to see you again." She stepped forward to try and give Lili another hug. However, this time, Lili pushed her away and stumbled onto a nearby sofa, collapsing.

Worried, Peony followed her into the house and saw a woman walking down the stairs. When the woman saw Peony, she became excited. "You must be the one my daughter sent here to pick up the air ticket. I am... well... everybody calls me Madam B. Sasha's mother. Take a seat," she said in Mandarin with a strong Vietnamese accent as she led Peony into the sitting room.

"Thank you," Peony said looking at her suspiciously and taking a seat next to Lili, looking at her friend with grave concern.

"Oh, don't worry about that silly girl," Madam B said. "She must be drinking too much again." She turned to Peony, looking at her up and down with a disgusted look. "Tea or coffee?"

"No, thanks." Peony felt awkward and uncomfortable. "What was wrong with Lili, and why was she here?" she wondered.

"What are you doing in Sydney?" Madam B asked. "I guess a beautiful girl like you must have an easy life. Are you with the rich and famous?"

"I am a student. I am going to study fashion design next year." Peony shifted uneasily in her seat.

"Yes. Once upon a time, I came here to study, too," Lili interrupted with a sarcastic laugh. "Look at me. I don't even know who I am anymore."

"You're just being stupid," Madam B said. "If you were not drunk and drugged all the time, you could be making lots of money from those men." She stared at Peony again. "You look like you have better sense than her. You could make much more money! I will train you and teach you all the tricks to make the men happy." She went on, "Have you had a man before? My clients pay up to ten thousand dollars for a virgin."

Peony jerked back in disbelief, "You are a disgraceful woman! Lili, is that what she makes you do? Has she made you become a prostitute?"

"Oh, you take it too seriously! She is a high-class escort! Serves rich and famous men! Easy money! What's wrong with that?"

"When you sell your body and soul for money, that is prostitution," Peony said, emphasising the word. "There is no such thing as high class or low class. I will never do that. Besides, I'm determined to save my virginity for my future husband, who I will truly love."

"Don't be stupid," Madam B scoffed. "Do you think there is such a thing as true love? Ha! Save your virginity? Those things are worth nothing! Get the money from those stupid old fools who think virgins keep them looking younger." She rolled her eyes and continued, "I have a client in Melbourne this weekend. It looks like Lili is unwell to serve him. I can line you up with him. Lili can tell you how easy it is to get those stupid mongrels' money. I trained her well!" She said as she smiled at Lili, who was in a world of her own.

"Lili. Can't you understand this woman gave you free accommodation but sold your body and soul?" Peony's voice shook with anger, "Surely this woman will give you a free ticket to hell as well!"

"Who cares?" Lili waved her hand slackly in the air before it dropped back down beside her.

"Where is my air ticket?" Peony shouted. "Give it to me now! Shame on you. Now I understand. You use your daughter to lure Chinese students like me to you so you can turn them into sex slaves."

Peony stood up and turned to Lili, "Please, it is not too late to get out of what you are doing. I will help you. You can come to stay with me."

"She is not going anywhere till she pays me all the money she owes me. The accommodation is free, but not the drugs and alcohol." Madam B became very aggressive, like a venomous snake about to attack and hissed, "Who do you think you are?

You think you are so pure. All women are prostitutes, one way or the other. Either you give sex to make money or get no pay for the sake of so-called LOVE! The ones willing to marry you are the worst of all. During the day, you are his slave, cleaning, and cooking, and at night you are his prostitute anyway. Even worse, if you have children with the bastard, you become his slave to him and his children forever! What is good about falling in love? You end up falling into hell."

Madam B, consumed with toxic anger, stood up and paced up and down the floor. "When I was in Vietnam, I thought I fell in love with my ex-husband. In the end, he forced me to serve men as a prostitute. Then he took all the money that I earned and spent it gambling. Even a few days after I gave birth to my daughter, he again forced me to provide sex to earn money. Which was worse?" She said as she threw up her hands. "After years of suffering, I finally found a chance to escape from him. I used all my belongings to trade places in a boat to free me and my daughter. We went from Vietnam to Australia in the boat, and we were not only nearly drowned by the huge violent waves, but we were also raped multiple times by the mongrel dogs in the boat. They raped my daughter right in front of my eyes, she was only nine years old! I begged the scumbags to leave my daughter alone, telling them I would give them whatever they wanted. They continued to rape us both until the boat arrived at Darwin, and we were rescued by the Australian Navy. I am telling you, all men are bastards. If they want sex, they have to pay! They are not only paying for our bodies, but for what they did to all the women they have hurt!"

Peony was horrified by what Madam B had said and tried hard to hold back her tears. "I am sorry about what happened to you and your daughter. Hurt people hurt other people. You can still do things to make things right. Stop giving these men the opportunity to hurt other women like Lili."

"No, too late! They must pay for what they did to me and my daughter!" Madam B screamed with blood-red eyes.

"Never too late," Peony said with sadness.

She turned to Lili, "Lili, don't listen to her nonsense. My mum and Dad were deeply in love with each other through good times and bad times. When my mum was sent to a re-education camp, Dad could have chosen to divorce her and make a declaration that he was against mum. Then he could 'come clean' and stay in Guangzhou. But he chose to go to the 're-education camp' with Mum. There are lots of good men out there. They will love and respect you. You mix with the wrong people. Come with me, it is not too late. You have the power to make the right choice," Peony said, desperately trying to get Lili out of this situation.

"She is not going anywhere unless she pays me back all the money she owes me," Madam B shouted.

"How much does she owe you?" Peony asked. "I can pay you back!"

"Too much. You can only pay it off by having sex with a lot of men," Madam B replied.

"Then I have no choice but to call the police," Peony said.

"Fine! You call the police, and she will be sent back to China!" Madam B threatened.

"Peony, you have a bright future," Lili cried. "Don't waste your time trying to save me. I am just a filthy, dirty slug, as many men told me. I have got in too deep now and have no hope of escaping. I don't want to go back to China. At least here, no one knows what I am doing. Just leave me alone. Go!" Lili pointed her finger at the front door.

"Here is my phone number." Peony wrote her phone number on a piece of paper and handed it to Lili. "Please call me. Remember, I will always be there if you need help."

"Just go!" Lili grabbed the paper and threw it on the floor

tearfully before stumbling upstairs to her bedroom.

"Here is your air ticket. Get out of here before I kick your ass." Madam B threw the air ticket to Peony.

Peony's heart sank as she watched Lili's weak, thin body disappear up the staircase. After Peony stepped out of the house, Madam B slammed the door shut.

On her way home, Peony could not stop thinking of how to get Lili out of her situation. "God, please help Lili and give her strength and courage to get out of her situation." She prayed desperately.

CHAPTER 9

In the morning, Matt offered to take Peony to the airport. The excitement of seeing her parent consumed her with joy. She told him that she looked forward to seeing her mum and dad in Hong Kong since she hadn't seen them for almost a whole year. They had so much to catch up on, and she couldn't wait to taste the special signature dishes that her mum cooked. Even though she had learned cooking from her mum, her dishes were never as tasty.

"It will be wonderful for you to see them," Matt said with a slight tremble in his voice.

"Sorry that your dad is no longer with us, but thankfully your mum is still here, so you can see her at anytime too." She said.

"Peony, can you visualize what your future looks like?" Matt tried to steer away from the topic.

"Ha-ha. Good question. My future looks as bright as the midday sun!" Peony replied with a joyful look on her face. "I will be accepted to study for double diplomas in fashion design and business management at the Sydney Institute of Technology next year. And after finishing my study, I will start my own business." Peony's English had improved dramatically after almost one year of living in Australia and with the help of Linda's family and Matt.

"Good to hear that. You are a wonderful lady, and you deserve the best...." Matt paused.

"How about your future?" She glanced at Matt. "It looks like something is bothering you. Is there anything I can help with?"

After a long silence, he decided to break the sad news, "Last week we found out my mum has pancreatic cancer. The doctor told us she may have only three to six months left with us."

"Oh, Matt! I am so sorry to hear that. Why don't you tell me earlier?" Peony felt devastated.

"I know how much you were looking forward to seeing your parents, and I didn't want to spoil your holiday, but I just couldn't hold it in any longer." He said apologetically.

"I can delay going to Hong Kong and stay here to help look after your mum and support you and Linda." Peony's eyes filled with tears.

"You're only going for a couple of weeks. I would rather you go now in these early days and come back to help us deal with the challenges ahead of us." Matt sighed, "I shouldn't have told you that. I hope that I am not spoiling your holiday."

"Matt, I'd rather you tell me now. We share the good and bad together. By now, you should know that we are family. I am one of your family members. Right?"

"Yes, I know. One thing Mum wishes for is for me to get married and start a family. She does not know that I am gay."

"Every time we are together, many people think we are a couple, but I know you are not interested in women. As a matter of fact, a few times I've caught you looking at attractive men." She rubbed Matt's arm gently, "Does Linda know you are gay?"

"Yes, Linda knows. She caught me kissing a guy when I was in year twelve. But we keep it a secret from Mum. Dad passed away when we were little. Mum did her best to raise Linda and me. She is a very faithful and traditional Christian. The last thing I would do is bring a man home and tell her I am gay. I don't think she would be able to cope with that."

"She is a wonderful woman," Peony agreed. "Knowing the tree by the fruit it produces, look at you and Linda. Both of you are the kindest and finest people in this world. Look how you both have kept this from me! You're so considerate, but your mum is my mum too—by choice."

"I know. You are not only my family but also my best friend. I have a... um... ridiculous request...." He hesitated.

"Tell me. I will do whatever I can." She gave Matt a serious look, "What? You don't trust me?"

"I'm wondering if you would consider marrying me to make my mum's wish come true. You know that she loves you very much. I think it would make her very happy."

There was a long silence, and then Matt added, "If it is too much to ask, just say no. I understand."

Peony thought for a while and answered, "Well, in the next few years, I need to focus on my studying, and I'm not in a hurry to fall in love and get married. So yes. If that will make her happy in her sunset moments on this earth. At least I can do something to repay the kindness that your family has shown me."

Matt tapped the top of her hand and said tearfully, "Thank you so much Peony. That means a huge amount to me."

When Matt parked the car at the airport car park, he picked up his phone and called his mother. "Hey, Mum. How are you feeling today? I have excellent news. Peony and I are going to get married.... Yep! I have just proposed to her, and she said yes.... When she comes back from Hong Kong.... In the middle of January, before she goes to college.... All right, I will come to see you after seeing her leave.... Yes, I am at the airport with her right now.... Love you, Mum." He hung up.

"The outside world doesn't have to know the kind of relationship between us." She smiled at Matt and added, "I don't think I will have time to make my wedding dress. I will get a dress from Hong Kong. Linda will be the bridesmaid. Hannah will be the flower girl. Raymond will be the page boy. Hey! I am excited because I am marrying my best friend." Peony smiled at Matt and punched his shoulder.

When they were inside the airport, Matt settled with Peony in the coffee lounge and ordered a café latte for her, "Enjoy your coffee. I will be back soon."

"Hey, where are you going?"

"Wait and see. You will know when I come back."

After about fifteen minutes, Matt returned with a little box in his hand. He sat next to Peony and said, "Give me your left hand." He opened the box and took out a beautiful opal ring. He slowly slid it onto her ring finger.

"By giving you this ring, I promise to be your best friend and always be there for you to protect, encourage, support, and help you be the best you that you were born to be. Will you promise me that you won't settle for the second-best and will wait for the best man who deserves you?"

"I will." Peony giggled, and from that moment, Peony knew that they would be best friends for life.

Hugging Matt, she saw the Westpac Bank over his shoulder and was reminded of the first day she entered Australia. "I wish Lili and Jasmine were here to share my joy. I miss them so much," she thought to herself and smiled at Matt.

CHAPTER 10

At the same moment, Peony was at the international airport waiting to board the flight to Hong Kong, and Lili was at the domestic airport waiting to board the plane to Melbourne. She was on her way to serve her client. As soon as the plane took off, she screamed in a raging voice, "Get me a glass of champagne! Does anybody hear me?!"

The air hostess rushed to her and explained that she had to wait until the plane completely took off.

"Your service is not good enough! I will make a complaint to the airline company once I get off this damn plane." She said, consumed by anger, bitterness, and hatred.

Finally, the air hostess handed her a glass of champagne. She gobbled the glass of wine down in no time." Give me another one." She shouted.

The man in the seat beside her stared at her. Glancing at him, she took in what she observed to be a short, bored businessman in his 60s. "Why are you staring at me? As if you haven't seen an Asian woman before!" Lili said rudely to the man.

He can't help but look at Lili's slim tall body. He fixed his eyes on Lili's full breasts half shown from above her low-cut mini dress before looking back up at her face and saying, "I am just admiring you," he said timidly.

"You have a wife?" Lili pointed to his ring finger with his wedding ring.

"Yes, but so what?" he said with a shrug.

"You should not look at me this way!"

"I am a naughty man. I prefer a provocative woman like you to my boring wife, just like naughty boys prefer junk food to healthy food. We know it is not good for us, but it is so tasty, and we cannot resist it."

"Another dirty bastard. I will fix you," Lili thought to herself.

She stood up and tried to get out of her seat with her face toward him, then pretended that she was out of balance and fell on him. Her full breasts 'perfectly' landed on his face. Then she slowly picked herself up, "Excuse me. I need to go to the toilet." The man gave her a wink and said, "No worries."

When Lili returned to her seat, she passed him with her back toward him and bent down a bit, so her bottom rubbed his crotch. She could feel his penis grow erect against her.

As she sat down, the man started the conversation, "You live in Melbourne, or are you visiting?"

"Visiting." She gave him a seductive smile as she thought, "I am running out of money. I need some money from this bastard to get drugs before I see my next client."

"You? Live there, or travelling?" Lili asked sweetly keeping her thoughts to herself.

"Business trip in Sydney. On my way home. By the way, you are so beautiful and extremely sexy" he looked at her like a hungry cheetah targeting a little fawn as its prey. Then he introduced himself, "I am Jack. What's your name?

"Lili, Tiger Lili," she said, putting her index finger in her mouth and slowly pulling it out.

"You are hot!" he licked his lips.

"Since you are a businessman, do you want to make a deal?" she licked her top lip seductively.

"Depends on if the deal is attractive enough." He glanced at her with his tempted eyes.

"Five hundred dollars. A quickie in the toilet. Are you interested?" Lili asked directly.

Jack, at first, was shocked by Lili's straightforward approach, but then his eyes lit up. He put his hand on Lili's thigh. "Of course. How can I resist a sexy girl like you? I'll go there first, then I'll let you into the cubicle, ok?" He asked.

"Money first. Cash! No money, no honey!" Lili replied.

The man bent over and took out his wallet from his briefcase, which was placed under the seat. He counted five hundred-dollar-notes and handed them over to Lili.

She carefully counted all the notes and then put the money in her handbag. She put it back under her seat, then stood up and walked toward the toilet. The man followed soon after, and they both locked themselves in the toilet.

After a while, the captain announced their arrival at the airport, and all on board made their way from the aeroplane into the terminal. As Lili was heading out, she saw a woman running toward Jack and hugging and kissing him. Soon after, he walked to the café with her. The woman found a table and sat down while Jack went up to the counter to place an order. Lili seized the opportunity to approach her.

"Are you Jack's wife?" she asked. The woman looked at Lili with a puzzled face and said, "Yes, can I help you?"

"You don't want to know, but I'll tell you anyway. Your husband is a dead fuck. You may be interested to know HOW I know?" she asked seductively. Before waiting for the shocked woman to reply, she said, "Well, we have just had a quickie in the aeroplane toilet. Yet, look at him; he looks like an innocent man and is acting like nothing has happened!" she smiled with a mixture of bitterness and anger.

"I don't believe you. He is a faithful husband and loving father. He will never do that! Go away! You liar!" the woman shouted.

"Oh, yes? By the way, the tattoo of a tiger's face on his left butt is... kind of ugly. Tell him to get rid of it." Then she walked toward the taxi stand. Just before she got into the waiting cab, she turned back around to see Jack's wife pick up the coffee he'd purchased and pour it all over him before storming off.

"Bastard, serves you right!" She thought with a victorious smile.

After leaving the airport, Lili did as usual; she went immediately to her contact to get drugs before seeing her client in the evening. By the time her client entered the hotel room, she would be numb and would not care what she was doing, or who she was with. She stayed in the hotel after she took the drug and continued drinking until late in the afternoon. When she looked at her watch and realised her client was about to arrive, she quickly took her clothes off and lay in the bed waiting for him. Zoned out, she didn't much care whether she lived or died anymore. She was barely functioning.

She heard the door opening. As she heard steps come closer, she did not even bother to open her eyes. "Help yourself, take your clothes off and go for it," she said.

"So, in the other words, it is a buffet dinner. Help myself in any way I like?" The man said with a sneer. Taking his clothes off, he looked at her sprawled on the bed, emotionless. He climbed on her attempting to have sex with her, but she did not respond. He finally gave up, frustrated and screamed, "You fucking whore!" Climbing off her, he complained furiously, "Madam B told me that you were experienced and knew how to satisfy your client's needs. Look at you! You're lying there like a piece of dead meat. You are not a high-class escort and nothing like what Madam B described to me. You should stand in the street at Kings Cross and fuck the old men who could not afford to pay top dollar for hotel rooms and air tickets! Waste of my money!" The man yelled and stormed off into the bathroom to shower. Still shouting at her, he screamed, "Disappear! I don't want to see your ugly face when I get out!"

Lili thought, "You dirty old bastard. You still have a wedding ring on—just like all the other scumbags! Their wives thought they were off for business trips while they were fucking other women."

While the man was taking a shower, she got up, got dressed, and put on some lipstick to mark a kiss on the inside of his used underpants. Then she carefully put the used condom in his pants pocket and sprayed her perfume on his shirt. As she was leaving the room, she whispered to herself, "Hope your wife does your dirty laundry. You bastard!" closing the door behind her.

CHAPTER 11

Two weeks passed, and Peony flew into Australia for the second time in her life. Matt picked her up from the airport, and once in his car, he took a deep sniff. "What's that smell?" he asked.

"I did not have a shower last night. Is that bad?" Peony asked.

"No, silly, I like the perfume you are wearing. From who?"

"I bought it duty-free. What?! Are you getting jealous already? We're not even married yet!" she said jokingly.

"Ha. I mean, from which company," Matt said, smiling.

"It's called Eternity by Calvin Klein. Do you like it?" she asked.

"Yes, the luxurious composition of the flowers, citrus, and softwood that holds the promise of lasting love... it suits you," he said.

"That's getting a bit too romantic! Should I be worried?" She asked playfully.

"You are going to be my wife. I need to look after you and take notice of your likes and dislikes," he said.

"I hope you don't change your mind and end up falling for me," Peony continued with a serious tone. "You need to stay true to who you are."

"Don't worry, I won't change my mind. You are beautiful, and I love you, but certainly not romantic love," he laughed.

"Phew! Now I can relax." She put her hand on her forehead and pretended to wipe her sweat off.

"I took the day off. I want to take you to Whale Beach for lunch, then I'll drop you back at Linda's. You can take a shower and have a rest. What do you think?"

"Sounds like a plan." She agreed.

"I will come to pick you up at around 4 pm and take you to my place, oh, and I should say our place. I'd like you to look around to see if there is anything you would like to do to make it your home."

"Your home is beautiful. It only needs a little bit of my girly magical touch, that's all. I can do that. I want to show you the wedding dress as well."

"Don't let me see the wedding dress," Matt laughed. "It is bad luck for the groom to see the wedding dress before the ceremony."

"You believe that?" she asked, stunned.

"Let's keep the tradition. I want to be surprised. I can't wait to see you and can only imagine how beautiful you will be in the dress. But I prefer to wait."

It was a brilliant and sunny day. The white fluffy clouds drifted across the clear, blue sky. Matt and Peony's wedding was at Linda and Jason's home. Linda had set up the house stunningly with a beach theme. She and Jason even made an arch by the pool with beautiful fresh flowers and evergreen vines. Linda helped Peony with her makeup. They kept it simple but magical. As Jason walked Peony down the aisle, the delightful sea breeze brushed across her face, and her long black silky hair danced behind her freely. The off-shoulder soft chiffon wedding dress Peony had chosen was elegant and fitted her perfectly. With graceful steps, and happiness radiating from her eyes and face, she stepped toward the arch where Matt was waiting.

After they had exchanged their vows, Linda came to her, hugging and kissing her, exclaiming with delight, "Now you are officially my sister-in-law! It's just a small ceremony, but I hope you feel as special as we do. Mum is over the moon happy!" She said, holding hands and looking over to her mum Joyce who sat with a big smile on her face and tears of joy.

Linda led her over to her new mum-in-law, who spread her arms out to give Peony a frail but warm, long hug. "My dear, you look stunning in your wedding dress. Welcome to our family," she said lovingly.

"Thank you, Mrs Williamson. It is my privilege to be part of your family." Peony hugged her tenderly.

"Call me Mum from now on. You know we all love you dearly."

"Thank you, Mum. I know I can feel that I am deeply loved." Tears of joy ran down Peony's face.

"Mum! You made Peony cry," Matt playfully said, picking up a napkin from the table and carefully whipping the tears off his new bride's face. He put his arm around Peony's waist and continued, "You know you have this whole new family here for you. Now you can spread your wings and fly as far and as high as you want. The sky is your limit!"

Jason walked up and kissed Peony, "From now on, you are my sister-in-law. How awesome!"

"Thank you for walking me down the aisle, Jason. By the way, even though I move to Matt's today, Matt and I still want to look after Hannah and Raymond every Wednesday night so you and Linda can spend time together." Peony hugged him and added, "You know you are my favourite brother–in–law."

"Ha! You say that because I am your one and only brother–in–law!" They both laughed.

The next day while Matt and Peony were sitting in their back garden having breakfast, she suggested, "Matt, I would like your mum to move here to live with us. What do you think?"

"We are a 'unique' couple, living together yet in separate bedrooms. What would Mum think when she found out?" Matt said thoughtfully.

"If Mum asks why we sleep in separate bedrooms, I'll tell her you snore very loudly. I was disturbed by your snore and couldn't sleep well."

"Do I snore that bad? Really?" He looked at Peony questioningly.

"Yes!" She laughed. "You do! I could hear it even in the sitting room with your bedroom door closed. You're like a freight train" She laughed.

"That can't be true!" He laughed back.

"It is true! But we love each other more than many husbands and wives do. So I won't complain."

"Are you sure Mum can live with us? I will be forever grateful if she can." He asked.

"I'm positive! In Chinese culture, we take care of our unwell or aging parents. It is our love and duty. In the Christian way, one of the Ten Commandments is to honour our father and mother. Honouring them means to love, respect, and take care of them."

"I am sure mum would love to spend time with her new daughter-in-law. You are so thoughtful. Thank you!" Matt said with an appreciative smile.

Peony looked around the garden and asked, "Where is this scent coming from? It is so familiar!"

"It must come from the Jasmine tree over there. It is blooming," Matt pointed to the corner of the garden.

She walked to the Jasmine tree and picked a bunch of flowers, then she put them close to her nose and inhaled deeply before murmuring, "I wonder where Jasmine is? How is she doing, and is she happy?"

CHAPTER 12

Arriving at Bob's home, Jasmine was met with a sink full of dirty dishes in the kitchen sink, empty beer bottles lying everywhere in the small, derelict three-bedroom fibro house in the suburb of Campsie. She looked around, thinking, "Oh no, what have I got myself into?!"

Dirty clothes were on the floor in the bathroom, used bath towels in the hallway, and used takeaway food containers with leftover food were on the couch. The spare bedrooms were full of empty beer boxes. The stench was so foul that Jasmine could almost not handle standing in the house. Everything was dusty. It was a complete mess.

She pointed to a window and asked quietly, "Open?"

"Go for it!" Bob replied as he went to the fridge to help himself to a beer.

Jasmine went over to the windows and heaved them open. Fresh air flowed towards her, which she eagerly and thankfully inhaled.

Jasmine, since she hardly could speak English, spent the whole Saturday cleaning up the house. But she did not mind because she thought it was the least she could do to repay Bob for his kindness, food and bed. After dinner, she cleaned up the dishes. She finally had the chance to sit down and have a rest. Bob took her hand and led her to the bathroom. "Have a shower," he demanded, then turned the shower on and pointed to her.

Jasmine waited for him to leave the bathroom and then closed the door before she got in the shower. Bob grabbed her and took her to his bedroom as she got out of the bathroom.

"No!" Jasmine refused to get in.

"Come on! You need to do that to repay me!" Bob insisted.

Without waiting for her response, Bob pulled her onto his bed and got on her.

The next day, Jasmine continued to clean the outside of the house all day. Bob looked around the clean house and said, "Hey! In the coming week, I will also teach you to mow the lawn." Bob laughed as he opened another beer and sat down on the sofa. "Hey, do you know how to cook my favourite food—sweet and sour pork?" Bob asked.

"What?" Jasmine could not understand what he said.

"I will buy the bloody ingredients, and you can cook it for me. Yes?"

"Yes." She didn't have a clue what he wanted her to do, but she assumed it was something about food since she recognised the word cook. She figured she knew how to cook and would work it out when the time came to do what he had asked of her.

The following day, Bob returned and dropped the shopping on the kitchen bench. Jasmine looked at a piece of pork and a bottle of vinegar and knew what Bob had requested immediately. She opened the fridge, got some other ingredients out, and started cooking dinner. Soon the aroma of sweet and sour pork was floating throughout the kitchen and into the sitting room.

The phone rang, and Bob dragged his half-drunk body up off the couch and went to pick it up from the side table. "Hey, Paul. What's up, mate? I am having a beer and waiting for dinner to be served. Remember I told you about the Chinese chick I picked up from the park? Yep, she can clean. Good cook. And guess what, she is my girl from now on... Yep!... Not bad ha!... Yeah, now I don't need to pay two hundred bucks for those bitches at Dee Why anymore. Every time I go there, I worry that I will get HIV because you don't know who they've been with!... Oh, yeah!... Mate, she is clean... Ha! Ha! How do I know?... Good question... I don't know, but I think she could be a virgin mate!... No, at first she said no, and pushed me away. But you know that I will not take no for an answer. She has no choice; where's she gonna go? She'll come around mate, but for now, I'll enjoy the feasts she cooks up and my clean house! I'll feast on her later!... Ha! Ha! I told her that's the way she could repay me... Nah, don't worry! Her English is poor, and she is cooking in the kitchen. Even if she heard me, she could not understand what I am talking about... What? Fair dinkum? You arguing with her again?! No good... I am telling ya. Your wife sounds like a real bitch. Divorce her. Get an Asian chick. They are easier to control. Just like the one I have. Because they have no friends and family here. Even if I treat her badly, she has nowhere to turn to! They do as you tell them, don't argue back and want to please—what's better than that?!... Ha, Ha!... Mate, my dinner is ready. I got to go." He said, hanging up the phone.

While they were having dinner at the table, Bob said. "Jasmine, I want ya to be my gal. You know I have been very kind to you. Don't ever forget that I picked you up when ya had nowhere to go, right?"

"Yes," Jasmine said, unsure. She didn't know what he said, but Bob's smile made her uneasy.

"Since you arc with me, you need to let me know wherever you go. You don't need anyone else since you have me. I don't want you to invite anyone to come here either. Understand?" he said, swallowing a piece of sweet and sour pork. "From now on, you don't need to go to college anymore," he continued.

Jasmine understood enough of his last sentence to figure out what he was saying, "Study 22 hours a week, or no visa stay." Jasmine answered with her limited English.

"You can learn English from me. I will apply for a visa for you to stay in Australia since you are in a relationship with me now. I want you to get a job." Bob insisted.

"English first. Then University... accounting." Jasmine said, looking down at her plate, fearful of having eye contact with him.

"Nah! You have me, you don't need that bullshit degree anymore! Just find yourself a job in a Chinese Restaurant as a kitchen hand. There you don't need to speak good English. Understand?"

"Friends... English college... say goodbye," she told Bob while she cleared the plates from the table.

"Don't be so selfish and only think of yourself. You don't need any friends! You have me, and you belong to me from now on. Do you know? You are a very lucky gal. You have food in the fridge and a roof over your head. You should be grateful!" Bob gave her an unimpressed look.

Jasmine recalled the night she slept on the floor with Lili and Peony on the first night in Australia and didn't want to go back to that place. Maybe she was lucky, she thought. Perhaps I should do what Bob suggested. Surely a man with a house would know a thing or two. The next day, she went to the nearest Chinese Restaurant, which was just a twenty-minute walk away, and found a job as a kitchen hand.

When Jasmine got her first pay, she asked Bob to help her to send some money back to China to her mum so she could pay the money back to her relatives that she had borrowed for her college fees. Bob was furious and screamed at her, "That's not your bloody problem. From now on, you give me your wages. That's what all women do in Australia—give the money to their men to look after."

"Money... back... relatives. Pay is three hundred... eighty dollars... week... give two hundred dollars... you... send one hundred fifty dollars to China... to Mum." She pointed to herself, "Me... thirty dollars pocket money?"

"No, your bloody relatives can wait. You give your wages to me every week. That's how we do things in Australia. The men control the money. Give my bank account details to your work and ask them to deposit the wage into my account, or the cheque has to be in my name from next week. I will give you a credit card for grocery shopping so I can keep an eye on what you spend. Also, every time you do the shopping, you must give me the receipt. I will check every item you buy to make sure you're not wasting money," he stated.

"But...."

"No but's. Do as I tell you. Now go and cook my dinner before you go to work."

From then on, the only money Jasmine got for herself was the money from tips she received in the restaurant. She asked her friend Mie from the restaurant to keep her share for her so she could send some money to her mum at the end of the year.

Jasmine had been living with and enduring Bob's unwanted sexual advances he forced upon her, when one morning, he rolled on top of her to have sex with her again. Jasmine sat bolt upright and told him, "No! Aaagghh here it comes again," she thought. "I'm going to be sick." She couldn't understand why she kept waking up feeling like she wanted to throw up. It wasn't like she'd eaten anything to make her feel sick.

Returning to the bedroom after being sick, she asked Bob to take her to a doctor. "Pull yourself together woman. Don't lie to me and try to pull the sick card to avoid having sex with me."

"I feel sick and dizzy all the time. Please take me to see a doctor. Today is my only day off." Jasmine begged.

"You are nothing but trouble Jasmine. I will take you there when I am good and ready," he said while forcing himself on her again. Done with her, he demanded angrily, "Get out of my bed now! Get me my breakfast."

After another week of Jasmine becoming even more ill, Bob finally took her to the doctor. The female doctor was lovely and asked some questions before saying to Jasmine she would also need to do a urine test. Waiting in her medical room, Jasmine and Bob sat in silence while the doctor left the room to retrieve the results of the tests. Soon after, she returned and exclaimed, "Congratulations, it looks like you are expecting!"

"What? Expecting? You mean she is pregnant?" Bob asked with disbelieving shock.

"Yes, from the urine test. However, I will take the blood test to confirm how many weeks along she is," the doctor replied.

"Bloody hell!" Bob shouted.

"It looks like you both did not plan to have this child?" the doctor asked with worry in her voice.

Jasmine sat in complete shock. She couldn't believe she was pregnant. She was going to have a baby! If she were in China, she would have been celebrating this fantastic news with her family, who would rally around her and be a great support in welcoming the news. But she didn't feel the excitement about becoming a mother. Instead, she was nervous about being all alone with just Bob, who was anything but supportive and definitely wouldn't help with the raising of a child.

"I want... baby," Jasmine answered the doctor's question nervously.

"We will discuss this at home," Bob said curtly, throwing her a disgusted look.

"When can we come to get the blood test result?" He asked the doctor.

"Next Monday." She replied, looking worriedly at Jasmine, who sat meekly with her eyes cast down to the floor.

"We will be back for the result on Monday," Bob said with irritation. As soon as they got in the car on the way home, he screamed at Jasmine, "See what you did to me! You are my nightmare!" The minute they stepped into the house, Bob grabbed Jasmine's arm and pushed her onto the sofa. He shouted even louder at her, "You stupid bitch! Why didn't you take the pill as I told you to?"

Fearful of Bob's physical aggression, she whimpered, "I am so sorry. I took it every day but forgot once?"

"We cannot afford to have this... this bloody little shit kid! I will make an appointment for you to get an abortion. Now I have to spend even more bloody money on you! He ranted. "If you had been more careful and remembered to take the pill, this would not have happened!" He yelled.

Jasmine burst into tears but dared not to cry out, "Wait... wait for the blood test result... no... no killing baby, please. Keep the baby please." Jasmine begged him hoping to borrow sometime between then and the next appointment to persuade Bob to keep their child.

"Shut up bitch! Who do you think you are? You are nothing. You are from a low-class country. You are far from fit to have my child! I can't even imagine taking little Ching Chung out there in public. People will laugh at me!" He seethed.

"You knew I was from China when you met me. If you think I am low class, you should not have took me," Jasmine said, straight away regretting it.

Bob saw red, and his face bloated in rage. He pulled back his hand and smacked Jasmine hard across her face sending her reeling towards the floor. Crying out, she tried to crawl away from him as he grabbed her hair, pulling her up to face him. "How dare you talk back to me!" He shouted into her face. "You think now, because you can speak a little more English you can talk back to me, hey? Let me give you a heads-up, I chose you because you were easier to control than those Aussie bitches. Don't think for a minute I love or care about you enough to marry you, or have my child. You're a slave, and that's it. If you had that little shit of a kid, you would be busy looking after it and not me!" he said callously, letting go of her hair and watching her drop to the ground like a bag of potatoes. He didn't say another word to her, just looked at her with more disdain before storming out the front door, leaving her on the floor sobbing.

Jasmine picked herself up and managed to pull herself onto the sofa. She felt helpless, lost and alone. She had nowhere to go and no one to turn to.

The weekend passed with very little interaction between the two other than Bob barking orders at Jasmine. Monday morning, Bob drove Jasmine back to the doctors in silence to get the results of the blood test. The doctor confirmed, "The test result has come back, and it confirmed Jasmine is 12 weeks pregnant!" she said happily.

"Since we are not ready to have a family yet. We want to book an appointment for an abortion," Bob told the doctor bluntly.

"I am sorry, you cannot just make an appointment for an abortion. This decision cannot be made lightly. Firstly, I have to refer you both to a counsellor to speak to. For such a big decision, there is a lengthy process. Furthermore, your wife will make the final decision since the baby is in her body." The doctor explained.

"I am the father and her partner. Her English is not good. It is not fair that I can't make the decision," Bob argued.

"I am not the one making these rules and regulations. We have to follow the procedure. We have to make sure that the abortion is not being forced unwillingly." She looked at Jasmine, who was quietly sitting next to Bob and asked with concern, "Are you ok?"

"She's fine," Bob answered.

"I asked her. Please allow her to answer for herself," the doctor said sternly, fixing Bob with a look to say, be quiet.

Jasmine glanced at Bob before looking down and answering in a quiet tone, "I... I... I am good."

"Jasmine, here is the information pack," the doctor continued compassionately. She opened the booklet and explained, "If you decide to abort your child, you will need to contact these people first and book an appointment to meet with them. If you decide to keep the baby, you need the information. It tells you where to get your regular check-ups and how to book the hospital for the birth. Oh, and see this page; if you need an interpreter, you need to call this number, and they will explain everything to you in Mandarin." The doctor circled the number and then handed the information pack to Jasmine before asking, "Any questions?"

Jasmine paused for a moment, then answered with a sorrowful smile, "No, thank you."

When they arrived home, Bob slammed the door so hard it nearly fell off its hinges, then he turned around and began punching and kicking Jasmine violently. "Who gives you the right to decide to have this little shit or not? Remember, you are nobody!" he screamed at her with every blow.

Jasmine cowered under the dining table, begging him to stop, but Bob kept dragging her out by her hair and continued to kick and hit her.

Jasmine kneeled and bent over her belly, trying to protect her unborn child by using one hand to cover her head, and the other over her tummy to stop the kicks from reaching her uterus.

"Please stop for your child's sake," she said, howling with desperation and pain.

"Please! Please! Do not harm the child. I will put you first and do anything to make you happy."

"I am not going to give up anything for you and that little shit! You better continue to work hard to save money before it comes out!" He said done with assaulting her. Leaving her bleeding and bruised, he walked to the fridge to get a beer. Opening it, he took a long slurp before adding, "Look at you! Useless! You better pull yourself together and try not to upset me. Don't you dare tell anyone about me hitting you either— you deserve this! Wear long sleeves to cover your arms and if anyone asks about the bruises on your face, tell them you fell down some steps or something. I swear, if you even think about telling the police, I'll kill you. They'll just laugh at you anyway. They won't know what the hell you are talking about because your English is so shit! They'll probably think you're crazy and send you back to China—pregnant and unmarried. How would that look?"

Jasmine was sitting in the corner of the dining room, shaking. Feeling worthless and shameful, she knew that what he said was probably true. She could not go back to China, she had no money, she still owed money to her relatives, and would be embarrassed to face her family and relatives pregnant without a husband.

"This is all your fault. Make sure you don't tell your fucking Chinese slug friends. Get up and go to get me another beer." Bob sat on the sofa with his feet resting on the coffee table. Jasmine sucked in a painful breath and pushed herself up. With unbalanced steps, she wobbled and weaved to the kitchen to get Bob a beer and handed it to him. Bob snatched the bottle from Jasmine's hand and screamed, "You fucking airhead! How can I drink it without opening it?!" Jasmine stumbled back to the kitchen to grab a bottle opener from the drawer and handed it to him. While he was opening the bottle, he ordered, "Start making my dinner now. I am bloody hungry! Cook me a piece of T-bone steak. The leftover from last night is good enough for you!"

Jasmine dutifully returned to the kitchen, trying not to make big movements and refrain from crying out from the pain bursting through her bruised body.

CHAPTER 13

Peony was planning to get her driver's license so that she could take Joyce, her mother-in-law, out while Matt was at work.

"I want to learn to drive. What do you think?" she asked Matt.

"Good idea," he said encouragingly.

"Could you please find me a driving instructor?" she asked.

"I will find you an instructor to give you the first five to ten lessons. Then I will take over to help you practice."

"Thank you. I'd like that!" Peony was thrilled and looking forward to her first lesson.

However, all did not go well. Peony stormed in the front door after her first driving lesson.

Matt looked at her and asked with concern, "What happened?"

"Bloody English!" She threw her handbag on the floor and slumped on the sofa.

"Hey, don't be upset, please. Take a few deep breaths. I'll go and get you a glass of water." Matt came back with the water. "Drink it slowly, and when you are ready, tell me what happened."

After drinking the water, Peony calmed down a bit. She explained, "When I was driving towards the intersection, I asked the instructor to give me directions. I asked him, 'Left or right?' He replied, 'Right ahead,' so I turned right and kept going. Then he screamed at me. 'I said right ahead, did you hear me?!' I told him I did exactly what he said—turned right and kept driving ahead. Then he screamed at me again and said, 'Right ahead means straight ahead.' He got more upset the more he talked. He said I'd better learn more bloody English before the next lesson."

Matt hugged her and suggested, "In the future, if anyone criticizes you for your English, ask them to criticize you in Chinese. I bet none of them could speak Chinese as well as you speak English." While he thought the instructor was rude, he could not help but think to explain the different meanings of the same word 'right' to Peony. But for now, she just needed his support, so he kept focused on the job at hand.

"It's all your fault! You told me that Aussies like to shorten words. For example, afternoon you say arvo. Breakfast you say brekkie; cuppa is short for a cup of tea, and I hate that when I ask someone a question, they answer 'Yeah, nah' I am confused with the answer; is it yes or no?" Peony complained.

"I will find you another instructor. English is not an easy language to learn, particularly with all the Aussie slang. You are doing extremely well and are a fast learner. Don't worry. I am very proud of you, and you should be very proud of yourself too." Matt encouraged her.

"Now, I worry about going to college this year. What if my English is not good enough? If I can't understand, I will fall behind or even fail!"

"Peony, look at me. Stop, you're worrying about nothing. It will be fine. He was just a jerk." Matt held Peony's shoulders and helped her to calm down, for he knew she could overreact and wind herself up sometimes.

"Feeling better?" Matt asked.

"Yes, thank you!" Peony gave him an appreciative smile.

"Trust me, you will be fine. Whatever you set your mind on, you will achieve it. I have read your information from your college pack. They will organize an English tutor for non-English speaking background students like you. On the first day of college, I want you to let them know you need the English tutorial support program, ok? Will you remember that?"

"OK, I will. What if…." She still hesitated.

"Most people are decent people and not anything like that bloody driving instructor," Matt ensured. "However, remember that you will bump into a few bad ones along your journey—just as you would in any country. Just ignore them. You only need to focus on where you're heading. By the way, I am going to cook dinner tonight."

"Now you are talking. What's for dinner?" she asked.

"Bangers and mash." He replied.

"Oh! What's that?" she queried, not sounding enthusiastic.

"It is a traditional family dish in Australia. Sausages served with mashed potato, onion gravy, and green peas. You will like it. Especially the way I cook it."

"If you say sausages with mashed potato and peas, I know exactly what I am getting. Bloody English!"

They looked at each other and burst into laughter.

"Hey, while Mum is with Linda tonight, shall we watch a movie after dinner? I am going to hire a video from Movie World. I'm thinking of Back to the Future."

"I'm thinking of Ghost." Peony gave Matt a puppy dog look.

"Ah! Ah! Don't give me that look. I know you well by now. You can't always get what you want. We'll toss a coin. Heads for Ghost, tails for Back to the Future. Agreed?" Matt took a one-dollar coin out of his pocket. "See the queen's head is the head, the other side is the tail. Don't ask me why we call the other side tail. Not because there is a tail on it. I guess because it is opposite of the head."

He tossed the coin in the air. "Tails. Back To the Future. You will enjoy this movie."

"I trust your choice. I am so hungry. I can't wait for the bangers and mash."

"All right, won't be long." He said, leaving to head into the kitchen and get started.

"Is there anything I can help with?" Peony asked.

"You can peel the onion and potatoes and slice them if you like?" Matt got an onion out of the basket from the pantry cupboard.

"Yes, chef." Peony said.

"Peony, are you crying?" Matt asked.

"No, I'm not, it's the bloody onion!" she laughed. "You know, I am so grateful to have you and your family in my life."

"You are crying! It's not the bloody onion, I can tell. We are family now. Come here, silly." Matt wrapped his arms around her and held her tightly, close to his heart.

"Well, they are tears of joy. Life is full of surprises. We were strangers a year or so ago. I was from thousands of miles away. Now we are a family. Promise me, no matter what, we will be family for a lifetime?"

"Sure, pinkie promise." He smiled.

"This one, I know. We also have pinkie promise in China." She locked her pinkie finger with Matt's.

"Hey, next Sunday is your birthday. I want to take you to the 360 Bar & Dining for dinner. It rotates three hundred and sixty degrees in sixty minutes. It is on top of the Sydney Tower. Three hundred and nine meters above the ground. You'll get magnificent views of Sydney – the Opera House, the Harbor Bridge, St. Mary's Cathedral, and Hyde Park. And you can see as far as the Blue Mountains."

"Mag-ni-fi-cent, magnificent views," Peony repeated quietly.

"It's a formal dinner. Which means you need to dress up. I will drop you at Linda's. You are a size similar to her, so I am sure she will be happy to help you with something to wear."

"I have never been to a formal dinner in Australia. I don't even know how to use a knife and fork properly," Peony said with concern.

"Yeah, I noticed that. Sometimes during dinner, I saw you with your knife and fork pointing upwards," Matt laughed.

"Stop it! If you want to pull my leg, you better pull the one with the bell on it." She put one leg out and shook her ankle, laughing.

"Trust me, everybody will stop eating and stare at you. No, just kidding! They will be busy enjoying their dinner. If I go to a Chinese restaurant, I don't care if I can use chopsticks properly or not. I would just focus on enjoying the food," he said.

"Well, in a Chinese restaurant, if you don't know how to use chopsticks, you can ask for a knife and fork. I am sure they wouldn't give me chopsticks there!" she giggled.

"Smarty-pants! Try to make any new experience fun. I will teach you a few more things in the next few days when we have some more time. How about I make a three-course dinner on Saturday, and we can practice at home?"

"I would like that."

"I think the potato is ready. Would you like to mash the potatoes?"

"Yes, sure." Peony turned the stove off and drained the water out of the cooked potato.

"Let me add my secret ingredients first. A spoonful of butter. Freshly shredded parmesan cheese. One clove of crushed garlic. Then a third of a cup of hot milk and salt. Now you can use this to mash the potatoes till they're creamy and fluffy." Matt handed her the potato masher.

Peony mashed it for a while and showed it to Matt. "Is this ready?"

"Looks good! Taste it and see if you like it."

Peony used her finger to scoop a bit. "Oh my God! I never knew you could make humble potatoes taste that delicious!"

After dinner, while Matt was preparing the movie, Peony washed the dishes and made Matt his peppermint tea.

They both sat on the floor, leaning against the sofa to watch the movie.

Halfway through the movie, Matt paused it, saying he'd be right back.

"Close your eyes and put your hands out," he asked, hiding one of his hands behind his back.

"Should I trust you?" she said.

"If you can't trust me, you can trust no one!" he quipped.

"Just kidding! Of course I trust you—with my life." Peony closed her eyes and put her hands out, one on top of the other.

Matt put a bar of Darrell Lea chocolate in her hands. "Now open your eyes. That is called Rocky Road."

"What's in it?"

"Marshmallows, peanuts, and chocolate. Go on, try it!" he urged her.

Peony took a bite. Then closed her eyes and chewed it slowly. "The taste of it is incredible. I love it!"

"When you go through rocky roads in your life journey, remember to focus on the outcome of the sweetness," Matt stated.

"Ok. I will remember that." Peony gave him a grateful smile.

"Should we go back to the movie now?" he asked.

"Yes, please."

Early morning on the coming Saturday, Peony woke Matt up to get all the ingredients for dinner. Peony looked at Matt on the drive to the supermarket and thought, "How come I am so fortunate to have these wonderful men in my life? First, my father. Now, Matt." They were both incredible human beings, and the best male role models she could possibly have asked for.

"What are you thinking?" Matt asked.

"Nothing!"

"Really?" he asked, not convinced.

"I just want to let you know that I appreciate you." She replied.

"I know. You don't need to tell me."

In the evening, Matt and Peony set up the table together. He showed her how to set cutlery and crockery out properly. Matt put the entree on the table. "The easiest way to remember is that you take the knives and forks from the outside first. Then as each course comes, you use the next set in. The last set closest to your plate is for dessert." He explained.

"Normally we start with the entrée, or starter, or appetiser. Then follow with soup, main and dessert. When we are in the restaurant, wait for the waiter or me to pull the chair out for you to sit down. You sit down and stand up again if you need him to adjust the chair. Try not to make a noise when you use the cutlery, and do not talk when your mouth is full. Put the knife and fork on each side to show you are still enjoying your food so the waiter will not take your plate away. Once you've had enough, you put the knife and fork together at one side so the waiter will take the plate away and serve you the next course."

"Too much to remember. But if you are ready to take me there, I am ready to embarrass you. Ha!" Peony made a funny face.

"Oh, one more thing. The dress code is cocktail after five."

"Now you're making things more complicated," she said, looking at him with a frown.

"Don't worry. Linda will help you. I will drop you over to her house after church so you can spend time with her and Mum."

Matt took three hundred dollars out of his wallet and handed it to Peony. "Take Linda and Mum out somewhere nice for lunch. Then spend the rest of the money to pamper yourself with a manicure and a pedicure."

"I can't take your money. But we'll still have girls' time, and I will take them somewhere nice for lunch to celebrate my birthday."

"What makes you think that you can't take my money? We are family, and family do things for each other. Anyway, that is also part of your birthday present." Matt took her hand and put the money into it, then folded her fingers over.

"So, what are you going to do while we are out on Sunday?"

"I will mow the lawn and tidy up the garden at home," he said.

"You sure you don't need me to help with the garden?"

"Nope, that's the other part of the birthday present. I want you to come home to a beautiful, tidy backyard and garden. I will come to pick you up at six o'clock."

Peony decided to take Linda and Mum to Warringah Mall for lunch, and she wanted to buy Mum a couple of sets of cotton pyjamas after lunch. They found a lovely café next to the fountain on the ground floor. Peony helped Mum sit down on a chair at a sunny table. "Matt gave me money to pay for our lunch. So, I want you both to choose something delicious. And spend the three hundred dollars," Peony insisted.

After they'd ordered, Joyce handed Peony her birthday present. "Here is a little gift for you. Happy birthday, Darling!"

"Could I open it now? Or should I wait?"

"Sure! It's yours, my dear," Joyce said happily.

Peony carefully opened the wrapping paper and the little navy-blue velvet box. Inside it was a vintage heart-shaped diamond pendant with a white gold chain.

"It is a family heirloom from my grandma," Joyce explained.

Peony hesitated. "I can't accept this. It's a family heirloom. Linda should keep it."

"I want you to have it. Don't worry, Linda also has something special," Joyce insisted.

"Peony, it is Mum's wish," Linda urged, "Please accept it. See, I got this diamond ring from Mum." She showed the ring to Peony.

"Thank you, Mum. I feel so honoured to accept it. I promise to cherish it."

"When you think of me, just hold this pendant in your hand," Joyce said.

"I'll help you to put it on." Linda got up and walked behind Peony to put it on her neck.

"It looks beautiful on you. You are the perfect person to wear it," Joyce cheered.

"I can't agree more Mum. It looks gorgeous on you Peony." Then Linda passed a cute little bag to Peony. "This is for you from Jason, the kids, and I."

"Thank you. Could I open it, please?" Peony asked.

"Go ahead," Linda said.

"Oh, I love it. I want to wear it now." Peony carefully removed the beautiful white gold bracelet from the box and put it on her left wrist.

"See the words engraved at the back," Linda suggested.

"You are loved," Peony read.

"I hope it will always remind you that you are loved by our family," Linda stated.

Joyce took Peony's hand and carefully inspected the bracelet. "Linda, it's so unique and beautiful. What a brilliant choice!" She tenderly patted Peony's hand and released it, then suggested. "While we are still waiting for the food to be served, I'll tell you a story."

"We would love that," Peony said, glancing at Linda for agreement. She nodded.

Joyce took the glass of water and had a sip, then started. "There were twins in their mother's womb. One said to the other, 'Do you think there is life after delivery?'

'I don't know,' the other said.

'I think that's the end of our lives after delivery,' one said.

'After we get out of here, we may enter a bigger, brighter, and more beautiful place. Maybe we can walk freely as far as we want, and we can do many other things,' the other said.

'It's impossible. The umbilical cord is too short for us to go far. Plus, no one has come back here after delivery. I think there is nothing but a big black place out there. That's all,' one said.

'Surely our mother will take care of us when we are out of here,' the other said.

'Mother? I never see her. I think mother doesn't exist,' one said.

'No, if you are still and quiet, you can feel her, you can sense her, and you can hear her heartbeat,' the other said."

Joyce finished her story, giving them a peaceful smile.

"I tell you both this story because I believe there is a heaven. We haven't seen it, but that doesn't mean it does not exist. I can see it through the eyes of faith. There is a saying—believing is seeing. I want you both to know that an ending is also a new beginning." Joyce sipped another mouthful of water and then carried on. "I want to make sure my loved ones are doing ok after I leave this world. I will be at peace when the time comes to be with my heavenly father, my husband Ron, and my mum and Dad. Remember, I will be in an even better and more beautiful place that what we call Heaven. My spirit will be with you even though my physical body is no longer here."

"How do we know when your spirit is here with us?" Peony asked.

"You will know. I will be the birds singing on the branch, the butterfly fluttering in the garden. I will be the sunshine to hug you. I will be the gentle breeze to kiss you. I will be the flower to smile at you..."

It was a delightful evening. Matt went back to Linda's place to pick up Peony. As she stepped out the front door and walked toward Matt, she spun around, and the full skirt of her red satin spaghetti strap dress flared out in a spectacular swirl. The late afternoon sunlight shone on her bouncing, long, silky hair. The red lipstick on her lips made her smile even more enchanting.

"Look at you! You look drop dead gorgeous! Elegant and stylish. My God! Are you Miss China or what?" Matt was astonished by her transformation.

Peony lightly lifted her skirt and held it to the sides, then put her right foot behind her and bent her knees. She bowed her head to make a curtsey like a princess. "Thank you. So, you agree that Linda did a fantastic job? She lent me this beautiful dress. Shoes and handbag to match. Oh! See this bracelet. A present from Linda, Jason and the kids. And Mum gave me this pendant as my birthday gift."

"It looks perfect on you." Matt put his arm up and asked, "Shall we?"

Peony put her hand around his arm, and they walked to the car together. Matt opened the car door, helped her get in the car, and then smoothly drove off.

Once Matt parked the car, he led Peony to the lift up to 360 Restaurant. The lift opened, and Matt gestured to Peony to go out.

"Here we are, the Sydney Tower! My princess."

"You should say—my lovely wife." She elbowed him lightly.

A beautiful lady in black greeted them at the entrance. She looked at the booking list.

"Mr and Mrs Williamson?"

Matt nodded and said, "Yes."

"Follow me, please." She led them to the table. A waiter pulled the chair out for Peony.

She smiled courteously. "Thank you."

Peony looked at the uninterrupted view of the sun setting outside the giant glass panels from the ceiling to the floor.

"What a magnificent view!"

Matt smiled at her.

The waiter replied, "Indeed! Mr and Mrs Williamson, would you like some drinks to start?"

"Yes, could we have a bottle of champagne to celebrate my lovely wife's birthday, please?" Matt winked at Peony.

"Certainly, Sir."

Matt handed Peony a birthday present, "Happy Birthday."

"Thank you! I can't wait! Could I please open it now?" she asked eagerly.

"Why not? It's yours now." He smiled.

Peony unwrapped the present with pleasure. Appearing in front of her eyes was The Holy Bible.

She turned to the page on which the birthday card was inserted. On the first blank page of the bible handwritten, it said,

To Dearest Peony,

May the Lord go before you to make your path straight as you travel through your life's journey.

May the Lord walk beside you to hold your hand if you stumble, so He can pick you up if you fall.

May the Lord be above you to be your guiding star and pour His blessings upon you.

May the Lord be the solid foundation below your feet so you can stand firmly and stand tall.

May the Lord be behind you and protect you so you can go forth boldly and confidently, for you know He has your back.

May the Lord live within you and His Holy Spirit lead you to a bright and fulfilling life.

Happy Birthday!

Love you always. Matt."

It ended with a love heart next to his name.

Peony finished reading and looked up at him with her teary eyes, "That is a most precious gift! Thank you!"

"All the beautiful stories your mum used to tell you are in this book. Now you will have your own bible when you go to church."

"My mum told me that this is the instruction book for humankind. It is the book of life. If we follow His instructions, we will have meaningful and fulfilling lives. It will give us wisdom and knowledge when facing obstacles and challenges in life."

Peony clasped the bible close to her. "Since I've been going to church with Mum and Linda's family every Sunday, my faith and my English are improving. Your mum told me you went to church when you were younger. What stopped you? Would you like to go to church again with me?" Peony suggested.

"I don't feel comfortable. I worry about people judging me."

"Judge you for what? Because you are gay?"

"Shhhhh!" Matt looked around and whispered, "I'm wondering what they would think if they found out you are having dinner with your gay husband?".

"I will tell them you are the best husband any man or woman can hope for." Peony giggled.

Then she went back to church subject. "Didn't the Lord say, 'judge not, will not be judged? Condemn not, will not be condemned? Didn't he also say, 'I am not sent to this world to judge and condemn but to love?' and 'whoever has no sin cast the first stone?' No one has the right to judge you for who you are, but to love you for who you are. Anyway, it is the relationship between you and the Father. So, will you go to church with me?" Peony asked again.

"Give me time to think about it," Matt replied.

The waiter bought out the entrée of lemon garlic prawn and the creamy crab meat soup. Lobster mornay for the main course and mango tiramisu for dessert. Last was Peony's favourite café latte.

"Delicious food and great company. I feel like I've been in heaven and back. Thank you so much. You made this birthday an unforgettable one. This is the best!"

"No. The best is yet to come," Matt replied with certainty.

CHAPTER 14

Jasmine went to work at the Chinese restaurant as usual. In the late evening, while washing the dirty dishes in the kitchen, she started to feel the contraction pains stronger and stronger. With one hand holding onto the kitchen sink, she took the other and rubbed her tummy, hoping she could ease the pain. When her friend Mie came in with more dirty dishes, she noticed Jasmine's pale face and excessive sweating.

"Jasmine, are you ok?" she asked, concerned.

"I feel pain in my tummy," Jasmine said, wincing.

"I think you are in labour. I will call a cab straight away to take you to the hospital."

Soon the taxi arrived, and Mie helped her to get in it.

"I am scared Mie." She squeezed Mie's hand as they drove off together to Canterbury Hospital.

"I will be with you. Don't worry. Just focus on the baby that will be in your arms very soon. Once we are in the hospital, I will call Bob and tell him you are there," Mie said.

"No. Thanks. He is not at home. He went to Jindabyne for trout fishing. He said he could not stand the way I looked like a big fat and ugly pig." Jasmine tried to hold back the tears.

"Oh, this is nonsense! Don't believe what he said. You are beautiful." Mie was holding her trembling body and tried to comfort her.

The following day the sky slowly turned bright orange to red, and the gentle sunlight radiated through the window, lighting up the room. Jasmine held the newborn baby boy in her arms, who was sleeping peacefully. She touched his soft, innocent face and then held his little hand. Her hope was renewed. Even though there were no friends or relatives with her to share this special moment other than Mie, somehow, she didn't feel alone anymore. "Mommy will do anything for you at all costs," she said tenderly, looking at her gorgeous little boy.

"Do you have a name for this adorable little man yet?" A nurse's voice interrupted her thoughts.

Jasmine looked up at her and back at her baby as she replied, "I have a name in Chinese for him, but I can't think of a name in English yet."

"Do you like the name Josh? It is a strong name and easy to pronounce."

"Jo-sh, Josh, yes, I like it very much. My little Josh." Jasmine gave a tender kiss on his forehead.

Just after Jasmine came home from the hospital. She received a parcel from China. "It must be from my mum!" she shouted joyfully, racing to the bathroom to get a pair of scissors to open it. Inside were a letter to her, a congratulatory card, toys, and baby clothes. There are more! Some clothes for her as well. There was also a man's T-shirt and a belt. She thought they must be for Bob.

"This T-shirt and belt are for you from my mum. I hope you will like them." She handed them to Bob and hoped they would bring a smile to his face, and he would treat her better.

"I don't want them. Everything made in China is crap and useless like you!" Bob grabbed them from her and continued, "At least this belt is good for one thing. Belt the shit out of you!" Then he flung them across to the other side of the living room. He pointed to Josh, their little son. Who was happily bouncing in the bouncing chair, "Even this little redneck is useless and will end up in jail."

Jasmine was devastated but dared not say anything. She thought gratefully. "At least he let me have my special little boy."

"By the way. It's time for you to go back to work again. I want you to get the evening shift this time. 5 pm to 11 pm is good. At least you still can cook dinner earlier and feed and bathe that little shit before you go to work. I will not work anymore since I have to put up with all this bullshit from you! See what you have done to me? Now I have to look after this little shit for you while you are at work. You stupid bitch!" Bob complained with anger.

Another few months passed by, and Bob became more abusive toward Jasmine and Josh.

He complained that the dinners were no longer on time since Josh came along.

"All this little shit knows is crying." He slammed Josh's bedroom door shut. The loud noise made Josh cry even louder.

Jasmine rushed toward the bedroom and tried to calm him down.

"Don't you dare to go in. Let him cry. Look at you—ugly pig. You have no idea how much I hate you! I am so embarrassed to have a child with you."

"Please let me get in to feed him. He is just hungry," Jasmine begged him.

"Since this shit of yours came along, you have no time to look after me anymore. Remember this, I am your number one priority. Look after me first. I am hungry too. Now go and cook my tea."

Jasmine was crying and begging Bob to let her feed Josh and settle him first, then cook dinner.

Bob smacked her and dragged her to the kitchen. "Cook for me first. That little shit can wait. Or do you want me to go in and smack him as well?"

Jasmine did not want Bob to smack Josh. She had no choice but to pull some food out of the fridge and start cooking. It seemed like it took forever to cook dinner, and her heart was ripping apart inside, hearing Josh cry out for her. Finally, she managed to put the dinner on the table for Bob, and then she rushed out of the kitchen to Josh's bedroom.

Between the mouthfuls of food, he screamed, "I can't handle this bullshit anymore. I am going back to the Snowy Mountains for a break from all this nonsense."

Jasmine was torn between working to make a living and looking after Josh. After Bob went to the Snowy Mountains, she called Mie and told her that she had to find someone to look after Josh; otherwise, she could not continue to work and needed the income to support the family.

Mie suggested, "Would you like to stay at our place while Bob is at the Snowy? My mum is retired. She was looking forward to having grandchildren. But hey, you know I don't even have a man yet. My mum will happily look after Josh while you are working."

"That would be wonderful. Could you please ask her if she is happy to do that? Please let me know as soon as you can." Jasmine breathed a sigh of relief.

"It will be fine. I will drive to your place to pick you and Josh up after lunch. Say at two o'clock? Meanwhile, pack some of your and Josh's clothes and the things you need."

"Thank you Mie. I think this is the only way I can keep on working. Bob doesn't like me to have any friends. But since he is not at home. You can come." Jasmine said.

"What? Why doesn't he want you to have friends?" She asked, shocked.

"Ah...." Jasmine swallowed back what she was about to tell her.

"I've seen you with some bruises on you Jasmine. I am your friend. There is no need to hide anything." Mie pointed out.

"Bob has a hot temper. But you know, I had nowhere to go when I first came to Australia. It was he who took me in. So at least, I could repay him for what he did for me and make sure to do as he tells me."

"No. If a man loves you, Jasmine. He will respect you and will protect you, not harm you!"

"Well, he told me that he does not love me. I am a second-class citizen, ugly, and he doesn't even like me. I am far from being good enough to have his affection."

"He is a horrible beast! I can't understand why you are still with him?" Mie could not understand.

"He said he would send me back to China if I didn't do as he told me. I still owe a great amount of money to my relatives, and because Bob takes all my wages, I only have my tip money to pay them back with. I would be embarrassed to go back as a single mother still owing them. People will look down on me, and my mum will lose the respect of her friends and family. I don't think Mum could handle it."

"You will have time to think it over while he is away. Either stay or leave. Whatever decision you make, I am here to support you. You know that." Mie said.

"You are a true friend. Much appreciated." Jasmine said gratefully.

While staying with Mie and her Mum, Jasmine started to experience peace and freedom once again. She realised living with Bob was like walking on eggshells and living with a ticking time bomb, not knowing when he would set off. She did not want to live in that nightmare anymore. She decided to leave Bob and asked Mie to come with her to pick up the rest of her belongings.

When Bob returned, he noticed Jasmine and Josh's belongings were gone. He was furious and screamed. "How dare that bitch leave me? Not that easy! Over my dead body!"

He finished the last mouthful of his beer and smashed the empty bottle on the front retaining wall of the house. "I have to find a way to get that Chinese bitch back here," he thought.

That evening, about the time Jasmine was let off work, he went to the restaurant with a beautiful bunch of flowers and waited for her.

When he saw Jasmine walking out of the restaurant, he marched up to her, "Hello, my darling. I am coming to pick you up." Mustering up the nicest and sweetest manner he could.

"I ... ah... I am not coming back to you." She was fearful but trying her best not to show it to him.

"Why Not?! I miss you so much, my sweetie!" he gushed.

"Because... you... you did not treat me right." Jasmine stammered.

"Well, while I was in the Snowy Mountains, I had time to think of my behaviour. I am so sorry. I promise you that I will be nice to you and Josh. I will give up alcohol and go and get a job. I will do anything you want, and take care of you and our son Josh. We are family, and you don't want Josh growing up with a broken family and without a father. Do you?" He added.

Jasmine was hesitant and did not know what to do. She turned to look at Mie, who was shaking her head to indicate she should not go back.

"You must be Jasmine's friend. I guessed you must have helped her a lot while I was away. Thank you for being her friend. I always encourage Jasmine to have her friends and come to visit us." Bob put his hand out and tried to shake her hand.

Mie refused to put her hand out and replied coldly, "People will not change overnight. Jasmine will stay with us. You have three months to prove that you are a changed man before she decides whether she should stay with us or go back with you."

"Jasmine portrays me as a monster. I am not. Yes, we have arguments over who is doing the house chores, and sometimes

I drink a bit more than I should. But hey, every couple disagrees with each other now and then. That's normal!"

"It is not normal that Jasmine often comes to work with bruises all over her!" Mie said furiously.

"Jasmine is quite clumsy. She either fell or bumped into something—she does it all the time. That's why you see so many bruises on her," Bob explained.

"Oh?" Mie replied with disbelief.

Bob then ignored Mie and turned to beg Jasmine, "Come on Darling! Listen to me. We are family. It is important that our son Josh be with Mum and Dad, and I don't want to live without you! I do love you."

Since Bob was acting so sincerely. Jasmine thought that at least give him another chance to prove that he was a different man. She did want Josh to grow up with a mum and Dad like other families. So, she accepted the flowers and got in his car, much to Mie's disgrace and worry. On their way back, they went to pick up Josh from Mie's mother.

"I don't want to leave you. I have no intention of hurting your feelings, Darling. I just could not bear it that you hit me all the time. It broke my heart whenever I saw you smack Josh and knock him around. I am glad that you want us back and you want to change. All I want is a happy family." She glanced at Bob with a smile.

Bob did not respond. In fact, he did not say a word at all on their way back. The car stopped at the driveway. He opened the car door and went straight to the house with Jasmine to get Josh. Josh was sleeping, so Jasmine carefully picked him up and let his head lay on her shoulder. When they got home, she walked up the steps, and Bob ordered her to put the sleeping Josh in his bedroom and come back out. Kissing her sleeping son, she smiled before walking out of his room into the hallway.

There she saw Bob standing waiting for her, his face blood-boiling red and holding a pillow in his hand. She knew in an instant she was in trouble. She tried to run into the spare bedroom to lock herself inside, but it was too late.

Bob grabbed her from behind and pushed her onto the floor of the room. He shut the door behind him. He put the pillow on top of her and kicked and punched her. "You stupid Chinese bitch. How dare you leave me? You think I am sorry! You fucking useless slug. If you try to escape again, I will kill you and your stupid Chinese friend's whole family. I know where they live now, and I will do it!" he screamed manically.

Even though the pain was unbearable, Jasmine bit her lips, trying not to cry, and wake her son up.

Bob waved the pillow in the air, "With this, there are no bruises and marks on you. No evidence to prove that I beat you up. One more thing. Make sure you don't tell anyone; if you do, you will cop this again! You ungrateful miserable tart. Don't forget I was the one who picked you up from the gutter and brought you here. That's how you repay me? Running away?" He threw the pillow at her as he stormed out of the room.

Jasmine lay on the floor in the dark, motionless. The excruciating pain in her body was hard to bear, but it was nowhere in comparison to the pain in her heart. She felt trapped and hopeless again.

After a short while, Bob came back and turned the light on and ordered her to, "Pick yourself up and go to my bedroom now."

"I am in so much pain. Can you not do it tonight?" Jasmine knew exactly what he wanted.

"What did you say?" he swung around to shout.

"I.... " Jasmine dared not repeat the rest of the sentence as she saw the raging anger burning in his eyes.

"I... I... I... what?! Do as I tell you! Right now! "he screamed.

With a sharp intake of breath, she managed to pull herself up. She took another deep breath, moved her leg with a small step, and finally dragged her body into the bedroom. Despite the unbearable pain, she took the last piece of her clothes off. Then laid on the bed and closed her eyes, hoping it would be over quickly.

Bob's heavy overweight body was on top of her. She nearly passed out from the pain and tried to draw her legs up to ease it somehow. It was worse, and her face was covered in a mixture of sweat and tears.

The next day when Jasmine went back to work. She dared not tell Mie what happened because she worried that Bob would hurt Mie and her mum. Instead, she told Mie that Bob is a changed man. He was pleasant and kind to her and their son.

CHAPTER 15

Peony got up earlier than usual as it was her first day in college. She caught the seven o'clock L90 express bus to Wynyard, then the train from there to St. James station, where she walked to Darlinghurst, where the college was located. In the almost two hours of travelling time, her only focus was how her first day at the Sydney Institute of Technology College would be. Standing in front of the college with excitement, she found herself nervous as she took a deep breath and stepped into the beginning of her new chapter.

As she went through the front gates of the college, she followed the path lined with beautiful Jacaranda trees. The morning sunlight shone through the branches onto her face, reminding her to adjust her posture, stand taller, and hold her head higher. She continued walking towards the old sandstone heritage building built by the first convicts to settle in Australia. Looking at the timetable in her hand, she read which classroom she needed to be in first and walked through the campus until she located it. Peony got into the class just as the teacher said, "Welcome, everyone. Today we will learn the history of European Fashion..."

Peony could only grasp half of the information the teacher presented during the class, as she spoke quite fast, and there were a lot of fashion terms she was not yet familiar with. During her lunch break, Peony went to the reception and asked to speak with someone in charge of English tutorial support.

A lady in her early 40's with fair skin, blonde hair and wearing an elegant dark sky-blue pencil line dress greeted Peony: "Hi, I am Ava. How can I help you?" she said cheerfully.

"Hi Ava, my name is Peony. I am here to discuss the English tutorial support," she replied politely as she followed Ava into her office.

"Sure. Take a seat," Ava instructed.

"Thank you," she smiled as she pulled the chair out and sat on it.

"How's your first class this morning?" Ava asked.

"Good. But some of the terms I could not quite understand," Peony said.

"Don't worry. That's what I am here for." Ava smiled.

Peony took the notebook out. "I tried to take as many notes as possible but still can't quite get it yet," she explained while fiddling with the study notes in her hands.

"I will give you a short, written test to determine your English level so we can work with you and give you the right support." She put the papers on the desk in front of Peony. Ava said, "How does 4 pm today sound for the test? We can do it straight after your last class. Will that suit you?"

"Yes, thank you," Peony nodded with a smile.

Later that day, Peony sat with Ava and conducted her English-level testing. Ava asked her several questions that required more than a yes or no answer, such as, "Peony, tell me, where can you see yourself in one year? Three years and five years?" Ava spoke clearly, and consciously so Peony didn't miss anything she said and could successfully find out her oral English level.

"By the end of this year, I can see myself mastering my English and passing all the subjects. I will be one of the top students at my graduation in three years. In five years, I will be running my own business. Manufacturing and selling my designs. And hopefully, my designs will be on parade at international runways," she said.

Peony expressed her vision with passion. As she breathed life into her dreams and goals, she could visualise the whole new world in front of her.

"Based on the level of your English, and considering you are still new to this country—what you aim to achieve, some may think is very far-fetched," Ava challenged her.

"As long as I don't lose my faith and have laser vision, keep my focus on my goals and continue to move forward. Everything is possible," Peony said with determination.

Ava was pleased to hear her statement and, with a satisfied smile, said, "your spoken English is quite good. We need to work on helping you with your comprehension and written English to achieve your goals. The government only provides one hour per week to non-English speaking background students like you. I think you will need more support than that, especially with sentence structuring, grammar, and how to write essays and create presentations that you will need to do in the course. Also, I can help you to extend your vocabulary and provide information on where to gather additional materials for your assignments," Ava said.

She stared at Ava in silence, contemplating the money this extra support would be, "I don't want Matt to pay for support for me. I need to get a part-time job on weekends before I take this offer," Peony thought.

"I love Chinese food. How about you bring me some of your cooking as my tutor and support fee?" Ava offered, seemingly reading her mind. "This Saturday at 3 pm at my place?"

"Can I let you know by the end of today?" asked Peony, as she wanted to discuss it with Matt first.

"Of course." Ava tore a page from her notebook and wrote down her phone number and address before handing the paper to Peony: "I really would like you to come. I don't offer this to all students. This morning when you were in my communication class, I noticed you straight away even though you were sitting at the back of the lecture room. Your body was slightly leaning forward, and your eyes were wide open and focused. I could see you trying hard to grasp the knowledge like a dry sponge absorbing water. Our conversation just then confirms that you are the right person for me to give you an offer of help," Ava said.

Peony had her first assignment and a presentation due by the following Monday. She knew that she would need the extra help, so decided, "I would like to see you at 3 pm this Saturday. Any particular Chinese food that you like?" she asked.

Laughing, Ava said, "Excellent! I like anything with legs except tables and chairs. Just kidding! Whatever you cook will be fine. Look forward to seeing you this Saturday." Ava stood up and shook Peony's hand. Then she walked her out of the office.

Saturday came around fast, and Peony travelled to Ava's semi-detached house in a suburb called Neutral Bay which wasn't far from where she and Matt lived. The place was as warm and inviting as its owner. Ava greeted her with a big smile, hug, and invitation to enter her home. As Peony walked in the front door, she was straight away drawn to a bookshelf that took up one entire wall of a sitting room. It was bursting with all sorts of books.

"Take a seat," Ava said, pointing to the dining table. "I made us some cheese scones for afternoon tea. Tea or coffee?"

"Tea with milk and honey please," Peony said, thanking her.

"I think you don't need honey. You are already sweet enough!" Ava said with her light-hearted laughter.

"Ava, I may not be as sweet as you see!" she said, returning her laugh.

"It is ok to be as sweet as you can, but only to the right people," Ava cautioned.

"I agree!" Peony nodded.

While Ava was making the tea, Peony could not help but walk up to the bookshelf. There were different varieties of books, all placed into sections. History, Biographies, Design, Communications, Business, Motivation, and Novels. Her face looked like a little girl walking into Disneyland.

"You are welcome to borrow any of the books. But two at a time. Once you finish reading them, you must tell me what you learned from them. Then you can swap the other two. Fair enough?" Ava handed her the tea.

"God! More than fair! Could I borrow the 'Think and Grow Rich book by Napoleon Hill? From the introduction, he said, 'whatever your mind can conceive and believe you can achieve.' It sounds like a book that I have to read. Also, this one, 'The Fundamentals of Art and Design'," she asked with excitement.

"Of course, you can," Ava replied and then asked, "Tell me which assignment is due next week?"

"A presentation. Each student has to choose and present their favourite designer and talk about what makes them famous and successful. I chose Christian Dior. I did my homework before I came here. I borrowed his biography book from the library and have already read it. I outlined his background, the elements of his designs, and why he is different from the other designers. I also printed out some of the iconic designs that represent him. For instance, see this one?" She handed Ava a photocopy of one of Dior's designs and continued, "It's called 'The Look', from his 'The New Look Collection', launched in Paris on 12th February 1947. Since then, Dior's well-known unique couture dresses changed women's fashion forever."

"Looks like you have already got all the information that

you need. First, you must create a storyboard to show and tell his story. Also, you need to use palm cards to write down the points you want to discuss. In point form, and with the use of keywords, it helps to remind yourself of what you want to talk about. Your tone of voice is very important as your body language, and hand gestures make your presentation interesting and could enhance what you want to present. Don't forget that eye contact is also important in interacting with your audience. Move and avoid standing still. Try to finish your presentation within the time frame. When you go home, I want you to stand in front of the mirror and present it to yourself. If you can, try to record it and listen to your tone of voice and your pronunciation. Practice, practice, and practice," Ava coached.

Peony listened carefully and wrote each point, "Ava, my English is not that good yet. I am worried I might disappoint at the presentation."

"Well, if you think you are going to make yourself look like an idiot, I encourage you to stand up and stand tall to make a good job of it!" she said jokingly.

Early Monday morning, Peony checked and ensured she had everything she needed for the presentation before leaving home. She nervously put the storyboard against the whiteboard as her name was called. She looked at the palm cards in her hand and took a look around the class with a tense smile. She began her presentation with her Chinese accent, "Normally when men look at women, they imagine undressing them. But this man looked at women and not only loved to dress them but dressed them elegantly in a style that made them feel good about themselves," she began. "Today, I have the privilege to present to you the most famous fashion designer in the late forties to fifties—Christian Dior..."

As her English tutor, Ava was invited to sit in the class watching Peony's first presentation. "Nothing can stop her now!" she smiled and thought to herself.

Peony was great during the presentation, except for some little blunders in her English, which people understood. She left the front of the class with many people clapping in appreciation for her presentation. She was happy that people accepted her and seemed to enjoy her presentation. As she took her seat, she breathed in deeply, feeling relieved it was over.

After the presentation, Lucina, Peony's classmate, came up to her, "Hi, Peony, your presentation was unreal!"

"Sorry? What do you mean by unreal? It is real! I spent a lot of time researching him and did the presentation myself. Ava helped me with my grammar, spelling, and sentence structure, and I practiced, practiced, and practiced many times at home," Peony said, feeling offended.

"Unreal means excellent, unbelievably good. I am Lucina Walker." Lucina introduces herself. Lucina had short curly black hair, black lipstick, and a black leather collar with metal rivets on it. Her exaggerated dark eye shadows drew attention to the sparkle in her eyes. With her friendly smile, she added. "Oh, in case you're guessing, I am Aboriginal—first nation Australian."

"Sorry for being rude. I thought you were saying I did not do the assignment myself," she said, relieved.

"That's fine, no worries; I am so envious of you. Your English is excellent! I wish I could speak another language as well as do with your English. Hey, do you want to grab some lunch at the Conner Cafe' with me?" Lucina asked.

"Sure," she replied, doubting whether or not to go with her.

It turned out she had nothing to worry about. From that first meeting, Lucina became one of Peony's closest friends.

Her class finished, Peony went to the tutoring sessions with Ava to help her to improve her English. To boost her confidence, Ava withdrew a notebook from her bag, drew a group of O's on it, and an X in between them.

OOOXOOO, Peony saw, puzzled as she watched and tried to work out what Ava was doing.

"Tell me, which one stands out? The O or the X?" she asked Peony.

"Of course, the X," she responded.

"Why?" asked Ava.

"Because the X looks different than the O, that's why the X stands out," she said.

"This is the X factor! Remember that young lady, don't try to fit in. You are born to stand out!" she continued. "You will always look different as you carry your Chinese lineage. That's ok. Because these elements make YOU unique. Do you like my English with a kiwi accent?" Ava questioned.

"What is Kiwi?" Peony asked curiously.

"A Kiwi could be a bird, a fruit, or a person," Ava laughed with a joking tone.

"What?" Peony was confused and stared at Ava intently.

"Kiwis are flightless birds native to New Zealand. Kiwifruit is originally from China. Your people called them monkey fruit. Kiwi is also the nickname used by people who are from New Zealand. People know I am from New Zealand by my Kiwi accent," she told Peony.

"Ava, Matt took me to watch a football match shortly after I came here. It was Australia versus New Zealand. The players from the New Zealand team did a strange dance before the game started. I could not understand a word they said, but they were shouting a lot. Do you know what they were doing?" Peony asked.

"Ahhhh! That's called Haka. The Maori war dance. Traditionally it is used on the battlefield. It shows strength and unity. The Haka is also used during Maori ceremonies. These days the Haka is used to challenge opponents on the sports field. That's what you saw before the rugby match."

"What are Maori's? Sorry to keep interrupting you," Peony asked.

"Maori is the name for the original people who lived in New Zealand. As the Aborigines were the first people to settle in Australia, the Maori were the first to settle in New Zealand." Ava stood up and encouraged Peony to do the same.

"Stand up, and I will teach you the Haka. Watch me. You put your hands on your hip like this. Bend your knees." She demonstrated to Peony. "Kah Mo! Hi!" follow me, "Kia kaha, kia kaha, kia Ora, kia Ora"... ok. This is the last step. You finish with your eyes wide open, your tongue pops out, and you shout 'Hi!' It spells H I, but it sounds H E, not Hi!"

Peony gently said, "Hi."

Ava corrected Peony, "No, no, no, you are too gentle. Imagine you are about to enter a battle. Your main aim is to intimidate your enemy before entering the battle. You say it with determination, authority, and strength."

Peony shouted as loud as she could, "Hi!"

"That's it," she said excitedly.

"Wow. This dance is incredible! Certainly, it has increased my confidence!" Peony cheered.

"At some point in our lives, we all will face battles. Try to avoid them if you can. But if you have no choice, make sure you put on the full Armor of God and stand up to face the battles confidently. Fight the good fight of faith," Ava said earnestly.

"Certainly. I will always remember the life lessons you gave me and apply them when I need to." Peony ensured her.

"Ava, what made you decide to come to Australia?" she asked.

"When I found out my ex-husband had an affair with one of his colleagues. The next day I put his dirty clothes in a washing basket and went to where he was working. I put the basket on her desk and told her that if she decided to share my husband, then she had to share washing his dirty clothes as well. I know I couldn't stay with an unfaithful husband, so we divorced, and I moved here to start fresh," she said, feeling emotional. Peony could tell it was an incident that still caused her some hurt.

"I am so sorry to hear that. They say every new beginning is disguised as a painful ending. That's so true, don't you think?" Peony asked.

"That's spot on! Now I am in love with Steven—the love of my life. As a matter of fact, last Christmas, I sent my ex a Christmas card and thanked him. Ha!" she laughed.

Ava suddenly changed the subject, "Oh! I almost forgot the world-class Sydney Symphony Orchestra is performing in the Opera House in the coming month. I would like to take you there. Should I book it for the first Saturday night of next month?"

"Please give me a moment to check my diary." Peony said before replying, "Yes, I would like it very much. But only if you allow me to pay for the tickets," Peony insisted.

"Well, looks like you are determined, and I would be wasting time fighting you to pay, so ok! It's a deal. The classical musical 'The Phantom of the Opera' is also coming up in July at the Royal Theatre. I think you will enjoy it. I will book and pay for that one then," Ava said.

Ava picked Peony up for the Symphony at the Opera House. Peony wore a Black halter-neck evening dress that she designed and made herself. She also made a dress for Ava to thank her for all she had done.

"You look beautiful. This dress is perfect for showing off your shoulder and neckline." Ava was delighted to see Peony dressed up so elegantly.

"Ava, you look fabulous as well!" Peony exclaimed.

"I love this dress. It fits me like a glove. It is from an upcoming world-famous fashion designer. I think you know her very well." Ava winked at Peony and laughed. "How do you know sky blue is my favourite colour?" she asked.

"Remember that I am an upcoming fashion designer?" They both looked at each other and burst into laughter as they walked into the Opera House.

Eventually, as Ava and Peony's friendship grew even stronger, their bond became one like mother and daughter.

The first semester at college was quite challenging for Peony. She was trying so hard in all of her units. Especially the one in computer design since she had limited computer skills. During one of her classes, she accidentally deleted her classwork. Panicking, she told the teacher what had happened. At the end of the class, most of her classmates left. Peony was collecting her things when she dropped her pen on the floor, which rolled behind all the seats. Bending down trying to look for it took some time, and Tracy, the computer design teacher thinking Peony had gone, said to the remaining students filtering out. "I can't believe how dumb Peony is. She asks the stupidest questions that all the other students already know. What the hell?! She even deleted her classwork!"

Shocked at what she heard, Peony stood up and replied, "Tracy. I am not as stupid as you think. English is my second language, and I am still getting familiar with the computer language. I didn't understand the word delete since I have only been living in Australia for a year. I ask you to be patient with me and give me a few months. I will show you I am not dumb as you think," Peony said confidently.

Lucina, who had just reached the door to leave, stopped upon hearing the conversation and said, "Peony is smart. I cannot imagine myself in a non-English-speaking country and speaking their language as well as her own."

Tracy's face turned bright pink, and she did not know what to say. She was embarrassed and speechless.

Lucina gave a reassuring smile to Peony, and waited for her at the door. Lucina had been helping Peony with her computer skills while Peony helped her with her pattern making, garment construction and fashion illustration. Their friendship had blossomed as days went by.

Tracy seemed to continue to have a problem with Peony. She always gave her low marks on all her assignments and tests. Lucina observed all of that and was very upset by it. During a class, students were asked to put their garments on mannequins to show their designs. Then the best to worst were arranged from the best on the left-hand side to the worst on the right-hand side. Tracy put Peony's design the last on the right-hand side. Lucina stood up and asked. "Who thinks Peony's design is the best? Put your hands up."

Most of the students put their hands up. Lucina walked up to the classroom and took the mannequin with Peony's design to the first on the left-hand side. Then she told Tracy, "This is the class's decision."

Tracy became angrier with Peony, and by the end of the year, she failed Peony in computer design.

When Peony asked Tracy which part of the subject she did not pass on, Tracy simply replied, "Your confidence to operate the computer."

Peony burst into tears, "I thought I passed all my classwork, assignments, and exams."

"If you have a problem with me, see the head teacher."

"I don't have any problem with you. I think it's the other way around. You have a problem with me!" Peony protested. Then she rushed to the ladies and shut the door behind her. Tears spilled over and flowed down her face like a river escaping a dam. Not because of the failed subject but because she was devastated as Matt's Mum was in the hospital. The family had been told to prepare— she only had days to live. She felt her world was crumbling down. She knew that she had to be there to support Matt and her newfound family. She finally dried her face, put herself together, and carried her exhausted body home.

When she stepped in the front door, she dropped her handbag and sat down on the floor in complete stillness and silence for a long while. She felt numb in her head and did not know what to do. The only thing on her mind was to pray, "God, please help me to face difficulties in my life from your perspective. Teach me to focus on your power of grace and strength. Today I bring these difficult situations to you. I ask you to help me to be strong and courageous in this tough time. Help me to walk by faith and trust in you. Guide me with your wisdom and knowledge and supply me with everything I need to overcome any obstacles and challenges in my life. Thank you, God, for counselling me and instructing me. In your mighty name, I pray."

Peony sat still until she felt calmness and peace. She then pushed herself up and went into the kitchen to prepare dinner. By the time Matt came home, she was able to be there for him and give him her undivided attention. She served him dinner and discussed his Mum's situation. She decided not to tell Matt what happened in the college as she could feel Matt was mentally exhausted.

The next day Peony put on a brave face when she returned to college. She went to see the head teacher Debbie and tried to solve her issue with Tracy. But things went from bad to worse.

Debbie told her that she had to repeat the computer design unit and pass it before she could continue the second-year units. Which meant she would waste one whole year doing the subject again.

She took a deep breath to calm herself down, and then she asked, "I don't want to waste one year doing just one subject. Is there anything you can do to let me continue the second-year units?"

Then Debbie thought for a while and suggested, "Peony, if you agree to repeat the failed unit at Lidcombe campus one evening a week for a half year with a different teacher until you pass it, I will allow you to continue with second-year units. Go home and think about it. Let me know your decision tomorrow," she said to Peony.

Ava learned what had happened to Peony from the head teacher. She invited Peony to her home after her last class. When Peony saw Ava waiting for her at the front door, she threw her arms around her without saying a word. Ava walked her into the house and let her sit comfortably on the couch. "It's not just the college issue that's bothering you; what else is it?" Ava asked in concern.

Peony nodded sadly, "My mother–in–law has only days to live. It is extremely hard to accept that and let her go. I am afraid without her, it will leave a huge gaping hole in my heart and Matt and Linda's—their father died when they were younger, so their mum is the only parent left." She began sobbing.

"Oh! I am sorry to hear that," she said as she put her arms around Peony's shoulder.

"She was diagnosed with cancer over a year now. The doctor predicted she only had three to six months to live, but from the grace of God, she has lived an extra six months. We should count each extra day as a blessing, I guess. She said that her heart is at peace, and she is ready to go home to her heavenly father and be with her husband," Peony's chin trembled as she spoke.

Ava was listening intently without interruption, letting her friend talk and get it all out. She comforted Peony with her arm around her shoulder and stroking her hair. Then with a gentle voice, "She must be so special to you."

"She is such an amazing person and being loved by her is an incredible blessing." She paused and clutched the diamond pendant tightly, which was on the necklace around her neck, "This was a birthday gift from her." Her breath hiccupped in her throat when she tried to take a deep breath. Silent tears rolled down her cheeks.

Ava let Peony lean on her shoulder, stroking her back gently, saying, "you know that she will always be in your heart, and her love will embrace you forever. Right? The best way to honour her is by living a happy and fulfilling life. It is ok to feel sad and heartbroken. I want you to remember that I am always here to listen and here for you, Peony." Ava passed a tissue to her so she could wipe away her tears.

"Thank you," Peony said gratefully, taking it and dabbing it at her eyes.

"Do you want something to eat and have a break before discussing the college issue?"

"No, thank you. Matt will come here to pick me up, and we will get some takeaway, then go to the hospital to see Mum," Peony replied.

"Regarding the college matter, I think there are two options for you to consider. Here are my thoughts; Option one; you have the right to challenge Tracy. This means all class work, your test, assignments, and the final exam will be sent to the education department of NSW. Other independent teachers will mark them. If they suspect discrimination or unfair treatment, they will investigate that matter further. If they prove it is discrimination or unfair treatment, she may be disciplined, or she may even lose her teaching job.

Option two, take up the head teacher's offer. I think she knew what Tracy did was wrong. Because all teachers in the office could not stop praising you, they all said that you are an outstanding student. You passed 11 other units with an A, except for Tracy's course and the reason she failed you was your lack of confidence to operate the computer. Really?! At least Debbie already knows it was unfair treatment or discrimination. If the education department investigates this matter, as the head teacher, she will also be responsible for Tracy's actions. She would not want that to happen because the college would have a bad record. Debbie wanted to send you to the Lidcombe campus because she did not want Tracy to be your teacher again, and she wanted to deal with this matter internally," Ava informed her.

"Yes, Debbie did mention a different teacher," Peony confirmed.

"The question is, do you trust that Debbie will take action and give Tracy a warning internally? Or do you think Tracy deserves a second chance? The decision is yours. Whatever your decision, I am here to support you; you know that," Ava asked, trying to console her as best as she could.

Peony thought for a while. "I think I will take the second option and give her a second chance. Now she knows all the teachers and staff in the office know what she did to me. I have to believe Debbie will ensure that such a thing will never happen again. Plus, I need to preserve my time and energy to support my family and to deal with my grief," Peony said thoughtfully.

"Of course, I will talk to Debbie and make sure that behaviour will not happen again. Either to you or other students," Ava said.

When Peony heard the doorbell ring, she said, "It must be Matt! Please don't mention my college issue to him. I haven't told him yet."

Ava put her right hand up with an ok sign as she went to open the door.

Matt greeted Peony with a soft hug and thanked Ava for doing such a great job of supporting her.

When Matt and Peony arrived at the hospital, Jason and Linda were already there. Linda ran over and threw her arms around him, "Oh, Matt." With her choking voice, "The nurse has just put in a heavier dose of morphine to help ease Mum's pain. It seems to be working. Mum is sleeping. The doctor just informed us she may slip away soon." Linda gulped back tears. Peony went up and hugged her. Then she and Matt approached

Joyce. They stood on each side of the bed, and Peony held her hand while Matt stroked her forehead.

"We are staying here tonight," Matt said to Peony.

"Yes, I think we should," Peony agreed.

"That's what we planned to do as well," Linda told them.

"Who is looking after Hannah and Raymond?" Matt asked.

"Our next-door neighbour. We took them there this afternoon after bringing them here so they could say goodbye to Nana," Linda said with a trembling voice.

Jason walked up to his wife and hugged her to comfort her.

Peony woke up by the first rays of sunlight shining softly through the hospital window. She found herself leaning on Matt's shoulder. Lifting her head and rubbing her eyes, she gently tapped him on his back to wake him up as two nurses entered the room to check on Joyce. After a while, one of them told the family compassionately, "I'm so sorry, but we need you to leave the room for a moment. I will call you in to say your final goodbyes soon," she said apologetically.

When they were called back into the room, Joyce was looking peaceful. The nurses had given her a freshen-up with damp, warm clothes and dressed her in a beautiful soft pink floral dress that Peony had made for her and brought in. Her silver hair was combed neatly and slightly backward away from her face, tucked behind her ears. She was covered with a pure white sheet to the chest. Her arms were outside the sheet, comfortably positioned one on top of the other over her heart.

"You will have a short moment to say goodbye. We will be waiting outside the room. If you need us just call out," one of the nurses said in a gentle voice.

Matt walked up and held his mum's hands while Peony was beside him, "Mum, thank you for your amazing love. You don't need me to tell you... you know that you are the best mother and are loved deeply by all of us. I am sure Dad is busy tidying up the house in heaven and preparing a banquet to welcome you. I am sure he is extremely proud of you for raising us so wonderfully. Grandpa and Grandma will hug you so tightly when they see you." Matt spoke in a quavering voice then he kissed her forehead gently.

Linda and Jason were standing on the other side of the bed. Linda stroked her mum's forehead tenderly. "Mum, thank you for loving me and being the perfect role model. You have shown me and guided me to be the best mother to my own children… Mum, we are not going to hold you back now. You have fulfilled your God-given purpose on this earth, and I bet God is very pleased with you. When you see him in heaven, you should be extremely proud to face him and say, "Yes, I did it your way." We understand that we have to let you go now…Please take all our love with you, and know that you are leaving us with the most wonderful memories we will keep close in our hearts and cherish dearly." Linda got a lump in her throat. There were tracks of tears on her face. Jason put his arm around her waist and pulled her close to him.

Next, Peony spoke, "Mum, I will miss you even though you promised that you will come back from heaven to visit us. You said we will know you are with us when we see the birds sing on the branch and the butterfly fluttering in the garden. The whisper of the wind, the gentle waves lapping on the shore. The star shining in the sky…." Peony could not continue. She paused for a long moment before she continued. "Mum, you told us you will be the ray of sunshine to hug us. The gentle breeze that kisses us. The opening flowers that smile at us." Peony's face contorted as struggling to hold in the tears.

Jason held and stroked one of Joyce's hands and then gently put it back on her heart.

"You are the best mother-in-law, as Peony will agree with me. Now you can be in your heavenly father's arms with his everlasting love. Mum, you can go in peace. We love you." The room fell silent as all of them tried hard not to cry and make Joyce sad.

At that moment, sunlight illuminated the entire room. It was as if the angels had arrived and were ready to carry her to heaven. She peacefully breathed her last breath and entered the heavenly shore to be with her husband, her mum and Dad, and her heavenly father. Only then did the four heartbroken relatives let their tears flow freely.

When Peony returned home from the hospital with Matt, she had a quick shower and headed to the college to the head teacher's office to see Debbie. The door was opened, but Peony still politely knocked on the door to inform her that she was there.

Glancing up, she said, "Hi, Peony, come in."

"Good morning, Debbie," she said.

"Take a seat," Debbie pointed to the chair next to the window.

"Thank you," Peony sat down and took a deep breath, "Debbie, I decided to take your suggestion and attend to Lidcombe campus to repeat the computer design subject, so I can continue to study my second-year units."

"That's great! Thank you for taking my suggestion. Oh, by the way, I have good news for you."

"I am sorry. I beg your pardon." Peony gave her a sad smile. She bit her lip and looked outside the window, trying not to let Debbie see her teary eyes. At that very moment, a beautiful butterfly landed on the Bird of Paradise plant, which she was staring at. Suddenly she felt the warmth of her mother-in-law's love flooding her heart.

"Peony, are you alright?" Debbie asked.

"I... I am ok. You mentioned... ah... good news?" she asked, trying to collect herself.

"Yes, I have good news for you. I just found out this morning before you came in. The Fabric Flair Committee chose your designs for the final competition. Ten students were chosen from different colleges in New South Wales. You will represent this college in the competition!" she said excitedly.

"Really?!" I am so pleased to hear that," she said in disbelief.

"And there's more good news... If you win this competition, your designs will be shown at the Australia Fashion Show! This is the biggest annual fashion show in Australia and is recognised worldwide! You have four weeks to complete making a full range of your designs. Nicola Fabrics & Co has offered to provide you with all the fabrics you need for your designs. Here is their letter." Debbie handed the letter to Peony and continued, "Show it to them when you go there to choose the fabrics. Best of luck!"

"Thank you. I will do my best and hope to bring back a prize for the college." She said, tears prickling her eyes in a range of mixed feelings. She felt sorrowful and mournful. At the same time, she felt encouraged, inspired, honoured, and blessed. She whispered, "Mum, I promise you to live a life to its fullest as you did." She looked out the window again to see the butterfly dancing cheerfully in the air. It also seemed The Bird of Paradise was smiling under the warm morning sun. The gentle breeze came through the window and kissed her face softly. She smiled. She was determined to channel her energy and concentration into preparing her designs for the competition. She wanted to make her mother-in-law proud.

The grand final of the design competition was held at the Regent Hotel, and the invited guests from the fashion industries gradually began arriving in their droves. Peony was sitting next to Matt at the same table as Debbie, Ava, Lucina, and Tracy, along with a few other staff from the college. After the last group fashion parade, she squeezed Matt's hand nervously, waiting for the announcement of the winner. Finally, the Prime Minister's wife got up the stage. Peony thought she was such an elegant lady and hoped someday she would be able to dress her in one of her very own designs. The Prime Minister's wife interrupted her thoughts as her voice echoed through the microphone and announced the third-place winner in her category. Peony's heart was beating faster and faster. Her palms were sweating, and she had to extract her hand from Matt's to wipe them, which brought a smile to his face and instantly made her feel calm again. The second-place winner was announced, and they all held their breath as the winner was announced. "And the winner of the Fabric Flair Competition is…" Of course, she did not say the name straight away. She wanted to draw out the nervous energy and build the drama, which was almost unbearable. Then finally, she pronounced clearly, "Peony Chen!" Peony could not believe what she heard.

Matt removed her sweating palm from his hand and gently reminded her, "Peony, go up the stage to get your award." Peony was in complete shock. All she could hear was the ringing out of hundreds of people clapping her as she made her way to her feet.

Accepting the award, she thanked the Prime Minister's wife and glanced down the stage to her table. Scanning each face at the table, she said, "Thank you. My family by choice." smiling at Linda, Jason and Ava. Then continued, "My friends and all the teachers and staff at my college, I would not be able to stand here to receive this award without you. Thank you, Mum. I hope your spirit is here with us. Of course, all members of the Nicola Fabric and Co., and Fabric Flair Committee for providing the gorgeous fabric for my entire design range. Last, but not least, Matt, my best friend for life. Thank you so much."

As Peony walked down the stage, her eyes settled on Tracy. "I need to let her know that I did not hold a grudge against her," she thought. She went to shake hands with everyone from the college while other people came up to congratulate her. Then she walked over to Tracy and hugged her. "Thank you for coming to support me. It means so much to me."

"I am so sorry for the trouble I put you through." Tracy apologised with teary eyes.

"Thank you. I appreciate you saying so, and I accept your apology," she replied with a smile.

A little later, Lucina got a chance to come up to Peony and whispered in her ear. "Are you crazy? You let her off the hook? That woman deliberately failed you in computer design."

"Forgiveness is not about letting someone off the hook. It is lifting the anchors. So, both of the ships can sail forward." Peony held her hands and smiled, "I still can't believe I won the competition. Crazy, hey?"

"You deserved it!" Lucina hugged her.

Peony strived daily to be her best in every subject in the next two years. In her final year of study, Peony was chosen as one of the models for the last year fashion parade. When the head teacher informed her that she would share the stage with the rotational models at The Four Seasons Hotel, she called Ava straight away. "Ava, do you know the college asked me to be one of the models to model our final designs on stage with the rotational models?" she asked.

"Yes, I do, it was my suggestion, and all of my colleagues agreed," Ava replied.

"No way! I can't believe you did this to me. I think I will die of a panic attack on stage," she exclaimed.

"Remember, if you do not dare to get on the stage, you will always be destined for the audience. Fear is a state of mind. It is a thief and a liar. It will steal your self-confidence if you allow it to. It also constantly lies to us, 'You are not beautiful enough. You need to be taller. You are not slim enough. You need to be more talented. You do not have what it takes.'"

"That's what exactly was in my mind when Debbie came to tell me that they chose me as one of the models. The rehearsal will be on Friday after class. I am speechless. I think that was a bad suggestion!" she said, still panicking.

"Hey Peony. Listen, the biggest fear is FEAR itself. That's what they say: you can interpret F.E.A.R. in two different meanings. You either Face Everything And Rise, or Fuck Everything And Run. The choice is yours. Remember that fear is also a huge stopping block for many people and prevents them from fulfilling their God-given destiny. But I know you are wise to take this stopping block and use it as your stepping stone. Anyway, too late now. Just tell the fear to bugger off. Another Aussie slang term that means 'piss off,'" she laughed. "I encourage you to step up and own the stage. God will step in and help you to overcome the fear. Your job is to give your best shot and have fun. I promise you that when you look back in ten years, you will be glad you did it," Ava insisted.

With all the support she needed, Peony took up every challenge in life to work toward her goals. She went from strength to strength. She ran, crossing the finish line of her final year of college with a distinction level in all units. Her hard work paid off! On graduation day, she went up to the stage to collect her awards, all four of them:

"The winner of The Excellence in Design Award goes to Peony Chen!"

"The Most Outstanding Student Award goes to Peony Chen!"

"The Gerber System Computer Design Award goes to Peony Chen."

"The Australia Wool Design Award goes to Peony Chen, and Peony, your designs have also been chosen to parade in Japan's fashion show to promote Australian wool!" the headmaster of the college announced, to loud and enthusiastic applause.

CHAPTER 16

Matt came home after work and cheered, "Hey Peony, put on something nice. We are going out for dinner tonight. I want to introduce someone special to you."

"Ah! Tell me, that person must be very special!" she said, intrigued.

"He is a local builder. I met him when I took up his electrical job at one of his projects at Avalon about a couple of months ago. Love at the first sight," Matt said, beaming. He could not wipe the happiness off his face, which made Peony laugh.

"So, you have been dating someone and having an affair behind your wife's back for a couple of months hey?! Now, finally you have the guts to tell me?" Peony pretended to be upset.

"Oh, my darling wife, please forgive me," Matt put his palms together, pretending to pray for forgiveness.

"Tell me, what is his name?" she asked, eager to know more about this mystery man.

"Tom, I call him Tommy," Matt said.

"Sounds like he is the one! I am so happy for you. Does Tom know about our relationship? she asked.

"Yes, I told him because I don't want any misunderstanding between him and I. He is the man of my life, I can feel it Peony, so I didn't want to get off on the wrong foot and lose him. When I told him about you, he said he would love to meet you. Go and get changed while I have a quick shower. Hurry up, we're meeting Tom at the Arm's Hotel at 7:30 pm," he said excitedly.

"Ok, ok! Don't hurry me! I have never seen you so serious. We will be there on time," Peony grumbled.

The restaurant was on the top level inside the Arms Hotel. Matt had booked a table by the window overlooking Pitt Water where boat lovers were sailing their boats back to the ramp, and dog lovers walked their dogs along the water's edge. It was quite beautiful taking in the view as the sun slowly said its goodbye for the day.

Peony and Matt entered the restaurant, and Matt pointed to a man sitting at his booked table near the back of the restaurant by the window with a view, "Tom is over there," Matt said nervously.

Peony observed Tom had short, neat hair and wore a pair of tight jeans, and a white shirt with the top two buttons unbuttoned, showing his smooth but clearly muscular chest. He stood up and kissed Matt on the cheek.

"This is Tom." He introduced him to Peony while he put his hand around Tom's shoulder, "Tommy, this is Peony," Matt said proudly.

"Nice to meet you," Tom leaned over and kissed Peony gently.

"Likewise," Peony gave him a warm welcome hug.

"Matt has not stopped talking about you since we started dating. Even though this is the first time we have met, it already feels like I know you," Tom said with a smile.

"This cheeky bear only told me this evening about you." Peony punched Matt gently and continued, "I am happy for you both."

After dinner, when they arrived home, Peony made Matt his favourite peppermint tea and handed it to him. She sat beside him and said, "I think we need to talk." She felt that she needed to bring the uneasy subject up. "Even though I am getting so used to being around you. I understand it would be awkward for you to date your man and yet still live with your wife. I think it's time for a divorce Matt. What do you think?" she asked.

"What?! You can't wait to get rid of me, can you?" Matt elbowed Peony playfully.

Smiling, she replied, "No. I don't want to get rid of you at all. But I can't be selfish and keep you all to myself now, can I? I will do what is best for you," she said.

"I know! Silly Billy! It has been my privilege to call you my wife for the last few years. That's why even after Mum passed on, I still wanted to remain to keep our titles of husband and wife. You are such a beautiful person Peony. I not only enjoy your company but your delicious Chinese cooking as well! It is so much fun when we go to places together, garden together, and even renovate together! We have had so many precious and amazing times together. I enjoy every moment with you. But I agree with you, it is the right time," he said.

"You have been there for me as my family and my best friend. You have been there to protect me and love me. I guess it is time for me to learn to be more independent." Even though Peony knew they could not live forever together as husband and wife. At some point in time, they had to live apart. She felt a wave of sadness rush through her heart. In a way, she felt like she had lost him somehow. She sighed, "I guess it's about time to find my own place," she said.

"Tom wants me to move in with him Peony, so I want you to stay here and remember here is always your home for as long as you want to stay. We are still soul mates and best friends. Right? I will always be there for you. As I promised I would be." Matt hugged her tightly.

"Oh! You're holding me so tight I can hardly breathe Matt!" she laughed. At that very moment, Peony felt and knew they would always have a special place in each other's hearts.

"I know you will. You and Tom are always welcome if you crave my Chinese cooking."

Matt held Peony's hands for a while, gently took the wedding ring and the engagement ring off her ring finger, then slid them onto the mirror finger on her right hand, "Leave this space for your wedding ring from your future husband."

"Ha, future husband? Where is he?" she asked with a chuckle.

"You never know? Maybe he's just around the corner. You will meet him in the most unexpected place, and in the most unexpected way. Just like I did with Tom," he proclaimed.

"When it happens, it will happen. I am not in a hurry. Anyway, I need to focus on building my business first," she said.

"Follow your heart. As you always do," he said.

"When are you planning to move to Tom's place?" she asked.

"The last weekend of this month. You are invited there for a housewarming BBQ," he told her.

"I will give you a helping hand to move," She stood up and tried to look up at the clock on the wall and hoped the tears would not drop down, "It is time to go to bed. Good night," she said.

"It is ok to be sad. I am sad too. Come here." Matt stood up. He pulled her close to his heart and gave her a long hug.

CHAPTER 17

Peony finished her double diplomas in Fashion Design and Business Management and was eager to open her first shop. She carefully read through the 'For Lease' pages in the newspaper and circled a few properties in a good location and had premises suitable for her shop. After finishing her morning tea, she made some phone calls to enquire about them and secured two appointments with agents to view them. The first one was at one o'clock in Palm Beach, and was close to her home, so it would be very convenient for her. The agent seemed a bit uneasy when he saw Peony at first. After she introduced herself to him, the agent asked her his first question, "Peony, how long have you been in Australia?"

"About four years," Peony stated.

"I'll be honest with you. This area is for the rich and famous. They are looking for designer brands. They will not buy brands that are unknown or cheap imported things," he cautioned. "I don't think this area will be within your target market. You better go to the West where more Asians live, as they are the ones who normally buy those kinds of products," he said dismissively. Peony tried hard to control her frustration and hide her annoyance at his comment. He seemed all too eager to get rid of her.

"How do you know I am not suitable for this area if I am not given any chance for the locals to know me and see my designs?" she asked him.

"I am just being realistic and giving you advice. Furthermore, I don't think the owner will lease it to you. She wants someone who has a well-established business, not a newcomer," he said over his shoulder on his way back to his car.

"Thank you very much for your time. I don't think this shop is suitable for me anyway. Because I need someone who believes in my abilities, qualifications, and determination to be a success rather than judge me by my look, where I came from, and my circumstances," she said curtly.

Peony was disheartened, but she managed to pull her courage together and head to the next appointment at Avalon. She was hoping this time she would have better luck.

When she arrived, the agent was already outside the shop waiting. "Manual," the agent said, introducing himself and stepping forward to shake her hand.

"Peony. Nice to meet you," she reciprocated.

"I didn't expect to be meeting such a beautiful lady," he stared at Peony flirtatiously.

"That's flattering! Thank you. Could you please show me the shop?" Peony felt uncomfortable and steered the awkward conversation towards the business at hand.

"Yes, of course, come in," he said, opening the shop door.

"I like the location, right in the heart of the shopping area and the strip of other fashion shops." Peony expressed her interest in the shop.

"Shall we go somewhere and have a cup of coffee and discuss this further? If you are interested in the shop, I will ensure you get it, and I can negotiate a better price for you," he winked at Peony and put his arm around her waist.

She quickly withdrew herself from his arm. "We can discuss it right here thank you, or over the phone," Peony stated adamantly.

"That's how things work in this country, something for something, you know what I mean?" he replied, somewhat irritated by Peony's refusal.

"I have a second thought. I don't think I like this shop. Coffee is unnecessary. Bye." Peony rushed out the door and headed straight to her car.

Peony was so disappointed with her experiences of the day. All afternoon she could not focus on her work. All she wanted to do was curl up on the couch and have a good cry. She forgot it was dumpling night with Matt. They had this night once a month while Tom was visiting his parents. Since Tom had not yet found the courage to tell his parents that he was interested in men only, he thought it wasn't the right time to take Matt to visit his parents yet. When Matt opened the door, he saw Peony was discouraged and not herself. "Hey, what's up?" he asked.

"I had a tough day!" Peony did not even bother to get off the couch to greet Matt with the big hug she usually gave him.

"Tell me what's happened," said Matt.

"I went for two appointments to view two shops I was interested in, and it all went bad. One was at Palm Beach, the other was at Avalon. One agent was a racist jerk, and the other was a dirty old bastard who wanted to touch me."

"You're kidding?!" Matt said with a hint of anger. "Bloody mongrels. Do you want to look further afield, so you don't need to deal with these kinds of people?" he asked.

"Where?"

"Maybe the CBD or big shopping malls?" he ventured.

"Really? What do you think the big shopping malls will do if the small shops in this area will not give me a chance? A newcomer with a Chinese background and no business experience? They'll just laugh at me," she said.

"No, they won't. I want you to look further and think bigger. Don't devalue yourself Peony. Look how far you've come and how much you have already accomplished! Don't let the few idiots out there dampen your spirit. If God closed one door, it's because He knows He will open another one with bigger and better things. Your job is to have faith in Him and keep on trying," he advised.

"I am not sure. The agents suggested I look at the western part of Sydney. There are more Asians, and those people will buy cheap things, one of them told me," she said.

"Peony, Stop there! Those turkeys are talking a whole load of rubbish! Remember, Eagles don't waste their time trying to prove to the Emu, Turkeys, and Chickens how high they can fly; they keep soaring with divine purpose. You have a big dream to accomplish. A strong woman like you will be tested by forcing you into obstacles and challenges again and again. I am asking you to keep soaring like an eagle with your head held high. I promise you that your gifts, talents, and strength will be recognised. You are equipped with everything you need to fulfil your God-given destiny. You know this," he said and gave her a big hug. "Sometimes you are just being silly! But I like your silliness. Anyway, are we ready for the dumplings or what?"

"You always say the right thing to make me feel better. I must confess that I forgot tonight was the dumpling night" Peony shook her head in disbelief.

"How about I take you out for dinner instead then to cheer you up?" Matt suggested.

"I would love that. Thank you," she said.

"Where would you like to go?"

"How about the Hong Kong Chinese Restaurant just down the road? Every time I get upset or down in the dumps, the shallot and ginger steamed fish with rice and jasmine tea cure me."

"No worries, I want you to put everything aside tonight. It is ok. Relax tonight, and then you can wake up in the morning refreshed, clear and ready to take on the world again," he said.

Dinner was great. A night out with Matt always made her laugh and feel better. After dinner, Peony returned and felt refocused and inspired to go after her big dream again. "If I have to, I will dance without the music until I get there," she said to herself determinedly.

As the brand new day unfolded, Peony chose not to look back at the closed doors and the disappointments, just as Matt had said. Instead, she rose brightly, took a long shower, prepared her favourite breakfast and was energised and ready to conquer the world!

She opened the front door. She stepped out determined to find her shop and the new opportunities that would open up for her with it. Was she scared? Oh, hell, yes! But she was not going to let fear get in her way to prevent her from moving forward. She knew that every time she stepped out, it would be one step closer to the destiny that she knew was to be created.

Taking Matt's suggestion, she made another appointment to look at a premises on Pitt Street in the Mall in the heart of the city. She had arranged to meet with the leasing manager at 10 am in his office at the Mall. When she arrived, the receptionist led her to the meeting room where the manager was, "Mr Artino, Miss Chen is here," the receptionist announced pleasantly.

"Come in please," a voice called out behind the door. The leasing manager looked up as Peony stepped in, their eyes were met, and Peony stood there frozen. Complete silence engulfed the room. "Is that you? The Greek Restaurant at Narrabeen? The 30 red roses?" he asked, surprised. She felt like the floor was falling out from beneath her. She felt all her confidence drain out of her. "It's him," she thought to herself.

He stood up and walked over to Peony. He put his hand out to offer her a handshake. When he reached her, he took both her hands in his and held onto them just a little longer than normal, before regretfully letting them go.

"Johnathan Artino, call me Nathan, I remember you. It's so nice to see you again." he said warmly, his eyes never leaving hers.

Peony could tell he was trying to remain calm and friendly, but she could sense that he was excited to see her. His unforgettable gentle, and warm eyes were locked with hers. "Oh, God! His voice is so calm that like water flowing gently down the stream, so soothing" thought Peony. There was something about him. He was memorable. He made her feel excited and nervous at the same time.

When she finally spoke, even she was surprised by her own voice, it was different, heightened. "Peony, Peony Chen. Nice to see you again."

"God, pull it together girl," she scolded herself, remembering why she was here in the first place.

"Take a seat, please. Coffee or tea?" he asked pleasantly.

"Water would be fine, thank you." She acted as calmly as she could, but looking down, she noticed her hands were still shaking from him holding them.

Nathan pressed a button on his phone and asked the receptionist to bring in some water.

"I was expecting to see you again in my friend Jimmy's restaurant, but you never came back. Jimmy told me that you were supposed to come in the following Saturday night. Tell me what you have been doing in the last few years since I last saw you," Nathan said, eager to know more about Peony.

"Well, since that night I saw you. I...." she looked at the wedding ring on Nathan's finger and snapped into business mode. "It's not important. Let's talk about the shop. What are the criteria for leasing a shop in your centre?" she asked.

"I'd really like to know more about you and what you've been up to, and sure we can talk about business too," he said.

"Ah… may I?" Peony looked at the chair opposite his desk.

"Oh, I beg your pardon." Nathan realised Peony was still standing there. He quickly pulled the chair slightly out and invited her to sit down.

"Thank you." She felt more comfortable and calmed down as she sat. "I have just finished studying fashion design and business management at the Sydney Institute of Technology. I plan to open a boutique to sell my designs. All my ranges will be made in Sydney. My target market is professionals, businesswomen, and office ladies. Some smart casual weekend wear as well. I mainly use natural fibres such as silk, cotton, linen, and wool. Here are some of my designs," Peony said, offering him the catalogue of her summer range.

Nathan took the catalogue and read each page carefully before saying, "I have three shops available at this moment Peony. To be honest with you, that's rare. Normally we have a waiting list for people wanting to lease a shop here due to its prime location, but after the recession, I think people are still trying to recover. Or, maybe they don't want to take such a big risk to start a business so soon after and are playing it a bit safe."

"You are right. Mr Artino," she agreed.

"Nathan, please call me Nathan," he asked.

"Nathan, in my opinion, there will never be the right time to start one's business. I believe one of the most important things is that we do our homework, find the right target market, have a budget, and carefully estimate the outgoing spending, and the income as well. One must take a calculated risk and do their best and let God do the rest," she said.

"How about I show you the shops, and we can talk more about the possibility of which one may suit you? We have one that is one hundred and five square meters, another is seventy three square meters, and the small one is thirty-five square meters," he told her.

"That sounds great. Thank you."

Nathan stood up and walked to the door, opening it for her. "After you," he said.

"Thank you," she replied.

"Follow me this way," Nathan said, leading the way to the first available shop, which was big but L-shaped.

"It is a good size, but half of the shop is hidden," Peony said.

He agreed, and they moved on to the second shop. This one was seventy-three square meters.

"It seems in a good position with lots of traffic passing through," observed Peony.

Nathan nodded and walked her to the last shop he had available.

"The last one is just around there." He said, pointing to the shop opposite the escalator. He opened the door to the thirty-five square meter shop and invited her in to take a look.

Peony thought it seemed too small for what she wanted, and it was hidden behind the escalator, which she wasn't in favour of. "Could you please take me back to the seventy-five square meter one for a second look?" Peony requested.

"Of course," said Nathan and exited the shop locking the door behind them before making their way back to the second shop for another viewing.

"It is next to the escalator. It's only 10.30 am, and plenty of people are already using the escalator to go up to the food court. I've learnt that people on an escalator have about 10 seconds to scan the shops in view before they step off. I suspect the traffic here at lunchtime would be much more than now." Peony thought out loud, Nathan nodded, confirming her thoughts.

"Would you like to have a coffee with me at the café over there?" Nathan pointed to the coffee shop opposite where they were standing. "We can discuss the lease further if you are interested in this shop, such as the terms and criteria we need," he said hopefully.

"I would love to." She said as their eyes locked again. Peony tried her best to avoid eye contact with him. It seemed whenever she looked at him, and he looked at her, she felt a weird sensation that he could read her mind and soul.

"Peony, stop it. You are going too far with this. He has a family. He is not your friend. He is a kind man who got you out of an embarrassing situation. Focus on business!" she thought to herself sternly.

Peony was still deeply in her thoughts as Nathan pulled the chair out for her to sit in. "What would you like?" he asked.

"I beg your pardon. What did you say?" Peony said with just a hint of embarrassment. She hoped he didn't pick up that she was fantasising about him.

"I asked what you would like," Nathan repeated his statement with a smile.

"Latté, please," she said.

Nathan waved to the owner of the café. "Hey Ben, we would like two lattés and two almond croissants. Please," he said.

"Yes sir, how's the start of your day Nathan?" Ben asked while pouring some water into the glasses.

"It's fantastic. Could not ask for better!" Nathan beamed and threw a brief look at Peony.

"Oh my God!" thought Peony, "he's flirting! And how on earth did he know I would love an almond croissant?! It was my do or die in the mornings with my coffee."

"They bake the best almond croissants here on site every morning. I can't wait until you try them. They are my favourite!" he said. If you decide to have your boutique in this centre, I bet you will come here often. I better warn you; their croissants are addictive." Nathan said with an affectionate smile.

"Please don't smile at me like that, she thought, you're killing me with it." Peony looked down, fidgeting with her long silky black hair. There was a long silence, and then Nathan suggested, "Ok, should we get on to business? Once you choose which shop you like, would you draw up a business plan that projects the sales of the next one, three, and five years? The landlord likes to see your business plan to make sure you are planning for success. He's pretty helpful and likes to help new businesses in the centre," he said.

"Sure. I am happy to prepare my business plan and present it to you." She said, sipping her latte'.

"Could we schedule our next meeting with your business plan then?" he asked. "Let's check. How about next Monday at the same time?" he said, looking at his diary.

Peony also checked her diary and replied, "That's perfect for me."

"Fantastic. We can meet in one of our meeting rooms. When you arrive on Monday, the receptionist will show you which meeting room we'll be in," he said helpfully.

"I look forward to it, thank you," Peony replied. No! No! No! Not that look again! She forced herself to disengage from her gaze and look at the waiter who had come to set their croissants down on the table.

"Your almond croissants." He said pleasantly, "Enjoy!"

Peony picked up the croissant and had a bite. "Oh! You are right. It is to die for, very delicious!" she said in between bites.

They chatted a little more about business in the centre before Nathan had to excuse himself to head back to the office for his next meeting.

Apologising, he thanked Peony for coming in and said he looked forward to seeing her again on Monday. Retaking her hand, his eyes lingered on hers as he said, "It's really good to see you again Peony," as he regretfully let go of her hand.

Peony thanked him for his time and said she'd see him with her business plan on Monday.

CHAPTER 18

After leaving the café, Peony immediately took out her mobile phone to make the call, "Hey, Ava, you're not going to believe who I saw today. I will tell you when I see you. But first things first. I was hoping you could help me with my business plan. I have it all in my head, but I need to write it professionally to present to the centre manager and centre owner of a shop I want to lease," she said.

"When do you need to have it done by?" Ava asked.

"Monday at 10 am," she replied.

"Piece of cake! Come and have dinner with me tonight at six o'clock. We can do it then," she said.

"Ok. Will we have fish and chips," Peony tried to speak the sentence in her best version of a New Zealander.

Ava laughed, "No fish and chips tonight. Good try though! Your Kiwi accent is getting there!" she giggled. "I have some venison from New Zealand just for you. I may be able to get a dozen New Zealand oysters as well. After dinner, we will put your business plan together," she assured her.

"Can't wait to see you," Peony said, thanking her.

After seeing the fabric samples for her next autumn / winter range at Alexandra. Peony picked up a bunch of Ava's favourite yellow roses from the florist and a bottle of Ava's New Zealand wine, then she headed to Ava's.

She parked her car in Ava's driveway and whispered, "God, I am so grateful to have her in my life. Thank you for putting the right people in my path," she said thankfully.

She knocked on the front door. Ava came out and greeted her with a long hug. "Glad to see you. Come on in. Dinner is ready to serve," she said happily.

Peony handed the flowers and wine to Ava, "These are for you," she said.

"Oh! You should not do that." She smelled her favourite yellow roses and then arranged them in a vase.

Peony put her handbag beside the coffee table. Then she went to the kitchen to get some plates and cutlery to set up the table. The first thing she could not wait to talk to Ava about was not her business plan, but Nathan.

"Ava, remember I told you the story about the man who gave me 30 roses? Well, I met him again today," she blushed.

"Where?" Ava said in astonishment.

"You wouldn't believe it! He is the Sky Paradise Centre Leasing Manager. His name is Nathan. I am going to present him and the owner my business plan on Monday."

Ava could feel the excitement in Peony's tone of voice and saw the twinkle in her eyes.

"I am sure that it is not a coincidence. So, what are you going to do about it this time?" she asked mischievously.

"The problem is that I don't know if I am attracted to his kindness, or what," she pondered aloud.

"In the last few years, you haven't stopped talking about him and the red roses. I hope you are not waiting for another few years to do something about this. You've got a second chance now. It may be your last." She warned.

Ava placed the food on the table, "Ok, young lady. Serve yourself as much as you want, and let's talk about this Nathan of yours."

"Thanks," said Peony, helping herself to the food on the table. "Somehow, the way he looked at me, I couldn't help but be completely lost in his eyes. I felt there was something between us that was unexplainable. Oh, Ava, the problem is that I saw the ring still on his wedding finger! I am tempted by the devil if he is a married man. My heart is troubled. At the same time, I want to do the right thing in God's eyes," she shook her head with worry.

"Well, you will find out soon. Sometimes things are not what you see. Sometimes you got to trust your heart, not your eyes," Ava explained.

"You have no idea how hard it was to pull myself together during today's meeting. Oh my God! My heart was beating so fast. Even now, when I talk about him, it's racing. I don't know if I can do the presentation properly!" Peony signed.

"Of course, you can present it. Just like the first time you did the presentation about Dior in College. And that time you modelled on stage. Scared, but you did it anyway and did it brilliantly," Ava reminded her. "I know your business plan is in your head, but let's pull it out of there and put it on paper, hey?" Ava got up and asked, "Tea as usual?"

"Yes, please." Peony quickly picked up the plates and put them on the kitchen bench. She wiped the dining table down so they had a clean, accessible space to prepare the business plan on.

"We should start with your qualification, experiences, and your achievements. You need to let them know who you are before you let them know what you are planning to do," Ava said, handing a cup of tea to Peony.

"That sounds great. After showing them my qualification and experiences, I should show them my target market, followed by my marketing plan. I also need to project the next one, three, and five years of revenue and the road map of how I intend to get there," she said.

"I am sure that you don't want to deliver your products by TRICK this time, though," she laughed.

"You still remember that assignment when I was in college? Ha, Ha! Not funny! I meant to say they deliver the garments by TRUCK, not TRICK! How embarrassing," Peony laughed.

"You see, only one letter different changes the whole meaning in English. It's no easy language to learn, but you, my friend, are nailing it!" Ava said proudly.

"Thanks. Let's get into the business plan," Peony said, trying to steer away from any more of her most embarrassing moments.

"Not yet. We have plenty of time!" Ava stopped her.

"Please Ava, don't bring up any more of my embarrassing moments," she pleaded.

"How about that time when we were in the pub in the Blue Mountains? You asked the bar attendant for some 'penis'," Ava said, laughing so hard she almost spilt her tea.

"Oh God! Don't mention it ever!" Peony put her hands over her face.

"The guy sitting next to us almost fell off his chair. And the bar attendant's jaw hit the floor! I wish that I had a camera to capture the moment. I tried not to correct you back in those days too much, but I fully enjoyed that moment for a bit before telling them that you meant to ask for some peanuts," she laughed.

"You are cruel. Ava," Peony said, laughing with her.

"Well, sometimes you gotta be cruel to be kind!" Ava said, smiling fondly at her friend.

"Remember that guy at the bar walked towards us, and I told you that I bet he comes up to ask you for your phone number? I suggested you not give him your real number unless you liked him. Otherwise, just make up a number like 666 296 instead?" Ava asked.

Nodding, Peony said, "I didn't like him, so I gave him the incorrect number."

Ava said, "Yes! I didn't tell you at the time, but I deliberately picked the number 666 296 as I knew with your Chinese accent you would pronounce the number as, sex sex sex tonight sex."

"Oh, Ava, you are so bad!" Peony said in hysterics.

"He thought that he hit the jackpot!" Ava laughed.

"Sometimes I wonder why I still hang around you! You are such a bad influence!" Peony said, enjoying their laughs.

"Even though I have been already living here for four years, I still have moments it all goes astray with my accent. Last weekend I was invited to a birthday party. In a conversation, I told a guy that we were so lucky. There are six beaches surrounding us in such a short distance. He looked over to a group of women and asked, 'Who? Those bitches?' I had to correct myself and say, 'Sorry, I mean beaches, like water and sand,'" she giggled.

Ava held her tummy and rolled forward and back, crying with laughter. "I am so glad you have developed a thick skin but have remained tender-hearted. Just like the Chinese deep-fried tofu, crispy and hard outside, but soft and tender inside," she said, wiping her tears away.

"Ava, how can I ever repay you for what you have done for me? I mean the good and the bad! "Peony said cheekily.

"There is nothing you need to repay me with the good. I am just sowing kind seeds in good soil. I know they will flourish and produce fruit to benefit many others. The bad hey? Ah! You can pay me back by embarrassing me at my 80th birthday party!" she smiled.

CHAPTER 19

The receptionist led Peony to the meeting room. She was so nervous that she could feel her palms sweating and her heart beating out of her chest. She walked in quickly, scanning the meeting room. Nathan was sitting with a man in his 60s at the end of a long table. The centre owner was tall and slim with silver-grey hair and looked up from a stack of papers in front of him as she arrived.

Nathan stood up and walked towards the door to greet Peony, "Good morning Peony," he said, then turned and addressed the centre owner, "this is Peony Chen. And this is Mr Callas," he said, making the introductions.

"Nice to meet you, Mr Callas," Peony smiled and put her hand out to shake his hand.

"Likewise. Call me Andrew. Please take a seat." Andrew gave her a firm handshake and directed her to sit in the chair opposite him.

The kind and friendly smile on Andrew's face instantly made Peony feel at ease.

"Thank you Nathan and Andrew, for your valuable time. Here is my business plan." Peony said, getting right to the point and handing each of them a copy of the business plan with her slightly shaking hands. She then took a deep breath and began the presentation.

"Sky Paradise is an iconic building in Sydney's CBD. It is truly a shoppers' paradise for both locals and tourists. The interior design of my shop will mirror and complement the centre's design to bring the outside in. The shop will be simple and elegant. In this way, less is more. I want to let my design do the talking. My marketing strategy is as follows," Peony said, going on to explain it in brief. "I believe my design will bring a striking look and add value to your centre. I will be grateful if you allow me to become part of your unique shopping centre. These are some of my designs from my summer collection."

After Peony finished her presentation, Andrew looked at Peony's business plan in front of him, then turned to Nathan and said, "I am more than happy to give Peony an opportunity. Could you please ask our solicitor to draw up the leasing contract? The term is 3x3 Peony, plus we will give you six months rent-free and $20,000 towards the shop's interior design expenses. He stood up and leaned over to shake Peony's hand. "Peony, it is our privilege to have you in this centre. Nathan will work alongside you and guide you on how we would like your shop to become part of this centre. He'll go over our colour scheme and lighting with you. By the way, Peony, I don't wish you good luck. Because you already have everything you need to be a success," he smiled.

Peony's eyes were wide. It all happened so fast that she didn't have a second to think about what they had just offered her to sink in. Quickly regrouping, she managed to say, "Andrew, I am extremely grateful for the opportunity."

Nathan looked at his watch and said, "I can't believe my eyes. It is almost lunchtime. Would you like to have lunch with me? We can discuss it further then, and I can go over the contract terms so I can forward them to our solicitor." He asked. "There is a restaurant not far from here. It is quiet, and the company has a room for us to take our clients for meetings and a nice meal," he advised.

A room set up in a restaurant to meet clients? She remembered what happened with Lili in China and worried she was stepping into something she couldn't get out of.

Seeing Peony's face change, Nathan asked, "Does that suit you? Or do you prefer to meet somewhere else? Andrew insisted the lunch was on us, so you don't need to pay for it; we will be," Nathan said reassuringly.

Nathan and Andrew seemed like decent businessmen, Peony thought. She had to trust her gut on this one and put aside her fears. "Your suggestion sounds great," Peony replied, letting Nathan lead the way to the restaurant.

"The restaurant is one of the top five-star hotels in Sydney, only 5 minutes walking distance to where we currently are. I hope you don't mind that we stroll there?" he asked.

"Not at all. I enjoy walking and taking in the sights," she said.

The room was set up professionally, as Nathan had promised. A conference table was positioned near a window overlooking the breathtaking view of the Harbour Bridge and the Opera House. On one side was a desk with two chairs and the essential office equipment such as a computer and printer. On the other side were a three-seated leather lounge and two single-seated sofas.

Peony stood in front of the window, "What a magical view!" she exclaimed.

"Yes, indeed. Andrew must like you a lot. Normally this room is for meeting his business associates. In this room, we have signed contracts worth billions of dollars. He is a well-trusted businessman and a great friend of mine. I have known him and his family since I was a kid," Nathan revealed with admiration.

During the lunch, Nathan and Peony discussed some more detail about the shop set-up, the terms, and the fit-out that needed to be included in the lease contract.

Slowly Peony's nervousness subsided. Nathan had a way of making her feel comfortable, even with something as momentous as this.

"I will ask our solicitor to send the draft of the lease to your solicitor. Is there anything you want to bring up or discuss?" he asked.

Peony thought for a while and replied, "Not at this moment."

"If you have any questions, please do not hesitate to contact me. Peony, I am so pleased that I have met you again," he extended his hand.

"Likewise." She said, offering her hand. Again, she could feel him hold her longer than normal. It was like he didn't want to ever let go of her.

Departing, Peony's first phone call after leaving Nathan was to Ava, "Hey Ava, I got the shop!" she squealed with excitement.

"It does not surprise me. I knew you would get it. Whoever does not give you the opportunity is missing out!" she said happily.

"Listen to this; I also have the shop for six months rent-free and twenty thousand dollars from them for the internal setup of the shop! Such as the new carpet and the new lighting," Peony said excitedly.

"That's amazing! Good on you! Great negotiating skills Peony!"

"Ava, the truth is that I did not even negotiate those terms. They offered it to me! According to Nathan, Andrew only offered it to me because he knows I have what it takes to be a success. Thank you so much for helping me with my business plan. Otherwise, I don't think I would get the shop lease and the generous offers," she said generously.

"Don't be silly. The idea of the plan is all yours. I only helped you to present it more professionally. That's all! The credit's yours!" Ava said.

"Thank you. Ava. From the bottom of my heart. Catch up with you soon," she said as she hung up the phone. The next phone call she made was to Matt.

"Hey, my gorgeous ex-husband. I got a shop in the city. Thank you for pushing me to look further and go bigger. I need your help. Could you please do all the electrical and lighting jobs for me?" she pleaded.

"Of course, I can. I am very happy for you. You know that I will do anything for you. Just let me know the time frame so I can schedule the time for you." He said, with the cheerful voice Peony always delighted in hearing.

"Ok. I will. Approximately within two weeks, I think. I will let you know as soon as possible. And when I see you, I will tell you another unbelievable story. Give a big hug to Tom for me," she said.

"You want to tell me you met someone?" Matt laughed.

"Um, no one yet." Nathan's smiling face crossed Peony's mind. She felt the unmistakable warmth flowing through her heart again.

"You will know when you meet the one. Like when I met Tom. Talk soon. Love you."

"See you soon. Love you too," she said.

Then Peony called her close friend Kang, who had come from Fujian in China. He was in his final year of studying architecture at the University of Technology Sydney. They met in the State Library. Since then, they got together to do painting, sketch, and discuss art and design. Eventually, they became very close friends.

"Hello Kang, I have good news," she said with uncontainable excitement.

"Ha-ha. You want to do live drawing again at lady bay beach?" Kang joked.

"No joking! That beach that you took me to is a one-off thing! I still remember when that naked guy asked me if I wanted him to be a live model, which was sooo embarrassing. Luckily you came up to rescue me. I swear I will not go there again!" she laughed hard.

"Then, tell me, what is the good news?"

"I have your first project for you. Interior design for a fashion boutique in Sky Paradise Shopping Centre."

"You are kidding. Right? You are opening your first shop?" Kang said, feeling excited.

"Yep! They are preparing the contract. I should sign the contract and have the key if everything goes smoothly by the end of the next couple of weeks. Nathan, the centre manager, said I could get into the shop to take some measurements and photos in the meantime. So, you can start the design. Do you have time tomorrow?"

"Yes, my lecture is in the afternoon. I can meet you there at 9 am if that suits you," he said.

"Perfect! See you tomorrow."

The following morning, Peony went to the shopping centre office to pick up the key. The receptionist informed Nathan that Peony was there. He came out of his office with the key and handed it to Peony. As he walked her out of the office, he turned to Peony, giving her a long, thoughtful gaze before asking, "Hey, Peony. Are you a good cook?"

"I believe I am a reasonably good cook. Why?"

"If I buy the ingredients, could you teach me to cook some homemade Chinese dishes at my place?" he asked.

A little taken off guard, she said, "Sure, when?"

"This Sunday, 5 pm?"

"Ok, I will get all the ingredients because you don't know where to get them. I assume that your wife will be there. Right?" She looked at the ring on his finger.

"No. She will not be there," he said.

Peony could sense some sadness in his eyes at the mention of his wife but wasn't sure if she was reading him right.

"What? It doesn't feel right that I come to your place when your wife is not at home," she said, "I... I don't think that's appropriate...."

Nathan interrupted her gently and said, "Don't worry. I will explain it to you on Sunday, but don't worry, ok?"

"Ok. See you on Sunday then," Peony said.

"I will send you an email with my address. I live at Seaforth, not far from Newport, where you live. Look forward to seeing you. Oh, by the way, do you drink?" he asked.

"A glass occasionally. Only at special events with special people." Peony jokingly said.

"Looks like I have to get a bottle then," he laughed. "Red or White?"

"Do you like seafood?" Peony looked down at her hands, twisting the key round and round with her finger in the keyring.

"Yes, I enjoy seafood," he noticed her shy and blushed smile.

"White will be perfect with seafood, is that ok?" She could feel her heart about to burst into fire. God he was sweet!

"Sauvignon Blanc?" he asked, not taking his eyes off her.

"Perfect," she said. Meeting his eyes, it was like time stood still. She could get lost in his eyes forever, she thought.

"Look forward to seeing you on Sunday." He broke the silence.

"Same," she said and floated off to her shop to meet Kang.

Kang was waiting in front of the shop when Peony arrived there. They hugged then Peony opened the shop. "Come in. Time to show your talent!" she said with an excited tone.

"I am glad that you chose this shop. It is a great location," he affirmed as he took a tape out and started to measure the shop so he could design the layout for her.

"I appreciate that you are taking this job Kang. I would like three change rooms in this part of the shop. What do you think?" she asked, pointing to the left corner of the shop.

"I agree with you. As customers walk in, psychologically they always look at the right-hand side first," Kang replied.

"I am sure we will work well together to achieve the best layout design," she said.

"Thank you for trusting me, my friend," he said as he wrote notes down on his pad.

"Hey, I know it will be an outstanding result!" she said confidently.

CHAPTER 20

On Sunday, Peony turned her car into a neat and impressive driveway that led to a stunning modern house nestled in one of the most beautiful gardens she had ever seen. The smell of freshly cut grass mingled with the aroma of several floral scents. Collecting her bag of ingredients from the back seat of the car, she walked towards the front door. She found the sound of the water soothing as it trickled from the fountain in the centre of the front garden. She could not help but stop to appreciate the homely and welcoming feeling the property exuded. Reaching the front door, she pressed the doorbell.

Nathan came out of the house to greet her. Extending his hand, he said, "Ni Hao (how are you), Huan Ying, ching jin (welcome, come in)" Nathan tried to speak Mandarin, but in such a strong Australian accent that took Peony tried hard to hold back a little giggle. He really is so cute, she thought. He was wearing a weekend casual white T-shirt, a pair of blue jeans, and was barefooted. He looked more relaxed than she'd ever seen him and more handsome too.

"Ni Hao. Where did you learn Chinese?" she said, a giggle escaping.

"Hope it sounded right! Gosh! It's harder than I thought. I learned it from the Chinese lady working at Sky Paradise's food court. I told her that I had a Chinese friend coming for dinner. I want to make you feel welcome and relaxed, so if I welcomed you in your own language, it might help." He took her bag of ingredients and led her into the lounge room, "Please take a seat. I will put these on the kitchen bench."

Peony followed closely behind him and recommended, "Could you please put the seafood in the fridge first? I have already prepared everything at home. I just need to cook it all. If I start cooking at 6.30 pm, it will be ready by 7 pm. How does that sound?"

"Really? Wow! Sounds great! You can really cook dinner in 30 minutes?" he asked, surprised.

"Chinese cooking is all about preparation. If you can simplify things, the actual cooking part is not that complicated," she said.

"Do you enjoy cooking?" he asked.

"Yes, I found it quite enjoyable," she replied.

As they walked back to the living room, Peony glanced around the room at the interior design. It was a beautifully designed home. The light brown leather sofa matched the natural tones of the feature stone wall. The rich jade green velvet cushions gave the room a luxurious, cosy feel. Standing commanding its own spotlight, was a piano that sat elegantly in an area of its own off to the side of the living room. Somehow, it looked lonely sitting there by itself with no other furniture next to it. Above it was a collage of photos. Peony could not help but draw closer to them. She could see theatre tickets, postcards, and pictures of Nathan and a stunning woman. "That must be his wife," Peony thought.

"I have the wine ready for us in the back garden," Nathan said, coaxing her away from the photo she was looking at.

"Oh... great, ok," she smiled and followed him outside.

Nathan led Peony to an outdoor setting by the large resort-style pool. On the table was a bottle of wine in a silver wine cooler, two wine glasses, and a plate of mixed berries.

"I forgot to ask you to bring your swimmers," Nathan said apologetically.

"I did not know you had such a stunning swimming pool overlooking this breathtaking water view. Otherwise, I definitely would have brought my swimming costume with me," Peony said, taking her sandals off. Standing, she strolled by the pool and sat beside it to dip her feet in the water. She swung her legs back and forward, making little splashes in the pool. "You have a beautiful home, Nathan. I can see the Spit Bridge from here. It's spectacular!"

Nathan turned around, pleased she liked his home. She could feel his gaze on her intensify and felt a sense of déjà vu. He was lost in thought when she looked up to see him so transfixed on her, that the glass he had been pouring champagne into began overflowing onto his hand. Realising that he had spilt it, he said, "Oh, I am sorry, I thought I saw... never mind," he said quickly, grabbing the other glass and filling it for her.

Using a serviette from the table, he dried his glass and returned to sit beside her. He leaned a little closer to her, saying, "See the yacht over there. The white one with the name ATHENA. It belongs to Andrew and his wife. They named it after her."

Nathan was so close to Peony, she could smell his aftershave. It smelled amazing, and the aroma penetrated her, possessing her like a potion. All she wanted to do was rest her head on his shoulder and breathe more of him in. "He must love his wife very much to name the yacht after her," Peony reflected.

"Yes, they were so in love. Their hearts, minds, and spirits combined and became one. You know they say some people's love is so strong that even death cannot separate them?" Nathan paused, looking at the pink clouds painted by the sunset to avoid the tears running down his cheeks. He continued, "The lady you saw in the photo collage is my wife, Bella. She passed away five years ago."

"Oh, I am so sorry to hear that...." Peony's breath caught in her throat. She didn't know what else to say.

"It was my fault. We planned to drive to the Hunter Valley that Sunday. It was on Valentine's Day—our wedding anniversary. It was raining in the morning, and Bella suggested staying at home, but I insisted we should go and do something. I thought watching the rain in the vineyard would be very romantic. On the highway, a truck lost control and hit our car... I often asked God why he didn't take me instead of her. I was the one who insisted on going."

"It was an accident, you know that." Peony stroked his back gently. "Often, we can't understand why bad things happen to good people."

"I haven't been with any other women in the last five years. I felt that I should remain faithful to Bella until...." he paused and looked deeply into Peony's eyes.

Peony looked at the ripples in the pool created by her feet gently kicking in the water. Then she looked at him with tenderness and asked, "May I reverse your situation?"

"What do you mean?" he asked, confused.

"Say, you were the one who died in the accident, and Bella survived. How would you like her to live the rest of her life? Would you want her to live alone and unhappy, with guilt, regret, and suffering?" she asked.

"Of course not. I would want her to remember all the wonderful memories that we shared. But I would want her to move on to live a happy and fulfilling life," he said with thought.

"I think that's what Bella wanted for you too. Don't you think so?" she asked.

"I guess she would." He paused for a while and looked away to the Spit Bridge.

"The first time I saw you at Jimmy's restaurant, it was our wedding anniversary. And also, it was the first Valentine's Day without her. That night Andrew was with me," he said.

"I saw a gentleman there with you. When you bought the 30 roses and gave them to me. I... um...."

"The way you looked at me somehow reminded me of Bella. You both look different but yet so familiar. You both look at me in the same unique way. Like the way you are looking at me right now!" he teased.

Peony moved her eyes away and then looked up at the sky. "I believe that God always gives us a second chance. We just need to follow our intuition." Peony stood up, "Should we start cooking?"

"Yes! I am happy to be your kitchen hand!" he smiled.

They walked back into the house. While she was taking some of the ingredients out of the fridge, she reviewed what she was going to cook. "Ok, tonight's menu is:

Prawn dumplings for entrée,

Chicken and sweet corn soup,

Steam coral trout with shallot and ginger,

Salt and peper king prawn,

Steam mix vegetables,

Dessert is a homemade mango pancake with my family's special recipe.

How's that sound?" she asked with a smile.

"It sounds fabulous. I can't wait! But that is so many dishes! Can we eat them all?"

"Don't worry. My Chinese cooking is quite light, and they are small portions. You can eat to your heart's content without feeling you are overeating," she said, taking a bowl out from the top cupboard to put some flour in it. Then she took a frying pan out from the bottom left-hand side of the cupboard and put it on the stove.

Nathan was astonished that Peony seemed to know where everything was in the kitchen without guessing or looking for them. "I'm so surprised. This is your first time here, yet you know where everything is. How is that possible?" he asked astounded.

"Good question. I just know. It all seems so familiar somehow. It's like I've been here before, but of course, I haven't," she said.

"Ok. Could you please give me my favourite coffee mug?" He said jokingly.

Without hesitation, Peony opened the cupboard under the island bench, took out a coffee mug with a hand-painted love heart, and passed it to him, "How come you need coffee at this time of the day? Dinner is almost ready," she said with a wink.

"How did you know that?! It's so weird! I don't need a coffee, I just wanted to see if you knew which one was my favourite mug and where I put it, and you did! So uncanny," he said.

Laughing, Peony said, "Well, don't ask me for any more party tricks. The first one is free, but the rest aren't," she giggled.

"It is unbelievable!" he looked heavenward with his palms opened in the air.

"I suggest we should start making the prawn dumplings." She turned around and opened the fridge. Then she took out a plastic container, "Here is the prawn and chicken mince I prepared." She took the lid off the container, and with a rolling pin she had retrieved out of the lower drawer, she began rolling it onto a piece of dough to make the dumpling pastry demonstrating to Nathan how to wrap the dumpling shape.

"You put the mince at the centre, fold it to half to make three pleats on the outside just like that."

Nathan watched Peony and followed her procedure, placing the mince and folding the pastry. He grumbled with disappointment, "Look at the one I made, it's nothing like the one that you made!" he said.

"Keep on practising, my friend. Practice makes perfect" she handed him another dumpling pastry and gave him a cheeky glance, "Ok, watch me, maybe this one you use less filling. Ok? Fold it this way and put three pleats this way. Easy enough?" Peony looked up and caught him gazing at her with admiration. There was a long pause of silence.

Nathan picked up some flour from the plate and wiped it on Peony's face to break the silence, "You look more like a chef now!"

Laughing at Nathan's spontaneity, Peony picked up some flour and wiped it on his nose. "Now we are even," she giggled.

"I love cooking and helping out in the kitchen. I came from an Italian background. Italians enjoy cooking."

"You don't have an Italian accent. Were you born here?" Peony asked.

"Yes," he answered.

"Can you speak Italian?" she asked.

"When I was little. I was encouraged to speak Italian, but only at home. It is fabulous to speak another language. I applaud you for learning a second language."

"How do you say hello, how are you in Italian?" Peony asked.

"Ciao Bella," he said with a smile.

"I am not Bella. I am Peony." She stared at him.

"The word Bella in Italian means beautiful. I just said hello, beautiful." He explained.

Peony's face turned pink. She could feel the warmth of embarrassment moving up into her face and turned to look at the ingredients on the table to avoid making eye contact with him.

"I'm sorry, I misunderstood," she said apologetically.

"You're not to know these things. You must be in learning overload with English, let alone Italian too!" he said.

"There's definitely a lot to learn," she said. "Now we make

traditional salt and pepper king prawns. Normally you deep fry the king prawns first, but I'm going to pan-fry them as it's healthier. You can help me coat the prawn lightly in the flour. Just like this." Peony did one in the flour to show Nathan.

"Ah! That's the secret of keeping your 3 T's," he stated.

"What are the 3 T's stand for?" she said.

"Trim, taut and terrific!" he exclaimed.

"I thought taut and terrific had nothing to do with food?" she laughed.

"Of course, it has something to do with food!"

"You're trying to make an argument out of nothing now," she said, still laughing.

"It is not an argument; it is a conversation," he said playfully.

"Ok, I'll let you win the argument this time!" she said, smiling mischievously.

Nathan went quietly observing and admiring her while she was cooking. For her, it seemed effortless. In fact, her movements in the kitchen looked so effortless and flawless.

"Right, done! Now is the moment of truth." she announced.

Nathan hesitantly picked up the chopsticks. He'd never used them before, so he was unsure of the fundamentals of eating with them.

Seeing Nathan fumble with the chopsticks, Peony picked up her set and explained, "The traditional chopstick is 7.6 inches long. The seven represents the seven emotions: love, joy, excitement, gratitude, anger, fear, and guilt. The six represents the six senses: sight, sound, smell, taste, touch, and intuition. The two chopsticks represent Yin and Yang. You cannot eat food with only one. You need two of them to be balanced. Traditionally, the end of the chopstick is square, representing the Earth, while the front of it is circular, representing Heaven. So, they bring the balance of Heaven and Earth. We hold the chopsticks with our five fingers representing the five elements:

metal, wood, water, fire, and Earth. So, everything must be balanced in life. Now you can see how important it is for the Chinese to express and share their emotions by eating together," she explained.

"Wow! I feel so honoured you sharing this knowledge with me. I had no idea. No wonder they said the best way to learn one's culture starts with food." Nathan tried to pick up a dumpling with the chopsticks, but it kept sliding off them. Peony took one and put it on his plate. "Do you want to use a fork instead?" she asked.

"No. Thanks, tonight I am determined to master these two little sticks!" he said, spearing a dumpling with a chopstick, putting it into his mouth and swallowing it.

Peony laughed, "Well, that's one way of doing it!"

Nathan laughed with her, "Mmmmm, your dumping is much better than I've tasted in any of the Chinese restaurants!" he complimented her.

"Don't jump in with the conclusion too fast." Peony giggled while serving a piece of the steamed fish on his plate. "Try this one."

"Tender and smooth with a hint of ginger and shallots. Delicious!" he proclaimed as he picked up the wine glass and said, "Cheers to the Chef."

"Cheers!" Peony picked up the glass, tapped his, and had a sip.

"Now try the prawn," Peony suggested picking up a prawn with her chopsticks and putting it in Nathan's mouth.

"It's succulent inside, and I love the crispy coating and flavour. The intense and unique taste exploded in my mouth. God, am I in Heaven?" he asked dreamily.

"We will finish with the homemade mango pancake and a cup of Oolong Tea," Peony said, putting on the kettle. "Drinking Oolong Tea after dinner will help to digest the food and has many other benefits too." She took the teapot and cups from the top cupboard and continued to make the tea. Looking up, she smiled at Nathan.

It wasn't lost on Nathan how she naturally went to the right cupboard to retrieve the cups and kettle. It really was uncanny, he thought.

"What are you thinking about? You seem world's away," she said.

"Oh....um....I was thinking about how home cook food is hard to beat," he said.

"It is not just the food. It is the enjoyment of the process of cooking, I believe." Peony said.

"Watching you cook is like watching an artist creating a piece of art." He complimented her.

"Next time, it is your turn to teach me some Italian cooking. Would you?" Peony asked.

"Well. I can cook a few signature Italian dishes like seafood risotto, homemade pasta and saltimbocca." He said with a smile.

"What is Saltimbocca?" she asked. It was a dish she'd never heard of.

"Thin slices of veal topped with salty prosciutto and flash herb leaves. Join them together with a string or toothpick, and sauté in a pan until the meat is cooked. You can also use chicken if there is no veal," he suggested.

"Sounds delicious! I'd like to try that," she said.

"I look forward to cooking it for you Peony. It was my mum's signature dish, but I still can't cook it as tasty as hers. I would like to take you to Mum and Dad's home for dinner soon if you are ok with that?" he said, surprising her.

After dinner, Peony suggested, "Can we look at the collage again?" she asked.

They walked to the sitting room that Peony had first entered when she arrived. Peony looked at the photo of Nathan's wife once more, and she whispered, "Ciao Bella" then, turning to Nathan, she said, "She looks so beautiful. How and where did you meet Bella? Where is her favourite place? What is her favourite food? I want to know more about her," Peony asked eagerly.

"We met at high school when she moved to our school in Year 12. We became besties straight away, and then she went to England to study. We wrote letters and called each other the whole time she was away. When she graduated, I picked her up from the airport, and from that moment on, we were inseparable. This photo was taken on top of Mt. Wellington in Tasmania. That was our first time travelling together. This one was when we saw the Phantom of the Opera at the Royal Albert Hall in London when I went there to visit her when she was still studying. This one was at Mt Etna in Sicily on our honeymoon. This one is from Mykonos, Greece—at Andrew's holiday house." Peony could feel his love for Bella and how much he had enjoyed those special moments with her.

"Bella used to play this piano almost every night," Nathan said, running his fingers over the piano's keys with sadness.

Peony gently touched the keys of the piano, looked up at Nathan and asked, "May I?"

"Absolutely, I would love that," he said, beaming.

She moved the stool, sat down, and adjusted her position before commencing to play "All I ask of you" from The Phantom of the Opera.

Her fingers danced gracefully from key to key. Each stroke of the keys seemed to stroke Nathan's heart. When she finished, she turned around and found tears streaming down his face.

"That's Bella's favourite song. The way you both play is almost identical! Soft, gentle, yet passionate. Even this afternoon, when you walked to the back garden, you sat beside the pool and put your feet in the pool, splashing them in water exactly like Bella used to do. You both have these unbelievable similarities." Nathan shook his head with a look on his face. He rested his hands on her shoulders, "I am so glad you came tonight."

"Thank you for inviting me to come here." She looked at the watch and stood up, "It's almost 11 o'clock, I'll have to head off now."

"Thank you for accepting my invitation to come here. I really did enjoy this evening," he said.

"I did too," she said with a smile.

Nathan walked Peony to her car and opened the car door for her. When Peony was about to get into the car, Nathan reached for her hand and gently pulled her towards him, "Thank you, it's the happiest I've felt in five years," he said. Under the moonlight, she saw the tenderness in his eyes. He held her so closed that Peony could feel his heartbeat and the warmth from his body. She leaned into his embrace and rested her head on his shoulder. Nathan could smell the fresh fragrance of orchid and frangipani wafting off her skin. As he gently lifted her head off his shoulder, she noticed that he was looking at her with a mixture of intensity and desire. She blushed with a shy smile. He smiled back softly. The chemistry between them ignited in the stillness and quiet of the night. She closed her eyes and drew in his scent as he drew her to him again. She could feel the sparks between them. His soft, warm lips found hers kissing her, loving her tenderly.

"You are my God-given second chance," he whispered.

CHAPTER 21

The next day when Matt walked into the shop to install the new lighting for Peony, he could tell immediately that something had changed in Peony. She was glowing. "Well, well, well, don't you look very happy this morning! Come on tell me, what's going on? I can tell something good has happened, you're beaming!" he said with excitement.

"Gee! I can't hide anything from you!" she said with a big grin.

"Never! Come on tell me," he urged.

"Remember I told you about the guy who gave me 30 red roses?" she asked him.

"Yes, the restaurant guy?" he asked.

"Yes, well, his name is Nathan. It turns out, he is the centre leasing manager here, and he invited me to his place..."

"Ah-Ha!" Matt exclaimed and gave her a cheeky smile.

"No! No! No! NOT what you think. Just purely dinner. However, he did kiss me when he walked me to the car." Peony could not stop smiling. "You know what? It was my first romantic kiss. I feel that I am the happiest person in the world."

"That's why you keep smiling!" Matt laughed.

They both kept chatting until lunchtime. Peony asked Matt to keep on working while she went to get some takeaway lunch. While they were sitting on the floor having their lunch, they kept chatting and giggling like two school kids.

"My basil and chilli chicken is so delicious; how's your satay chicken?" Peony asked.

"Yum! Try it." Matt picked a piece of chicken and put it in Peony's mouth. After they finished, they got to work again fitting out Peony's shop and chattering about everything and anything as they always did. Peony loved her time with Matt. It was great to hang out, especially for a whole day which they hadn't done for a few weeks.

In the following few days, Peony was expecting Nathan to contact her. She had no idea why, but she hadn't heard from him or seen him. She couldn't wait any longer, so she took the initiative to call him. "Hey, it's Peony," she said when he picked up.

"Peony, is there anything I can help you with?" Nathan answered with a business-like tone of voice.

"No, nothing. It's been almost a week since I saw you, and I haven't heard from you, so thought I'd call to say I was thinking of you. I was wondering how you are doing?" Peony asked.

"Peony, do you have a special man in your life?" Nathan asked directly, completely catching Peony off guard.

"I don't quite get it. What do you mean? Could you please be more specific?" Peony asked, puzzled.

"Last week, when I went to the food court to get some lunch, and I saw you and a guy in your shop, you both were having lunch. You both seemed to be in a special kind of relationship. I could tell by the way you shared each other's lunch and the way you were with each other."

"Ohhhhh! He is, ah..." Peony thought for a second about how she would explain Matt to Nathan.

"Look, you don't need to tell me. You don't owe me any explanation. Let's keep our relationship strictly business. If you need any assistance, please let my secretary know, ok? Sorry Peony, I need to attend my next meeting now. Bye," Nathan hung up so quickly she didn't get a chance to talk.

Nathan's straight business tone made Peony feel as if a big bucket of ice water had poured on her. She was so shocked she couldn't even think straight.

She finally pulled herself together and headed off to the shop where she knew Matt would be finishing the lighting installation.

Seeing Peony enter, Matt said, "Good timing. Could you please pass me the box of light globes?" Peony just stood, still. "Peony!" Matt called.

"What?" she said, annoyed.

Her tone immediately made Matt stop and look around at her. "What's up?" he said with concern.

"Don't want to talk about it. Let's focus on what we are doing," she said abruptly.

"No way. Come on, let it out. What's going on!" he said insistently.

Peony was silent for a while. Finally, tears sprung to her eyes as she said, "Nathan saw us at the shop having lunch and giggling and laughing that day when I told you about him. I think he thinks we're in a relationship, and he was so short about it that he didn't even give me a chance to explain before hanging up."

"If he gives up easily like that, he will miss out on the best thing in his life. I will talk to him. Leave this to me. You don't need to worry; promise me?" he assured her.

Matt stepped down from the ladder. "Come here, give me a hug," he said, reaching out to her and giving her a big hug. "Love you," he said.

"Love you more!" she cried.

The next day, Matt found the chance to see Nathan at his office.

"May I see Nathan, please?" Matt asked the receptionist politely yet with an impatient tone.

"Please wait; I will see if he is available." She walked toward Nathan's office. Matt was following her. She tried to stop Matt, but it was too late. He stepped into Nathan's office and asked, "Are you Nathan?"

"Who are you?" Nathan demanded.

"I am Matt. Peony's ex-husband," he declared.

"Ex-husband! She never told me she married before. She lied to me," Nathan said.

"Did you ask her if she married before?" Matt quizzed him.

"No," Nathan admitted.

"Let me put it straight. She did not lie to you. She hasn't had the chance to tell you about it. It's complicated, and she would have told you had you given her the time to." he said.

"I don't need any explanation. Don't waste my time," Nathan said, waving him away.

"I hope you are not that stupid to let go of what I know would be the best thing in your life. Peony is amazing, and if you spend just a few minutes listening to me, I'll tell you why." Matt insisted.

Nathan nodded, "Ok, let's talk. I'll give you a few minutes. I have to visit a retailer in the centre. We can talk in the coffee shop on the way." He said, picking up his phone and leading Matt out.

They walked in silence to the coffee shop a couple of shops away from his office. Both men were annoyed for different reasons.

They found a vacant seat at the coffee shop, ordered, and Matt began to tell Nathan of his relationship with Peony and how she had married him to give his dying mother her wish. He also told him how special Peony was and the relationship they still had even years later.

Nathan was dumbfounded and felt terrible. With his eyes cast downwards at his coffee cup, he said to Matt, "I could tell you were both not just ordinary friends. I am so sorry that I acted like a fool Matt, I really am. I feel so bad about this," he said.

"Don't need to say sorry to me. But you owe Peony a BIG apology. She was devastated. She deserves the best. That day you saw us chatting. She was telling me how excited she was to see you again. Do you know what she did with the 30 roses that you gave to her? She carefully air-dried them and preserved them. They are still in her bedroom! If Peony gives you a second chance, I would hope you don't act like an idiot anymore," Matt cautioned him.

"I am sorry. Thank you for telling me. I owe you one mate. How about dinner on me. You and Tom, Peony and I. Oh God, I hope she will forgive me. Do you think she will?" Nathan asked worriedly.

"I have no idea. But you better see her sooner rather than later and sort it out, then we'll see about dinner. I have to get back to work. Good luck with that mate," Matt said, standing, and patting him on the shoulder before leaving.

Nathan didn't waste a second and called Peony straight away. "Hi, Peony, I am very sorry that I misunderstood you. Matt came to see me and explained everything about the relationship between you two. I could not understand why we had such a lovely time on Sunday. With that kiss, I was overjoyed and knew our relationship would flourish. Then, the next day, I saw you were leaning your head on another man's shoulder, feeding him, hugging him, and I was confused, hurt and jealous. I am so sorry. Could you please forgive me?" he asked.

"You have no idea how devastated I was when you didn't give me a chance to explain to you!" she said.

"I will make it up to you. Please allow me to take you to a special place this Saturday. I will pick you up at 11.30 am, and I promise I will make this right. Is that ok? I'm so sorry," he said.

"Apology accepted. Ok, I will look forward to Saturday," she said.

It was a gorgeous Saturday morning when Nathan arrived at Peony's home. Arriving in a taxi, he asked the driver to wait, as he got out carrying a big bunch of red roses and went up to Peony's door and knocked.

Peony opened the door and her face lit up. First to see Nathan on her doorstep looking handsome, and secondly to see the beautiful red roses he was holding out to her.

"They are so beautiful!" she exclaimed, accepting the flowers and inviting him in while she found a vase to put them in.

"Not as beautiful as you are though!" he replied.

"Smooth talker. But I humbly accept your compliment."

Peony was wearing a delightful white linen dress. It was a simple style, with a boat neckline and semi-fitted on her slim body to the mid-calf length, and she looked relaxed and elegant in it.

Nathan was staring at her; he couldn't help it. "You look so stunning! If you were not wearing your straw hat and sunglasses. I think you are an angel who just came down from heaven!" he said.

Peony blushed again as he moved toward her to embrace her. She could smell his fresh aftershave and thought she could easily stay like this in his arms forever.

"There are 31 roses," Nathan said. "Matt told me you kept the roses I gave you the first day we met. Well, there are many more to come! I will add one more each year," he said with a big smile, holding her in front of him and looking lovingly into her eyes.

"Thank you. Imagine when I turn eighty, the roses I will have?!" she laughed.

Nathan thought for a while, "So eighty years minus twenty-three, plus the thirty-one roses today... I guess when you turn eighty years old, I will be presenting you with eighty-eight roses. Looks like you are willing to spend the rest of your life with me then hey?" he chuckled.

She put the roses close to her nose and inhaled deeply, "Depends if you could keep your promise!" she said cheekily.

"That would be my honour if you could give me the chance to do that of course! "Nathan took a bow.

"Where are we going?" Peony asked.

"Ah! You have to wait and see. I don't want to tell you and spoil the fun," he said cryptically as he took her by the arm and led her out to the waiting taxi.

After they got in the taxi, the driver drove straight to Palm Beach Wharf and pulled up in front of a seaplane. A pilot waiting beside it saw Nathan and waved. Peony could not contain her joy. She looked at Nathan expectantly, and he nodded, confirming they would be taking a ride. Peony let out a little squeal and threw her arms around him. Nathan laughed, returned her hug, and kissed her, happy she was excited by his surprise.

Nathan helped Peony get on the plane.

"Where are we going?" Peony asked again with excitement and curiosity, just like a little girl going on an adventure.

"Just be patient my princess, as I told you I don't want to spoil the fun." Nathan sat next to her, giving her a gentle kiss on her cheek, and interlocking his fingers with hers.

After a short while, the plane landed beside The Cottage Restaurant at Cottage Point. Nathan stepped out of the plane, and holding Peony's hand, he helped her out onto the jetty.

"Good afternoon," a waiting assistant said cheerily.

"Good afternoon," Nathan replied. "I booked a table for Mr Artino and Miss Chen."

"Welcome, Mr Artino and Miss Chen. Please follow me," the assistant said and walked towards the restaurant.

They were led to a waterfront table overlooking the tranquil and picturesque river. "What a view!" Peony gushed.

Just then, a pair of friendly Kookaburras landed on the railing next to them. They were so close to Peony that she could almost pat them.

"They are so cute and friendly! Please take a photo for me with them before they fly away." Peony asked, passing her camera to Nathan.

"Would you like me to take a photo of both of you?" asked a waiter who had arrived with the menu.

"Yes please," Nathan said quietly so as not to scare the birds away, and slowly got up and moved another chair next to Peony's and sat down next to her. Peony leaned her head on his shoulder and held his hand. With a sweet smile, they both looked up at the waiter smiling while he manoeuvred Peony's camera around to get the perfect picture.

"You are a perfect couple," the waiter said as he took the photo and handed the camera back to Peony.

"Thank you," she said and took over the camera from him. Glancing at Nathan, she said, "Did you hear that?"

"Yes, I believe so," he squeezed her hand proudly.

"Should we start with a drink?" the waiter recommended.

Nathan picked up the wine list, studied it, then replied "Yes, please, the House of Arras thank you."

Then turned to Peony, "I think you will love it."

"Are you so sure?" she asked.

"The tastes of grapefruit, jasmine flower, and lychees are perfect. I know you'll love it. This sparkling wine was crafted in Tasmania where it is significantly cooler than the mainland, which is the ideal growing condition for the fruit to develop and create what is known to be a world-class sparkling wine," he said.

Peony listened, impressed with his knowledge. She looked at the wine menu and whispered to Nathan, "It's quite an expensive bottle."

"For you, nothing is too expensive. You deserve the best." He ran his fingers tenderly from her forehead through her silky hair to the back of her head. Then he picked up the food menu and passed it to her. "This place is famous for seafood. Most of them are locally caught."

"Seafood, now you are talking straight to my heart," she said happily.

"They say the way to a lady's heart is through her stomach," he chuckled.

"I thought it the other way around?" she giggled.

Peony looked at the menu and said, "I would like you to choose for me. I want to relax and let my man lead today."

Nathan liked the way she called him her man. "I had the feeling that you would like me to do that, and of course, would love to. Would you believe me if I told you that I had already chosen what we would have when I booked the table?" he asked, mischievously.

"Really?! You are good! And confident!" she proclaimed. "Of course I trust you, and I love surprises!" she said.

The waiter approached them and poured the sparkling wine into the glasses, then put the bottle in the cooler next to them.

Nathan lifted the glass and said, "Cheers to our new beginning." He was gazing at Peony as she sipped the wine. She noticed his intense look and blushed with a shy smile. He smiled softly back at her. She was soaking in the warmth of his eyes and watched his lips when he sipped the wine, which made her recall their first kiss. She blushed again. She had another sipped from her glass and looked down. Slowly lifting her eyes to his, they both got lost in the moment. It seemed they could see through each other's eyes straight to the deepest part of their souls. They were lost in a world of their own.

The waiter quietly placed the entree on the table without saying a word, not wanting to interrupt the divine atmosphere he had observed.

Reluctantly they broke their gaze to the arrival of the food. Nathan watched her as she picked up an oyster from the plate and moved her face slightly upward, slowly and gracefully pouring the oyster into her mouth. With each bite, you could tell she was tasting the finest Sydney oyster without saying anything. She gazed at him as she put the empty shell on the plate.

There was complete silence, yet anyone could see the chemistry between them, the connection of their souls and their spirits that made this magical moment in their universe.

The main course arrived. They ate slowly but heartily. They shared each other's food and fed off each other's forks until the plates were empty. Time seemed to stand still for them.

A single dessert of Crème Brulé was served. There was just one spoon. Nathan passed a small spoonful into her mouth. Creamy yet not too heavy. She was delighted with his perfect choice. Her child-like enthusiasm and smile made their way straight into his heart. His heart melted. He could not help but fall in love with her. He put a spoonful in his mouth and smiled back at her. At this very moment, he was testing the sweetness of both the dessert and the tenderness and joy Peony brought into his world.

Finally, their favourite—café latté was served. Peony stirred the coffee slowly in one direction. Then she had a sip, milk froth remained on her lips. He reached towards her, cupped her cheeks in his hands, and leaned towards her locking his lips with hers. They were in a world of their own, lost in each other and the moment.

CHAPTER 22

In the following couple of months, Peony was focused on preparing the shop while Nathan was busy with the new development project his company had at Chatswood. They gave each other freedom and space to do what they needed to do, and not hinder each other in their goals, while still catching up as often as possible, even if it was for a quick cup of coffee and an almond croissant. Their relationship was going steady and strong.

Nathan had just returned to his city office from Chatswood, and as usual, he called Peony. "Hey, Honeybun, are you in your shop?" he asked.

"Yes, my Sweetie Bear," she said.

I am going upstairs to the food court, would you like to join me for lunch?" Nathan asked

"Sure, I will be up in a few minutes. See you there," she said excitedly.

While they were having lunch, Peony suggested, "We both have been busy. I think we need to have some time out for ourselves. I wonder if we should drive away for this coming long weekend. We can drive to Wollongong and spend a night there. You have a nice car in your garage, and I haven't had the chance to be your passenger yet," said Peony joking around.

"No. Never!" Nathan suddenly raised his voice anxiously.

Peony was taken by surprise, "Umm, are you busy? We don't

need to go right next weekend. We don't need to stay overnight either. Maybe the next month or so?" she asked.

"I said no. Can't you hear me? We are not driving away anywhere. That's it. No further discussion," he said angrily.

Peony had no idea what had happened or why he was suddenly so upset. "What's the matter?" Peony asked, confused. Right now, she couldn't recognise her Nathan, what on Earth was going on?

"I don't want to talk about it. In fact, Peony I'm going to need some space right now."

"Well, it appears, I do too!" Peony said, getting up, grabbing her handbag and storming out of the café without finishing her meal. Nathan watched Peony leave the café. He felt helpless, but the flashback to the accident that took his wife's life, wouldn't disappear.

Nathan tried to call Peony a few times later in the day, but she wouldn't pick up his calls. She had gone home upset and furious with Nathan's attitude and began cleaning her house to try and distract her from the overwhelming emotion and confusion she was feeling.

"Peony, I booked the Japanese as you requested tonight. Are you ready? I am hungry!" Matt cheered, as he came in the front door.

"No, I'm not!" she said, frowning as she continued cleaning the house.

"What? Did you forget about our dinner plans for tonight?" He asked.

"No! I don't feel like going out tonight," she said flatly.

"What's going on? You sound like someone has just killed your cat!" Matt said, following her around as she cleaned like a mad woman.

"Nothing!" she said as she chucked the dirty clothes into the wash basket.

"Oh, yeah... nothing? Peony, I've known you for too long. I told you—you can't hide anything from me."

"Don't ask me any more questions. Ok, I'll change, and we can go out." She said as she walked to her bedroom. She cried out, "Ouch!"

"What's happened?" Matt turned around and saw Peony on the floor.

"I just kicked the edge of the coffee table and tripped." She was holding onto the shin of her leg.

Mat went over and checked. He took her hand off her shin and saw the blood on it. He quickly went to the bathroom and got a Band-Aid out of the first aid box, and carefully wrapped it around her wound, "Look at you; you look like a sad sight. Tell me, what's bothering you?"

"Nathan and I argued," she said miserably.

"See! I knew it," Matt exclaimed.

"You knew nothing!" she said, rolling her eyes.

"Do you still want to go out? I can call and cancel the booking and cook you something if you're not in the mood," Matt suggested.

"If you don't mind. Sorry, but I'm not in the mood at all to go out," she admitted.

"That's perfectly fine with me. What do you feel like for dinner?"

"I don't know. Just cook something nice to cheer me up, would you please?"

"Sure thing." He went to the kitchen and opened the fridge. He pulled out a pack of mixed seafood from the freezer. "I know exactly what you like. I will cook your favourite seafood mornay."

"I'll help?" She said, trying to lift her attitude.

"No, you won't. But you can come here, and we chat while I cook," he stated.

"Ok. Sounds good," she said.

"I think you guys are the perfect match. Everyone who knows both of you will agree with me," Matt said.

"Well. Maybe you don't know him well enough." She moved her hurting leg slightly and put her weight on the other one; by doing that, she could ease the throbbing.

Matt pulled out a stool under the island bench and helped her sit on it. "Dinner won't be long," Matt said as he went to the pantry to get some garlic.

"You are just interested in cooking, not listening!" Peony complained.

"I am listening! I can multi-task you know!" he said proudly.

"I suggested to Nathan a drive-away for a weekend. He got very irritated by my suggestion—it was totally out of character. Then I got upset and stormed off," she said.

"Well, I agree. It is out of character for him." Matt said, thinking it over. "Maybe something happened to him driving? Did you ask him?" Matt questioned her.

All of a sudden, Peony got it... "He lost his wife in a car accident on their way to Hunter Valley," she said with tears brimming.

"Oh, that's why he behaved that way! Poor Nathan, my heart goes out to him. I was so insensitive and just didn't think!" she said, visibly upset by what she had done.

"I don't know what to do," she said, looking up at him for the answer.

"Why don't you call your friend Fiona to seek some advice while I finish cooking our dinner?" he suggested.

"It's a bit too late at this time of the night. She has a life too."

Matt picked up the phone, found the number from her phone book beside it, dialled it then handed the phone to Peony. Then he signalled to her that he would continue to cook the dinner.

"Hello," Fiona answered.

"Hi, Fiona. Hope it is not too late to call you," Peony asked.

"No, not at all," Fiona said.

Peony told Fiona what happened between her and Nathan.

"Oh. It sounds like he was traumatised by that car accident and the loss of his wife. I suspect that he is suffering from PTSD," she said.

"What is that?" Peony asked worriedly.

"Post-Traumatic Stress Disorder. A disorder characterised by failure to recover after experiencing or witnessing a terrifying event. The condition may last months or even years. When you asked him to drive away for the weekend, that triggered memories of the trauma accompanied by his intense emotional reaction to something incredibly traumatic for him," Fiona explained.

"I understand. I feel so bad for storming off without any concern for his feelings," she said.

"Peony, don't be hard on yourself. I want you to know that you did not cause him to feel that way. Also, you did not understand why he behaved that way. He probably needs to see a therapist who specialises in this area," she suggested.

"Can you help him?" Peony asked.

"Perhaps not because I am so close to you. However, I will share with you some techniques to support him. The best support is to be there for him. I can recommend one of my colleagues to see him if he's open to it. This way, he can get the help he needs for his recovery. At the same time, it's important you are supportive and considerate of what he's going through," she said.

"I will need to be more mindful and not go off like a rocket, but if you can suggest anything else I can do, I would really appreciate that," Peony said.

"You must be patient and not take it personally. It will take time to heal from something so significant. Next time something like this happens, take a deep breath to calm your own heightened emotion and place your hands on his shoulder. Gently stroke his shoulders to his hands about 20 times. Say nothing, allow him the space to process his feelings, and provide lots of love and care with your body language and eye contact. If he feels comfortable and safe in that moment, he should begin to feel calm and get through the triggering moment knowing you are there for him." Fiona explained to her calmly.

"Thank you, Fiona. Hope we will catch up for lunch soon. I won't take up any more of your time tonight." Peony said.

"Bye, take care, catch up soon. Don't hesitate to call me if you need some more help," Fiona said.

"Thanks, I will," Peony said and hung up the phone.

"I invited Nathan for dinner while you were talking to Fiona. He will be here soon. I will take some dinner home and watch the footy to give you both the chance to talk it through." Matt said.

"Thank you, Matt. You have no idea how grateful I am to have you in my life." Peony said, giving Matt a grateful hug.

"Hope you two will sort things out. Remember, love is patient and kind."

Just then, the doorbell rang. Matt gave Peony a knowing look and went to open it. "Hey, mate, good to see you." He said to Nathan.

"Good to see you too. You are not staying for dinner?" Nathan looked at the takeaway container in Matt's hand.

"No, mate. Getting this takeaway and heading home to watch the footy." Matt said, as he lifted the container box of food.

Matt waved to Peony, "See you later, enjoy!" then he closed the door behind him.

Nathan walked up to Peony and pulled her close to him. There was silence. The only sound were the two hearts beating.

After a long while, Nathan broke the silence, "I am sorry for my behaviour today."

"I am sorry for storming off. I should have been more thoughtful in the beginning and sensitive and understanding afterwards." Peony's head rested on his shoulder as she rubbed his back gently.

"I love you so much. I cannot afford to lose you like I lose Bella. I don't think I can handle it," Nathan said.

"It was a terrible and tragic accident, but Nathan, it heartbreakingly could happen to anyone at any time," she said sadly.

"In the last five years since the accident, I have taken taxis to work and back home. Or I use a driver from the company. I haven't driven since losing Bella. It's just too hard," he said.

"Oh. That's why I have never seen you drive. I completely understand and am so sorry for putting that on you. We don't have to drive away for weekends. I want to be your first passenger when you are ready to drive again," Peony said.

"I know that I have to overcome this fear. I don't want to end up having you driving us everywhere. I want to be your co-driver, not your passenger. I will not let this fear hinder the rest of my life. But please allow me some time to work my way through it," he said.

"Take all the time you need, baby steps Darling. I love you. I am here to support you," she said.

"Thank you, that means the world to me," he said, smiling.

"Have you ever got any counselling?" Peony asked.

"No, I thought it was a complete waste of time. How can anyone understand the pain of losing someone who means the whole world to them?" he said.

"I understand. Now that your world is expanding, it might be a good time to revisit that to help you overcome the trauma," Peony encouraged.

"I guess I could have to try. Because I love you so much, I will do anything to be the best person I can be for you," Nathan assured her.

"Thank you. I appreciate that. My psychologist friend Fiona's colleague is very good in this field. If you like, I can get the phone number for you so you can chat with him to find out if he is the one who could help you," Peony ventured.

Nathan thought for a while. "Ok, please pass on his details, and I'll give him a call," he said.

"Done, I will."

"Do you know the car in my garage is brand new? The insurance company replaced the damaged car with a new one. I have never driven it. I've never even sat in it. Would you like to come over sometime this week and just sit in the car with me?" He asked, trying his best to take a step forward.

"Sure, I would like to. Of course! Let's have some dinner now. I am starving." Peony held his hand and led him to the dining table. She served the dinner that Matt had made on the table and sat next to him. "Do you want me to come to yours for breakfast tomorrow?" she asked.

"I'd love that," he replied.

The next day after breakfast, Nathan asked Peony nervously, "Shall we?"

Peony nodded, understanding what he wanted to do. She stood up and held his hand, "Let's do it, and if you think you are not ready, just let me know," she said gently.

They walked to the garage in silence, and Nathan unlocked the car with the remote control. He held onto Peony's hand firmly with one hand and managed to open the door with the other hand. Peony noticed his hand was shaking, and she could feel the sweat on his palm.

"If you feel it is too much, we can do it some other time, but you are doing really well." Peony held his hand a little tighter, encouraging him.

Nathan took a deep breath and took his hand off Peony's hand. He sat in the driver's seat and put his shaky hands on the steering wheel. He closed his eyes. His whole body was trembling. Peony kept stroking his back to help him calm his anxiety.

"Would you like to come to the house? I will make you a cup of coffee." He said, clearly, it was a big enough step for him.

Nathan got out of the car and closed the door. Peony put her arm around his waist as they walked back into the house.

CHAPTER 23

Matt and Tom finally arranged to meet Nathan and Peony for the double date at The Cantonese Kitchen Chinese restaurant at Campsie. They detoured to pick Nathan up on their way there.

"It is small, but well known for its Hong Kong-style Chinese cuisine in Sydney. Normally, people have to book at least two weeks in advance. I know it is a bit far away but trust me, it is worth driving there," Peony explained as they walked into the restaurant.

"Good evening, do you have a booking?" the waiter came up and asked.

"Yes," replied Peony.

"Under what name?" the waiter asked.

"Peony," she answered.

"Oh, yes, booking for four people. Please follow me." The waiter then took them to their allocated table in the corner and presented them each with a menu.

"Could we have some Jasmine tea, please?" Peony asked the waiter.

"Sure, will you require a knife and fork for your meal tonight?" the waiter asked.

"I can use chopsticks very well. How about you guys?" Nathan glanced at Peony with a proud smile while he asked.

"If you can use the chopsticks to catch a fly, then you can

say you used the chopsticks properly." Matt picked up a pair of chopsticks and clicked them like scissors to show Nathan he was all over it too.

"Where are the flies? I am sure I can catch one with these," Nathan picked up the chopsticks and mirrored what Matt did, laughing.

"No, we don't need them. Thank you," Tom replied to the waiter. He looked at Peony rolling his eyes at Matt and Nathan with a smile.

"Come on guys, whatever you do, do not embarrass me at my Chinese territory. Ok! Everyone pick your favourite dish, but we are going to share as the Chinese do," Peony stated.

"Sweet and sour pork as usual," Tom looked at Matt.

"Tommy, I know it's your favourite," Matt agreed and asked, "Peony, what are their signature dishes here?"

"Shallot and ginger steam oysters. Chilli mud crab. Garlic king prawn, black pepper veal spare ribs. Combination seafood hot pot. Just name a few," Peony replied.

Matt looked at Nathan and asked, "Are you thinking what I am thinking?" Nathan nodded and smiled, agreeing with Matt without saying a single word.

"Peony, you place the order. It is so hard to choose. Every dish you mentioned sounds delicious," Matt requested.

At the end of the dinner, Matt asked, "Who is going to have the last piece of black pepper rib?"

"How about we play scissors, paper, rock," Nathan suggested.

"Good idea!" Tom agreed.

"Guys! Enough!" Peony shook her head and protested.

"Tom, you can have it. Not you, Matt," Nathan said.

"Peony, excellent choice. We definitely would come here again. How come you never showed me this restaurant?" Matt asked.

"Well, I discovered this little restaurant when I was at college. You were busy enjoying the time with Tom," Peony said with a wink.

"Yes, the food was delicious. But it will never compare with your cooking," Nathan said.

"Our Peony! The one and only!" No one can compare her cooking!" Matt said jubilantly.

"Peony must have spoiled you with her cooking when you were living with her," Nathan said, resting his hand on Peony's.

"Sure, she did! She still does. Now that she has you, I am worried I will miss out on her cooking." Matt said.

"Yep, quite often when Matt craves Peony's delicious Chinese cooking, he invites himself to her place," Tom disclosed.

"Tom. Anytime Matt is coming; you are also invited to come as well, except for the dumpling night. I divorced my husband because of you. You should be grateful for that," Peony said jokingly and patted Tom's shoulder.

"Well, in the first place, Matt, to be fair, was not interested in you in that way," Tom looked at Matt and gave him a wink and a kiss.

"You are right, Tommy," Matt put his hand on top of Tom's and said, "Hey, Nathan, one day you and I should go out for a beer. I will tell you all the funny things and embarrassing things Peony did when she first came to Australia." Then he whispered: "Have you ever heard her swear?"

"No, Matt! Don't you dare to embarrass me! Or no more Chinese cooking for you," Peony declared.

"Ok, Boss. Since you are the one paying the bill for tonight's dinner. I wouldn't embarrass you. But I do not guarantee in the future though," he laughed.

"Well, I am so glad that everyone enjoyed tonight's dinner. See! I told you guys that I guarantee I would not disappoint you." Then Peony waved her hand and signalled for the waiter to come with the bill.

On the way out, Peony saw a woman pushing a trolley full of dirty dishes. The woman was so familiar. She had a second look and exclaimed with surprise, "Jasmine?!"

The woman looked up, and shock quickly spread over her face. However, she quickly lowered her eyes and continued to push the trolley toward the kitchen.

Peony quickly got up and walked up to her, "Jasmine! Wait!"

"Not here. Please don't talk to me. I don't want to get in any trouble. Bob would not be happy if he saw you talking to me!" she whispered while her fearful eyes scanned around. "If you go to the ladies and wait for me. I can meet you there." She quickly went inside the kitchen with the trolley.

Nathan, Matt, and Tom were waiting by the front door for her. Peony informed them she would be right back. "I need to go to the ladies. Could you guys please wait for me here for a few minutes? Thanks." she rushed to the ladies without waiting for an answer.

Jasmine was already there. "I hope no one noticed that you know me," she said, worried.

"Jasmine. It is very nice to see you. Why are you scared? And who is Bob?" she asked quickly.

"Bob is my partner. The guy I met in the park, he was the one who took me to his house. He warned me if I contacted anyone, he would kill me and anyone that I contacted as well. That's why I never looked you up." She said sadly.

"Jasmine, I am not afraid of him. I am concerned about you! Tell me what is going on in your life."

"No, I don't want to put you in danger," Jasmine said, with deep concern.

"Tell me, please. I want to help you. That's what friends do!" Peony insisted.

"Ok, give me your phone number, and I will call you tomorrow," Jasmine said.

Peony noticed her body shaking as she took out her newly printed business cards and handed it to Jasmine.

"No, can you give me something smaller? Bob will find it." Jasmine said.

Peony searched her handbag and tore a small piece of paper from her notebook. She wrote her number on it and handed it to her. "How about this? Is it ok?" she asked.

Jasmine folded the paper as small as she could get it, and then bent down to carefully insert it inside one of her shoes. Without saying goodbye, she quickly scuttled out of the bathroom and back into the kitchen before anyone noticed her absence.

The following day after dropping Josh to the preschool, Jasmine quickly went to the public phone booth and called Peony. She briefly told Peony about her life, and the abuse both she and her son Josh had to endure from Bob.

"That's terrible! I am so sorry you've been through this. You should have told me earlier. I would have come to get you," Peony said, full of worry.

"Even if I had your contact, he would not have allowed me to have anything to do with you. He forced me to cut all contact with everyone. I am only allowed to go to work, get groceries, get some second-hand clothes for Josh and me from the local Red Cross from time to time, and drop and pick up Josh." Jasmine said with her voice full of fear.

"Tell me, are you and Josh ever alone?" Peony tried hard to think quickly, knowing Jasmine couldn't talk for long.

"Bob is home most of the time but has a nap around 3 pm each day. That's the time I go and pick up Josh from day care," she said.

"What is the name of the day care?" she asked.

"Little Angels Day Care."

"And the address?"

"38 The Fifth Street. Campsie," Jasmine said.

"Ok, let me think." She rubbed her head, looked up at the sky for a few moments then continued: "Listen carefully. Here is the plan to help you and Josh get away from Bob for good. Tomorrow I will wait for you outside the day care centre. Act as normal as you can in case he decides to follow you. Don't pack anything. I will buy everything that you and Josh will need. If you can, please get your passport and Josh's birth certificate. My car is a white Holden Commodore. I will keep an eye out for you. I will stand near you, pretending not to know you to make sure the coast is clear. Then when we know for sure it is safe, get Josh and follow me to my car."

"I am afraid Bob will hurt my friend Mie. He knows where she lives. He said if I dared to leave him. He will kill her and her family," Jasmine said, scared.

"Once I have you and Josh in the car safe, I will inform Mie and the police immediately. Have you got Mie's phone number?"

"Yes, even though I did not write it down, I memorised it in my head," she said.

"Give me the number, please. In case you forget it when you are nervous. We will make sure that Mie and her family are protected."

"7260356"

"Thanks," Peony said, quickly writing it down.

"Peony, are you sure that will work? This is the only hope I have," Jasmine asked nervously.

"Yes, don't be afraid. I will do my best to get you both out of there Jasmine; it will be ok. We are not alone, I have reliable friends and will make sure to get them on board to help us. See you tomorrow," Peony said.

"Ok, see you," she said as she swiftly returned the receiver to the pay phone.

After finishing the phone conversation, Peony called Nathan and told him what was happening to Jasmine and her plan to rescue her.

"The way that scum bag treated her makes my blood boil. Count me in; I will go with you in case he shows up," Nathan said assertively.

"Jasmine and Josh deserve a better life. I can't believe that type of man exists!" Peony said in disbelief.

"I think you should let Matt know as well. We can't fail her. We need to make sure this mission is successful," he said.

"Yes, I agree with you. I will let him know. We need both of you," Peony agreed.

When she spoke to Matt, he suggested. "Why don't we call the police and let them handle it?"

Peony explained. "Matt, how often have we learned that when a domestic violence victim informs the police, they do nothing much but take out a court order for an AVO? We've seen this so many times on the TV. Then the victim has nowhere to go but back to their abuser. Worse, the police go and knock on the front door and tell the abuser that there was a complaint about them! Scumbags like Bob would tell the police it was just an argument, and they would sort it out between them. And then, guess what? The next minute, the victim faces even worse abuse or is murdered. We will get Jasmine out of the situation before we call the police," Peony said defiantly.

"Yes, ok. I agree with you. Let me know how I can help," Matt said, convinced.

The next day Peony, Nathan, and Matt arrived at Campsie half an hour earlier. Nathan went across the road to get some coffee. When he came back, he gave one to Matt and handed one to Peony: "Honeybun, I think you need it. You look a bit nervous."

"I just hope our plan works." She said, taking a shaky sip of her coffee. "She cannot go back there. Bob said that he would kill her if she tried to escape. I'm so worried. What if Bob shows up? What is our plan B?" she asked.

"I will call the police and try to distract him. Nathan, you help Peony. You both make sure to get Jasmine and her son in the car safely and drive!" Matt responded.

Nathan paused for a little while and replied, "I will go and distract him. You help Jasmine and Josh get into the car and drive off."

"I am a Tradie, and I carry heavy things all the time. I can easily lift that scumbag and drop him in the garbage bin," Matt said frankly.

"What are you talking about? Do you think I am not strong enough? It is my job to protect Peony. You think all I can do is sit in the car and wait?" Nathan asked, offended.

"Guys. Jasmine is over there. I am going over there to let her know we are here," Peony interrupted their argument.

"Can I go over there with you to get them?" Matt suggested.

"No, Jasmine has never met you. She doesn't know who you are. She will be scared and might not go with us," Peony said.

"Please be careful. I will not be far away from you. I will keep my eyes on you," Nathan assured her.

"Ok, will do," Peony replied as she walked toward Jasmine.

Peony arrived at the entrance of the day care centre. She stood not far from Jasmine and made sure Jasmine spotted her. She was acting as if she was there to pick up her child.

Josh came out of the front gate and ran toward Jasmine. She hugged him and took his school bag, swinging it over her shoulder, and then took his hand and held it tightly as if she thought Bob would turn up any time and snatch him away from her. Her heart was pounding faster and faster as she turned and followed Peony towards her car. She was so scared she thought she would have a panic attack. The whole time she scanned every face, she could see to make sure none of them was Bob's.

Peony was just a step in front of Jasmine and heard her

whisper, "I worry that Bob is here, walk faster," she said, shaking.

"My shoelace is undone, Mummy, can you please tie it for me?" Josh suddenly stood and came to a stop.

Peony, hearing the young boy, quickly turned around and took Josh's school bag from Jasmine's and suggested she pick Josh up and carry him so they could get to the car faster.

Matt walked a few metres behind them to intervene if necessary.

"Mummy. Where are we going? Home is the other way," Josh questioned.

"Mummy's going to take you to a new place to see my friend" Jasmine held him tighter and made sure he was safe in her arms.

"We are not allowed to see anyone. Daddy will be angry if he could not see us when he woke up. He would hit us again." Josh's eyes grew wide, and Jasmine could see him starting to panic.

"Shhhh! don't worry, my little man, we are going to be ok." She was walking even faster behind Peony as they approached her car. When Jasmine saw Nathan sitting in the driver's seat with the engine already running and noticed Matt behind them, she hesitated.

"It's ok Jasmine, they are my friends," she signalled Jasmine to get into the car. "I am your Mummy's friend," she told Josh while she helped him to get in the car.

Jasmine's heart rate was increasing, and she was wildly looking around to make sure Bob was not there.

"Everybody's seat belt on?" Nathan said as calmly as he could, looking in the rear-view mirror.

Peony looked back at Matt as she was getting in the backseat of the car beside Jasmine and Josh. He gave her the thumbs-up sign and slid into the passenger seat next to Nathan before quickly closing the door.

"Yes. We're all ready," Peony replied, slamming her door.

Nathan gunned the car and drove off quickly.

Nathan handed his mobile phone to Matt. "Matt, call the police immediately, and Peony call Jasmine's friend to let her know what's going on."

"Here is Mie's address. Let the police know they'll need someone to go there to keep them safe," Peony said, passing a piece of paper to Matt.

"Peony, when you call Mie, ask her and her Mum to leave home for a while to make sure they are safe in case the police are slow to respond." Nathan said.

Peony dialled the number. "No one is picking up the phone!" Peony turned to Jasmine, who looked terrified.

Matt, who was talking to the police, heard Peony and said, "Could you guys please make sure to get there as soon as possible? Please before he gets there... ok. Thanks."

When Matt got off the phone, he announced, "The police are on their way to Mie's. Keep calling her Peony."

"I hope they are safe and sound. If anything bad happens to her, I will not forgive myself." Jasmine said with tears in her eyes.

Finally, Nathan turned the car into Peony's driveway.

Peony pressed the remote control to open the garage door, and Nathan drove the car straight in before Peony hit the button again to close it, so they were out of sight.

"Mission accomplished!" Peony shouted with excitement.

As they got in the house, Matt put his hand up, "Mate, give me five. You have just driven from Campsie to Newport! Another important mission accomplished! Congratulations!" he said proudly, giving Nathan a big hug and clap on his shoulder.

"I guess when your mission is bigger than your fear, anything can happen! Yay! Onwards and upwards," he said, scooping Peony up and kissing her.

"Congratulations to everyone! This is the first step. The

next step will be getting a Domestic Violence Order to protect Jasmine and Josh," Nathan stated.

"Definitely. That bastard should be in jail." Matt added with anger.

"Yes, I agree. But first things first, let's get you both settled Jasmine." Peony said, turning to Jasmine. "Jasmine, you and Josh will stay with me. Come on in, and welcome." She said, leading them through the hallway to the first door and opening it. "This is your bedroom. I set it up with a double and single bed so you and Josh can sleep in one room."

"Peony, I just want to say thank you so much. You give us hope when all the hope and will to live was lost," Jasmine said appreciatively.

"Don't mention it," she said.

"Hey Josh, Uncle Matt needs to go. But Uncle Nathan will be here to play with you for a little while. Your mummy and I will go and buy some new clothes for you. Guess what? We will have pizza for dinner. Do you like pizza?" she asked Josh.

"Yay! I like it that much!" Josh stretched his tiny arms from one side to the other side.

"Peony, I am too scared to go out," she stated with a concerned look on her face.

"Jasmine, it is ok to be scared with what you've been through. It's probably a good idea to lay low anyway right now. You stay here with Nathan, and I'll go and get you some things, ok? What size clothing is Josh? I will grab a few basic pieces for you, and you can also share my clothes too if you like. Anything else you need?" Peony asked.

"I cannot think of anything I need. Just some clothes for Josh would be fine. Thank you."

"Won't be long. I will be back in a couple of hours. She hugged Nathan, "Thank you, Darling, you are amazing. I am very proud of you. Love you!"

"Love you too, Honeybun!" Nathan kissed her.

"Hey, you love birds, wait for when there is no one looking when you do that," Matt winked and looked at Josh, who sat looking at them both with the widest of eyes.

Matt went with Peony outside to her car. "Thank you, Matt. I hope you don't mind that Jasmine is staying with me for a while. I am thinking that I should start to pay you rent." she said.

"Peony, don't be silly. I am not going to take any rent from you. I don't need the rental income from this property. The truth is that in the past few years while I was living with you, the renovations we both did and paid for increased the value of the property. Not to mention all the things you have done for my family and me. It's beyond any amount of money. You cooked, cleaned, and gardened, and almost every evening you made me my favourite peppermint tea. I am most grateful for you helping to take care of Mum in her last life stage. You taught me what unconditional love is. You are the best wife a man could ask for. Nathan will be the luckiest husband of all. In the future, when you move in with him, maybe I can use this house as temporary accommodation for people like Jasmine." He said thoughtfully. "I wonder how many women are out there in the same situation as her," he said sadly.

"I don't know. I only hope that we help as many as we can," Peony said, thinking of Lili as well.

"Ending domestic violence one life at a time," Matt said. "Has Nathan asked you to move in with him yet?"

"No. We've only really begun dating. It is too soon to think of moving in together. I think I will agree to live together when we are married."

"Nathan is the best Peony. I think that will come around quicker than you think. He loves you so much." Matt told her.

"You think so?" Peony asked.

"I know so," Matt with a definite answer.

"You know us more than we know ourselves!" Peony hugged him, then she waved goodbye and got in her car. Peony drove to Warriewood Shopping Centre. She bought most of the things that Josh and Jasmine needed, and on her way back, she picked up the pizza from her favourite Italian restaurant at Mona Vale and headed straight home.

"I am home!" She cheered as she walked in the front door. "Hey Josh, come here. See all these new clothes I bought for you." she waved a big shopping bag in the air.

Josh and Nathan had been playing with a Lego set Nathan had brought him, and he looked up at Peony and then looked at Nathan to see if it was ok.

"Go on, let's see what Aunty Peony bought for you," Nathan said.

Josh jumped up excitedly and took the bag off Peony's hand. He started to pull the clothes out of the bag: "Wow! Mummy, come and see! I have heaps of new clothes. Oh! A superman T-shirt. Here is a batman one! Oh, a Power Rangers one! I like them all!" he said and broke into the theme song from the Power Rangers show, "Go, go Power Ranger!"

"I haven't seen Josh that happy ever before. Thank you again, Peony," said Jasmine, with tears of delight.

"You are most welcome. Here, these bags are for you. Whatever you need should be in it. If not, you can borrow some from me. Hope you will like them, in case you don't like them, I have the receipts so I can take them back to exchange them," she said, handing the bags to Jasmine.

"These beautiful dresses. Jeans, tops, pyjamas. Oh! Peony! These are fancy undies and bras. Oh my God! Shoes as well!" She was fanning her face with her hands and trying to dab at stop the tears of happiness from rolling down her cheeks. But it didn't work! Happy tears cascaded uncontrollably. "I haven't worn new clothes for many years. Most of my clothes and Josh's clothes are from the Red Cross. Thank you!" She hugged Peony.

"Well, I am glad to see you are happy." She wiped the tears from Jasmine's eyes and then suggested, "Come on, let's eat! The pizza is getting cold."

Nathan bought some plates out and put them on the table, and pulling Peony aside, said, "Darling, shortly after you left for shopping. I got a call from the police. Bob went to Mie's place to look for Jasmine when she didn't come home. They have taken him into custody and have charged him with carrying a dangerous weapon and entering private property with the intent to harm others."

"I hope he will be sentenced to jail so Jasmine, Josh, Mie, and her family will be safe," Peony said quietly.

After dinner, Nathan left to follow up on a few things with his work. Peony served Josh some rainbow ice cream, made Jasmine a cup of hot chocolate, and handed it to her, "It will help you sleep better," she said. "You both must be exhausted after your ordeal. Why don't you go and have showers, jump into your new cosy beds, and get an early night and some rest?"

"Thanks Peony, that sounds perfect. You too Peony. It was a big day for everyone. See, this little angel? He's already falling asleep," Jasmine said, looking at Josh, who was nodding off at the table. She picked him up and said to Peony, "Thank you again. This means so much to us. Good night!"

"Good night!" Peony smiled and hugged her friend.

Just as Peony began drifting off to sleep, she was woken abruptly to someone screaming.

"No! No!" It was Jasmine. Following the scream, Peony heard Josh cry out and call, "Mummy! Mummy!"

Peony rushed to their bedroom and turned the light on. She saw Jasmine curled up in the corner of her bed with her hands over her head, cowering and crying, "No! Please!" Josh was sitting up and screaming, "Mummy! Mummy!"

Peony sat next to Jasmine on the bed and said, "Jasmine, it's ok! You're safe!" and put her arms around her. Jasmine was shaking violently while Josh looked on, worried for his Mum.

Waking up, Jasmine's tear-streaked face looked at Peony and realised with relief where she was. Picking Josh up, then held him tightly. In a calm and gentle voice, Peony said, "Jasmine. I am here with you. You're ok."

Peony could feel Jasmine's shaking begin to subside. She stroked her hair and instructed, "Take a few deep breaths. Jasmine, breathe in... and breathe out... breathe in... and breathe out. When you are ready, only if you are ready, please tell me what frightened you?"

Jasmine stuttered, "I dreamt about Bob... Bob was stomping on my friend Mie's head. Blood was everywhere. Then he grabbed... grabbed me and hit me. And... Josh tried to stop him, but he kicked Josh on the ground. He tried to force us to go back with him."

"Oh, Jasmine, you and Josh must have been through hell. I wish that I had found you earlier. The real nightmare is over Honey." Peony gently calmed Josh down, put him back in his bed, and waited for him to fall asleep again. Then she laid next to Jasmine to settle her back to sleep.

"Peony, am I that stupid and useless as he said? Every time he abused me, he told me it was my fault. I deserved it. Perhaps if I tried harder and did better, would he have treated me better?" Jasmine questioned with guilt.

"Jasmine, listen to me; it was not your fault. You are a beautiful angel. You didn't deserve to live in the hell that Bob put you through. I want you to know that Angels don't live in hell. No one has the right to harm another human being in any shape or form." Peony stroked her hair and continued: "Remember this place—it's called Newport. It is your new port, your new beginning. You are like a ship in a safe harbour after sailing through the stormy sea. We will be with you each step of the way toward your new life. I am so proud of you for your courage. You are not only making this new life for yourself, but most importantly for your son Josh as well."

"I am so scared. Can you stay here with me?" Jasmine asked with a quivering voice.

"Of course I can," Peony assured her. They kept chatting until she fell asleep again.

CHAPTER 24

Andrew invited Nathan for their usual weekly lunch after they met with a new client. When they arrived at their favourite harbourside restaurant, Nathan asked him, "Please help me to understand how come at the meeting you did not ask the client a single business question, and instead asked about his family?"

"Well, at the first meeting, I always want to know the client first. You know your clients by how they treat their families. If they treat their families with integrity, loyalty, and wholeheartedly, then you know they will apply those principles in doing business with you. I never do business with unfaithful people or anyone who is disloyal to their family and friends. Remember, you can always find people with skills, but you cannot always find people with good character," Andrew told him.

"Thank you, that's valuable advice. Now, let me update you on the progress of the shopping centre at Chatswood," Nathan said.

"Nathan, we have just finished the meeting. Now it is lunchtime. Let's talk about something not related to business while we eat. How are you and Peony going?" Andrew asked.

"We are going strong and in the right direction. It's only been a short time, yet it seems we have known each other for years. I consider myself a very lucky man. Yesterday we went to rescue her friend Jasmine from an abusive relationship. Peony was amazing. The more you know her, the more goodness you discover in her. She doesn't only have a pretty face, she's incredibly clever. I adore her for her beautiful kind heart and admire her courage in standing up and doing what is right to help her friend. She's compassionate, loyal to friends and family..." Nathan replied with admiration.

Andrew smiled and nodded, "There are many heroes out there without the capes. They look like ordinary men and women. In the same way, that day when you stood up for Peony in Jimmy's restaurant. I enjoyed watching you turn the situation around without saying one word to that idiot who humiliated Peony. I will never forget the way she looked at you. You were her superhero that day, and it looks like you still are. She didn't even notice me. That's why at our first meeting with her, she didn't realise that I was the one with you that night. I am pleased to see you and Peony reconnected, and your relationship is blossoming. You two are meant to be together. I firmly believe Nathan; she is the woman for you," Andrew said sincerely.

"Now I know that's why you helped Peony with the six-month rent-free plus the twenty thousand dollars to help her with the interior decoration of her shop!" Nathan looked at him with an understanding smile. "I didn't realise you remembered her as well!"

"Well, since you own a twenty percent share of the company, I didn't think you'd mind." He chuckled. "We both know that she earned it. From her business plan, I know her vision is clear, and she works hard towards achieving what she wants. She's focused and diligent. With all that aside, she's a real sweetheart, pure of heart and brave like a lion. Look at how she helped Jasmine without hesitation. I like that." Andrew said as he picked up his glass and drank some water.

"This country has just come out of recession. There is still a widespread drop in spending. While many people have a wait-and-see mentality, she's shown real courage to start her very first business in this climate. Peony will succeed. She knows exactly what she wants and goes after it," Nathan added.

"I agree with you." Andrew went on, "Within relation to her friend Jasmine, I've been giving this some thought. I am thinking of funding a charity organisation at Northern Breaches to support women and children who experience domestic violence by providing a haven for them. Maybe a women's and children's refuge centre? Get Peony involved in this project. I'll leave it to you to work out how this all gets up and running, son. We need to do everything we can to protect her and Josh from her abusive ex-partner and other women like her. As Australian men, you and I have a duty and obligation to build a safe and secure environment for all women and children. Abusing women and children is a cowardly act. The majority of Australians will not tolerate and should not tolerate it. We need to do our bit to help where we can," Andrew concluded.

"I am more than happy to take on this project. Sadly, I think there are many more like Jasmine and Josh who could do with some help," Nathan said.

"Nathan, I am so proud to see you become the person you are today," Andrew patted his back.

"You and Athena have been very kind to me and been unbelievable role models. I'm grateful that you took me under your wing and helped me to become the best person I am. I'll make you proud by continuing to do my best every day," Nathan said.

"Son, I'm already proud of you. Never forget that. Why

don't you and Peony come for dinner this Friday night? Athena hasn't seen you for some time. I am sure she would love to meet Peony. It's time. More so, we can have further discussions about the project. I am sure Athena will give some valuable input too," Andrew rose and patted Nathan's shoulder, "Keep on doing the good work. Son! Your parents would also be proud of you. You are their pride and joy."

"I'd like that. I am sure Peony and Athena will love each other. They have so many outstanding qualities in common," Nathan stated.

After lunch, Nathan called Peony:" Hey Honeybun, I miss you. How's Jasmine doing?"

"Getting there. She seems to be settling down a bit. Would you like to come here for dinner? I miss you already!" Peony said.

"Would love to. What's for dinner?" Nathan asked.

"Jasmine wants to cook Peking Duck. That will do her good to keep her occupied and take her mind off what had happened to her. Hey, we have already found another daycare for Josh too—he can start next Monday," Peony said happily.

"That's awesome! I just finished lunch with Andrew. He gave me a new project. I need your help. I will tell you more about it when I see you tonight. Bye, Honeybun."

"Ok, Sweetie Bear. I can't wait to see you," Peony said, blowing a kiss down the phone line to him.

When Nathan stepped into Peony's place, he shouted out while he hugged Peony, "Oh. I can smell five spices from something that smells amazing!" He followed the aroma, walking into the kitchen. Nathan tapped on Jasmine's shoulder and said, "Smells delicious!"

Jasmine jumped and stepped back a couple of steps, screaming, "No!" She stared at Nathan with her eyes wide open.

"Jasmine, Jasmine, it's ok, it's just me. Are you ok?" Nathan asked with concern.

Peony rushed into the kitchen when she heard the scream. She held Jasmine in her arms and whispered, "Everything is alright. Remember that you are in a safe place now."

Jasmine was frozen, and then confusion spread over her face as tears rolled down her face. "I am sorry. I was in another world. Bob used to beat me up if I did not cook the food that he wanted or if I was later getting it on the table."

At that moment, Josh came into the kitchen and asked, "Mummy, are you Ok?"

Nathan picked up Josh, "Hey, my little buddy. Your mummy is ok. Would you like to help set the table with me?" Nathan asked.

"Yeah!" Josh put his arms around Nathan's neck and leaned his head on Nathan's chest as he carried him to the dining room, then gently put him down, "Let me show you how Peony and I set our dinner table ok? The serviette goes on this side, and the chopsticks on this side. See? Just like this. Now, would you like to do a set?" Nathan asked.

"I can do that," Josh said with a proud voice.

"Peony, Nathan is going to make an excellent father one day. I hope it will be very soon. I am so happy for you," Jasmine said while they both watched Nathan and Josh setting up the table. Peony blushed with a shy smile.

During the dinner, Nathan assured Jasmine, "The police said that they would do their best to make sure he will not come near you and Josh. We are all doing our best to protect both of you."

"Why me? I don't understand. I am a good woman. I work hard. I was doing my best to look after him," Jasmine said, still trying to make sense of it all and find the answers.

"Jasmine, I know you are still hurting. Sometimes bad things happen to good people. It is not making sense and you may not understand it now, but everything happens for a reason." Nathan patted her shoulder gently.

"Don't think about it too much. Now your mission is to recover from the trauma. I want you to remember that for every bad thing that happened, something good must come out of it. Josh is one of those good things. Furthermore, you can use your experience to help others in the future." Peony said, picking up a piece of Peking duck and putting it on Jasmine's bowl and continued, "Jasmine, remember I told you about my mum and my dad who were sent to the re-education camp for 'confession'? I was left at home by myself in the dark when I was only four years old. Probably about Josh's age. When I look back, I thank God for the experience. Out of the suffering came compassion," she said reflectively.

"We want you to know that you are not alone. We are here with you and for Josh," Nathan added.

"I feel that I am stuck at the moment, but with both of you by my side and supporting me, I hope I can move forward," Jasmine said hopefully.

"You are not stuck; you are just taking a moment to reflect on what has happened to you while you regain your strength and confidence." Peony continued. "After everything is settled, if you agree, I will recommend a psychologist to help you and Josh. So that both of you can heal faster from the trauma," Peony suggested.

"I am longing for a normal life. In addition, I commit to doing whatever it takes to provide a safe and secure place for Josh, "Jasmine responded.

"Your home is here now. We are your new family," Peony promised.

Finishing dinner, Peony said for Jasmine to take Josh and get him bathed and into the bed while she and Nathan cleaned up.

Chatting away, Peony suddenly remembered that Nathan

wanted to talk to her about his new project, "Darling, you said you have something you need to discuss with me?"

"Oh, yes. You and I are invited to Andrew's home for dinner this Friday night. His wife Athena would love to meet you," he said.

"Lovely. I look forward to it." Peony said. "I will ask Matt and Tom to come for dinner with Jasmine and Josh on Friday night. They will stay with them until we come home just to be safe."

"Great idea," Nathan said. "I have to head home and do some more work, we'll talk about the project later on or on Friday night, ok?" he said.

"Sure, sounds good," Peony said, walking him out and kissing him good night.

Peony took Jasmine to her first session of therapy the next day. After introducing Jasmine to Fiona, she stayed for about ten minutes longer to ensure Jasmine was comfortable with Fiona before leaving to take Josh to a park nearby to play. They had all sorts of adventures and fun in the park before returning to pick Jasmine up.

Fiona was born in Australia, but because both of her parents were from China, she could speak fluent Chinese. She was friendly, and the atmosphere she provided was calm, safe, and peaceful. Therefore, it didn't take long for Jasmine to start opening up and telling her about her traumatic experiences with Bob. Fiona listened with compassion, understanding, and non-judgment. When she noticed Jasmine could not continue at one point, she asked her to take a break and deep breath, a strategy she had shared with Peony for Nathan. Occasionally, she passed a box of tissues to Jasmine to dry her tears which were plentiful throughout the session. At the end of their time, Fiona explained, "Jasmine, you are extremely courageous to revisit those painful events. I want you to know that it is not your fault. The truth is that no matter how hard you tried to please him, you would never have been good enough for him. No one would have been. He planned to clip your wings so you couldn't fly away from him and remained in his cage to serve him—that's all he cared about. There might also be something that happened to you when you were a child that led to the result of drawing that type of man to you, so we'll have to do some work from your childhood too, ok? This will help to prevent you from falling into the same trap again, which many abused women do. Now, I want you to close your eyes and take a deep breath. Go back to a time when you were a child and recall any trauma that may have caused you great pain. I want you to visualise what the younger you was going through. Describe how you felt. Try to find words to describe these feelings. For example, were you frightened? Angry? Hurt? Abandoned? Rejected? Shameful?" Fiona questioned.

Jasmine closed her eyes and recalled the time when she was about five years old. Her father was smacking her, screaming at her, and telling her that she was useless and wished she was never born. He hated her because she was not a boy. She felt scared, rejected, shamed, abandoned, and helpless. After a moment of silence, Fiona used her calm and gentle voice to instruct her, "Now, in a kind and compassionate voice, I would like you to ask the younger you what she needs. Does she need a long hug to reassure her that she is loved? Does she need understanding? Nurturing? Perhaps acceptance? Or all of them? I want you to tell the younger you that you know what she's been through and how much she's hurting. Tell her she will survive that experience. Tell her that you are here with her and for her, and ask her what she needs from you. She may ask you to hug her or take her to a special place where she feels safe and secure. I give you a moment with her." Fiona fell silent to let Jasmine visualise. After a couple of minutes, Fiona continued, "Once you know that this younger you has accepted your kindness, caring, and love, let her be. Now I want you to bring awareness to your breathing and open your eyes."

Jasmine opened her teary eyes; she was sobbing. Fiona passed her some more tissues and asked, "Would you like some water?" Jasmine nodded thankfully while she wiped the tears from her face.

Fiona poured some water into a glass and handed it to her, explaining the activity they had just done. "What we just did is called 'compassion for the younger you', Jasmine. Recently, a study showed that the type of partner we choose has something to do with the first man introduced into our lives. To heal, we sometimes have to start from our childhood and work through it from there. In each session, I will apply different techniques to help you get your life back on track to what it was that you wanted it to be when you were a very young girl. Just remember, it takes time to heal, be kind to yourself. To take care of Josh, you must first take care of yourself."

CHAPTER 25

Soon after Nathan finished working at the Chatswood site, he went back to Sky Paradise to pick up Peony. "Hey, Honeybun, are you ready?" he asked as he walked into her boutique.

"Yes," she hugged him and went to turn the lights off, "Let's go," she said, locking up her shop. Nathan led her into the lift, and after they got in, he pressed the basement car park button. Peony could not understand why they were going there and asked, "Oh, you just hit the basement level button; I'll press level one so we can get the taxi." She said, thinking he'd got confused.

Nathan put his hand on her arm gently to stop her from pressing the button. Peony looked at him questioningly. Nathan did not answer. He just looked at Peony with an affectionate smile. Peony followed him to get out of the lift, then he took car keys out of his pocket and pressed the unlock button on the remote. Peony eyes followed the sound of the beep... beep. Then she saw his car parked just a few meters away with the light flashing. Nathan smiled broadly and casually said, "I am driving tonight." As his pace quickened to open the passenger door of the car for Peony.

"My first time as your passenger!" she shouted with glee.

"Well, the second time actually," he laughed.

"I know the first time was when we rescued Jasmine. I meant the first time in your car just you and me with me in the passenger seat," she said excitedly.

"I can't believe how excited you are by seeing me drive again. What are you waiting for? Get in please ma'am," he grinned.

As Nathan was driving off, Peony couldn't stop staring at him and couldn't stop smiling. "For me it is the best not only seeing you drive again, but also knowing that you are an overcomer!"

"I didn't think I would ever drive again, but with you by my side, I feel like I can do anything!" he said.

Finally, Nathan stopped the car in the driveway. Looking at the house, Peony would have thought she was somewhere in Greece. The mansion's walls were whitewash with deep sea blue accent doors and windows, and a deep pink Bougainvillea arch draped itself around the top of the front door. The different varieties of Greek native flowers beautifully grew on large terracotta pots in the front garden. Nathan got out of the car and walked to Peony's side to open the door for her. Then he went to open the boot. He took a bottle of wine and a bunch of flowers out. They walked to the front door where Andrew and Athena were already standing at the front door to greet them. "This is Athena, my wife; this is Peony." Andrew introduced them to each other.

"It is lovely to meet you," Athena said in a rich and colourful Greek accent. She presented herself elegantly and gracefully as she walked forward to give Peony a warm hug.

"Likewise, Mrs Callos. Nathan has spoken fondly about you many times." Peony replied respectfully.

"Call me Athena." She smiled and turned to Nathan, "Nathan,

come here and give me a hug. So nice to see you."

"Athena has been busy preparing a delicious Greek dinner for us," Andrew said as he led them through to the kitchen and picked up a serving tray with four dips and pita bread.

Sitting at Andrew and Athena's dining room table, the foursome chatted away, enjoying each other's company and getting to know more about one another. The dips were followed by an octopus with lemon and fresh herbs appetiser that Andrew served, and a Greek-style slow-roasted leg of lamb that Athena put on the table.

"Look at this. It's so tender and falls off the bone. There is no need to use a carving knife at all," Nathan said as Andrew served the meat on the plates.

After the main, Athena took out the dessert, "Nathan, I made your all-time favourite. Hope Peony likes it as well." She said.

"No one can ever beat her Portokalopita with mango desserts. And you can't have it without the Greek coffee I made." Andrew said as he poured the coffee.

"That's what makes you the perfect couple," Nathan stated, feeling thrilled with how the night had progressed.

"The best Greek food I have ever tasted. A home-cooked meal with heart and soul is incomparable. Thank you, Athena, and you too Andrew," Peony said with gratitude.

"Athena had all the fun of cooking. I am just her kitchen hand," Andrew said, giving Athena a playful and loving look.

"Peony. You know we love you. You are welcome any time," Athena said with a delightful smile.

"I appreciate both of you for the warm welcome. I would love to learn to cook a few Greek dishes from you if I might?" Peony asked.

"I am more than happy to teach you. And you can teach me to cook Chinese too!" she replied.

"Peony's Chinese dishes are unbelievably delicious too," Nathan looked at Peony with pride.

"Women. We cannot live without them." Andrew looked at Athena and gave her a wink.

"Yes, good women are worth more than all diamonds in the world. They are invaluable." Nathan took Peony's hand and gave it a gentle kiss.

"You are right. I am so fortunate to have this special one," Andrew pulled Athena a bit closer to him and continued, "Peony, when Athena and I left Greece for Australia, we had only our suitcase with a few clothes in it. Soon after we arrived, I worked at a construction site as a labourer during the day, and I studied English in an English college at night. On weekends I worked in a fruit and vegetable market where I met Nathan's mum and dad. Since then, we have been very good friends. Athena has always been wonderful to me. She never complained about the little time I spent with her. Instead, she made sure I was being looked after. They say there is a woman behind every successful man. So true. Those women could be wives, mothers, girlfriends, sisters, daughters, teachers, and best friends. Our job is to love, cherish, respect, and protect them." Andrew stated with a determined look on his face.

Nathan nodded, "My father told me that he came here from Italy the same year you and Athena came here. He told me that when he first came here, he slept in his relatives' shed for a few months until he found a job and rented his first flat at Marrickville. Then he met my mum, she is a wonderful wife and a lovely mother. Since I was very young, Dad taught me to respect women. He showed me by example how to respect Mum and all women," Nathan said.

"A coward would slam the table and shout 'I am the head of this house! Do as I told!' while a real man will stand up and declare, 'I am the man of the house, it is my duty and responsibility to love, provide and protect my family," Andrew stated.

"Peony. You can see why I gracefully submit to my husband being the head of the house," Athena announced.

Peony nodded with an admiration smile to Athena.

"Well, put it this way, real smart men know that women are the body. The head could not survive without the support of the body. Isn't that right Honeybun?" Nathan looked at Peony with a cheeky smile.

"That's an interesting statement!" Peony laughed.

"In the book of Ephesians, it said that 'Husbands ought to love their wives as their bodies. He who loves his wife loves himself," Nathan explained.

"Peony, we both are fortunate to have these two amazing men," Athena said, with a tender smile and glanced at her husband.

"I wholeheartedly agree with you, Athena," Peony replied with an appreciative look at Nathan.

"Darling, speaking of looking after women, I mentioned to you about the refuge centre for women and children. I've spoken to Nathan about this. Let's bring Peony in on the conversation too," Andrew said to his wife.

"Andrew, thank you for involving me in this project. After Nathen explained your intention to set up a women's and children's refuge, I did some research and gathered some information before I came here," Peony said enthusiastically.

"Yes, I think it's important everyone puts together some ideas. I think we should let Peony share her idea first," Athena insisted.

"I am the one with the least experience in setting up this type of charity organisation," Peony hesitated.

"You have just had a hand on experience helping your friend. I am sure you have gained a great deal of knowledge and information," Andrew backed his wife up.

"Thank you for trusting in me. I will give it a try. We can set up the centre with a home-like environment. The community room should be set up like a family room to make them feel at home. It would be best if each bedroom had an ensuite and a fridge. Some rooms could be set up with one double bed and two bunk beds. Some rooms with a baby cot. We could allocate them according to each need." Peony paused for a while and continued, "We also need volunteers such as social workers, counsellors, and psychologists. We need to nurture women and build them up again mentally, physically, and psychologically. Furthermore, we should provide them with job training as well to further their education and build new skills so that the women can go back to the workforce when they are ready and learn how to be financially independent, so they don't have to feel they need to go back to their abuser to feed their kids. I'd like to see them as domestic violence victors, not victims. They will no longer be survivors; they will become thrivers." Peony gathered her thoughts for a while, then continued, "As a designer, I learned to put fabrics and trims together to create unique designs. Sometimes the smallest piece of fabric that was considered insignificant that people wanted to throw away, became the element in a piece that made the design stand out. In the same way, I hope the centre will provide temporary food and shelter and put them in the right place to help them to see their true value," she expressed her desire.

"That's why we need your input. You have great insight into what the women and children will need. You and Nathan will become the powerhouse for this project and our community," Andrew said, pleased.

"What should we call the centre?" Nathan asked.

"Grace Women and Children Centre?" Athena suggested.

"It is a great name," Andrew agreed.

"We are standing strong by God's grace. Indeed, it is a wonderful name!" Peony, with a cheerful tone, added, "I think the centre should accept not only people who are experiencing domestic violence but also people who have been experiencing other abuses such as drug and alcohol and sexual abuse." At that very moment, Lili came into Peony's mind again, and she silently sent a prayer in the hope her life could turn around.

CHAPTER 26

" The shop is ready for you to display your designs. Peony, it is your chance to rise and shine." Kang was pleased with the result of the interior design of the shop.

"Well done with your first project. I am delighted with the result." Peony could not be happier to see Kang show off his talent.

"Check if the lighting is shining to all the right places. Otherwise, let me know, and I can adjust them," Matt said.

Peony checked around. "Yep. It's exactly where I want it. Except for this one. Could you bring it down a bit so it draws attention to the display, rather than having it shine into people's eyes? You are amazing my bestie," Peony patted his shoulder.

"All the invitations have been sent out for the launch. The advertising is placed in this month's issue of the major fashion magazines and the newspaper. The brochures have been placed at the entrance of the centre too. A catering company will take care of the food and drinks. I can't wait for the opening party!" Nathan said.

"Thank you, my sweetie bear. You are awesome!" Peony said, throwing her arms around him and kissing him.

"The garments are ready in the warehouse. I have organised the truck to deliver them here at 8 am tomorrow. Oh, and I almost forgot, I have already sent out some of your designs to the people on the list Nathan gave me," Lucina added.

"Awesome! Lucina. You are my right-hand girl. I couldn't do this without you," Peony cheered.

On opening day, Nathan was the first to arrive at the boutique with a beautiful bunch of purple-pink peonies. He scanned the shop, "Wow! These designs are stunning! Very proud of you Honeybun. You surprise me all the time!"

"Thank you! I think you like surprises!" she said knowingly.

Then Matt, Tom, and Jasmine arrived, followed by Linda, Jason, Kang, Ava and her partner Stephen, Lucina, Andrew and Athena came in after them.

From there, other guests slowly arrived. Some of the guests Peony had never met before.

"Oh! See that lady walking towards her. She looks like the Prime Minister's wife," Peony whispered to Nathan.

"Yes, she is indeed our Prime Minister's wife!" Nathan replied quietly, impressed.

"No way! She is wearing one of my signature pieces! She looks so elegant in it," Peony said, surprised.

"Yes! She is a very good friend of Athena. I asked Lucina to deliver one of your designs to her and make sure it fit her perfectly," Nathan said.

Peony was astounded by his thoughtful surprise, "You did that?! Why don't you tell me about that?" she asked.

"If I told you, that would spoil the fun. Stay tuned for more exciting surprises!" he laughed.

"Oh My God! Is that the celebrity Kate Ledger from the

movie Second Chance?" Peony asked.

"Yes, she is my childhood friend. She had no choice but to drop everything and get on her private plane to come here," Nathan smiled.

"How many things do you hide from me? Tell me the truth!" she playfully demanded.

"Well. You have lifelong to find out, my honeybun," he said lovingly.

"I can't take any more surprises!" she exclaimed.

"Wait and see. Come with me, I will introduce you to Kate," Nathan held her hand and walked toward Kate.

"Wow, wow. This must be the lovely Peony. Very nice to meet you." Kate hugged Peony.

"What a nice surprise! It is my privilege to meet you! You make my design look so beautiful, and I cannot find anyone more perfect than you, to wear it," Peony said, thrilled.

"Nothing to do with me. The other way around. Your design makes me feel so beautiful. I just love them," she said.

"May I borrow you for a moment Peony?" Athena said, accompanied by the Prime Minister's wife, "This is our upcoming designer, Peony," she said, introducing her.

"It is my great honour and pleasure to have you here tonight," Peony said with the greatest respect.

"The honour is mine to be invited to share this special event. You are a fine example of those who come across the sea, call Australia home, and take the opportunities it offers. You are treasured assets for this country."

"Australia is my home now, and I plan to do my best to contribute in any way I can," Peony replied.

At the end of the party, when all the guests left except Peony's family and close friends, Nathan pulled out a chair and asked Peony to sit down. "I told you that will be more surprises to come. I guess this will be the biggest. Are you ready?" he asked mysteriously.

"Are you serious?" Peony said, staring at Nathan amazed there were even more surprises.

"Close your eyes," Nathan insisted.

"What trick have you got up your sleeve now?" she closed her eyes waiting eagerly.

"Now you can open your eyes," he said.

Peony found Nathan kneeling in front of her, holding up a beautiful box in his hand. He slowly opened it to reveal a stunning sparkling diamond ring.

"Peony Chen, my heart was a desert until you came and watered it with your love. When I look into your eyes, I know that no one else can ever hold my heart the way you do. I know that you deserve the very best. Will you let me be the one who supports you in all you want in life, without limits, and inspire you to grow without holding you back, and love you with all my heart? You are the only one I want to spend the rest of my life with. Would you marry me?" Nathan proposed.

She stared at Nathan in total shock. Tears of joy sprung to her eyes, and a wave of overwhelming love went through her entire heart and soul. She turned around and looked at a beaming Matt, who nodded and said, "Well, what are you waiting for?"

Jasmine shouted, "Just say yes!"

Peony giggled, giddy with the love she felt and said, "Yes, of course, yes! I can't think of anything I want to do more than spend the rest of my life with you!" as she put her left hand out.

Nathan slid the ring gently onto her ring finger and leaned forward to hug her and kiss her tears of happiness.

Matt turned to Tom, "Looks like we have to take Jasmine home after the party. We should leave those two love birds alone tonight." He said, going up to Nathan and Peony to congratulate them.

After everyone congratulated the happy couple, they parted, leaving Nathan to take his fiancé to Darling Harbour for a midnight walk. As they strolled along the magical harbour hand in hand, the streetlights reflected off the buildings in the water, making it look like they had just walked into a movie. They were looking heavenward at the midnight velvet sky littered with stars that seemed brighter than she had ever noticed before. Peony thought it was the perfect ending to a perfect day.

"I still can't comprehend and digest all the surprises tonight. I feel like I am in a dream. What surprised me the most was your proposal. We have known each other for not even three months." Peony said.

"Technically, we have known each other for years." He glanced at Peony under the streetlight, which illuminated her beautiful face, "You are beautiful in every way. But tonight, you look even more beautiful. You are glowing!" He pulled her close to him, put his arm around her waist and continued, "The first time we met was when I was still grieving the loss of Bella. That night before you left the restaurant, you turned around and smiled at me. The way you looked at me reminded me of Bella. Somehow, at that moment, I felt a heaviness lift from my shoulders, and I felt I could breathe again. Please don't get me wrong, I don't want you to replace Bella. It is unfair to both of you. I was disappointed to not see you again in the following days and months. I hoped I would, and you have remained on my mind since I first laid eyes on you. When you came into my office that day, I was so shocked and so happy that I could barely contain it. I realised then that it was meant to be. We were meant to be. I think I already loved you then." He said.

"That night, I felt something so magical that I had never felt before when our eyes met. That look was so familiar. I felt as if we had met before, or that I had known you forever. Then I saw the wedding ring on your finger and felt deflated. I thought that I had to do the right thing by God. So, I quit the job to avoid seeing you again," Peony disclosed.

"Thank God for meeting you again," he cheered.

Peony was going to say something, but she hesitated and held back.

"Is something troubling you?" Nathan noticed.

"Something... I don't know if I should tell you or not?" Peony spoke quietly.

"Try me. You can tell me anything!" he insisted.

"If I tell you, please promise not to laugh at me or judge me, alright? Because this is my choice and my belief. It is important to me," she requested respectfully.

"Alright, I promise," he agreed.

"I had never fallen in love with any man but you. This means I have never had an intimate relationship with any man. I promised myself to save my virginity for my husband," she looked at Nathan, waiting for his reaction.

"Since Bella passed, I haven't had any other woman. I thought that I would never fall in love again, that was until I met you. If I could wait for intimacy for that many years, I can wait for a bit longer! But hopefully not too long." He joked with a cheeky smile.

"You are putting pressure on me now!" Peony gave him a gentle squeeze on the hand that she was holding.

"Just relax, I know all the good things come to those who wait. You don't need to worry when it comes to physical intimacy. Everything will fall into place naturally at the right time." He glanced at her and continued, "Intimacy is not just physical. In fact, intimacy in a relationship is in four areas. Emotional—sharing our deepest feelings, fears, and thoughts; Intellectual—sharing our ideas, opinions, and life perspectives; spiritual—feeling closeness, validation, and beliefs on life's purpose, and last but not least, Physical—body closeness, cuddling, kissing, hugging, holding hands as we are right now and making love after we marry. When we connect with our emotions, intellectual and spiritual first, then the physical connection happens naturally. So, in my opinion, done in that way, it makes for a fulfilling marriage. In contrast, many marriages fail because they only have the physical connection without the other three elements which build the strong foundation." Nathan said wisely.

"Well said. What about the chemistry? I still clearly remember the first time our eyes met," Peony said.

"Oh! Yes, I felt it too. When our eyes met, I felt like there was an invisible connection from your heart to mine—it felt like you had penetrated my soul. It was almost indescribable. Perhaps this is chemistry? Love at the first sight?"

"I believe so." Then she asked, "Could I share a lovely story with you?"

"Yes, I'd love to hear it," he said.

"While I was studying in college, I worked part-time as a dressmaker at Dee Why. I remember one day an elderly couple came in. He asked me to make a dress for his wife for their 50th wedding anniversary celebration. I asked them what the secret of their successful marriage was. He said chose the right one to start with. When they first met, he was seventeen, and she was sixteen. He told me that when he saw her, he knew she was the right one. Every time he says he loves her, he says it means more than saying these three magical words. He told me that when you truly love someone, the loyalty, faithfulness, respect, patience, tolerance, understanding, and caring for your loved one assures them you love them more than the words themselves." Peony told him.

She turned to Nathan, kissed him, and said, "I know you are the right one for me."

CHAPTER 27

At the Grace Women and Children's Centre opening ceremony, Nathan and Peony stood side by side. She looked at him with a proud smile and a slight nod of her head. He smiled back and let go of her hand, which he held tightly. He walked up to the front of the stage to deliver his speech.

"Good evening! We want to let you know that we appreciate those who have given their support and helped us to create this amazing organisation. You will be participating and witnessing life-changing beginnings in this centre. It is not how much we have, it is how much we give that counts.

For those who come here to ask for support and help, we say thank you. Because you dare to take your first step in changing the world, but more importantly, your world.

Like our good friend Jasmine, because she accepted the help and dared to change her circumstances, now she can help others. At some point in our lives, we all need help. So don't be afraid to ask. Life is a gift, we are all here not by accident but instead with purpose— a purpose to fulfil. We all have the ability and obligation to make this place a better world.

Ava and Linda, who are our volunteer English tutors, and Matt and Tom, who have worked tirelessly on weekends and every spare minute they have to construct the centre, we thank you.

Together, we will be helping people like our friend to let go of their past, gain confidence and self-value and step into brighter, healthier, and happier futures. Our friend did this and studied hard in her recovery to qualify as an accountant here at Grace Women and Children's Centre, and we're incredibly proud of her and what she's achieved.

We look forward to the centre's official launch and helping those in need live the lives they deserve," said Nathan to the applause of those gathered.

Nathan and Peony had been heavily involved in the refuge centre development. While Peony was running her business, Nathan still managed the shopping centres and building projects. They hardly had time for themselves. After the official opening, Peony decided to book a dinner for just the two of them at The Beach Restaurant and Bar at Dee Why to celebrate Nathan's birthday. When they arrived, they sat at the bar for a drink and waited for their table to become available as the early bird customers still occupied the table till 8 pm.

Peony barely noticed a group of women dressed erotically sitting at a table in the corner as she and Nathan sat enjoying their drinks and long overdue time together. The women were drunk and talking and laughing loudly as if there were the only customers in the room. Peony excused herself and went to the ladies' room. One of women noticed her departure and got up and walked over to Nathan. Giving him a seductive smile, she said, "Hello, want company?"

Nathan looked at the way she dressed and the way she behaved. Straight away, he knew what she was up to, "Thank you for asking. But no, thank you." He replied politely.

"Don't be shy. I promise you that I will give you the best service you have ever experienced before. Satisfaction guaranteed!" She said, trying her best to persuade him.

"I said no, thank you. I am happily in a relationship with my fiancé. She has just gone to the bathroom and will be back in a minute." He said firmly, trying to get rid of her quickly.

"I can meet you another time if you wish?" she persisted, using her last attempt to get herself a client.

"I am not your type of client. Sorry." Nathan started to become annoyed and wanted her to leave.

As Peony walked towards Nathan, she saw a woman sitting next to him, leaning her body very close to him. When she came closer, she noticed who she was. She cried out, "Lili?"

Lili turned around, and when she saw Peony, her mouth gapped open. Stunned, she responded, "I don't know you," she said, and quickly moved back to the table of women.

"You know her?" Nathan asked in disbelief.

"Yes, I am sure that's Lili. Do you mind if I go over to talk to her?" Peony asked.

"No, I don't mind at all. Do you want me to come with you?" he asked with some worry in his voice.

"No, thank you. Won't be long," Peony said confidently.

When Lili went back to her table, one of the women made fun of her. "So, you got the wrong guy. Ha. Shame! I just finished serving my client. The room up there is available."

The other woman responded, "You weren't with him in the room long. Looks like you had another dead fuck. But that's exactly what we want! Who wants to waste their time on these bastards," she sneered.

"Unfortunately, he is one of many of these wankers in my experience, not only a dead fuck, but he had a chilli dick as well." The first woman responded which had all the women at the table burst into more loud laughter.

One of them managed to stop laughing long enough to say,

"Don't you get it? That's why they need to pay us for sex because any decent woman would not get into a relationship with these fuckwits who are useless in bed."

"I agree, they are a bunch of selfish jerks in bed, they get what they want and haven't got a clue how to satisfy women's needs. That's why their wives give up having sex with them." The other woman added. "Or they are cheaters who have no respect for themselves and are morally bankrupt."

"I guess he is not one of them," The other woman looked over to Nathan.

"He is someone's fiancé," Lili answered with an uneasy tone.

"Uh oh! You mean that woman coming over here now? It looks like she may have found out that you tried to get her fiancé into bed! You're in trouble now!" The other women in the group said with more than a bit of concern.

By then, Peony had reached Lili's table, "Lili, can we talk out there? Please!"

"If you want to have a go with me for talking to your fiancé, go ahead! Otherwise, I have nothing to talk about," Lili said smartly and turned away from her.

"I missed you. I think of you all the time. How are you?" Peony said.

"Don't you see I am with my friends?" Lili snarled.

"I understand, I promise it won't take you long," Peony insisted.

"Go away! Don't bother me!" Lili said dismissively.

"Here is my business card. Please call me. I want to catch up with you." Peony handed her business card to Lili.

Lili read the card and said sarcastically, "Wow! Wow! Wow! Look at you! Now you are a businesswoman and a fashion designer. I am just a hooker. We have nothing in common, and we have nothing to talk about."

"Lili! I have worked hard for the last few years to achieve

where I am now."

"You work hard to get where you are now. Unlike me. Ha! Stupid, and know nothing other than open my legs. Get easy money from the scumbags." Lili said agitatedly.

"I am sorry. I don't mean that. I don't mean to upset you," Peony said apologetically.

"Whatever! Go back to your handsome fiancé, he is waiting for you."

"Please Lili. Call me. I can help you. It is not too late," Peony pleaded.

"I am in a dark tunnel, and there is no way out. Don't waste your time!" Lili said flatly.

"Sometimes, when you are stuck in the dark tunnel, you may not see the light at the end of it. I can help you until you get out at the other side of the tunnel. I promise you at the other side is a brighter and better place."

"Don't try to preach to me! Who do you think you are? My saviour? Just leave me alone," Lili spat.

"Please, call me. Will you?" With teary eyes, Peony walked back to Nathan.

"Is everything ok? Hope you don't think that I had something to do with her?" Nathan said, concerned.

"No, from the moment that I saw you at Jimmy's restaurant, my intuition told me that you are not that type of man. I trust you," Peony assured.

"You look upset though."

"Lili is my friend. I met her the first day when we arrived in Sydney. More or less, you know what Lili is doing. I am concerned about her well-being. Somehow, she did not want to talk to me. The only thing I could do was give her my business card. I hope she will change her mind and contact me," Peony said, hopeful.

The waitress came up and interrupted their conversation, "Excuse me, your table is ready. Please follow me," then she led them to their table.

"Let's celebrate your birthday. It is your special day. You have been working so hard, we need to relax and enjoy your special night. I hope you can take this moment to recharge your batteries," Peony tried to focus on celebrating his birthday with him.

After dinner on their way back, Nathan suggested, "It's still quite early. Do you want to drop by my place for a while? We can watch Sleepless in Seattle. I got the video at home."

Peony looked at her watch, "Oh, it's only a quarter to ten. I have already watched the movie with Jasmine, it is such a classic romantic movie, but I am happy to watch it again with my mister though," She glanced over to Nathan and gave him a smile.

Peony put her feet up on the footrest stool. She cuddled Nathan and rested her head on his shoulder while watching the movie. In his arms, she felt content and safe. She tried to focus on the movie but could not get Lili out of her mind. "Is Lili safe tonight? What's her life like?" Peony thought.

"Would you like a hot chocolate?" Nathan looked at Peony and found her fell deeply asleep on his shoulder. He murmured, "Ha! Sleepless in Seattle becomes Asleep at Seaforth." He said looking at his love, feeling overjoyed and grateful. He gently stroked her forehead and whispered, "You are an immeasurable blessing from above. I adore you Peony Chen, my princess."

The gentle morning sun poured through the window. Another new day brought with it new hope and an aspiring beginning. "Oh! God, that scent. It belongs to Nathan." Peony thought as she slowly opened her eyes and found herself in his bed. She rolled over and pressed her face into the pillow. The scent of the bed somehow made her feel so calm and peaceful, like a baby in her comfort blanket. She rubbed her eyes and then stretched her arms in the air. She rolled out of the bed and walked to the window. As she admired the rosy glow in the morning sky, a pair of lorikeets was chatting cheerfully in the bottle brush tree in the garden. The yachts in the distance still slept calmly in Middle Harbour. She could feel the morning breeze sweeping gently like a feather across her face. She looked down at her light pink silk thin-strap pyjamas. "I can't remember getting up here and changing into these pyjamas. Oh! These are not my pyjamas!" She thought with sudden confusion.

The aroma of the coffee wafted up from the kitchen to the bedroom. She went downstairs to the living room and saw Nathan in the open kitchen preparing breakfast.

"Good morning Darling." Peony chirped.

"Good morning Sunshine. I am making you breakfast. With you in this house, it is a home again." He handed her a freshly squeezed orange and grapefruit juice and gave her a gentle kiss on her lips.

"Thank you." Peony wondered if anything had happened between them last night. She asked, "Last night?..."

"You are safe." He laughed, seeing the look on her face. "Nothing happened. I slept in the guest room. Oh, by the way, those are Bella's pyjamas. I thought you would be more comfortable sleeping in some pj's instead of your clothes. You were out like a light. Hope you don't mind?" he asked.

"No, not at all. That's weird. I can't recall changing into them. I knew they weren't my pyjamas, but I felt like I had worn them before. They are so comfortable!"

"I put them on you. You were sound asleep. You know I respect you. I will never do anything to you without your consent. I promise I didn't look." He said cheekily.

"I know you wouldn't have. But I am your fiancé now, and you know I would not refuse if you... um... right?"

"Yes. I know; I have to admit it was tempting. But I was a good boy." He smiled.

"That's why I trust you, you are a true gentleman." She proclaimed.

"Furthermore, I would not take advantage of you after you had a drink. Also, I could see you were very tired, plus you could not hide from me that you are concerned about your friend Lili. All I wanted was for you to have a good restful night's sleep and wake up fresh as a daisy with enough energy to face the new day. As you are now!" he delighted.

"Thank you for your respect and for taking good care of me. Tell me, what have I done to deserve you?" Peony put her arms around Nathan's waist from behind, leaning her cheek onto his back.

He turned around and cupped her cheeks with his palms. "Your love inspires me to be a better man for you. A wonderful, loyal woman like you is the greatest thing a man could have in his life, but it takes a real man to realise and cherish her. Remember, love is patient, love is kind. It does not envy, it does not boast, it is not proud, it does not dishonour others, it is not self-seeking."

Peony carried over, "'It is not easily angered, it keeps no record of wrongs. Love does not delight in evil but rejoices with the truth,'" she recounted.

"'It always protects, always trusts, and always perseveres.'" then he wrapped her around his arms.

"Love never fails..." they both said simultaneously.

"Corinthians 13: 4-8. That is one of my favourite verses. I uphold those words like one of my most valuable treasures," Peony stated.

"I will not take your first time lightly. As I told you, it will happen naturally. I hope it will be an unforgettable experience for you," Nathan smiled and assured her.

He got the knives and forks out of the drawer and handed them to her.

"Beautiful sunshine out there. Should we have our breakfast in the garden?" Peony suggested.

"Great minds think alike! I was going to suggest the same thing," Nathan replied.

A gentle breeze swept Peony's silky black hair to her face while they were having their breakfast in the garden. She flipped her hair back, ran her fingers through it, and then tucked it behind her ear.

"Could you not do that? Please," Nathan with a straight face.

"Am I annoying you?" Peony asked.

"No, but you are driving me crazy!" he laughed.

"I am sorry," Peony said sarcastically, giggling.

"You look so damn sexy when you flip your hair like that. Don't make me lose my self-control!" he said with a pained look on his face.

"We need to prepare for church." Peony blushed, changing the subject. She stood up and picked up the plates.

"Ok, I won't tease you. What's your plan for the rest of the day after church?" Nathan asked while they were tidying up the table.

"Other than going to the Church, I haven't planned anything. I want to take a day off to recharge my energy," she said.

"Good idea. After Church, should we come back here, take it easy and relax?" Nathan asked.

"I would love to. I can't ask for a better place than with my mister, but promise me no teasing—deal?"

"Deal, I will behave myself," he laughed.

Peony looked at the pyjamas she was wearing and asked, "What are you going to do with Bella's clothes and other belongings?"

"I guess it is time to let go of them and make room for you. She is in here," Nathan said, putting his hand on his heart.

"It is fine with me if you want to keep some of her things.

She will always be remembered, and she is part of you. If you like, I can help you go through all her items. I would like to keep the collage above the piano—they are all your best memories with her. I would like to add a new one next to it for our new chapter if it is ok with you?" she asked.

"I love that idea," he said smiling.

After they came back from the Church, Peony lay at the poolside chair reading a fashion magazine. Nathan was inside the house and started sorting Bella's items from his bedroom.

"I guess all her clothes will go to Red Cross.' He thought while he was putting Bella's clothes on top of the bed.

Peony came inside to find him in their room surrounded by Bella's things, "Could I keep some of her clothes?" she asked, coming up behind Nathan and cuddling him.

"Oh! You must read my mind! When did you come in? I thought you were relaxing in the back garden."

"I came in just then. I can't bear you being out of my sight even one minute!" she said playfully.

"Oh! You smooth talker," he laughed.

"Can I help you in any way?"

"If you insist. All the clothes here are yours to sort out. Then I would like you to help me to clear the rest of the things from the wardrobe and make space for you. Is that ok?"

"Sure, alright. I feel unexplainably comfortable in these pyjamas," she said, perplexed at why she would.

"Well, she must like you! You should feel comfortable because you are not taking over for her. In fact, if she is watching us from heaven, she would be happy to know that we are deeply in love with each other, and you make me feel alive again."

"I feel quite emotional sorting out her things," Peony looked at the wardrobe.

"How about you sort out what you want to keep first? Will that make it easier for you?" he asked.

"I guess so," she said.

The rest of the items you don't want, you can put in this box, and we will decide what to do with them later," Nathan passed her a large plastic box.

As Peony sorted out Bella's items, she found a small box in the wardrobe behind the clothes. "Sweetie Bear, what's in this little box?" she passed it over to Nathan.

"I don't know. I haven't seen it before!" He took it from Peony's hand and opened it.

In the box were two letters. One was to 'My dear husband, Nathan.' The other said to 'Dear Nathan's future wife.'

Nathan and Peony looked at each other, not quite believing what they were seeing.

Puzzled, Nathan turned the letters over in his hand.

"From the handwriting, I know they are from Bella. Should we read them together?" Nathan asked nervously. Peony could see his lips were shaking. He sat down on the floor and propped himself up against the bed.

Peony sat next to him, "Yes, you read yours first."

Nathan carefully opened the letter. He started to read with a trembling voice.

"My Sweetie Bear,

If you are reading this letter, that means I am at home with my heavenly father.

Sorry I went there before you even though we planned to grow old together. Life is not always according to what we planned, there are twists and turns.

I want to let you know that I have lived a life without regrets because I was loved by you – my amazing man. I consider myself the luckiest woman in the world. Each day with you is a blessing. I lived my life with fullness and would not have chosen any other man to share it with than you.

It's ok to be sad, but just for a little while. You must be strong and move on with your life without me. Please take each day as it comes and enjoy it to the full. Promise me that you will open your heart to the next love of your life. You will know when it

will happen, just like the first time we met.
You have my blessings, and you know that. I will be your angel
from above, watching over you.
Love you to heaven and back!"
Bella

Nathan's letter ended with a kiss and a love heart.

Nathan tried his hardest to read the last words of the letter without breaking down. Peony gently stroked his back. They both were sitting there completely silent for a long while.

"Now it is your turn to open your letter," Nathan managed to find his voice, breaking the silence.

Peony nodded and carefully opened her letter.

Dear Nathan's future wife,

If you are reading this letter, congratulations, you are loved by the most amazing man. Thank you for loving him back and sharing your life with him.

By the time you sort through my belongings, I will know that he is ready to move on with his life.

I love him very much. All I want is for him to be happy and enjoy his life to the full.

There are a few tips for you though...

When the day is done, he will look forward to coming home sharing the cooking and sharing the quiet time with you. I want to remind you that he does not like the taste of anchovy even though he comes from an Italian background. Unbelievable, ha! Sometimes he acts like a big child. But hey, we all do! Just give him a hearty hug and a tender kiss, and he will be a man again.

Bella had added a smiley face to this line.

Peony was sobbing. Tears streamed down her eyes blocking her vision to continue reading.

Nathan wiped the tears from her eyes and put his arm around her, "Do you want me to read it for you?"

Peony nodded and handed the letter to him.

He cleared his throat and continued reading the letter, *"I am so happy you found each other. I assure you that the more you get to know him, the deeper you will fall in love with him. As I promised Nathan, I will be in heaven watching over both of you. With my best wishes and deepest love for both of you."* *Bella.*

Bella ended her letter with a love heart next to her name.

"Well, now you know that you have Bella's blessings," Nathan said.

"She is an extraordinary lady. I understand why you love her deeply. God bless her soul. God must have needed more angels like her in heaven. I feel overwhelmed. I'm still trying to digest all of this," Peony inhaled deeply.

"I am sorry. You are supposed to be relaxing today. Should we have a break?" Nathan got up. He put his hand out to reach Peony's and pulled her to her feet.

"Good idea. Should I make you a coffee?" Peony asked.

"Yes please, I'd love one. I got some almond croissants from the baker down the road too we can have."

"Yum. You know they are my favourite!" she said.

"Ay, our first meeting in Sky Paradise. I watched you with each bite. You looked as if you were in heaven," he smiled, remembering.

"I can't hide anything from you! You read me like a map!" she said.

While Peony was making the coffee, Nathan pulled the almond croissants out of the bag and put them on two plates.

"I am so pleased to see you so comfortable here, your future home; how do you like it?" Nathan asked.

"Yes, somehow I feel like I lived here before. Maybe my past life? Everything seems so familiar. I find everything in this house effortless!"

"How do you want our wedding to be?" Nathan asked.

"Packing up Bella's things, I know purple is her favourite

colour. I used to love dusty pink before I came to Australia, but for some strange reason, purple has become my favourite colour. I think I'll have a bouquet with purple flowers," she said.

"You can organise the theme and colours. You are the designer. I trust you," he said.

"I want the wedding to be small and simple yet unforgettable. I just want to invite immediate families and close friends. However, the location must be waterfront. Water always makes me calm and peaceful. I will design my wedding dress. Lucina, my friend, promised me she would make my wedding dress when we were in college. Now it is your turn to tell me, how would you like our wedding to be?"

"Well, having an Italian background, it is almost impossible to have a small and simple wedding. Would you meet in the middle ground with, say one hundred and fifty guests?" he asked.

"That is too many! In my mind, I was thinking it would be about fifty," she said.

"You're kidding me! Normally on my side of the family, we would be talking two to three hundred guests; I was being conservative saying one fifty," Nathan said.

"Oh my God! I probably only have about twenty guests!" Peony exclaimed.

"Trust me, with my mum and my dad, plus Andrew and Athena it will fill up one hundred and thirty guests without any problem," he said.

"You're making me feel nervous now," she said, worried.

"Relax!" after the wedding, let's go to China for our honeymoon. I would like to learn more about your culture and meet the rest of your friends and family there. We could even have another ceremony there. Would you like that?" Nathan asked.

"Now you've got me thinking. Can you imagine being in a new country and not being able to speak the language? Would you be comfortable?" she asked.

"That's the exciting part—getting into unknown territory! When I am with you, I can go anywhere because I'll have my own personal translator! Furthermore, I am planning to learn Chinese with the best Chinese teacher around, and guess what? I can kiss her if I like!" he said mischievously.

"Sure, if you do well, that may be your reward. I promise not to be jealous," she laughed.

"Can I have my first lesson?" Nathan asked eagerly.

"Right now?"

"Yes, why not! How do I say I love you in Chinese?" he asked.

"Wo ai ni," she replied.

"Wo ai ni," Nathan repeated after Peony.

"Now you can kiss your teacher," she giggled.

CHAPTER 28

Lili finished seeing her client at Gold Coast and came back to Sydney. When she opened the front door, Madam B heard the door open and stormed downstairs and screamed at her, "I have just got off a phone call from my client who complained about you! He was so disappointed with your service he demanded his money back! You have no idea who he is and how powerful he is in this country. He threatened that if I sent you again, he would destroy my business and send me to jail. Pack your bag and leave immediately. You're done!" she yelled.

"Whatever! You stupid old bitch!" She screamed back.

Madam B was so furious that she went upstairs to Lili's room, grabbed her clothes and threw them down the staircase. She kicked whatever remained on the stairs to the floor as she walked down. Then she got a couple of garbage bags out of the kitchen cupboard and angrily stuffed Lili's clothes into them before shouting, "Get out of here!"

Lili picked up the garbage bags, and her unpacked suitcase that had also been thrown down the staircase and raged, "Cross my heart and hope you die horribly. You fucking witch!" as she walked out the door and slammed it.

Lili walked to the Burwood Shopping area. It was still early in the morning, and none of the shops were open. She sat on a bench in front of an Asian grocery store, thinking about what to do and where to go. A short time later, the shop owner arrived and opened the store. She went in and bought a Chinese newspaper hoping to find a job and accommodation. With the paper tucked under her arm, she walked to the noodle bar nearby, ordered a bowl of noodle soup, and laid the paper open at the job section. 'Asian escort women wanted' she circled a few ads. After finishing the noodles, she made use of the public phone booth outside and made several enquiries. Finally, she got an appointment for an interview at Dee Why in the late afternoon.

By the time she got the train from Burwood to central and caught a bus to Dee Why it was almost dark. She was following the directions the owner gave to her, walking through a narrow lane. The neon sign saying "The Asian Massage Palace" caught her eye. It was an old building just off Pitt Water Road. As she rang the bell, a woman came out and let her in then led her into a room with curtains closed.

"Looks like you've done this type of job before." She said sizing Lili up. "I guess I don't need to explain to you what to do. I will get straight to the point. We will find you the customers and pay you fifty dollars for each. Sometimes if it is a good day, you will have up to eight to ten customers, depending on your popularity. The aim is to service as many bastards as you can. Get them in and get them out if you want to make more money. The more you give them what they want, the more repeat business you will build up and the less you will need to work hard to get new clientele."

"What about accommodation?" Lili asked.

"We have shared accommodation; it is two hundred dollars a week. Are you interested?" The Madam asked.

"I will take both the job and the accommodation," Lili replied.

"I will ask one of the girls to show you your room. It's just around the corner" she said.

"Ok. Thank you," she said, suddenly exhausted from the emotional day.

"Oh, will you take customers tonight?" the woman asked.

"Yes, I guess," Lili answered with a deep breath. All she really wanted to do was to have a good night's sleep, but she had no choice but to work—she needed the money.

A woman took her to the accommodation. It was a basic three-bedroom flat. There were five other women there. She had to share a bedroom with one other woman. Later on, she discovered that all five women came from China on holiday visas. The owner of the Massage Palace had held their passports for ransom and forced them to be sex slaves to have them returned.

One of the women begged Lili within minutes of entering her room, "Could you please help us? All we want is to go back to China to our family," she sobbed.

"How could I help you? I can't even help myself!" she sighed helplessly.

As soon as Lili got the money from her last client, she went out and tried to get some drugs even though it was after midnight. She was so drunk that she ended up wandering along the street and had no idea where she was.

A group of men in an old van drove past her. They suddenly stopped the car and reversed back. Two men got out of the car and grabbed her, pushing her into the car before driving off. She didn't even have the energy to scream. She knew what they would do to her. She could hear them taunting her and bragging to each other about how they would 'do her'. All she could hope for was that they finished quickly, so she could get out of the mess she was in once and for all.

They stopped the car at Warriewood and dragged her stumbling along into bushland, where they gang-raped her. Afterwards, one of them asked, "What are we going to do with this bitch now?"

The other one suggested, "We should finish her and bury her here."

Then another voice said, "You stupid or what?! If they find her body, we are definitely going to go to jail for a long time. I have a better idea. We drug her and dump her at the side of the road. If people find her, they won't believe her anyway because she'll look like the drugged dumb hooker she is. They'll think she overdosed and collapsed on the road."

One of them grabbed her hair and said, "Listen up bitch, if you tell the police who we are or what we did, we will find you and kill you."

"Anyway, the police won't believe you. You are just a waste of space junkie. No one cares about you. They have more important things to do. They won't waste their time on a whore."

Lili was hoping they would inject as much of the drug into her body as possible. She hoped she would never wake up again. She longed for release from the shitty life she had.

CHAPTER 29

As the paramedics pushed Lili into the emergency department at Mona Vale Hospital. One of them told the doctors, "Drug overdose."

"Any relatives listed to call?" asked the Doctor.

"She's not on the system, so that's a negative as far as we can tell. She did have a business card on her though, maybe call that number and see if anyone knows her." The paramedic said retrieving Lili's few things, including the business card, and handing them to the Doctor.

"Ok, thanks. Nurse? Please try this number and see if we can get in contact with her next of kin," he asked while examining Lili's dirty and limp body.

After being informed by the nurse that Lili was in the hospital, Peony and Jasmine rushed to the hospital, where they were told to wait in the waiting room. They were anxiously waiting for what seemed forever. Finally, one of the nurses came out from the emergency theatre and said, "She is in the safe zone now; you can both go in and see her. She is weak, so please do not stay for too long," she asked.

When the girls entered the room, they were shocked to see how poorly Lili looked and gasped. Lili slowly opened her eyes:

"What happened? Where am I?" Her face was so pale. She tried to put both her arms on the bed to support herself and sit up, but she was so weak that effort barely could be seen.

"Thank God! You are safe! You are in Mona Vale Hospital," Peony said with a soothing voice. She held Lili's hand with one hand and gently stroked her forehead with the other hand.

"Peony? How come I am here?" she asked weakly.

"The doctor said you took a drug overdose," Peony replied.

"How are you feeling?" Jasmine came a little closer and put her hand on Lili's other hand.

"Jasmine! You are here too? But how?" she asked barely above a whisper.

"Yes, it's me. You collapsed in the street at Warriewood. Someone called the police, and you were brought here." Jasmine explained then added, "Luckily, the nurse found Peony's business card in your handbag and contacted her."

Lili closed her eyes for a while, then she remembered what had happened and her eyes blinked rapidly, and her heartbeat raced. The sound on the monitor was beeping fast.

"Lili, Lili. How are you feeling?" Peony asked worriedly.

"I was gang raped. But please don't tell anyone, they said they would kill me," Lili sobbed.

"What! We need to report it to the police," Peony held her hand tighter, perhaps tighter than she should.

"No. They wouldn't believe that. To them, I am just a prostitute. What they know is that I was drunk and had a drug overdose. They probably think those men were my customers," she said despondently.

"But the truth is you were raped," Jasmine insisted she should speak to the police.

"You can't let those mongrels run free and get away with it," Peony tried hard to control her anger.

"I was working before I was raped, so I had already had sex

with a few men that night. How could I explain to the police?" she asked.

"You only need to do is tell the truth. Could you remember what they looked like?" Jasmine asked.

"No, I was too drunk, and it was dark. I only remember there were three of them. That's why I don't want to report it to the police. The police won't care about a hooker that's been raped," Lili sighed.

"I think they will care. Otherwise, you wouldn't have been taken to the hospital, and no one would have informed me you were here." Peony carried on. "I still think that you should report it to the police. Give them as much information as you can. If later on, you can recall what they looked like, you can let them know so they can add it to the report. I hope they will be caught so they can't do this to anyone else," she said hopefully.

"Even if the police try to help, what is the difference between those men paying for sex and those men who raped me? It's all the same. I don't care anymore," Lili stared ahead, then shook her head.

"The ones who paid had your consent Lili. The ones who raped you didn't. That's a big difference in a court of law," Peony explained.

"Can't you see? They'll think I'm a drunk and drugged hooker walking the street in the middle of the night, probably deserved it," Lili said.

"I hear what you are saying. Some people out there will victim blame, but not everyone will. They would argue that you shouldn't get drunk, shouldn't go out in the middle of the night or shouldn't dress too sexy. There is no excuse; a raper is a raper. Even if you were walking in the street in the middle of the night and naked. I wonder how many women were raped and did not bother to report it to the police because they didn't want people blaming them or thinking that they deserved it. We need to bring those criminals to justice, you and other women in your situation as well," Peony stated passionately and emotionally.

"I'm not sure. Give me some time to think about it, would you?" Lili said hesitantly.

"Of course, whatever your decision, we are here to support you," Peony put her hands on Lili's and looked into her eyes with compassion and understanding.

"If I listened to you in the beginning, I would not be in this situation," Lili said regrettably.

"Listen, Lili, we can't change what's happened in the past. From now on, everything is going to be alright. You have me and Jasmine by your side," Peony assured her.

"The doctor said you need to stay in here for observation for one or two more days, gain your strength again and then you can be discharged. I will come to pick you up then. You will stay with us at our place until you fully recover. Peony and I will take good care of you," Jasmine said.

"But I..."

"No buts! You are coming to our house, and that's the end of it." Jasmine said, looking over at Peony. "Actually, it was Peony's home, she rescued me and took me and my son Josh in," she told Lili.

"No, actually, it was Matt's home. But now it's also our home," Peony said smiling.

"Who's Matt? Your fiancé, the guy I saw with you that night?" Lili asked.

"No, not him. We have plenty of time to catch up and explain it all later. Right now, all you need to focus on is getting well my precious friend," Peony said, patting her shoulder.

The next morning, Jasmine got a call from the hospital to inform her that Lili was recovering well and would be ready for discharge that day. After she dropped Josh off at school, she went straight to the hospital to pick Lili up. When they got in the car, Lili asked, "Could you please make a detour to Mona Vale police station? I want to report the rape." Jasmine looked at her proudly, "Good on you Lili and thank you. Let's do it so they can work on putting those mongrels away," she said firmly.

"Where is Peony?" asked Lili.

"She is preparing for the fundraising event for the Grace Women and Children Centre," Jasmine replied.

"What's that?" Lili said interested.

"It's mainly for women and children who have been abused in some way. I will tell you more about it later." Jasmine said, helping Lili into the car.

When they arrived at Peony and Matt's Newport home, Jasmine carefully helped Lili out of the car, and slowly walked with her supporting her as she took each uncomfortable step towards the house. Even though Lili was on the mend, the injuries she had sustained from the rape and kicks she received, were still healing.

"What a beautiful garden!" Lili exclaimed, looking out the huge window overlooking the back garden.

"Thanks to our beautiful friends Matt and Peony, we are lucky to call such a lovely place home. I would never have the courage to leave my abusive partner Bob had it not been for Peony, Nathan, and Matt," she said.

"Who's Bob, Jasmine? Is that the father of your son Josh?" Lili asked.

Jasmine confirmed it was and told Lili how badly he had treated her, "He told me if I left him he will kill us, and he said anyone who helped us would also be killed. He kept saying Josh would grow up to become a criminal, and I would have to visit him in jail, all because I was such a useless woman." She paused and tried to stop the tears from coming, "Luckily, I ran into Peony, and she put an escape plan together. Within 24 hours, I was out of Bob's cruel hands, and now both Josh and I have a meaningful new life that we love very much," she said, reminiscing.

Lili moved toward her and hugged her old friend. She whispered, "I wished I had your courage and strength to break away from my toxic lifestyle and drug and alcohol addiction I've had in the past five years."

"Lili, you are stronger than you know. You need to make the decision to be who you were born to be. We will be by your side and support you until you succeed. Come, I will show you your bedroom." Jasmine led Lili to the bedroom Peony had prepared for her. At that very moment, Jasmine had a flashback to the day Peony showed Josh and her their room on that first night of their freedom.

"Let's have a long afternoon tea and catch up. I have lots to tell you." Jasmine said, switching on the jug.

She handed the tea to Lili, "We will have the afternoon tea in the back garden. Could you carry the tray with the teapot, cups, saucers and spoons out and put it on that table? I will bring the tea and the blueberry muffins out. I can't wait to show you the garden later. You'll love what I've planted in it," Jasmine said.

"It's so peaceful out here," Lili observed, putting the tea set on the table and taking a deep breath.

"Indeed! See those herbs and vegetables over there. That's my new hobby. This garden helps me keep grounded," Jasmine said, pouring some tea into the cup and offering it to Lili.

"Um, nice tea, very familiar. What's the flavour? Don't tell me, don't tell me… let me have one more sip. Ah! Lychee! Am I right?" she said, guessing.

"Yes. You are right. Do you like it?" Jasmine asked.

"I love it!" said Lili. Then Lili asked, "Tell me, what do you mean by grounded?"

"That's the technic I learned during counselling. I suffered from Post-Traumatic Stress Disorder, but I am on my way to restoring my mental health. When bad memories come into my mind, and I feel I will have a panic attack, I use my five senses to help myself to be grounded. Five things I can see; four things I can touch; three things I can hear; two things I can smell; one thing I can taste. In this garden, I can find all these things," Jasmine explained.

"I have never heard of that before. When I found I could not cope, the only thing I found to help myself through it was drugs and alcohol."

"Now you know there are more options to choose from. Knowledge is power!" Jasmine had a bit of the muffin.

"You must think I am so stupid and ignorant," Lili said.

"No. Lili, you are not. You just got in with the wrong people. Like I did with Bob," Jasmine said.

"All these bastards just use my body. There are no decent men out there. If there were any, they wouldn't look at a woman like me regardless."

"That was exactly what I thought after my abusive relationship. I thought nobody would ever love me. I am damaged goods. Probably only those men like Bob who use women as slaves would be interested in me. But my psychologist told me something profound that I would never forget. She told me never to waste my time worrying about trying to capture the moths fluttering around, and instead focus on looking after my garden and growing beautiful flowers. A beautiful garden will attract beautiful butterflies, not moths. So, in other words, we don't need to worry about anything else but focus on rebuilding our lives. Then we will attract beautiful things in our lives," she said.

"That seems to make sense!" Lili said, pondering on it.

Jasmine smiled and continued, "But you know what? Now,

every time Bob enters my mind, I use another technique she showed me. I have four phases I repeat. 'I love you, I forgive you, thank you, goodbye.'"

"What?! How can you love, forgive, and thank him? He almost ruined your life and your son's life! I can't understand it," Lili shook her head.

"It's called mental and spiritual cleaning. I love him as a human, but not what he did to me. I forgive him so I will not let hatred take root in my heart, and I have the space for love. I thank him for the experiences so I can understand and help others. I say goodbye so I can let go of the past and move on to start a new life."

"I can't do that! How can you forgive and love and thank someone who has hurt you that much? I just don't get it!"

"As you learn and grow, you will understand. I cannot promise you it will happen overnight. It will take time to practice. One day at a time. Once you grasp it, you feel the peace and freedom within. Then you will feel the harmony with the outside world," Jasmine explained.

"Too much for me to comprehend," Lili said confused.

"Just park things aside. Wait until your mind is clearer, then revisit it then." Jasmine changed the subject, "Come, let's pick some vegetables and herbs for tonight's dinner," she said cheerily.

"See these bitter melons? I love them. They are perfect for cleaning the digestive system."

"I don't like the bitterness," Lili grumbled.

"That's the thing. Many people don't like them with the first bite, but if you chew for a little longer, the bitter taste passes to a unique sweet, tangy flavour, just like life. Sometimes the sweetness is hidden at the beginning of the bitter experience," she winked.

"Still not convinced," Lili shook her head.

"Have you ever heard the expression 'If you eat food like medicine, you will not eat medicine like food?' I will cook some this evening. Stir fry with scrambled eggs, garlic and oyster sauce—my grandma's recipe. I encourage you to try it. You might find you like it this time."

"Fine, I don't trust you, but I trust your grandma. If it is Grandma's recipe it must be good!" Lili laughed.

"Hey, let me tell you about something else pretty cool too," Jasmine said.

"What?"

"Tomorrow, we have a fundraiser at the Grace Women and Children Centre. All the funds raised—one hundred percent go to running the centre. Andrew, Peony and Nathan's friend is the founder. He provided the place. Peony and Nathan manage the centre. I work part-time there to manage the accounts and teach women to manage their finances. A group of volunteers help out and provide their services for free to anyone who needs them. There are volunteer psychologists providing counselling to the women to help them with any mental issues they have so they can get back to normal life. Businesswomen like Peony provide skills training. There are also nurses and doctors. The place is quite well-established now. Each room has an ensuite and contains every essential thing women and children need— even spare clothes. Imagine most of those women and kids forced to leave their homes to free themselves from an abusive situation with only the clothes they have on and nothing else? If you are well enough, I would like you to come and see it. Peony and Nathan will be there."

"I would love to," Lili replied.

Jasmine looked at her watch, "Oh, it's time to pick up Josh now. Do you want to stay here or come with me?"

"I will stay here. If this is OK with you."

"Other than the bitter melons, what else do you feel like for tonight's dinner?" Jasmine asked.

"You don't need to cook anything else. I still feel quite full from the muffin."

"How about some chicken and rice soup in our Chinese style?" Jasmine suggested.

"Oh! Now that sounds good. Exactly what I need," she said.

That night while Jasmine was sleeping, Lili was still wild awake. Her drug addiction was kicking in, and she twisted and turned in her bed. Finally, she could not handle it anymore. She got up quietly, and on tippy toes, she reached for Jasmine's handbag, which was up on the shelf in her wardrobe closet. She took the wallet out quickly and quietly walked to the front door. Suddenly, she recalled what Jasmine had said to her during the day, "You are stronger than you know." She collapsed in the hallway, breaking down and crying aloud, "I don't want to do this anymore. God! Help me!"

Her cries woke Jasmine up, who quickly ran out of her bedroom and found Lili sitting on the floor, leaning against the front door, sweating, and shaking with her wallet beside her.

Jasmine sat down next to Lili, "I know it's not easy." Jasmine acted as if she did not see her wallet beside her. She stayed on the floor with Lili and put her arm around her until she calmed down. Then she got up and helped Lili up, "I will make you a cup of camomile tea with honey, it will make you feel better and help your sleep."

Lili handed the wallet back to Jasmine. "I'm so sorry. Why do you still try to help me? I am not worthy of your help!" she exclaimed.

"You are my friend. Friends help each other. Peony helped me, and now I am in a position to help you. Can you still remember when we were on the airplane to Australia? One of the instructions was that in an emergency, when the masks were dropped down, we had to attend to ourselves first and then help others. Now is the time to attend to yourself and put on your 'mask'. Sometimes to help others, we must help ourselves first. If you make better choices and take care of yourself right now, you will be in a position to help others in the future. We make the right choices to not only benefit ourselves but also benefit our loved ones, our community, and others." Jasmine helped her sit on the couch comfortably. Then she went to make the tea and handed it to Lili. "Remember, you are not alone. We are doing it together."

The next day, Peony met Jasmine and Lili for lunch at the Palm Beach Café.

"Good afternoon ladies. Sorry for being late. With Nathan, time always seems to pass so quickly," she said, smiling.

"You look fabulous. So, tell us what happened last night?" Lili gave Peony a cheeky look.

"Nothing! Believe me, not what you are thinking. We slept in separate bedrooms." Peony replied.

"Just you and him in the house. You must have been tempted?" Lili questioned.

"If I tell you I wasn't, I'd be lying. Gosh, he looked so damn sexy in the kitchen washing the dishes," she laughed light-heartedly.

"Don't you need to try before you buy?" Lili asked jokingly.

"The answer is no. Somehow I have a gut feeling that everything will fall into place," Peony said with a proud smile.

"Yes, sure, FALL INTO the RIGHT PLACES," Lili said, emphasising the words.

"Don't be too cheeky," Peony blushed.

"Peony said she wants to save herself for her wedding day," Jasmine explained.

"Peony, I don't think I could ever do that. Anyway, I am damaged goods, a bitch. Those men could not wait to jump in bed with me, and not for love either. They were just like mongrel dogs in the street. When they had the urge, they just found a bitch to jump onto, had their way, and left," Lili sighed.

"Lili, I want you to change your mindset about how you see yourself. Imagine that you had a treasure box. You put an irreplaceable treasure inside the box and locked it. Will you give the key to anyone who wants that treasure? Or do you give the key to the one you can trust, love, and respect? The one you know who will protect and cherish the treasure inside the treasure box?"

"Of course, I only want to give the key to the one I trust and know would look after the treasure."

"You are the irreplaceable treasure. From now on, do not give the key to any man who wants you. Keep the key in a safe place until you find that special one who deserves you—the treasure. Will you do that?" Peony asked.

"Peony, I am different from you. You worked hard to achieve what you wanted in life. You have upheld your true value and dignity. You deserve respect. I am nothing. Nobody. Worthless as those bastards said."

Peony took a $100 note out of her purse and said, "This is going to pay for our lunch. Lili, please tell me the value of this note."

"I know I am stupid, but not that stupid! I still recognise it is one hundred dollars." Lili said with an offended tone.

Peony crunched up the one hundred-dollar note, "Now, could you tell me what the value of this note is? Will the staff accept this note?"

"Still one hundred dollars. They will take it. Now you treat me like an idiot, and I don't like it" Lili started getting upset.

"Well, don't say you are worthless anymore. You made a few mistakes. Your life may look a bit crunched up at this moment, but you have not lost your value. You are my friend, and I know your value. I don't look at the crunched up. Lili, you are wonderfully made. From now on, do not let anyone or anything make you doubt your value. Furthermore, true friends will not judge and condemn you for the mistakes you made, but love you for getting through them and trying to better yourself."

"Peony, you might not judge and condemn me, but the rest of the world will!" Lili exclaimed.

"Can I tell you a story that happened about two thousand years ago?" Peony asked.

"I have nothing else to do. So go ahead, as long as you have time," Lili responded.

"I will take as long as it needs to make you see your value. But let's order our lunch first. I like the grilled salmon and salad. How about you girls?"

"It sounds good, I'll have mine with chips," Jasmine said.

"I will have the same as yours Peony," Lili said.

"Great!" Peony waved the waitress to come over to take their order.

"Ok, Peony, story time," Lili urged.

"From Chinese history, we learned that ancient Chinese men could legally have as many women as they want. But a woman who committed adultery would be put in a cage and dropped in water to die by drowning. It was similar to the biblical time about two thousand years ago. Men can have more than one wife. But if a woman committed adultery the law said that she must be stoned to death. One day the Pharisees brought a woman before Jesus and wanted her charged with adultery..."

"Hang on, that same Jesus you mentioned on the first night we arrived in Australia? And we thought he is your imaginary friend?" Lili interrupted.

"Yes. The same Jesus." She smiled and continued, "So they challenged Jesus to judge the woman. Jesus thought for a moment then he replied, 'He who has no sin, let him cast the first stone at her.' The accusers and congregants departed realizing not one of them is without sin either. Jesus asked the woman if anyone condemned her, and she answered, 'No.' Jesus told her that he also had not condemned her and asked her to go and sin no more."

"So, the moral of this story is that no one is perfect, and no one has the right to judge. The most important thing is that I do not go back to that stupid lifestyle anymore. Is that right?" Lili asked.

"You got it! When you fall, don't be afraid to get up again. Try again, dream again, and live again. Do not let the hard lessons you receive harden your heart. Put one foot in front of the other. We are here for you. Allow us to walk through this journey with you," Peony concluded putting her hand on top of Lili's.

"I don't want to give you guys trouble. It is not your responsibility anyway. I am the one who made the wrong choices, so I am the one who should face the consequences and make it right," Lili stated.

"Lili, please count us in," Jasmine insisted.

"Thank you. I don't think I can do it on my own anyway. I guess I need all the help I can get. I just don't want to become your baggage that's all," Lili said.

"Lili, if it is ok with you, I will organize a meeting for you to see one of our psychologists, she specialises in helping people with addictions and trauma. Her name is Fiona. She is a friend of mine. She is not only very professional and experienced but also compassionate and understanding. I think you will feel comfortable with her," Peony told her.

"Oh, Fiona, you will like her!" Jasmine said enthusiastically, "Remember I told you about my counselling? It was with Fiona. She explained to me the typical cycles of abuse patterns and helped me to understand what Bob did to me that was not my fault. I have the right to walk away from anyone who harms me and my boy. She also gave me the strategies to build my confidence step-by-step including some techniques to handle anxiety and panic attacks, which I used to have all the time. One of them I mentioned yesterday to you was the grounding technique. Slowly but surely, we will make our way through this," Jasmine said.

"Together, we are going to get you through this," Peony assured.

Lili put her hand on Peony's and gently squeezed it "Thank you Peony and Jasmine. You are the strongest people I know. You are my strength and my rock." She said gratefully.

"I thank my tough childhood. Struggling and suffering builds resilience and compassion. I am sure you will be stronger as each day comes. Today is the day we celebrate the new life ahead of us. We can't change what happened to us in the past. But we have the power to re-build a new life out of what seemed a hopeless situation. 'Ash for beauty' that's what my mum always said," Peony smiled and asked, "Another coffee?"

"Sure, I need the caffeine before my addiction shakes kicks in again," Lili said which made them all laugh.

"After lunch should we take a lovely easy walk along Palm Beach?" Peony suggested.

Jasmine looked at her watch and replied, "I am sorry I need to pick up Josh. You two enjoy the walk," she said rushing out.

"Alright. No need to prepare dinner. On our way back, we will go to the Chinese restaurant at Avalon to get some takeaway," Peony called out after her.

"Sounds like a plan! I will take Josh to the playground for a while. See you two at home," Jasmine said as she slipped out the restaurants front entrance.

"Peony, can we walk up to the lighthouse? I can imagine

how amazing it would be standing up there!" Lili pointed to the Palm Beach lighthouse.

"Yes, the view up there is breathtaking. You can see it from the Central Coast on one side, and from Manly Beach on the other side. But not today. I think you need to take it easy, your body is still on the mend. Why don't we just stroll along the beach instead? We can make another time to go up there when your body becomes stronger."

"Ok. You are right."

Peony asked for the bill and paid for it, "Let's walk across to the beach."

"Since the first day I met you, I knew you were a clever lady. You warned me about Madam B's free accommodation and easy money being a scam and it was. You are so level headed and calm. How can you keep yourself away from things that aren't good for you in life?"

"I just use my gut feeling and common sense to tell me what kind of person someone is. In most cases, if it is too good to be true then it probably is. For instance, when the average student earns around three to four hundred dollars a week, Madam B's ad said one thousand dollars a weekend. I asked myself what special skills or knowledge I would have to have for someone to be willing to pay that kind of money, and what also would I have to sacrifice."

"I never thought of that!" Lili said amazed.

"Lili, from now on surround yourself with people who want to see you succeed for you, not for them. You need people around you who are wise and have your best interests at heart, not the ones who want to make money off you. Good people are the ones who will help you to bring out the best in yourself. Be ready to expect the best!" Peony splashed the water on Lili and ran. Lili ran after her and splashed it back to her. They were like two little innocent, happy girls on the beach. Then they both walked side by side to the end of the beach in comfortable silence. The only sound was the rhythmic pulse of the gentle waves bringing the sand to the shore. The late afternoon sun stretched its arm around the horizon to hug the beach with its warm light. The golden sand responded to the sunlight sparkling back, until the sun turned saffron painting the sky.

CHAPTER 30

Lili worked in Peony's boutique as a shop assistant, and also became involved in helping at the Grace Centre during her spare time. Now and then, the old life still tried to claw her back, however, the knowledge that her old lifestyle no longer served her kept her on the straight and narrow. With the help of her friends and also professional counselling, she gradually realised her past didn't reflect who she truly was. With her strong mind and determination, she had started to transform and evolve into living a more meaningful new life, and she was happy about it.

Peony was nervous about the big wedding. She suggested Jasmine and Lili meet her at the Manly Starfish Chinese Restaurant for a long Yum Cha lunch so they could all help her plan her wedding and give her some moral support.

Peony planned to catch the ferry from Circular Quay to Manly, while Jasmine would drive her car there with Lili. After lots of hunting to find a park, she finally found a parking spot on the side street close by. As they got out of the car, Jasmine recognised Bob walking towards them. She whispered to Lili, "Oh God! That is my ex—Bob walking towards us." Jasmine began panicking and didn't know what she should do.

Lili replied quietly, "Go, find Peony in the restaurant, stay safe there with her, and I will meet you in a few moments. Let me handle him," she said firmly.

Lili turned around and undid the top two buttons of her shirt dress to reveal her cleavage. She then turned back around and walked towards Bob. As she got close to him, she said provocatively, "Excuse me, I am lost. Could you please tell me how to get to the Novotel Hotel?" Lili knew the hotel well because she used to meet her clients every so often there.

Bob disregarded her question. Instead, he answered her with another question, "Do you know the woman who was next to you?"

"You mean that woman I just walked past and tried to ask directions from? Oh, she hasn't got a clue what I was asking. Either she is not familiar with this area, or she could not understand English." Lili rolled her eyes dramatically, acting like she did not know Jasmine.

"That woman looks like my ex-wife," he said with a frown.

"You are such a drop-dead gorgeous and sexy man, why do you need to chase your ex-wife? Anyway, that woman is kind of ugly and dumpy. There are many much better-looking women dying to have you, I bet!" Lili licked her lips and winked at him as she tried to use all her old tricks to make Bob forget Jasmine.

"So, tell me. Do you know where the Novotel Hotel is?" she leaned forward and made sure her cleavage drew Bob's attention.

"Sure. I could walk you there, and we could have a drink if you have some time," Bob said, gazing at her chest.

"Oh, I am sorry, not today; I am meeting my mum there," she said casually.

"I am happy to join you."

"No, not this time. But if you give me your telephone number. I will call you and go out for a drink with you. Maybe even more than a drink." Lili said suggestively, giving him another wink.

Bob put his hand in his pockets and tried to search for a pen and paper. He couldn't find any.

Meanwhile, Lili took a pen out of her handbag and said, "Tell me your number." After writing down the number, she remembered her act, "Now, how about those directions to the Novotel?" she asked. Bob gave her the directions, all the while looking at her cleavage; at one point, he even turned his head to peer over her shoulder to get a glimpse of her bottom. "He's so disgusting," Lili thought to herself.

She thanked him, and keeping up her act, as she began walking away, she turned and put her hand up to her ear in a… 'I'll call you' gesture. "Call you tonight!" she said brightly in the direction of the Novotel.

Scanning to keep an eye on Bob, she saw him get in his car and drive off. "Finally!" Lili muttered as she looped back around to the restaurant.

"Here comes Lili," Jasmine said with great relief when she saw Lili walking into the restaurant.

"I was so worried about you!" Jasmine pulled the chair out for her.

Lili sat down and took the cup of tea that Peony handed to her. She had a sip and replied, "Easy peasy. I have seen quite a few men like Bob or even worse than him. I know how to handle these types of scumbags." Then she added, "What I can't understand is how he is still walking the streets—he should be locked up!"

"They need to make the consequences and penalties for domestic violence heavier. That would make them think twice about hurting women and children. There is much more that needs to be done. Most people still think they should not get involved in a private family matter, but domestic violence is not just a family matter. It is a crime. There should be education programs at the workplace and home for prevention. Especially at schools while they are young. Educate them on what is unacceptable and give them clear guidelines and firm boundaries so that they will not become abusers or victims of abuse in the future." Peony stressed.

Jasmine agreed, "The other day, I asked Josh if he wanted to see his daddy. He said no because he didn't want Daddy to hurt us anymore. He told me he doesn't hate Daddy. I asked him what would make him say that, and he said because maybe his daddy didn't have a good daddy to show him how to be a good one."

"You would be surprised. Some people still can't understand the seriousness of domestic violence. They still believe children should see their parents no matter how abusive they are. They don't know that if children are forced to stay in abusive families, it causes them more harm than good and in some cases, even puts them in more danger. The most dangerous or even life-threatening time is when women are in the process of leaving or shortly after leaving an abusive relationship." Peony stated.

"I believe all parents who are protecting their children from abuse will do all they can to prevent their children from going back into an abusive environment again," Jasmine stated.

"If it is that bad, why don't you just leave?" Lili asked.

"It's not that simple. Leaving a violent relationship is much harder than people think. There are lots of other elements that influence it. Some stay for religious, cultural or social pressure, while others feel embarrassed to admit their partner is an abuser and have no one they can turn to for help. They fear how others will react negatively towards them and fear being judged, blamed, pitied or looked down on." Jasmine shook her head sadly and continued, "In some cases, relatives may point the finger or blame the victim for even hinting they want to leave. They isolate the victim and make them feel wrong for leaving their abusive partners. Also, many survivors believe if they stay things will go back to how they were at the beginning—it's called the Love Bombing Stage. Most perpetrators start with emotional abuse by chipping away at the victims' self-confidence, self-worth, and independence to prevent the victim from recognising they are in an abusive situation. Also, the perpetrator manipulates the victim to increase their dependency on them. On average, a person in an abusive relationship will attempt to leave seven times before finally leaving for good."

"Gosh, Jasmine, you are a fast learner! Looks like you gained a lot of knowledge from your counselling courses," Peony said astonished.

"Is it the course you are both attending in the evening?" Lili asked.

"Yes, two evenings a week. To help others with compassion, strategies and knowledge while providing access to resources they need." Jasmine looked at Peony knowingly.

"We need to provide the survivors with as much information, wisdom, and skill as we can so they recognise the abusive patterns and understand that these behaviours should not be tolerated," Peony added.

"Well, I would like to enrol in the course. Could you guys please let me know when the next one is available?" Lili eagerly asked.

"I will give you the information tonight when we are home," Jasmine stated.

"We also learn how to provide financial resources such as crisis funding from the government if needed. Once they become financially independent, they know they can choose to leave their abusive partner for good. You would be shocked by how many women (especially mothers with children) can't leave their abusive partners because they worry about becoming homeless. After the women are free from domestic violence, often the child support from the father is minimal so it's important they have access to funds. In Jasmine's case she doesn't get any child support," Peony explained.

"We are the lucky ones because you provide us with a home

and your ongoing financial support until we are able to stand on our own two feet. Many aren't that lucky," Jasmine gave an appreciative look to Peony.

"That is the least we could do. If I was in your situation, I am sure you will do the same to help me," Peony stated.

"Even though I got all the support that I needed, I was emotionally exhausted and felt like I was on the edge of a mental breakdown. I cannot imagine those women in an abusive relationship having to face all of this alone," Jasmine sighed.

"We are going to launch a campaign called 'It's not ok, mate.' This campaign encourages mates to watch out for their friends and family members if they see violence towards women and children. They are encouraged to stand up for the women and children, confront abusers and say it's not ok, or report them," Peony divulged.

"I am so glad to be part of all this, even if it is a small part," Jasmine said.

"You are a great example of going from a victim to a victor, from a survivor to a thriver. We are so proud of you," Peony gently rubbed her back.

"Ok, the spotlight is focused on you now. We are going to talk about your wedding. How can we help you?" Lili enquired.

"Nathan said the wedding would be at least one hundred and fifty guests. I counted on all my fingers and toes the number of guests I have on my side. Many of his side of family and friends I haven't even met. You guys have no idea how nervous I am!" she said.

"What things else is worrying you, Peony?" Lili asked.

"I want to make him proud when I walk down the aisle," Peony explained.

"You have already made him proud by just being you! I can

tell from the way he looks at you. Wow! This is the first time I have ever seen you insecure and vulnerable Peony," Jasmine expressed.

"That's why I need your moral support," Peony stated.

"It is our turn to support you. Right, Jasmine?" Lili asked.

"Yep, just let us know what you need," Jasmine agreed.

"I need you both to be my bride's maids. I will be more grounded if I know you are both beside me," she said.

"That would be our privilege and honour. I am so excited!" Jasmine looked at Lili and squealed with childlike delight."

"What do you both think of tiffany blue for bride's maids' dresses?" Peony asked.

"I am not sure. It seems a bit too loud for me," Jasmine stated.

"How about purple and pink?"

"That sounds nice," Jasmine replied.

"I agree," Lili said.

"My friend Lucina will make my wedding dress and all the bride's maids' dresses. After lunch, shall we go shoe shopping?" Peony asked.

"Do you think Bob is still hanging around this area?" Jasmine asked.

"How about we drive to the Pitt Street in the city? There are few shoe shops near my shop, and it's doubtful Bob will be lurking around there." Peony suggested.

"Sounds like a great idea. We can discuss the hairstyles while we are driving there," Lili said.

On their way to the city, they talked some more about Peony's upcoming wedding; Lili announced, "I want to let you both know that I am thinking of going back to Shanghai, China, to help those who were trapped in the same situation I was. The idea has been on my mind for some time now."

"Follow your heart. We will fully support you. Right, Jasmine?" Peony looked at Jasmine for her seal of approval.

"I am glad that you have found a purpose. Definitely, I will be there for you," Jasmine agreed.

"My friend Kang returned to China to start his Business in Shanghai. I will let him know of your intention. When you are ready to go there, I will make sure he can give you a helping hand," Peony addressed.

"That would be wonderful! I need all the support!" Lili replied.

"When are you planning to go there?" Jasmine asked.

"In the next few months," Lili replied.

"We are going to miss you!" Jasmine signed.

"Hey! I won't be gone forever. I will be back for Peony's wedding. Anyway, it's only a nine-hour flight—you could come to visit me!" She said, smiling broadly.

"We can handle that!" Peony said, excitedly.

"I have Josh. I can't just get up and go!" Jasmine said.

"You can come with him during the school holidays. No excuse!" Lili said.

"I am sure between Matt, Tom and Nathan, they will be able to look after Josh. He needs role models and father figures in his life to show him how to be a decent man. You just need to trust them and give them the opportunity," Peony added.

"Don't get me wrong, I trust them. I do. I just don't want to burden anyone," Jasmine explained.

"Actually, it is a blessing, not a burden. Nathan needs the practice before he becomes a father to kids of his own," Lili glanced at Peony with a cheeky smile.

"Ha! When we're ready, give us time to get married first!" Peony blushed.

CHAPTER 31

"Peony, since I started to wear your designs, I feel so ladylike. People have also started to show me more respect and are more polite towards me too." Lili mentioned to Peony while helping her change the window display for the new season.

"That's great Lili!" Peony said. "How you feel is important. Positive feelings and vibes attract positive people and opportunities. When you dress and act like a queen, you will attract the king!" Peony said, laughing.

"I wish I knew then what I know now!" Lili sighed regretfully.

"Well, you do now, and that's all that matters," she said.

"I still want to look sexy and show off my long legs though," Lili admitted.

"You got a beautiful figure! Why not! You still can wear a mini skirt, but five centimetres longer than what you wore previously. The ideal length is just like the one you are wearing now. Take Princesses Diana, for example, she always dressed elegantly but still looked sexy."

"That's true. She always dressed with such class, yet she was always sexy too." Lili sighed.

"Hey, don't be too hard on yourself." Peony reminded her.

"I am trying! But how do I know that I am not overdoing it?"

"The golden rule is, when you are dressed in public, make sure people cannot see the colour of your undies and bra." Peony giggled.

"I am serious!" Lili protested.

"Like many other skills. Practice, practice, and practice until you get it. Try as many styles as you can while standing in front of the mirror to see if the style enhances and achieves the look that you want. Then close your eyes and feel it. If you feel fabulous, uplifted, and comfortable, then that is a suitable outfit."

"Lucky my bestie is a fashion designer! Thank you!" She glanced at Peony with an appreciative smile and added, "What made you want to be a fashion designer?"

"Growing up, I heard stories of my grandmother narrowly escaping foot binding. Seeing how my mother lived through the Cultural Revolution in China, where all they could wear was grey or khaki, I longed to see colourful clothing again. I wanted to create stylish, comfortable, colourful ranges and styles and encourage women to be themselves and showcase their personalities."

"Style really isn't just about clothing, is it?" Lili tried to comprehend.

"Not at all, remember the best make-up is your smile. The best thing you can wear is your confidence. Whatever you have inside will show outside. Let your personality and character tell the story. You gained respect not just because you were wearing my designs but also because you changed your behaviour and attitude. I am so glad to see you become the person you are now. You are a beautiful person inside and out. You deserve respect and 'good' attention you are getting now," Peony stated.

"I still need your help finding the right clothes to wear on my return to China though." She said.

"Sure, you can take as many pieces as you want from the shop. I will help you mix and match them so you can wear heaps of outfits but still travel lightly." She said.

"That will be wonderful," Lili said happily.

"Have you booked the air ticket yet?"

"Yes. I booked it yesterday."

"When do you fly out?"

"In three weeks' time."

"I have a spare hour now if you want to take a break from the window display and look through the designs and choose a few? We'll do that, then head to Chinatown for dinner. What do you think?" Peony asked.

"Sounds fantastic!"

"I will also call Kang tonight and let him know your arrival date so he can pick you up from the airport."

"Are you sure that will be ok?"

"Yes. I know him well. Otherwise, I would not ask him."

After dinner, Peony dialled Kang's number and put the call on speaker phone.

While they were waiting for Kang to pick the phone up, Peony whispered, "You will like him."

"Wei! (Hello)," the voice said in Mandarin.

"Hello, my precious friend. How are you?" Peony responded.

"Hello Peony!" I am very well, thank you. How are you?! It's so great to hear from you!" Kang answered with excitement.

"I'm great. The shop is going well, and we're busy making wedding plans. Listen, I have a very good friend planning to go back to Shanghai. She has a mission that is an extension of the work we do here in Australia. She wants to save women who are trapped and forced into prostitution. We need your help."

"Wow! That's an amazing mission. I am more than happy to

help."

"Her name is Lili, and she is here with me now. You are on speaker." Peony said.

"Hi, Lili," Kang said cheerily.

"Hi, Kang," Lili replied smiling.

"It is a very good cause. You have no idea how badly the 'escort' business is affecting Chinese society right now. While their living standard is rising, the moral standard is decreasing. You know the history of China. This poor treatment of women goes hundreds and thousands of years ago—back to when men openly had as many concubines as possible. The more they had, the higher their status was in society. Some women are tricked into escorting and end up being held captive and forced to be sex slaves for gangs of men in China. Some are even sent overseas to work in prostitution," he said.

"I know," Peony sighed. "That's why I recommended Lili to connect with you. I am sure you two will start something amazing over there. And, of course, you have all our support here from Australia."

"Lili, when are you arriving?" Kang asked.

"In the next few weeks. I have just booked the air ticket. Peony will send you all the details of my flight when I've received it." Lili advised.

"You will just make it here in time for the Chinese New Year. Please allow me to come to pick you up at the airport, and I will organise a place for you to stay too."

"Thank you, Kang! Greatly appreciated." Lili responded.

"It's my pleasure; I look forward to meeting you."

It was a beautiful summer day in January. Peony was driving Lili to the airport. Jasmine was sitting next to Lili at the back of the car and noticed Lili was quiet. The only sound she could hear was Lili's heavy breathing. Despite the car air-conditioning being on, Lili's face was covered with sweat. She ran her fingers through her long hair and tried to comb it back and unstick her hair from her sweating forehead.

"Lili, how are you feeling?" Jasmine asked, concerned.

"I... I don't know if I really can face the giant monster within my head. Going back to China to face my past, which still... um.... haunts me... when I think about it," Lili fidgeted with her hair.

"I know it is not easy. I want you to know that you are not fighting the monster alone. We are here to support you," Jasmine held her hands and squeezed them a little tighter than usual.

"You will be there just in time for the Chinese New Year! Kang will support you and take care of you." Peony glanced at her from the rear vision mirror.

"I do look forwards to the Chinese New Year and all the yummy food," Lili seemed to relax a little bit.

"I am glad that there is something that you look forward to! Kang has already contacted many of his friends. He told me last night on the phone about the local government, some companies and charity organizations who want to be involved in this project too! When you get there, you can present them with your vision and see how they can support your mission. Once you have them on the same page, then we can campaign throughout the country. Remember, changing lives one person at a time," Peony reminded her.

"Peony, I still remember that story you told me once—about an old man who got up early every morning to go to the beach. He picked up a starfish that had washed ashore and put them back into the sea before sunrise to save their lives. A young man passing by said to him, 'You old fool. There are too many starfish, you can't save them all, and you're wasting your time.' The old man picked up another starfish, threw it back to the sea, and replied, ' At least I saved this one.' You may not save them all, but at least you can go out there and do your best to help those young women. It is such a good cause. If I didn't have Josh to depend on me, I would come with you and help you," Jasmine said.

"It may be overwhelming, but with you guys supporting and encouraging me, I think I can face the challenge ahead of me," Lili breathed with a deep sense of relief.

"We are very proud of you," Jasmine said.

"We are here. I will drop both of you off at the departure drop-off zone. Once I park the car I will walk back and join you inside." Peony said.

"Just drop me here. You both can go back." Lili responded, worried about parking fees.

"Don't be silly, we're not going to just drop you off and leave you! We will help you with your luggage and wait with you until you board the plane," Jasmine said, getting out of the car and walking around to the back of the vehicle to retrieve Lili's luggage from the boot.

"Peony, we will wait for you at the Qantas check-in", Lili waved and shouted to Peony as she drove off.

As Lili was checking in her luggage, Peony caught up with them. Lili suggested, "Should we go over there for coffee?"

"That's the same coffee lounge where Matt proposed to me," Peony said, reminiscing.

"What! I thought you both were besties. You are going to marry Nathan!" Lili said in pure astonishment.

"Matt and I are still besties. It's a long story. I will tell you over the coffee." Peony answered.

Once they sat down, Lili could not wait any longer and asked, "So, tell me what happened between you and Matt."

"I was married to Matt for a few years. We love each other deeply, but our love is Philia love."

"What's that? I have never heard of it." Lili looked at Jasmine, confused and more than a little shocked at what she had just heard.

Jasmine put her arms open and said, "Don't ask me! I don't have a clue. Ask Peony."

"There are eight types of love, according to the Ancient Greeks. Philia love is one of them. Philia love is known as 'brotherly love,' it is love without being romantically involved. It occurs between friends and family members. Both parties are open, trustworthy, share the same values, and respect each other...." Peony began to explain.

"Wow, it is too complicated for me to digest right now," Lili said interrupting.

"Well, you don't need to know and understand all eight types of love. But I would like to encourage you to practice Philautia love." Peony said.

"Please explain to the dummy then," Lili pointed to herself and rolled her eyes.

"Philautia love is a healthy form of love. Known as—self-love. You recognise your personal needs and self-worth, nurture your well-being, and take good care of yourself. You show compassion to yourself as you have shown to others and spend time with people who support you. Just like us." Peony smiled while she put one hand on her own heart and the other hand pointed to Jasmine.

"I promise that I will try," Lili said.

"Good, I'm glad to hear that," Peony said.

"I am afraid it's about time for the departure." Jasmine looked at her watch.

"I am going to miss both of you," Lili said with teary eyes.

"We are going to miss you too. Now you going to make me cry," Jasmine hugged her.

"Group hug!" Peony put her arms around Lili and Jasmine.

CHAPTER 32

As the plane landed slowly at the airport in Shanghai, Lili's heart beat faster and faster. She was looking outside at the runway. Snowflakes gently floated down past the plane window and fell softly onto the tarmac. The early morning lights shone like diamonds dancing in the pre-sunrise darkness. Shanghai was slowly waking up. Lili felt the familiarity of her country of birth, it hadn't seemed to have changed, but she had. She was a brand new person.

"Ladies and Gentlemen, boys and girls. Welcome to Shanghai…" The captain's voice brought Lili back to the present.

Kang was waiting for Lili's arrival with a sign that said, "Welcome Lili." He hoped that he could recognise her from the photo Peony had sent him. He thought, "At least she will see the sign if I miss her," he mused. "Ah! There she is!" he said aloud. She is more beautiful than in the photo, he thought, walking towards her. "Lili?" he asked.

"Kang?" Lili responded.

"Yes, Welcome to Shanghai!" Kang put his hand out.

"Nice to meet you, finally! Peony has told me a lot about you." Lili stretched her hand out and shook his. Kang's friendly smile calmed her nerves straight away.

"I hope she told you only the good things about me. Let me take the suitcase for you. My car is parked not far from here," he said, as he took Lili's suitcase and walked with her outside to the car park.

"Thank you," Lili said. "I really appreciate all your help," she said, as she dug her beanie out of her handbag and put it on to starve away the chilly air.

"It is very cold compared to Australia. Hope you have brought enough warm clothes with you?" Kang said.

"Yesterday was forty degrees in Sydney. Today it is minus 15 degrees in Shanghai. I have lived in Sydney for the past 6 years and can't remember it being this cold in Shanghai," she said, wrapping her long coat tightly around herself. As they approached Kang's car, he walked a few steps faster so he could open the door for Lili.

"Please be careful. The ground is a bit slippery." Kang carefully helped Lili get into the car before loading her suitcase into his boot and jumping in the driver's seat to start the car and drive.

"I've booked you into lovely accommodation I hope you'll like," he said.

"I'm sure I will love it; thanks for doing that," she replied, smiling.

They arrived at an impressive modern building overlooking the Huangpu River at Shanghai Harbour. Kang retrieved Lili's luggage, took it into the apartment, and helped her settle in.

"I hope you like this apartment," he said hopefully.

Lili looked around and replied, "It's very warm and inviting, I love it! I can see your architectural talent here that Peony told me about."

"Thank you. I designed this building. I loved the location here so much that I purchased this apartment. I lease it out mostly, but I booked it out for you. Try to have some rest. I will pick you up this evening for dinner, 7 pm?" Kang shook her hand.

"Yes, I look forward to it. Thank you," Lili replied gratefully.

After Kang left, Lili took her coat and boots off. She walked over to the window and gazed outside. Bittersweet memories flooded her mind. "The harbour is still as beautiful as I remembered," she thought, "But do I have the strength to face my past here and have what it takes to start over here?" she wondered.

She worried what she would do if she saw Hung again and thought of Jasmine's words about loving, forgiving, thanking people who have wronged you and letting them go. Lili could feel her heart beating faster and faster just thinking about it. She was sweating, and her head was spinning. She quickly went to the bathroom and turned on the cold tap splashing the water on her face. She dried her face, sat on a chair, and closed her eyes. She took a deep breath and murmured, "Lili, you have more than what it takes. Don't let the setback stop you from bouncing back," She said with determination.

After a while, she calmed down and ran a hot bath allowing the water to engulf her. She took another deep breath and tried to relax. After the bath, she felt much better. She stepped out of the water and put her dressing gown on, then she picked up the phone and called her mum.

"Wei Mama (Hello Mummy)," she said nervously.

"Is that you, Lili?" answered her mother with a trembling voice.

"Yes, Mama," she said, twisting her just-washed hair.

"Your voice is so clear. It's just like you are calling me from up the road. You have no idea how happy I am to hear your voice," she said, full of love and excitement.

"I am back here in Shanghai. Mama. I just flew in," she paced up and down the room while biting her middle fingernail.

"Am I dreaming? Are you at the airport? I can come to pick you up," asked her mother in a flurry of questions.

No, Mama, I am in an apartment not far from you. Could you come here to meet me?" she asked.

"Your father is out. He will be back soon. I will come with him once he is back. He would be so happy to see you."

"No, Mama. I want you to come here by yourself. I don't want to see him. Don't bother telling him I am back here either." Lili said firmly.

"You haven't spoken with him for more than six years. You probably don't know, but your father is a changed man. Please allow him to show you. Please!" begged her mother.

"How could you forgive him after what he did to us?" Lili started to feel her cheeks burning and her stomach twisting.

"After he saw you in the hotel room that night, he finished work and came home and locked himself in the bedroom. A week later, he finally told me what had happened, I was so angry with him, and at the same time, I was hurt and devastated. So many times, he came to me asking for forgiveness. I asked myself the same question. How can I forgive him? I could not stand the pain of it, and I told him to move out, get lost and never come back. In the following year, he kept showing up and asking for forgiveness. He focused on his business and proved in every way he could that he had changed. He was persistent in trying to win my trust and my heart back. Don't get me wrong. I was so sad and heartbroken when I found out your father played with younger women out there. It was very upsetting, and I was angry for a long time. But what hurt me more Lili was knowing what you were doing... um... that type of job," she said quietly.

Lili recalled that night Hung set her up in a hotel room for a client. She was waiting in her see-through sexy lingerie when the door was slowly knocked on three times—the signal for her client to announce their arrival. She went to open the door and was horrified to see the client was her father! She tried to shut the door, but he quickly forced himself inside and slammed the door shut behind him.

"What are you doing here? Shame on you!" he screamed at her.

"The one who should feel shame about all this is you!" she screamed back at him. "You are no different from all the filthy men out there. All you think of is how your life sucks that you have an old mutton at home. All you want is to get yourself off with a young juicy lamb like me. You play with someone's daughter while someone else is playing with your daughter, and you think that's ok and fair? Do you want to know how many men I have had sex with so far?"

"Stop it! I don't want to know. Put your clothes on and go home where you belong!" he cried out painfully.

"So many men that I lose count now! Get out! Get lost! I don't want to see your face for the rest of my life! You're disgusting!" Lili shouted.

"A fluffy slug. That's what you want to be?" His hand came flying through the air and smacked her face.

"You dirty old bastard! Get out of here!" she screamed.

"Lili, Lili. Are you still there?" her mum's voice said as some painful memories of the past began seeping through her consciousness.

"Yes, Mama, I am listening. Meet me at the Cherry Blossom Tea House where we used to go. Just you and me."

"Ok. I am so glad that I have my daughter back," she said happily.

After the call, Lili sank into the chair. She reminded herself to breathe deeply, in 1,2,3,4,5, hold, out 1,2,3,4,5,6,7, she repeated until she could feel a calmness settle back over her once more.

She then set off to meet her mother at the tea house. As she walked into the peaceful, familiar place, she spotted her mother eagerly waiting for her. They hugged for a long time as if they would not let each other go again before they sat down. While they are enjoying the bonding between mother and daughter, Lili told her mother about her mission of coming back to China, and her mum was so pleased to hear that and see the change in her daughter.

That evening Kang took Lili to The Dragon Chinese Restaurant for dinner. "I chose here because I think you must miss the delicious authentic Chinese food. I am sure that you will like the atmosphere here." He pulled the chair out for Lili to sit down on and then passed her a menu.

"Excellent choice! I like it here Kang. Thank you," she said, scanning the menu before noticing aloud, "The food here is very expensive."

"This is one of the best restaurants in Shanghai. This dinner is on me. Order whatever you like," said Kang proudly.

"Thank you. I haven't got the money to pay for such expensive meals. Peony employed me so I could save some money, and Jasmine taught me to manage my finances, but even then, I still have money only for the basic things I need, not extravagant things like this," she said, a little embarrassed.

"What made you decide to come back here for this life-changing mission?" Kang asked.

"Peony didn't tell you of my past?" Lili answered Kang's question hesitantly.

"No. Peony told me that you are her very close friend, and she told me about your mission and asked me to help you and support you in every way possible. That was all," Kang explained.

"She is such a beautiful person. Such a privilege to be her friend." She smiled and tried to put on a brave face before continuing. "I am unlike Peony. I lived a life that I was not proud of. I used to make my living by sleeping with men. I also had drug and alcohol addictions until the day I almost died from a drug overdose. Luckily Peony and other friends helped my life turned around."

"That's amazing Lili. You have shown great courage to turn your life around for the better. You are like a phoenix rising from out of the fire and ashes. What doesn't kill you makes you stronger. I can see how you coming back to China to fulfil such a big mission shows everyone just how brave and incredible you are," Kang said, then added, "You have a beautiful soul Lili. A flower blooming from adversity is the rarest and the most beautiful of all," he said sweetly.

"Thank you for your kind words," Lili said, blushing and dropping her eyes to prevent eye contact with him. She wasn't used to such compliments from a man.

"They are the words from Hua Mulan. Remember what Mulan's father told her?" he asked her.

"You mean the Mulan who replaced her aging and ailing father in the army by disguising herself as a man to lead China to victory? She was such an extraordinary and courageous woman with a strong sense of family honour. Yes, I remember the story."

"Yes, that's the one! Lili, you have the same courage. It's in your blood," Kang stated.

"I appreciate that you can see past my flaws and imperfections to see my soul. I don't think I've ever had a man do that. They've only ever been interested in my body, not my mind," she said quietly.

"You can call those jerks males, but don't call them men or even a man, they aren't. Real men would never do that; they would respect and protect you as Matt and Nathan do."

"They both are exceptional. I adore both of them. I think any good man who learned of my past would run away from me in a million miles a second."

"We all have scars. Whoever cannot handle your worst, doesn't deserve your best," he said adamantly.

Toward the end of the night, as Lili felt more comfortable with Kang, she finally gathered all her courage and told Kang about the relationship between her and her father. She still found it hard to forgive him and felt she needed some guidance.

"I am sorry to hear what happened between you and your father. It must be hard. I understand. Is there anything I can do to help?" Kang asked with compassion.

"I don't even know what to do or how to help myself to handle it," she admitted.

"Un-forgiveness is a cunning thief. It robs many people's joy, peace, and emotional well-being. Lili, you had the courage and strength to turn your life around; you'll have the courage to face your father and give him a chance as your mother has suggested, so you can all have a new start. If your father is a changed man, as your mum said, he will support you," Kang suggested.

"The truth is that I also feel shameful to face him too. I will never forget the shocked look on his face that night when I saw him in the hotel room."

"Have you finished the dinner?" Kang asked.

"Yes, I ate more than I should. I can't remember the last time I had such a delicious Shanghai-style meal." She looked at Kang hesitantly and continued, "Sorry to go on about my life. Am I boring you?" she asked.

"No. Not at all. I asked if you finished eating because I need to borrow your chopsticks," he smiled.

Kang picked up Lili's chopsticks and passed one to her. He instructed her, "Break it." Lili took it from Kang's hand and broke it into two pieces without effort. Then Kang picked up his chopsticks and added them to the one remaining from Lili's pair. He gave all three in a bundle to Lili and said, "Now break them all at one time."

It didn't matter how hard she tried, she couldn't break them, "What game is this?" she asked, looking around the restaurant feeling confused and uncomfortable.

Kang explained, "That's the power and strength we have if we are united together."

"Unbreakable?" Lili said, getting where he was going with the exercise.

"Would you please allow me to be your other chopstick?" Kang asked.

"Yes, I'd greatly appreciate that," Lili blushed.

"Great, it would be my honour. Hey, should we take a walk along the Rangpur River after dinner?" Kang suggested.

After living in Sydney's warm climate for six years, Lili could hardly bear the cold winter in Shanghai while they strolled along the riverbank. She was shivering even though she had put on a thick wool coat.

After noticing her shivering, Kang took off his coat and wrapped it over hers. "Here you are; it will keep you warmer."

All the men she met in her escort life treated her as a cheap toy. They just came to her, got what they wanted and left. Kang took care of her in such a caring way and respectful way, and he made her feel like a real lady for the first time in her life. "Peony was right, there were many good men out there," Lili said to herself in deep thought.

"You seem very quiet. Do I bore you?" Kang asked.

"No, not at all Kang. I appreciate your hospitality and enjoy your company very much," Lili said, feeling a tender and warm feminine energy surface from the inside out. She thought, "This is ridiculous! Why am I suddenly feeling this way in front of him?"

"Glad to hear that. I am afraid I must take you back to your apartment now as I don't want you to catch a cold. We have a mission to accomplish, anyway, and should rest up for it," Kang said, giving her a gentle smile.

Kang walked Lili to the front door of the apartment.

"Would you like to come in for a coffee?" Lili asked.

"Maybe next time. It is quite late. Let's get a good night's sleep, and I will pick you up at 7 am for breakfast, then we need to head to our first meeting. Good night Lili. I had a lovely evening with you. Welcome back to Shanghai!" Kang waved cheerfully as he turned and walked away into the night.

"Good night, and thank you!" Lili said and walked inside her apartment. She sat down, took her shoes off and then went to the wardrobe to get her pyjamas out. Changing, she murmured, "What a decent real gentleman Kang is. I like him." She loved how she felt with him and could see her dignity returning.

She stared at her reflection in the dressing mirror. "Well, Lili, remember in China they called escort women 'the toilet bowls in the men's public toilet', men go there to dump their dirt and leave? A fine man like him would not be interested in you! Especially after you told him about your past. You should know that's why he avoided getting in for coffee. You've embarrassed yourself, and he was just being polite because he is Peony's friend," she scolded herself.

She put on her pyjamas. It had been a long day, and she was exhausted. She climbed into bed and tried to focus her mind on good things, "Get a good night's sleep and focus on your purpose for coming back here," she said to herself as she drifted off to sleep.

The next morning, Kang arrived at Lili's apartment just on time, "I will take you to a special place for breakfast," he announced.

"Where?"

"Wait and see. I think you will like the breakfast there."

Kang parked the car on a side street, and they walked a short distance just around the corner. She could smell the familiar smell of street food. The delicious traditional Shanghainese breakfast on the go, "All the typical breakfast foods—you name it will be found here. You can choose anything you feel like!" Kang revealed excitedly.

"You have no idea how much I miss this street food," she cried out in surprise and happiness.

"Let me know what you like. I am going to get the four big Warriors as usual," he said.

"What's that?" she frowned.

"Ha, you are Shanghainese, and you don't know that?"

"Don't forget I haven't lived here for six years. There's probably a lot of new dishes with fancy new names I don't know."

"Yes, of course! Well, it isn't the bacon, eggs, tomatoes or avocado on toast you're probably used to in Australia. Come, let me show you." He pointed to a nearby street menu board and said, "Da Bing (Sesame Pancake), You Tiao (fried Cruller) with Ci Fan (Glutinous Rice Roll), and Dou Jiang (Soy Milk).

Lili pointed to the one at the bottom of the menu board and said. "I will choose this combination. Sheng Jian Bao (pan-fired dumpling) and the Xiao Long Bao (soup dumpling), Cai Bao (vegetable bun), and Dou Jiang (soy milk)." She said with her mouth-watering to taste it.

Once they got the food, they sat on small stools and ate while watching Shanghai life buzz around them. Everyone from grandparents, construction labourers, factory workers, and children to business people were here.

"Great choice Kang. Just like the olden days when I was living here." Lili said, biting into a bit of the soup dumpling. A stream of soup squeezed out the side of the dumpling and spilled out onto her jumper, "Damn! I can't go to the meeting like this!" Lili said, panicking.

Kang grabbed a serviette and tried to wipe it off. Lili moved quickly away from him with embarrassment as the soup stain was right on top of her breasts. "I don't think you can get it off by just using a paper serviette," Lili said, blushing and looking down at the stain.

Kang looked at his watch, "Don't worry, we still have time. I will take you back to the apartment to change before heading to the meeting," Kang said calmly.

They quickly made their way back to the car, with Lili apologising for her abrupt reaction to Kang's help. She told him she was still learning to trust men. Kang looked at her knowingly and said he completely understood.

"You've been through hell Lili, there is no need to explain. These things take time. The most important thing is to do what's right for you. You're safe with me Lili, I would never treat you with anything other than respect, ok?"

"Thank you, I am grateful for your understanding Kang; you are a true gentleman," she added, meeting his kind eyes.

Lili changed her jumper, and they still managed to be the first to arrive at the meeting. Following Kang and Lili, local government members, large groups of businesspeople, and a local charity organisation arrived.

Kang stayed beside Lili and introduced her one by one as they came in. After settling the guests, Kang indicated to Lili that it was time to start.

"We greatly appreciate you attending this meeting today. As you already know, there is an underworld of organisations running prostitution in this country. They are targeting women who are poor or with nowhere to go because of personal circumstances or those tempted by what they're told is a good lifestyle and easy money. But there are numerous cases where these gangs kidnap very young women and underage girls to use them as sex slaves to make money. They actively conduct human trafficking activities in other cities and states throughout China, and this extends to overseas countries such as Australia, which has become a focus for them. They lure women in with the promise of a better life overseas with short course study visas or three to six-month tourist visas. Once the women arrive in Australia, the gangs seize their passports, lock them up in guarded houses, and force them into sex slavery. The gangs hold all the money they make. In addition to this, they are coerced into trying drugs and alcohol to cope with the trauma, which they ultimately become addicted to, and the women become dependent on the gang, so there's no escape.

The Chinese government is cooperating with the Australian Federal Police and working earnestly together to defeat these organisations one by one. Where there are villains, there are also knights in shining armour working hard to eliminate this horrendous activity. Business people and other charity organisations like yours are working together in Australia to protect women from China and other countries that have been lured into this disgraceful industry. You may ask why I am so passionate and want to save these trapped women and stop this from happening to many more… It is because I was one of those victims. I know how it feels. It took me a long time to get out, but not without the help of my friends. It has taken a lot of ongoing support to turn my life around, start a new life without addiction, and even understand that I deserved anything more than I had.

The mental conditioning and brainwashing these women go through strips everything away from them—their dignity, their sanity, their self-esteem and confidence, and their bodies. That's why I decided to come back and help those needing our help and support. We also hope to provide education and information to prevent young girls and women from being trapped in the same situation as I was. Your generosity of time, support, finances, and resources would be much appreciated to help in this quest," Lili concluded.

Kang was so impressed with Lili's presentation that he clapped heartily as the delegates rose in their seats with tears in their eyes and applauded Lili. Filtering out of the meeting, several people promised to join Lili in her mission and said they would be in touch regarding the support they could offer.

Lili was elated. Kang beamed at her as they talked excitedly on their way back to the apartment. As soon as they walked in the door, Kang made a beeline for the phone to place a call to Peony while Lili got changed.

Putting the call on speaker phone when Peony picked up the call, Kang announced proudly, "The first meeting was very successful!" he said with excitement, looking at a blushing Lili who had just come back in the room.

"I knew it! It is not a surprise to me!" said Peony, thrilled. "Well done Lili! I'm so proud of you. Is Kang giving all the help that you need?" she asked.

"Yes. He's amazing. I am lucky to have him here with me. He gives me confidence and makes my workload with the mission much lighter and easier." Lili praised.

"Sounds like a perfect match!" Peony said cheekily, teasing them.

"Stop it Peony!" Lili laughed with a hint of embarrassment. "I don't think he is interested in a woman like me. He helps me because you are his best friend and he is a decent man! That's all!" Lili stated.

"But you are interested in him, right? I spoke with him last night. It seems you both get on very well." Peony said to which Kang found himself blushing.

Changing the subject, Lili asked, "Hey, when will you and Jasmine come to visit?"

"Don't try to change the subject," Peony said, not letting

them off the topic.

"No. I am not. I miss you guys already," Lili said.

"Well, it looks like you have to wait till Josh's school holiday in early April, so for now, you two will have to just enjoy each other's company," she said with a giggle.

Ignoring the last comment, Lili and Kang said together, "Can't wait!"

CHAPTER 33

Nathan was agitated in the driver's seat. He was so frustrated to be caught in the middle of the traffic jam, now of all times. He yelled under his breath, "Damn! Come on! Move!"

"God, please, I hope he is ok," he said, willing for the traffic to disperse so he could get through. Finally, he arrived at the Northshore Hospital. He quickly parked the car and ran into the hospital's emergency reception, where he was ushered through the doors to the intensive care wing. When he entered the room, he saw Athena sitting, holding onto the hand of Andrew, who had just come out of emergency surgery. She looked up at Nathan with a tear-streaked, weary, and worried face as she rose to greet him. Nathan walked towards her and gave her a firm hug.

"Thank you for calling me Athena. How is he doing? I can't

believe he's had a heart attack. He's so fit, energetic, strong, and healthy." Nathan said in disbelief, holding her as she sobbed. After a while, he released Athena and walked to an unconscious Andrew's bedside. With a soft voice, Nathan took his limp hand and said, "I know you will be all right. Just focus on recovering, my dear friend. I will take care of Athena and the business. You have nothing to worry about other than getting well," he assured him.

"The doctor said that he is out of the life-threatening stage and is in a stable condition. But I don't know when he will be out of the coma," Athena said with concern.

"Athena, I understand your worry. We pray and trust in God that he will pull through this ok." Nathan said as he pulled out a chair beside Andrew's bed. "Please sit down and have a rest. I am going to get you some food and a drink."

"No, thank you. Nathan. I don't feel hungry," she said, feeling sad.

"At least let me get you a juice. It will give you some energy and keep you going." Nathan said, heading downstairs to the café. After a while, he came back with a bottle of juice for Athena and a cup of coffee for himself. He opened the bottle of juice and handed it to Athena.

Athena had a sip and asked, "Nathan, do you have the instruction and authority from Andrew to run the company in his absence?"

"Yes, I do. So don't worry. I will take care of the company for Andrew until he fully recovers."

"That's great. At least that's one less thing I need to worry about. I would like to take him back to Greece for a while when he recovers. He works too hard and needs a holiday."

"It is a wonderful idea." Then Nathan added, "Oh. I just spoke with Peony when I was at the café. She is on the way to pick you up and take you home for some rest. I will stay here until you return."

"I want to stay here with Andrew, I want him to see me when he wakes up," she said, worrying.

"You need to rest Athena, it won't be good if you are both unwell. Peony will stay with you tonight, and she will drop you back here tomorrow morning."

"Ok, if you insist. I am happy for you Nathan. Peony is going to be a wonderful wife. I can tell," she said, smiling.

"You are right. I feel she is my soulmate," he agreed.

Just then, Peony rushed into the room. Athena asked, "Were your ears ringing? We were just talking about you!"

"Hope you two are saying good things about me. How's Andrew?" Peony hugged Athena and kissed Nathan before leaning down to take Andrew's hand.

"Of course, all wonderful things. Andrew is in a stable condition but still in a coma," she said, looking at her husband.

Peony leaned down, kissed Andrew on the forehead, and said, "Wake up soon, Andrew. We all need you."

Peony stayed for a while, then she took Athena home to leave Nathan to sit with Andrew.

A couple of days later, Andrew came out of his coma and was recovering well, to the point that he was finally allowed to be discharged from the hospital another couple of days later.

With Athena's tender loving care, he recovered slowly but steadily at home. Soon he was back talking business in meetings with Nathan from his home. "Thank you for taking care of Athena for me and managing the company while I've been in hospital and recovering Nathan. You have more than proved to yourself and me that you can run this company. With that said, I want to hand over the reins and appoint you as CEO of the company." Andrew said.

"I can't do that!" Nathan exclaimed, shocked. "I don't know if I am ready for that position. I am happy to do anything while you recover, but not take on the CEO title. Please?" he begged Andrew.

"While in the hospital, I realised I needed to spend more time with Athena. She always wanted to go back to Greece and live there for some time Nathan. Athena has said, and I trust her, that the only way I can be fully recovered is there, away from all the business dealings, so I can relax and focus on healing and spending precious time with her, which is long overdue," he stated.

"How about you put me as an acting CEO while you are away then? When you return, you can step straight back in as CEO of the company?" suggested Nathan.

"Well, to be honest Son, I am thinking of retiring. You are ready for this position, and furthermore, it is not about what you can or can't do, it is about what you should do Nathan. There are a lot of families out there who rely on our company. Our employees need to feed their families. Our company's continuous success will secure their futures and also provide a helping hand to those in need. Remember that when you have the faith to step up, God will step in to help you. Do your best, and God will do the rest. I can't think of anyone more suitable to take on the CEO position than you. You're a good man Nathan. I've watched you grow up, and Son, I trust you and believe in you. Now you have Peony by your side, I am certain that she will support you like Athena has supported me in successfully running the business." Andrew insisted.

"I am so grateful you took me under your wing. Your mentorship and guidance have meant the world to me Andrew. While my father taught me the value of hard work, you taught me skills and wisdom to run a successful company. I can't thank you enough." Nathan said.

"I will do all the legalities required to transfer the CEO role to you before I leave for Greece. Oh, by the way, I will also transfer a further 35% of the company share to you. So, you will own a 55 % share of the company. In that way, you can make decisions for the company without me there."

"I can't take over your shares just like that!" Nathen said, in shock and disbelief.

"When money is in a good hand, it will benefit many," Andrew said

"The responsibility is too great!" Nathan objected.

"This is the beauty of having money Son. The more money you get, the greater the responsibility, but also the greater opportunity to help others. People that need you to succeed so they can too. You will be ok, trust me and believe in yourself." Andrew said with finality.

Nathan and Peony took Andrew and Athena to the airport and said their goodbyes to the very relaxed and happy couple. On their way back, Nathan suggested, "We cannot get married without Andrew and Athena. It looks like we will have to postpone the wedding. Are you ok with that?" Nathan asked.

"That's ok. As a matter of fact, it will give me more time to prepare for the fashion show I've got coming up."

"What is the theme of the show?" Nathan asked eagerly.

"There will be three categories. The first one is called The First Australian. This range will be casual wear. It will be based on the first Australian living here—the Aboriginal. I am using the art of Aboriginal paintings and artists to print on fabric. I want the vibrant colours of the outback to acknowledge and represent the first people who lived on this land. I hope to showcase Aboriginal art and promote Australia in the international tourism industry at the same time.

There will be the 'East meets the West' category that will represent my Chinese background and integration into the western world. I will use oriental prints and patterns to make modern western styles that will be stylish and fun...." She said, enthused.

"Just like you and me, Honeybun," Nathan interjected, giving Peony a cheeky smile.

"Hey, do not interrupt me," she laughed and gave him a puppy dog face before continuing.

"And the final range will be called 'Elegance of Australia.' I will use the shape of the Opera House to create a range of stunning after-five evening dresses."

"Sounds amazing babe. I can't wait to see all the designs in the fashion parade," he said, looking at her proudly.

"I am extremely nervous. This is my first fashion show on an international platform."

"You know that I will be there with you and support you," Nathan said, patting her shoulder as they drove.

"You already make me feel so much better. Thank you, Sweetie Bear."

"That's what I am here for."

"Now it is your turn to tell me about your work," she prompted.

"Well, the Chatswood project is in the final stage now. The new project in North Sydney is still in the process of being approved by the council. This afternoon I have a meeting with the town planner, the civil engineer, the architect, and the builder. I estimate it will begin construction in the next couple of months depending on how fast we get the council approval."

"How can you get the final approval faster?" she asked.

"Corruption and bribery," he laughed.

"No, I am serious."

"I am serious too. But Andrew would never go down that path. He would rather put the matter in the Environmental Court. We did that many times. Besides, we have many projects in the pipeline, if it's necessary to put it on hold, we can always start another one. I don't think it will be the case though," he said confidently.

"How are you feeling about taking on the CEO job?"

"Honestly, I am ok with it now. I have been working with Andrew for many years and gathered everything I needed to know for the role, plus I have you by my side, so I feel like I could take on the world!" he said with a smile.

"That's brilliant my clever man," she said, gushing.

"You have already given me tremendous support by being here by my side and loving me. I honestly feel that I can do anything when I am with you," he said, glancing her way.

"Sweetie Bear, I am so glad that you feel that way. The joy you have given me is immeasurable. I have gained so much confidence by being with you and being loved by you too! The ancient Chinese philosopher and writer Lao Tzu once said. 'Being deeply loved by someone gives you strength while loving someone deeply gives you courage,' I believe that."

"So true." Nathan replied, then continued, "Oh, I almost forgot to tell you. We are looking for a construction site to build a new Grace Centre in the inner west of Sydney as you suggested. Thanks to you!"

"So, you did consider my input and idea?!" Peony shouted cheerfully.

"You know that we always value your input and take your ideas into consideration," Nathan said with a laugh.

"Oh, regarding the delay of our wedding. Even though I can't wait to be Mrs Artino, I think we should set the wedding date for October. By then, my fashion show will be finished, and I hope Andrew will be fully recovered and be able to fly back to attend our wedding. What do you think?" she asked.

"I think it is a good idea. Thank you for your consideration and patience, the more I discover about you Peony, the more I love you," he said, blowing her a quick kiss.

"I love you more. Sweetie Bear. Oh, I do have one special request though."

"Tell me. I am listening."

Do you mind if I keep Williamson in my name? So, after I get married to you—my best friend and soul mate, I'd really like my full name to be Peony Chen Williamson Artino."

"Yes, of course, I love it, Mrs Attino!" He laughed light-heartily.

"Not yet, but I am looking forward to being your Mrs though." She said, winking at him.

"Should we grab a coffee and your favourite—almond croissant at Sky Paradise before we go back to work?" he asked.

"What a good idea. I can't wait."

As Peony got out of the car, she lost her balance. Luckily Nathan, who had come around to open her car door, caught her in time to prevent her from falling.

"Are you ok?" Nathan asked with concern.

"I'm just dizzy. It happens now and then since the accident I had while I was in Hong Kong the year before coming here." She said with a frown on her face.

Nathan took her arm, walked her to the café, and pulled out a chair for her to sit down on, "How are you feeling?" he asked.

"I am feeling a bit better now." She said.

"What accident did you have? I've never heard you mention it before."

"It was a rainy Sunday; I was going to get my mum a birthday present because the next day was her birthday. When I was going to the underground railway station to catch the train, I slipped and hit my head on the stairway railing and fell unconscious. A stranger took me to a nearby hospital. Luckily,

I regained consciousness shortly afterwards. Mum and Dad said I acted a little differently after the accident." She said, recalling the experience.

"Acted differently, how?" Nathan stared at Peony.

"It was strange. Before the accident, I never intended to visit Australia, much less live here, but after it, all I thought about was wanting to come here. Most people would prefer to study fashion design in Paris. Millan or New York. But I had my heart set on doing my training in Sydney."

Nathan thought for a moment before asking, "When is your mum's birthday?"

"15th February," she said.

"The accident happened in 1988?" he queried her.

"Yes."

"Can you remember at what time?" he asked urgently.

"In the morning at about 11 am Hong Kong time. Why? I had almost forgotten about that accident, it's only when I get these strange dizzy spells that I remember it."

"That's the exact day and time we had the car accident, and Bella died Peony." He said in shock.

They both look at each other speechless.

CHAPTER 34

As Peony and Jasmine walked out into the arrivals lounge at Shanghai Airport with excitement, Lili ran toward them, and they group hugged for a long time.

"You guys have no idea how happy I am," Lili shouted happily while wiping her tears.

Kang walked up to the happy group of girls and hugged Peony and Jasmine, "So glad to see you. Welcome to Shanghai!" he said, putting his arm around Lili's waist. He pulled her closer to him and complained, "As soon as she spotted you, she ran off and left me behind! She clearly loves you two more than me," he said joking.

Peony looked at Lili with a cheerful smile and said, "Lili! You two?!"

"Yep," Lili nodded, turning her head to the side and giving

Kang a tender look.

"See! I knew it! I knew you were both perfect for each other!" Peony shouted with joy.

"So, you set us up?!" Lili said accusingly but with a broad smile.

"No," she laughed, "I just created the opportunity for you guys to connect. I knew you'd love each other!" she said happily.

"Both Lili and I greatly appreciate your help." Kang took Peony and Jasmine's luggage from them and said, "Come on girls, let's go. I have my car outside ready in the car park."

"You and Nathan are inseparable. I am surprised he let you go away from him for two weeks," Lili said, surprised.

"Actually, he encouraged me to take this trip with Jasmine. He said it was important to him that I retain my freedom to have time with girlfriends and do the things I want to do. He wants to ensure I know that marrying him doesn't mean losing my freedom and independence. Plus, he said it would do me good to party with you guys before I get married. You both know it is kind of a western tradition for the woman to go out and party with their girlfriends before her wedding. It's called a 'Hens Night' in Australia. And also, and more importantly, we need to spend some time here to support you too!" she said fondly to Lili.

"You are very lucky! But you create your luck. You always do Peony," Lili said.

"So do you," Peony tilted her head and looked at Kang, smiling.

"You girls, get in the car while I put your luggage in the boot," Kang said, opening the doors for them. As Kang drove them to Lili's apartment, Jasmine looked out the window with surprise. "Wow. China has changed a lot! This is my first time in Shanghai—The city that never sleeps."

"Well, Shanghai has been described as the 'showpiece.' It is the most popular and most beautiful city in China and one of the largest seaports and major industrial and commercial centres in the world. It is also well known for art, fashion, and design." Lili explained. "Hey, can you remember that song 'Shanghai Nights'?" Lili started to sing, "Shanghai nights, Shanghai nights, you are a city that never sleeps. Bright lights, singing, and dancing...."

Peony and Jasmine joined Lili, "Just seeing her smiling face, who knows her inner sorrow...?"

"Do you know the restaurant where I worked? The one where I met Hung and was enslaved? It's also called 'Shanghai Nights'. "That sentence sums up how I felt working there for him," Lili sighed.

"Oh. I am so sorry. Are we upsetting you?" Jasmine asked apologetically.

"No, that's ok. Now and then, something triggers and haunts me, but now I have an excellent technique someone special showed me to deal with it. Hey, Jasmine? It's called 'grounded,'" she said, smiling at Jasmine. "I am much stronger now. Physically, mentally and spiritually."

"I am so glad that you recognised that. I still say that you are stronger than you think. Otherwise, you would not come back here to face those demons." Peony praised her.

"I agree with Peony," Jasmine said, then changed the subject, "Hey, since this is my first time in Shanghai, where will the first place you take us to be?" she asked excitedly.

"Don't worry! Kang and I will show you all the most wonderful places—such as Yu Garden, Nanjing Road, and the Bund to name a few." Lili paused for a while and then continued, "But first things first, tomorrow morning, we will show you the New Women's Centre we set up for women in need," she glanced at Kang and continued, "Kang, my darling are you thinking what I am thinking for tomorrow's breakfast?" she asked him.

"Yep, I think they will enjoy it as much as you did, but you must warn them about the hot soup from the dumplings!" Kang said, bursting into laughter.

After Kang helped to carry the luggage into the apartment, he announced, "Now I have some business to do. I bet you girls have lots to catch up on, so I will see you for dinner tonight— it's on me. I will take you all to the same restaurant I took Lili to when we first met. I'll be back at 7 pm to pick you all up! Have fun! Bye!"

Lili walked Kang to the door and kissed him, "Thank you, Darling, I can't wait to see you tonight," she said sweetly.

"He is such a wonderful guy, and he is handsome as well!" Jasmine commented to Lili when she came back into the living area.

"Yes, he is. I thought no decent man would ever want to be with me after what I did in the past. I am so fortunate that Kang loves me as I am now," Lili said with uncontainable joy.

"Lili, I am glad to see you happy and living a fulfilling life. The most satisfying part is seeing how deeply in love with Kang you are and enjoying living with a purpose that is fulfilling. You really deserve it." Peony said in a cheerful tone.

"The trauma of my past still surfaces and hinders me a little though. Last week, I had a panic episode, and I accused Kang of having sex in a massage place," she said guiltily.

"How did he respond to that?" Jasmine asked anxiously.

"Well, first let me give you a bit of the background so you can understand why I reacted the way I did. When I worked at the Dee Why Massage Palace, men came in for a 'massage' and ended up having a happy ending, a blow job, or having sex. Last week Kang went to a massage place, and when he came home, I could smell the same sort of scent on his body. I asked him where he had been, and he told me he had gone for a massage after work. My heart just about exploded. It was beating so fast that I raged in anger at him and told him I did not trust him. I accused him of not only having a massage, but of also having sex with the woman as well. I demanded he tell me the truth." She said with flushed cheeks.

"I know Kang is not that type of man," Peony said.

"Well, he sat me down and explained that about a year ago, when he went to a construction site to check the progress of the building, he fell and hurt his shoulder. Since then, he has had what is called 'frozen shoulder' every now and then and needs physio massage to help ease the pain. He told me the massage therapist was a male. But I still did not believe him," Lili explained.

"Oh no! How did Kang respond?" Jasmine asked.

"The next day, he took me to the physio massage place and pointed out the person who did the massage. He also requested that they show me the record of the massage therapist's name so I could see he was a male. When I went home with him, I was so embarrassed and shameful. Fortunately, Kang knew my past and assured me he was not one of those bastards. He was so patient and understanding, and through it all, he created a secure environment, so I felt safe to show my vulnerable side and get through the episode. He helps me to deal with my trust issues by helping me to build my self-worth and self-love. He's quite amazing."

"I'm so glad you could overcome this issue. You've come a long way, my friend." Peony said. "Fill me in on more information about the centre. Would you, please?" she asked eagerly.

"Come and sit over here in the comfortable lounge. I will tell you over a cup of the best Oolong Tea you will ever taste. I have just made some for you both. And these traditional Shanghai sweet cakes my mum made for you," Lili said, passing the plate of cakes to Peony and then to Jasmine.

"Well, it has been very successful. Financially, I don't think you need to worry so far. Because many business people have got on board and are providing financial assistance. Also, the local government has provided us with the property to operate out of. We already have a team of employed staff and also volunteers. Some of the volunteers have had family members or friends who were held captive and forced into prostitution. My father is one of the very good examples. After I came back, I worked hard to build the courage up to finally contact him. Ever since, he has devoted his time and finances to the centre as he doesn't want any parents to go through the nightmare he did."

"Wow, that's incredible! I am so happy that you and your father have forgiven each other and are doing this amazing work together." Peony cheered.

"Trust me, it was not easy for either of us," Lili replied.

"I can only imagine", Jasmine stated.

"Without you both being there to support me from Australia and Kang there for me, I don't think I could have achieved reconciliation with my father. So, thank you from the bottom of my heart. Ganbie! (Cheers!)" Lili lifted her cup of tea and clinked it with Peony and Jasmine's, who jointly responded with a happy "Ganbie!"

"Oh, and one more thing—the authorities here are getting in touch with the Australian government to find those missing young girls who did not return to China after their visas expired."

"That's awesome! See, you are doing a fantastic job. I take my hat off for you!" Jasmine shouted.

"I will never forget those girls who were trapped at the Dee Why unit. They begged me for help. But back then, I couldn't even look after myself, let alone help anyone else. Mind you,

I did report it to the police and gave them the address when I went to the police station to report the gang rape," she said.

"I hope the police have rescued those girls," Jasmine said hopefully.

"I didn't follow up on the matter back then because I worried if the gangs found me, they would hurt me," Lili said with guilt.

"You did your best with what you knew then," Jasmine said.

"Actually, back then, it was in the news that the police cracked down on human trafficking at Dee Why, so maybe they did take action? It was probably related to your case Lili," Peony mentioned.

"I hope so," Lili sighed.

Peony took a bit of the cake, "Oh, my God! That's the best Chinese cake I have ever tasted. Could you please ask your mum to make more for us to take back to Australia?"

"Sure thing! Mum would be pleased knowing that you guys appreciate her cakes." Then Lili asked, "Jasmine, do you want to bring some of those cakes to your mum? You must be very excited and look forward to seeing her."

"Yes, I would love to, only if you have enough though. I am sure Mum would love them. I am so glad that you and Peony could come and stay a few days with me. Don't forget the flight to Beijing is this Friday." Jasmine reminded them.

Finally, when they were on the plane bound for Beijing, Lili asked, "Tell me, what can we see in three days in Beijing?"

"You really need three weeks to enjoy all the yummy food and visit the well-known places. However, I have already organised a full-on three days—you won't be disappointed, I promise. The first day I will take you both to the Temple of Heaven, and then we will take a taxi to Badaling to see The Great Wall. There you can see the famous walls of China snaking through the mountains in all directions around the gorgeous landscape." Jasmine said.

"Can we see the part of the Great Wall where the famous love story about Meng Jiang Nu happened?" Lili asked.

Recounting the story to both Lili and Jasmine, Peony said, "That's such a great story— Meng Jiang Nu's husband was forced to be a labourer and build the Great Wall by the imperial officials. She had heard nothing from him since his departure. As winter approached, she made him some winter clothes and set off to see him. Sadly, by the time she arrived at The Great Wall, she learned that her husband had already passed away, and the officials had buried his body inside the Great Wall. Her heart was broken, and she wept so bitterly that the part of the Great Wall collapsed." Peony recalled the story.

"Unfortunately, we do not have enough time to see that part of the Great Wall. It is in the Shandong Province and is quite far from here." Jasmine explained.

"After that, where will you take us?" Lili asked eagerly.

"The second day, we will be visiting The Forbidden City in the morning, then after lunch, we visit The Summer Palace. You'll need to wear comfortable outfits and shoes that day. We will be doing plenty of walking. On the third day, we will be going to Tiananmen Square. The Palace Museum. And, of course, I will take you to taste different traditional Beijing street food." Jasmine added, "Oh, we must taste the Peking Duck while there. You think my Peking Duck tastes good? Wait until you taste theirs!" Jasmine added with glee.

"Definitely! We can't leave Beijing without tasting the well-known Peking Duck" Lili licked her lips hungrily.

"After you two go back to Shanghai, I will spend two more days there with Mum and my sister," Jasmine said.

"Two days is not enough. You haven't seen them for six years," Lili exclaimed.

"I know, but I need to return to Sydney with you two to prepare for Peony's wedding. I will come and visit them again with Josh in the Chinese New Year, that's only a few months away," she said.

"You must come to visit Kang and I again on your way through." Lili requested.

"Of course! I promise," Jasmine assured.

"Who is looking after Josh?" Lili asked.

"Matt and Tom are taking care of him during the weekdays, and Nathan looks after him on the weekends," Jasmine replied.

"I guess two weeks goes by in just a blink of the eyes," Lili said.

The flight back to Sydney via Hong Kong was part of the plan because Peony wanted to spend time with her parents.

"Last time, when we were on the flight from Hong Kong to Sydney, we were strangers. This time we are flying back as besties. May I have the honour to show you this 'Oriental Pearl'?" Peony asked proudly.

"Only Two days in Hong Kong though?!" Lili complained.

"First day will be at The Peak for breakfast. Lunch at Victoria harbour followed by Shim Sha Chui for some night shopping.

On the second day, I will take you guys to Monkey Mountain and spend time with the cheeky monkeys. Then to Ocean Park to have some fun, and then we head to the airport for our evening flight." Peony said.

"Sounds like a plan! I am in," Jasmine said.

"Ha! You can't be out anyway. You are with us girlfriend." Lili stated.

"I am so happy I have you both to help me prepare for my wedding. I am more relaxed already," Peony said.

"Kang will fly to Sydney the day before your wedding. He has heaps to catch up on in Shanghai, but definitely will not miss out on attending your wedding," Lili said brightly.

"Nathan was right. We really did need this trip to spend some quality time together. See how far we have come since that first day we met each other six years ago. We have a whole new world in front of us, and we have all the reasons in the world to celebrate together!" Peony cheered.

The girls enjoyed their last couple of days together, with Peony playing the perfect host and showing them the sights. They went wedding shopping, saw the sights, ate at all the best places on offer, and laughed until they cried.

By the time they got on the plane to head back to Australia, they almost needed another holiday to get over the busy two weeks they had shared together. Just as they had six years earlier, they each slept on the flight, waking only when the Qantas Boeing 747 pilot's voice boomed happily throughout the plane, "Ladies and Gentlemen, girls and boys... Welcome to Sydney, Australia."

Lili, Jasmine, and Peony looked at each other knowingly with big beaming smiles. Unlike the first time they had taken this journey, they knew exactly what their futures held. There were no nerves, no worries. The three now best friends walked towards the familiar customs counter, sharing in the excitement that was to come.

"Welcome to Australia! May I see your passport please?" the customs man said. The girls looked at each other, responding in perfect English, "Sure, here you go Sir!" and laughed and hugged one another.

CHAPTER 35

In the late afternoon, the sun slowly set on the breathtaking South Pacific Ocean and guests started arriving at the Cardinal Cerretti Memorial Chapel on Manly Headland.

The golden sunlight shone through the magnificent stained-glass windows like thousands of diamonds dancing on the walls and red carpet. The red rose petals scattered from the entrance to the marble altar. Purple and pink peonies, white gum blossoms, oriental lilies, Chinese star jasmines, and silver ferns were arranged elegantly and placed along the sides of each aisle seat. Thirty-three red roses were carefully arranged at the centre of the altar.

Peony in her ivory silk satin dress was excited, yet she waited nervously in the limousine she had just arrived in. She had always dreamed of her wedding, even before she met Nathan and became a fashion designer. She had imagined the dress she now wore hundreds of times—a simple A-Line full-length silhouette with V shape neckline and a long train fanning behind her at the back. She knew exactly how she wanted it to look and had used her designer skills to sketch it on a piece of paper. Lucina helped her bring it into reality, and it turned out perfectly. She was elegant, graceful and had poise as she walked up the aisle with her arm draped through her proud fathers towards her love, Nathan and their wedding party.

The priest was standing at the sanctuary marble altar watching her, along with all the guests, as Nathan and Peony's theme wedding music, "All I ask of you" from The Phantom of the Opera, played. Nathan's childhood friend and well know actress Kate sang from the church pipe organ..." The bride's girlfriends—Lili, Jasmine, Linda, and Lucina in their purple-pink bridesmaid's dresses waited with tears of happiness in their eyes. Smiling at them all through her own tear-filled eyes, Peony's heart was full of divine joy, love, and gratitude to have such amazing friends.

Her eyes met Nathan's, and her body tingled in delight, she could feel the overwhelming love he had for her, and she for him, a deeply powerful connection she knew would never be broken. Her life from now, she thought, would not be the same; it would be even better than it was before.

Nathan waited nervously and eagerly for her to reach the altar. To him, it seemed like a slow-motion dream. "God, she's more beautiful than ever!" he thought as emotion welled up inside of him.

Finally, Peony's father took her hands and placed them on Nathan's trembling hands with a proud smile. They gazed at each other with deep love in their eyes for a long while. Then Peony turned around and smiled at each of her wonderful friends and families—each one a special light in her life—Matt,

Tom, Linda, Jason and their children, Lucina, Ava, Steven, Andrew, Athena, Lili, Kang, Jasmine and little Josh. Last but not least, her mum, Dad, and Nathan's parents proudly sat in the front row.

The Priest began, "Dear beloved families and friends, you may now be seated. We are gathered here this evening to witness this man and woman join together in holy matrimony. I invite Peony's mum, Mrs Chen, to read 1 Corinthians 13:4-8."

Mrs Chen walked up to the altar and smiled at the couple with her softly spoken voice in a rich Chinese accent, and she said, "Love is patient, love is kind. It does not envy, it does not boast, it is not proud. It does not dishonour others, it is not self-seeking, it is not easily angered, and it keeps no record of wrongs. Love does not delight in evil but rejoices with the truth. It always protects, always trusts, always hopes, and always perseveres. Love never fails," she concluded and smiled again at the happy couple before returning to her seat.

"Thank you, Mrs Chen," then the priest turned to Nathan, "Now you may say your wedding vows."

Nathan's hands began sweating as he held Peony's with excitement, looking deeply and lovingly into her eyes, he began:

"Do you remember the very first day that we met? The very first moment I saw you, I knew that this love we cherished was a gift from God. I knew we were meant to be together for the rest of our days. You are my strength and my joy. Your unwavering love brings out the best in me, and you have made me the happiest man on Earth. I promise to cherish and respect you, care for and protect you, comfort and encourage you, and love you for who you are and who you are yet to become. I promise to be patient, nurture your dreams, and help you to reach them. I promise to share my whole heart with you, to love you as Christ loved the Church and gave Himself for. I promise to stand by your side as your husband, your best friend, and soulmate in sickness or health, in times of prospering and decline, in peace and turmoil, as long as we both shall live." Joyful tears rolled down his face.

"Now I invite the bride to say her vows," the priest said. Peony squeezed Nathan's hands tight before looking at his beautiful eyes and saying lovingly:

"From this day forward, I choose you to be my husband to love and to be in your arms, and by your side, I vow to support you, inspire you, and love you with all of my heart. You have encouraged me to grow. You helped me to believe in myself and become the best version of myself. I know I can do anything with you by my side. I thank God for the love that has bound our hearts and lives together in the spirit of marriage. I promise to always allow God to be the foundation of our marriage. I promise to share with you my hopes and dreams, as we build our lives together. I promise to trust, appreciate, cherish, and respect you. I will always be with you for better or worse, richer or poorer, in sickness and in health. As long as we both shall live. I am so proud to call you, my love—my husband."

"With the power invested in me by the name of Jesus, I now pronounce you husband and wife. You may kiss your bride." The priest announced.

Nathan leaned over and kissed Peony's lips tenderly like it was the first time he had kissed her. Peony closed her eyes and felt a wave of warmth flush through her from her tingling throughout her entire being. She locked her fingers with his even tighter as they turned to be presented to the guests and walked along the aisle of the Church.

At the reception, Peony looked at the specially arranged bouquet in her hand—a combined posy of purple-pink peonies with oriental lilies and Chinese star jasmine represented the friendship with her two best friends. The white gum blossoms represented her Australian family and friends, the silver fern was sent from New Zealand, representing her Kiwi mum Ava. The white stylised Lily represented Nathan's Italian background and family, and the Acanthus Mollis honoured Andrew and Athena's Greek background. It was tied with a purple ribbon in remembrance of Bella. As they got to the reception stairs, Peony threw her bouquet backwards into the group of guests before getting into the waiting limousine, where it landed perfectly in Jasmine's hands.

As she was looking at the beautiful bouquet in her hands with astonishment, Nathan's cousin, Chris, one of the best men standing next to her, bowed politely and asked, "Jasmine, would you like a dance with me."

Peony turned back and gave Jasmine an encouraging smile and a wink. Once in the car, she nestled her head onto Nathan's chest and whispered, "They will make a perfect couple," as they drove away to begin their life as husband and wife.

ABOUT THE AUTHOR

Kitty Liu is an award-winning fashion designer, businesswoman and mother of two children, who are her pride and joy.

Kitty was born and raised in Guangdong, China, having immigrated to Sydney, Australia in 1990.

Kitty's personal mission has always entailed striving to be the very best version of herself - focusing on a positive attitude to encourage and inspire others.

Kitty enjoys skiing, walking at the beach, cooking and reading. She has also discovered a newfound passion for golf.

The Oriental Bouquet is her first book - one of many that she hopes to bring to life.